SO(

DROPOUTS

KAY C. BARROW

SILENT CRICKET
PUBLISHING

For Kahle,
Thanks for always being there to support me when I
needed it the most.

THE OPENER

Farah Vishwakarma had always been an introvert, so when her best friend suggested following a band on tour it wasn't something she thought she would ever agree to.

"Social Dropouts are playing in all these states over the summer. It's going to be so much fun! You have to come with me, Farah! Please!" Max Kayori pointed towards her phone, aggressively zooming in and out of the bizarre-looking tour poster that had been placed on social media to promote the shows.

Farah furrowed her eyebrows as she took the phone from her best friend and attempted to read the writing at the bottom of the poster. The only time she had ever heard of the band had been the times Max had raved about their music. She had an interesting taste and Farah appreciated her ability to find bands nobody had ever heard of. However, that didn't mean it was the kind of music Farah listened to.

"They're going to a lot of states..." Farah gave an uneasy look as she studied the poster. The art was of a humanoid figure with a wolf skeleton as a head pulling a trick on a skateboard. They were in a fiery inferno surrounded by other hellish creatures.

"That's what's so good about it. Trust me, you don't want to miss this! This is your last summer before you finish college, isn't it time you live a little? You need stories to tell, otherwise, your future kids will grow up and tell everyone how boring you were." Max folded her arms and shook her head.

At first glance, it was strange to see the two girls calling each other friends when their personalities were nearly opposite.

Most of Farah's outfits consisted of turtleneck sweaters and skinny jeans, wanting to be more subtle with her style than Max was. There was nothing that particularly stood out about the college student, but that was exactly what she liked. Not being able to be spotted in a crowd was her speciality.

Her ash brown hair flowed down past her shoulders, which she often tied up in a bun during intense studying sessions or during her morning run. She was a few inches taller than average height and her figure was slim, a pair of rounded glasses balanced on her nose. There was no doubt about it, Farah was attractive, but she never would have admitted it.

Farah was twenty-one years old; she should have been allowed to do anything she wanted and yet the fear of her parent's ruling loomed over her. After her parents came over from Pakistan to further their careers as a doctor and an engineer before she was born, Farah was always expected to follow in their footsteps of success. As much as it was something she *could* do, it wasn't necessarily what she *wanted* to do.

"I don't know..."

"Just think of it as a road trip." Max shrugged. "Just every night we go to a cool concert."

Max was a black student from outside Detroit, Michigan. Attending the prestigious university in North Carolina was a way to get onto the career path she desired. With exceptional grades, despite her fun-loving wit, her determination for success far surpassed anything else. Apart from one thing...her love for music.

Max spent most of her time in college wearing black ripped jeans, leather jackets, flannels, oversized band t-shirts and a pair of big black boots that had seen better days. Her hair was black and curly, a tatty red beanie struggled to balance on top of her unruly afro that burst from either side. Sometimes

Farah was convinced the hat was glued to the top of her head, there was no other logical reason for it being able to sit so perfectly in place.

Farah didn't hate any of these stylistic choices, they just weren't things she had any interest in.

Despite Max's alternative styling, the two had become friends in their college dorm. Living together for the past couple of years had forced them closer and allowed them to become the best of friends. They were both incredibly smart individuals, yet, Max led the life of a party-goer whilst Farah preferred being tucked up in bed by ten reading a fantasy novel.

Max was right in saying Farah hadn't done much with her college experience other than, well...college. Farah occasionally joined Max in attending parties, but other than drinking now and then, Farah wasn't into the raging party lifestyle that a lot of the students on campus loved.

"What kind of music do they play?" Farah looked at the poster again, it wasn't as if it gave many clues.

The only thing it revealed was the band name, tour dates and locations. It wasn't giving away any hints on what the shows would have contained.

"It's emo. The Midwestern kind, not that mainstream pop-punk crap. I'm talking edgy alternative rock. It's *mostly* just a bunch of whiney white dudes singing about their problems." Max explained, not selling the idea to Farah whatsoever.

"What do they have to whine about?"

"Heartbreak and hating their hometown."

"Is it like *punk*?" Farah cocked an eyebrow, passing the phone back to Max.

"Um, if you're talking anti-authority, then maybe not so much. But yeah, it's pretty post-hardcore."

"I have no idea what you're talking about." Farah snorted, it wasn't the first time she had to listen to Max yammer on about her love for music.

"Whatever, man. It's good! It'll be an experience of your lifetime and if you want, when we visit different states we can do all the nerdy shit in between. How does that sound?" Max tilted her head, trying her hardest to convince her friend that following a band on tour would have been the best thing to do with her summer.

3

It was Farah's last year of college next year and knowing that made her a little more open to the idea. As much as she had never been one for drinking or mosh pits, the idea of the adventure started to appeal to her. Sure, it would have been different, but perhaps that was what she needed.

"Oh come on, you love the nerdy shit too." Farah insisted.

"Well, duh. Do you know how many stupid museums and landmarks I want to see along the way? I've already made a document about them. I'll drop you the link." Max rolled her eyes, Farah should have known her better. As much as she liked music, she also enjoyed the vast amount of history the country had to offer. They were both huge nerds.

"Can I think about it?" Farah asked, still unsure.

"You think *too* much." Max groaned as she glanced down at the paperwork in front of her, distracted by the last-minute studying they had been trying to complete.

Farah chuckled as she looked around campus, it was a beautiful day and studying together outside had been a good idea. Max began to scroll through her phone and search for her favourite song by the band to show Farah. Max pressed on the screen and a song began to play through the speaker on her phone.

"Is this the band?" Farah questioned, listening to the melodic drum beat and twinkly guitar sound.

"Yeah! The band has a pretty gnarly backstory too. The frontman is the son of the lady from that cheesy nineties pop band that died. They were super famous! Uh...you know the one..." Max snapped her fingers and closed her eyes, attempting to remember the name of the girl group.

"Who? *The Flower Children?*" Farah cocked an eyebrow, vaguely remembering what had happened. It was a well-known story and she had heard Max speaking about it in the past.

"That's the one! God, I hate that name. This dude's band isn't that well known. It's not the same audience as the people who listened to his mom's music." Max shrugged again. A lot of the people who listened to his mother's pop band wouldn't listen to the sad drivel that was currently blasting through Max's phone.

4

Max began to flick through her phone as Farah listened to the song. The man who was singing wasn't singing...he was *shouting*. It wasn't something Farah would have chosen to listen to in her free time, but something she had heard being blasted through Max's dorm room door. Most of the music she listened to were songs she consumed whilst studying. Most of which were slow and acoustic.

Despite him shouting into the microphone, there were moments during the song where you could hear him sing. Notes being held in the right places to convey the emotion that needed to be heard. Farah was impressed with the singer's vocal range and was curious to know how different they would sound if they were to sing a love ballad on an acoustic guitar opposed to a grungy electric.

"The band is full of these super cool dudes and this one girl who rocks on bass. They're fantastic and if we're not friends with them by the end of all of this...our mission has failed." Max gave Farah a serious look from the opposite side of the table.

"Wait, we're not going to be groupies...are we?" Farah's expression dropped, realising what Max's plan may have been.

"You know what a groupie is, right?"

"Yes!"

"You shouldn't use that terminology. We're fans. *Fans.*" Max gave Farah a fraught expression as she repeated herself.

"*Fans...*" Farah rolled her eyes. It wasn't just about the music and that was the risk Farah would have to take if she wanted to go on a road trip with her friend.

After leaving her home in Delaware to go to college a few years ago, it had given her a breath of fresh air. Although she hadn't found herself growing much in the sense of trying new things, she certainly had come out of her shell. Unlike school, she had a social life. College allowed her to be whoever she wanted to be and if it wasn't for people like Max, she would have fallen back into her antisocial ways within the first year of being there.

Farah didn't want to be considered 'boring', it was just a lot of the things the other college students participated in didn't appeal to her. She was paying thousands in student loans to study, not to drink and smoke pot. She didn't want college to be a waste of her time.

Travelling across the country would have allowed her to experience more. Sure, it was mostly about the music and attending concerts, but it wasn't as if that was *all* they were going to do. The concerts were just a compromise and excuse for travelling. If they got to do something culturally interesting every day then would going to a concert in the evening be such a bad thing?

Farah would have gotten to experience some of the country and Max would have been able to see her favourite band. There was nothing wrong with that. The perfect arrangement.

She had originally planned for a backpacking trip through the summer to fuel her enjoyment for the outdoors but getting to see more of the country in a different capacity felt like a better option. Especially since Max wasn't willing to go on a backpacking trip and not going at all was better than going alone.

"So, what do you think?" Max questioned as the song came to an end.

It was moody and Farah wasn't sure what to think. She would have to listen to the song a few times before she could say she liked it.

"It's very...*shouty*?" Farah observed.

"Yeah, that's what this genre is about."

"It's *creative*?" Farah wasn't sure how else to describe it. She had never listened to anything like it before and wasn't sure how to feel. The tone was catchy, but the melodies were harsh and although she couldn't entirely hear the lyrics she knew they mentioned depressing topics.

"You hate it, don't you?" Max smirked.

"N-no! I don't hate it. It's just...*different*." Farah glanced to the side, she didn't want to hurt Max with her opinion. She didn't have any grounds to stand on in terms of criticism. The genre of music was out of her range of judgement.

"I know you're a woman with a vast respect for creative culture, Farah Vishwakarma. You're going to love this. It's passionate and raw...unlike that weird vampire book you read that got described by critics in the same way." Max wiggled her finger.

"I'm not having this conversation." Farah laughed, slightly embarrassed, suddenly regretting telling Max about a book she had once read.

"Sexy vampires aside, what do you say? Are you coming?" Max questioned, desperate for a response.

"Did I not just say I would think about it?"

"It's been five whole minutes. Is that not enough time?"

"No."

"Farah, I'm a very patient person, but this is getting ridiculous." Max pouted jokingly, placing her hands on her hips.

"I'll get back to you in three to five working days." Farah confirmed, shaking her head in response. She knew this was one of Max's many techniques in getting her to say yes to things.

She was thankful for having a friend like Max. Max was good at pushing Farah out of her college dorm, especially when she was in the mood where she only wanted to curl up in a ball and eat overly expensive ice cream.

"Okay, fine, but I need to know by the end of the week! I have to get the tickets." Max groaned, growing impatient with Farah's indecisiveness.

Max was used to it. Farah always had to get to the point where she was overthinking everything before she could decide on an answer. Max didn't mind, but she did find it hilarious.

As much as Farah wasn't into the idea at first, it was starting to grow on her the more Max spoke about it.

What was there to lose?

Both she and Max knew how to drive, despite Farah not owning a car. They could take it in turns. It had been a long time since she had gotten the opportunity to drive a long distance.

She hadn't thought about the logistical side of everything they were going to do. Luckily, Farah had a lot of money saved up for after college. Despite her parents not enjoying the idea, it would have been nice to have taken a gap year before diving into a career. Farah knew the gap year would have easily turned into a gap month if her parents had anything to do with it. Going through the summer would have been her only opportunity.

Travelling across the country? That seemed like a good thing to pour her money into. Hopefully, she would come out of the trip with new experiences. In that case, money didn't matter.

She had picked up work at a local coffee shop by the college for the past two summers and barely spent money on anything other than food, so keeping her finances in check was relatively easy.

Max placed her chin on the palm of her hand and kicked her feet out as she sat on the bench. She twisted a pen around her finger and huffed deeply.

"Farah...I need an answer." Max sighed heavily, unable to hold on much longer.

"Max, this sort of thing needs planning. I can't just agree to go on the spot. You have to know the ins and outs of everything. We have to make a *budget*!" Farah argued, looking at Max's vacant expression. "You haven't thought about a budget, have you?"

"It's more punk to not have a budget."

Max chewed her bottom lip anxiously as Farah stared back down at the page she was currently studying from. She gently tapped the pen against her forehead and sighed slightly louder than before. Farah glanced up from the textbook and shook her head.

"Y'know...I'm not going to decide any faster with you sitting there pouting at me, right?" Farah smirked, unable to hold back. It was hilarious to know her silence was torturing Max greatly.

Max stared back, taking a deep breath in as she placed the pen in front of her. She gripped the sides of the table and looked Farah directly in the eyes.

"Farah, I love you. You are my best friend. I would want nothing more than to share this adventure with you. I will make sure this will be the most fun you will ever experience in your entire life so you have something to tell people in social situations so they don't think you're boring. I will show you the world, something something...sorry, I never watched that movie." Max looked awkwardly to the side, refusing to make eye contact. "Farah, I am asking you from the very bottom of my cold, cold heart...will you follow a shitty emo band across the country with me?"

Farah blinked rapidly at Max's proposal; it was an excellent speech.

"Do I *have* to?" Farah snorted, her best friend's smile fading.

"*Yes!*"

"You're kidnapping me?"

"Yes..."

"Oh. I mean..."

"I'll be nice. I promise. I'll even get you a cushion for the trunk of my car." Max winked before throwing a finger gun at her friend.

"Wow, thanks." Farah sighed, burying her head back into the textbook knowing that at that moment, despite not explicitly telling Max she had made a decision, she was going to be going on a road trip.

Farah Vishwakarma was going on tour...

BROOKLYN, NY

Max nearly combusted when Farah agreed to go on the road trip with her. As much as it was about discovering everything the country had to offer, it was also about having fun. It was about the music and following a band they enjoyed.

The excitement for the music mostly came from Max.

Farah, on the other hand, still had to learn to like the music the band played. She wouldn't have typically listened to the genre and admittedly...she was struggling. After listening to their debut EP a couple of times, it still hadn't caught her attention.

She thought about telling Max to call the whole thing off, she couldn't see a band eighteen times when she had no idea how to feel about their music. Max had attempted to convince her that listening to a band live was different from hearing it on a streaming service. Nothing matched the live experience.

Farah was sceptical, she had never been to a concert and had no idea what to expect.

Farah hoped Social Dropouts would live up to their perky yet worrying sounding name. It gave the impression that unlike Farah and Max they were lacking on the educational front. Their music was energetic and moody, she imagined they would have been able to keep a crowd's attention for a forty-mi-nute-long set.

It wasn't a very long drive from Delaware to New York and they had set off from Farah's parent's house the same day as the first show. Her parents had been encouraging of the trip, but probably wouldn't have been if they knew the true nature of her journey.

Max handed the tickets to the doorman as their hands were stamped with ink and they were informed of no re-entry.

Farah didn't mind standing around and waiting for the opening act. Max spoke to her about what other venues she had been to were like in comparison to the one they were currently standing in. Considering it was the first venue Farah had visited, she didn't have much to compare it to.

Max was convinced it was one of the nicer venues she had been to in her time as a concert-goer. Farah would have begged to differ, but once again, she had no grounds to stand on in terms of judgement.

When the opener began to play, Farah stood beside Max and made sure to watch out for the rest of the crowd. She was worried everyone would have gotten too close. She was getting used to the atmosphere and didn't mind if she was bumped into occasionally. At the end of the day, everyone was there to have fun.

The opening band were loud and rowdy, but Max claimed they weren't as loud as Social Dropouts.

"I'm going to get drinks." Farah pointed at the bar as she shouted over the commotion.

"Beer!"

"What?"

"Beer! I'd love a beer!" Max held her hands in front of her and suggested her preferred size of beverage.

Farah nodded, finally realising what she was trying to communicate over the noise. She was happy for the short break before the headliner started, offering to get them drinks was a great escape.

Farah stood by the bar and waited patiently for a bartender, a young man was standing beside her, leaning on the bar with his elbows. Farah looked over at him, his body language shouted the confidence she lacked. It was as if he had ordered a million times before.

Just another smarmy guy who spent more time drinking than thinking. A culture Farah took an instant disliking to but was surrounded by in college.

He was wearing an open short-sleeved red flannel shirt that hung over a white t-shirt. The short sleeve revealed his arms which were covered in different tattoos that she couldn't entirely make out under the dim lighting. His hair looked as if it had a mind of its own, scruffy blonde on top and shaved sides revealing the dark brown of his roots. The young man had a round face, covered in a small amount of dark stubble that was prominent across his jawline and chin. She noticed the black studded earring in one of his ear lobes, it wasn't an uncommon thing for people there to have piercings or tattoos. Farah had neither.

The young man turned, looked at Farah and smiled. Farah awkwardly smiled back, nervous he may have noticed her staring. She knew she was being judgemental, but it was hard not to be in such a new environment.

"Are you enjoying the show?" The young man shouted over the generic musical tracks the venue had lined up between the shows. It didn't help that everyone else in the room was also yelling.

"Sorry?" Farah couldn't hear him inside of the venue. She leaned forward, hoping the next time he spoke she would have been able to hear him.

"Are you enjoying the show?" The man repeated, leaning towards Farah and shouting in her ear.

"Yeah! This is my first concert. Super cool!" Farah admitted, it was nice to strike up a conversation with a stranger. Her words were phrased in a way to help her fit in with the crowd. Max would have been so proud of her.

"Woah? *Really?*" The man in the red flannel raised his eyebrows in shock.

"Yep!"

"Are you here for the headliner?" He questioned as he pointed towards the stage that was dimly lit during the intermission.

"They're my friend's favourite band. We're planning on following them on the tour. We're going to every show." Farah explained, attempting to make conversation with another fan. She couldn't wait to tell Max she had already attempted to make new friends.

"Oh, really? That's pretty sick! I might see you around." The man nodded at Farah, his smile was kind and inviting.

"Are you doing the same?" Farah was interested to know if following bands on tour was a normal thing or if it was just something Max had dragged her into.

Just as the man was about to answer the question, the bartender walked over to them and requested their order, mistaking them to be together. Farah gestured for the man to take his order first, she wanted to be polite.

"What are you having? I'll get it." The man suddenly offered.

"N-no, it's okay. Thank you though."

"No, really. I'll get it! What are you drinking?" The man insisted as he gave her another sweet smile.

Farah hadn't been to many bars in her lifetime. After all, it was only last November she had turned twenty-one and even then, there hadn't been much opportunity to do so. That and going to parties in the area was usually a lot cheaper than going to a bar, most college kids chose to drink at home.

Was someone buying you a drink at a bar seen as a sign of flirtation? She didn't know. It wasn't as if he had seemed very...*flirty*.

"Really? Are you sure?" Farah was unconvinced he was going to buy her a drink out of the sheer kindness of his heart. She refused to be up for negotiations in the future.

"Really." He nodded in confirmation. "On one condition..."

Farah knew she had to be careful, bars could occasionally be filled with a vast amount of creeps. She didn't want to owe this man anything, it could have been a simple ploy to get to her. To get into her pants.

"What's that?"

"What's your favourite Social Dropouts' song?" He quizzed, interested to know where her interest in the music sat.

13

Farah didn't know how to answer the question. She didn't have a favourite. They were all just as equally noisy and she found it hard to distinguish the difference between them. Even Max playing them on her record player hadn't helped.

"I don't have a favourite. It's not my kind of music."

"What is your kind of music?"

"British boys in indie bands who like sticking their noses in American politics." Farah shrugged, admitting her taste in music. At least the coolest sounding genre of the ones she *did* listen to. It was the closest she was going to get to alternative rock. The closest she would have gotten to *fitting in*.

Even though she could barely hear him over the music, Farah could see the man sniggering at her answer.

"Are you guys ordering anything?" The inpatient bartender leaned forward and shouted at them both.

"Can you add it to our tab? Three beers, a diet soda and whatever this pretty girl would like." The man ran his fingers through his fluffy hair as he spoke before turning back to his newfound friend, Farah couldn't help noticing how non-traditionally attractive he was as he looked back at her. He had called her *pretty*. She was sure he did that to *every* girl he met at the bar.

"Um, one beer and some water, please." Farah requested, feeling awkward over his choice of words.

Pretty?

The bartender nodded as the stranger gave her a small smirk.

"Are you drinking the water or the beer?" He questioned, curious to know more about the girl.

"Are you drinking the beer or the soda?" Farah countered as she folded her arms with a smirk. The stranger was taken back by her sass.

"Soda. How about you?"

"Water."

"Sober squad!" The young man cheered. He was certainly...different.

"Sober squad!" Farah cheered back awkwardly; the slight wave of her fist reminiscent of some of the college parties she had been to. Most of which included cheering at other people drinking.

14

The stranger looked back to the stage as his beers were placed on the bar in front of him. He turned around and pushed the drinks together before picking them up carefully and balancing them in his hands.

"I'll see you around?" He tilted his head, holding the drinks in plastic cups the best he could, trying his hardest to keep his footing. Farah watched him concentrate on the task at hand.

Farah's drinks were placed on the counter and she grabbed them both before turning back to him.

"Yeah! Thank you for the drinks." Farah shouted over the music as he walked away, probably unable to hear her.

The stranger nodded, it was clear he had no idea what she said but went with it anyway. He was in a rush to get back to his friends. She knew it was best to let him go, if she caught him at the show later she would have thanked him for the drinks. At least a thanks for Max's beer, she was certain the water was free.

Either way, it was a nice gesture for a stranger to buy her a drink. That had never happened to her before and in a way, it was sweet. It had felt like an attempt to flirt with her and she appreciated his efforts.

Farah smiled as she watched the man disappear into the crowd. She found herself following him as he opened the perfect space in the sea of people for her to get back to Max. The stranger had completely disappeared by the time Farah had reached Max.

"How much is going on my tab?" Max joked as Farah handed her the drink.

"It was free!" Farah exclaimed with a grin, proud she had managed to get the drink for nothing. Considering it was their first night, it was already going incredibly well.

"*Free*? What? Did a cute boy give you it or something?" Max snorted before she took a sip of the beer.

"Well...yeah..."

Max nearly choked on the beer.

"*What*? A cute *boy* bought you this?" Max pointed to the drink.

"Yeah, he seemed nice." Farah shrugged casually; she didn't want to make a big deal out of nothing.

"Where? You've got to point him out to me!" Max stood on her tiptoes and turned around, attempting to look through the crowd for the boy who had provided her with the alcoholic beverage.

Just as Max stood on her toes the crowd erupted into cheers. Farah and Max both turned to face the front of the venue, the band taking their place on the stage. Farah watched in awe as the lights beamed down on the band members.

A young black woman with long dark two-tone hair walked on first and picked up a purple bass guitar, dressed in a black bralette, leather jacket and skinny black pants. Her face was covered in several different types of piercing and Farah found herself concentrating on how one side of her hair was a natural colour and the other a bright teal.

The bassist was followed by a skinny man with long brown hair wearing nothing but a pair of khaki shorts and an oversized white tank top that showed off the various tattoos on his body. He had a tan complexion and a pointed chin. His upper lip was littered with patchy brown facial hair. He took his position on stage behind the drums.

Next came a shorter than average white man with auburn hair that poked out the bottom and top of a backwards black snapback. He was wearing a pair of rounded glasses similar to Farah's and a pair of white denim overalls, arms littered with tattoos. He walked across the stage to pick up a well-loved sunburst painted guitar that was sitting on a stand.

Farah was entranced as a fourth band member took to the stage. A man with pasty white skin, scruffy blonde hair and stubble running down his jawline to his chin. He was wearing a red flannel with a white t-shirt underneath. He looked incredibly familiar. He was—

"Him!" Farah grabbed hold of Max's sleeve to get her attention before pointing up at the stage. Max's jaw dropped.

"*Him?*" Max shouted, pointing up at the man who was taking the position in front of the middle microphone.

"Him! He bought me the drink!" Farah rudely pointed up towards the man who was currently placing a checked strap of a red Telecaster over his head before pushing down on a pedalboard by his feet.

16

"Farah, what the fuck? That's *Brian Blossom*! He bought this?" Max aggressively gestured at the cup she was holding.

"Yeah! I swear— it's him." Farah reluctantly pushed aside the name of the frontman, desperately wanting to question how bizarre it sounded.

"Holy shit!" Max gasped. As much as she wanted to get close to the band, she hadn't expected Farah to make the first move. "You have to tell me everything later, the show's about to start!"

Farah couldn't believe her eyes. Although the band wasn't that well known, she felt as if she had run into a celebrity. He *was* a celebrity to a certain group of people, despite her having no idea who he was until thirty seconds ago.

Farah stared up at the man who adjusted the microphone before nodding to the rest of his bandmates. He pressed his distinguishable red sneaker against one of the pedals on the board in front of him before gently strumming the guitar once, the crowd erupting at the sound.

"Thanks for coming, everyone. We're Social Dropouts and we're going to play a bunch of cool songs. I hope that's okay!" The man, who according to Max was named 'Brian Blossom' shouted into the microphone. Unlike their exchange at the bar, his voice was rough as he yelled at the top of his lungs.

Brian took a step back as the crowd cheered in anticipation. He exchanged glances between each of his band members, the droning of a single note from his guitar humming in the background. A simple drumbeat began to play as the stage went dark and the crowd buzzed, occasionally disrupted by a singular person shouting 'woo!'.

Brian ran his fingers through his thick blonde hair before grasping onto the neck of the guitar and striking a single chord, the lights behind him flashing on as the crowd abruptly shouted back. Nobody held back as the infectious beat began to play, everyone in the crowd jumping into one another without hesitation.

Farah watched Brian through the gaps between the crowd as he ran his fingers up and down the guitar as if it was second nature, the alternative rock song wasn't anything like what she had heard online.

Brian took his mark in front of the microphone, still aggressively sliding his fingers back and forth down the frets as if his life depended on it. Farah watched in awe as he began to shout into the microphone.

"*I'm starting to forget my purpose. I'm cracking on the surface!*" Brian shouted the lyrics to one of his many songs, Farah listening contently as Max began to teeter on her heels and nod her head.

Farah thought she remembered the song. It sounded completely different live.

She wasn't sure whether it was because seeing them playing in person was different to a recording or if it was because she had become interested in the frontman of the band.

He had been nice enough to add her drinks to his tab. It was a kind and friendly gesture, but Farah only assumed he did it to all the women he encountered.

That was the problem with people in bands, a lot of them were in positions of power where they felt as if they could have flirted without consequence.

Was she going to fall to his feet over a *drink*? No way!

None of the songs had happy lyrics and yet most of them had upbeat melodies. Twinkly and complex. It was strange, although Farah was beginning to tolerate the genre after having Max blast it in the car on the way there.

He was fluent in his movements and his voice was powerful, showing off his musical talent as he tapped the guitar and sang lead vocals. His voice was gravelly when he shouted, not matching the smooth tone he had spoken in at the bar.

She watched as sweat dripped down each side of his face, the whole crowd gasping for more. Farah was stood somewhere to the side, having found herself there sipping on the water halfway through the show. Max had promised she would always come back to find her, but Farah hadn't seen her since halfway through the set.

Farah didn't mind, she knew Max was currently being swept away somewhere in a mosh pit having fun.

Besides, the concerts were for Max and the nerdy road trip was for Farah.

After finishing her water, Farah walked to the back of the venue to place the plastic cup on the bar. It was as if nobody else cared, throwing their cups on the floor. It was a health and safety hazard and Farah would have preferred to have a clear conscience knowing she didn't have any input in someone slipping on a cup.

Upon heading back to the edge of the crowd, Farah watched the band on stage with wide eyes. Everyone was passionate about the music they were playing, nobody missing a note. Brian shouted with such emotion in his voice that even the slight voice cracks he managed were in tune.

It wasn't always about making sure the right notes were hit within the genre. It was about emotion and the amount you were able to express within the songs. Brian had a fantastic way of getting his emotions across with his music, his voice showing a lot more baggage than expected.

Farah cheered along with the rest of the crowd as the show came to an end, even letting out a slight 'woo!' for the first time. It didn't matter, nobody else could hear her over the other people shouting and clapping as the band finished their set, but it felt nice to be included.

Farah watched as the band disappeared off the stage, each member waving as they left. Farah was convinced it was over until the crowd began to stamp their feet against the sticky wooden flooring.

"*One more song*!" They began to chant, expecting an encore.

Farah couldn't believe it, there was going to be *more*? She didn't mind, but she hadn't expected the set to go on for so long. Just a couple of hours had felt like a lifetime.

As the crowd continued to chant the words over and over, Max appeared from between two other people. Farah smiled, happy to see a familiar face in the room that wasn't the guy on stage who had bought her a drink. Max was dripping with sweat, gasping for air as she stood beside Farah.

"Are you having fun?" Max shouted as she touched her warm hand against Farah's shoulder.

"Yeah! They're...really good!" Farah wasn't lying. Social Dropouts were, in fact, *good*! She had gained some appreciation for the loud music. She didn't know if they were a band she would listen to in her own time, but she could appreciate how they played.

19

"See! I told you that you would like them. Next time, I'm getting you in the pit!" Max patted Farah on the back as the lights on the stage lit up once more, the band walking back out and picking up their instruments.

"Next time!" Farah chuckled nervously as she looked back up at the stage.

This time, the frontman caught her eye. She stared up at him in awe as he smiled back.

Was he looking at *her*? Did he recognise her from the bar? Was he looking at someone behind her?

Farah looked away, not wanting to keep eye contact as he adjusted the guitar and began to change the tuning for the last song. Max glanced over to Farah and nudged her violently.

"Dude, he's looking at you! You!" Max's eyes were wide and full of wonderment as she nearly knocked Farah over from her excitement.

"No, I don't think so." Farah blushed.

Brian Blossom stepped up to the microphone and smiled.

"We've got one more song for you guys!" Brian's voice sounded kind as he spoke into the microphone, unlike the aggressive singing he had been doing earlier on in the evening. "We're Social Dropouts and it's been a pleasure playing for you tonight. Please enjoy the rest of your evening and I hope you all get home safely. Thanks."

There was a slight pause.

"...and I'll see *you* tomorrow night!" Brian nodded towards the section of the crowd where Farah was standing.

"What?" Farah suddenly mouthed, praying the frontman hadn't seen her shock.

"Farah, what the actual fuck! Farah! What the *fuck*?!" Max screamed, her jaw-dropping at the sight. She was certain Brian Blossom had looked at Farah as the smooth words fell from his lips.

Max was freaking out. She was sure it would have taken them a few shows for the band to have picked up on the fact they were touring with them. Farah's natural beauty and charm came into play almost instantly.

"I don't know what's happening." Farah sweated nervously as the song started. The beginning of what was considered the encore and the end of the show.

"Did you tell him? Did you tell him we were following him on tour?" Max turned towards Farah, gripping onto her shoulders. Farah rejected the eye contact as she struggled to hear Max over the music that was beginning to play.

"Not exactly. Well, sort of. Maybe? I don't remember!" Farah shouted back over the music, her memory of the bar a little faded as she tried to compose herself in the crowd. She wasn't sure if it was the room that was hot or her bright red cheeks radiating sheer embarrassment.

"This is *awesome!*"

Max let go of Farah and looked back up at the stage, Farah brushed herself off as she too looked up to watch the band.

Each band member played their chosen instrument, with Brian having such a large stage presence, he was the only person Farah could focus on. He was so eloquent with his movements, the way he shouted into the microphone and how he played the guitar.

She was mesmerized by the way he played; she had never seen anything like it. The way his powerful music made the crowd move was something else.

The song wasn't long, but impactful enough to make the finale worth it. A great way to end the show. Farah clapped her hands violently as the crowd cheered along to the band's final performance of the night.

Farah watched as each member of the band exited the stage with a small wave, only to disappear behind a curtain not wanting to be seen until the next day.

WILMINGTON, DE

"He was checking you out."

"No way."

"You saw the way he looked at you, all cute and bug-eyed!"

"I don't think—"

"Farah, why can't you just accept that a cute guy might be into you? He's super-hot and he's the frontman of a band. Y'know...the band we're *following*! We've *got* to get in with the band."

"He's not into me. He doesn't even *know* me."

"Have you ever been with a guy before? They don't care about getting to 'know you', as long as you're cute, which you are, by the way, then you're good!" Max exclaimed at the wheel of her old car, which was riskily embarking on a long journey with incredible resilience. One of Max's brothers was a mechanic and a good one at that, her car had been made practically indestructible for the journey.

"Hey! I've been with guys before."

"I'm talking about guys that *you* choose to be with, not your parents."

"I don't know..."

"It's not Hasan or that weird adjunct you were with that one time. Give it a chance."

"I'd rather not think about it."

"Look, if Brian likes you then that's our way into hanging with the band."

"I'm not pretending to like a guy so we can hang out with a band." Farah argued.

"C'mon, it's not pretending when you're into him. I saw the way you looked up at the stage last night." Max glanced over to Farah and winked before focusing her attention back onto the road ahead.

Farah folded her arms and shook her head. Sure, the frontman was attractive, but that didn't mean she was going to leap into his arms and wish to be swept away. She had no idea who he was. Farah wasn't a groupie!

Fans. They were fans. This was not some kind of sexual pursuit.

"The way I *looked?* I was probably just squinting because of the lights. I don't know this man or his intentions. Men like him have a lack of understanding on how to treat women and I refuse to be roped into a role where I'm expected to fall for him due to his supposed position of power." Farah rolled her eyes. Max was blowing something small out of proportion.

"Okay, go off—"

"N-no, sorry. It's not because he's in a band or anything. It's just—" Farah immediately backtracked, not wanting to continue her rant on the topic.

"Dude, I'm not mad."

"I didn't mean to offend you. It's not about the band, or him...I'm sure he's a nice person." Farah began to panic, worried her words would only serve to offend.

"Farah, it's fine."

"Okay."

"Either way, it's our opening. You saw the bassist, right?"

"Yeah, I did."

"That's Zoe and she's awesome. If you can get us with the band just by looking at Brian, I *might* have a chance with Zoe." Max proudly pointed to herself; Farah was slightly disturbed by her friend's mind-set. Max's social life was different to Farah's, but she didn't expect to contend with her friend attempting to sleep with a member of the band.

Oh no, they *were* groupies.

"Really, Max?" Farah sighed as she stared out the window and watched the world pass them by, travelling through another state to their desired location.

"All I'm asking for is some cooperation so I can make a friend." Max shrugged.

"I'm not good enough anymore?" Farah smirked, finding a golden opportunity to snap back.

"What? You're the only one for me! Although, saying that...I think we should start seeing other people." Max gripped onto the front of her t-shirt dramatically. "It's not you, it's *me*."

"So, you want me to try and get with the frontman of some emo band so you can spend a night with the hot bassist?"

"Yes..."

"I'm not doing that."

"Farah! Far! F-Dog! The *big* F! C'mon, when was the last time you hooked up with a guy? When was the last time you lived a little? Did something for yourself? It's fun! I'm not going to force you to do anything you don't want to do, but I think it'll be good for you. We can hang out with them, pal around, potentially even spend some quality alone time with them...it'll be great!" Max attempted to explain the plan she had formulated in her mind. She had briefly mentioned some of these things before the trip had started, but Farah hadn't expected them to be things she was *serious* about.

Max was right in thinking it had been a long time since Farah had been with a guy, considering it wasn't something she had ever done before, she had never done anything *more* than kissing. Who had time for a relationship when studying was in the equation?

As much as Farah wanted to use the trip to break out of her comfort zone, she wasn't sure sleeping with a stranger was what she had in mind. It wasn't what she wanted.

"I can't believe I agreed to this." Farah laughed, trying not to regret her decision to tag along.

"Seriously? You're going to have the time of your life!" Max assured. She was determined to show Farah things in the world that weren't inside of a textbook. She was desperate to get

Farah to experience life for what it was, outside of the four walls of her dorm room. Outside of a college campus.

"We'll see about that..." Farah sighed once more as she turned the radio up to drown any further conversation.

They had spent most of the day hanging out in Brooklyn, the journey between Brooklyn and Wilmington being nowhere near as long as some of the other drives they would have to face along the tour. Despite being in Delaware, they weren't in a position to drive back down to Farah's childhood home for the night.

Whilst Max and Farah made their way to the venue, the band sat backstage making the most of their time together before a show.

Most of the time, venues only provided them with a very basic room to hang in before a show. It usually consisted of a few tables and a couch or two. It was never much, but then again, the band never expected much from the amount of money they were receiving for playing the shows. They weren't playing arenas and they weren't earning much for their time. If it wasn't for people buying merchandise, some nights they would have found themselves struggling to pay for food or cover their tab.

Living their lives in a band wasn't glamorous, but it was something each of them wanted to do. For now. Brian dreaded the day they would disband and he would have to find normality in his life. He couldn't imagine not shredding a guitar for a living.

"I was speaking to this girl at the bar yesterday and she said her and her friend were following the band. Isn't that cool?" Brian sat on a beaten-up couch situated at the back of the venue. There was just enough to keep them entertained between talking to the opening act and sound checks.

As by entertainment, they were referring to the copious amounts of weed and alcohol they had stashed away. The venue wouldn't *let* them smoke inside, but there was no harm in heading to the van to get their fix.

"Woah, we have *groupies*?" A man who went by the bizarre name of Catfish gasped as he sat on the edge of a table in his usual attire of khaki shorts and a tank top, no matter the weather. His straight brown hair flowed to his shoulders and helped counteract his struggle of growing facial hair. The stubble on his upper lip resembling that of a teenage boy hitting puberty was all he could manage.

Catfish's arms and the rest of his body were covered in ridiculous tattoos. Ranging from a lawnmower on the inner of his left arm to a cartoon sun with a pair of sunglasses on the right. Admittedly, these were considered the least strange out of his collection of body art.

His hands gently tapped a beat on his knees. His mind was always working on new material, whether that was for the band or electric drumbeats to sell online to wannabe rappers.

"Groupies? *Cute!* We've got to meet them!" Zoe gasped as the conversation drew her attention away from her phone for a split second. Her bubbly personality shone through to the boys in the band she had managed to put up with for years.

Zoe sat beside Brian on the couch wearing a leather jacket and a black bralette. Her hair was straight but held more shape than Catfish's sorry excuse for a haircut. Not only that, but she had gotten one side of her hair dyed a bright teal colour before the tour started. She was covered in all kinds of piercings, from her ears, eyebrow, nose, lip, belly button and it was likely some places only certain people knew about.

She was wearing grey skinny jeans to compliment her jacket. Her nails were painted black but were regretfully short. She had tried to play the bass with long nails before, but it never worked out the way she wanted it to.

"Groupies only have one intention and that's trouble." Russ commented with a deadpan expression as he sat opposite Brian on a wooden chair in his white denim overalls that had been stained in all kinds of materials. Beer, sweat, paint and probably blood masked as more paint. Nobody could be sure when it came to Russ. Most of the words that came out of Russ' mouth were ones the other members of the band continuously questioned.

Held tightly on his head was a black snapback, turned around so that a tuft of his thick brown hair flicked up and over the strap. He had a brown goatee on his chin and his thick-lensed rounded glasses that Zoe called his 'goggles' sat on the bridge of his nose. His creative nature curved him into having artistic tattoos, both his arms filled with complete sleeves. He had a lip ring and another tattoo on his neck of the word 'revo-lution' in a cursive font.

"They didn't *look* like trouble..." Brian defended the two women. He wasn't sure if they had been groupies. The girl he had met at the bar seemed reserved and based on their conver-sation it didn't feel as if she knew who *he* was. She had been dragged to the show by her friend.

"Groupies only have one intention and it's usually sex-re-lated." Zoe glanced around the room before shrugging. "I ain't complaining..."

"Hey, it's our call. Should we ask them to chill after a show?" Catfish questioned as he kicked his legs back and forth on top of the table.

"Care should always be taken amongst strangers." Russ had always been a little anxious around new people and hearing about two women following the band was a little nerve-racking.

"I'm voting, yes." Zoe agreed with a nod. "Brian?"

Brian wasn't sure how to respond. He had seen the two women in the crowd and had spoken to one of them at the bar. He felt terrible he hadn't gotten her name. It hadn't been the first time he had attempted to flirt with someone at a bar. He liked to think he was good at it and he was, his track record of sexual partners proved this. Although, people didn't like flirting with Brian, they preferred dragging him somewhere quiet and convincing him to partake in sexual acts. That was always easier than starting a conversation.

It was easier for *them.*

He didn't need convincing. As long as in his mind he be-lieved for a split second he would eventually find someone to be with, it was worth the shot. The only thing sex ever did for him was fill a temporary void that was desperate for compan-ionship.

How was he supposed to love someone if nobody was willing to give him a chance past a single night?

"Sure, we could do that. If they're here tonight." Brian shrugged; he was unsure of what inviting them backstage after a show would entail. They had invited people backstage before, but this felt different.

He had found himself encapsulated in the presence of the woman he had spoken to at the bar. Her eyes glistened under the lighting of the venue, her hair tied up in a messy bun, she was awkward about being there, but Brian appreciated that. She wasn't there for the music and surprisingly, that was nice to hear. It would have been good to speak to someone on the tour who didn't...*know* him. He hated to think it, but he had changed his flirting technique the moment he discovered she had no idea who he was.

Usually, he would have shamefully made a flirtatious move as they boosted his ego. He would ask to meet after a show and that was it. They'd both get what they wanted. He hated the thought. He was only hurting himself, knowing they were there for one thing and one thing only.

"If you don't invite them, I will. They better be cuties, Brian, else I'm calling you out on your bullshit again." Zoe sighed, recalling the last time Brian had gotten caught up with some fans. It never ended the way he wanted it to.

"Uh, they're cute! *Really* cute!" Brian smiled awkwardly before scratching the back of his head. He hadn't even seen her friend, but as far as he was concerned, the girl at the bar was cute enough to qualify.

"Don't get emotionally attached, man. You know how it is." Russ nodded towards his bandmate. Brian was a few years younger than them all and despite being the frontman of the band, they were often the ones to look out for him.

"Emotions are for music." Catfish inputted.

"All I said was they were cute. Nothing more and nothing less." Brian defended his actions, not wanting to admit his true feelings.

When he had seen the girl at the bar, he wanted to get to know her so badly. There was nothing he wished for more than being able to find out who she was and what she did with her life outside of being dragged around the country by her friend.

"This isn't going to be like that girl in Portland? Is it?" Catfish cocked an eyebrow.

"The girl in...*no*!" Brian recalled the memory before defending himself, flushing red.

"We all know you wrote that angsty song about *her*." Russ smirked as Brian gritted his teeth together.

"There's nothing wrong with being a romantic." Brian shrugged, closing his eyes and pouting.

"You can't fuck your way into love, Brian. It doesn't work like that." Zoe snorted, referring to the many times Brian had wanted one-night stands to be more than just that.

"I don't do that!" Brian shook his head. He was lying through his teeth.

"That's *exactly* what you do." Russ added, concern in his tone.

"I don't!"

Brian had always been so desperate to find someone to love but being in a band made that harder than it needed to be. Everyone he was ever interested in was only there to share weed or tick an adventurous box to say they had slept with someone 'famous'. Nobody ever wanted to *stay*. Nobody was ever willing enough to love Brian as much as he was willing to love them back.

"Jeez, save some for everyone else." Zoe laughed as she held her phone out in front of her.

Brian sighed as everyone went back to their own business. He continued to think about the girl at the bar and how she had looked back at him with such kind eyes. There was something different about her and he wanted to find out what it was. Yet, unlike a lot of the other times he had attempted to invite people backstage he was nervous. She didn't look like the type of girl to want to sleep with him for the sake of sleeping with him.

He had to muster up the courage to ask her to hang out with them after the show.

Brian eventually prepped himself to go on stage, speaking with his bandmates and hyping themselves up as usual. Unlike the previous night, Brian had managed to finish just over half a beer before going to perform. He wasn't a heavy drinker, but he sometimes needed liquid courage to be as confident as he was in front of a crowd.

He pulled the guitar over his head and began to play each string, making sure everything was in tune for the show ahead. He scanned the crowd, looking for the girl and her friend that mentioned they would have been there the next night.

Brian felt a sense of dread in the pit of his stomach, unable to see them. Unable to see *her*. She couldn't have been lying to him, especially after he had already told his bandmates they had people willing to follow them across the country. That would have been a disappointing blow to them all.

He tried not to let it get to him as he played, the rest of the crowd feeding off his energy as he aggressively strummed his guitar. They had never played in the venue before, despite playing in the city last year. With Brian's dad having a decent number of contacts in the industry they managed to get into most venues they requested.

Social Dropouts weren't a big band. If you were to speak to the average person, they would have no idea who the band were. If you mentioned that the frontman of the band was the son of Cherry Blossom from the nineties hit sensation *The Flower Children,* then perhaps they would have followed. Other than that...nobody wanted to listen to a shitty emo band.

He didn't want the same level of fame as his mother held. He enjoyed music and he enjoyed making music for himself and the people around him.

If fame was the thing that killed his mother, Brian didn't want to have anything to do with it.

"Good show, man. We crushed it." Russ pushed Brian's shoulder as they exited the stage.

Brian saw them like older siblings, from the way they had adopted him into their band to the time they spent looking out for him. Social Dropouts were their own little family and nothing could break them apart.

"No, *you* crushed it!" Brian argued as he tapped him back, a small laugh escaping from his lips.

"You guys want to pack up and order celebratory pizza?" Catfish questioned as he jogged up behind them, still sweating profusely from the show. It hadn't taken long for Catfish to decide that wearing a tank top was too warm of a choice.

"We *always* order pizza." Zoe groaned.

"Pizza is punk." Russ nodded. Russ was correct, pizza *was* punk.

Brian liked pizza but had become numb to the ritual. His mind suddenly plagued with the thought of spending the night in someone's basement or attic. They lived to couch surf and had managed to find themselves a place to stay for the night.

Each of them had gotten comfortable staying in a stranger's house. Brian didn't mind, it was just a way of life. He was never one for material items, the jacket on his back and his guitar were all he needed.

Brian made his way through the back corridors of the venue, he knew a part of him should have gone back to be with everyone before packing up, but he needed a moment alone. It had been a great show, but he kept thinking about the girl at the show the previous day. Zoe was right in saying he was a romantic, the words repeating within his mind.

He hadn't seen the girl. Not like last night. She probably hadn't gone to the show. As much as he wanted to stumble across the mystery girl at a bar again, he had too much anxiety to get the drinks himself, afraid he would have seen her again. He knew his words wouldn't have been as smooth the next time they communicated. It was unusual for him to be so jittery about a girl, but the girl from the bar was throwing off his confidence.

Brian went through the fire exit at the back of the venue and into the smoking area, sitting down on a small brick wall and running his fingers through his hair. It felt nice to have the cool air on his skin as his ears buzzed from the overexposure to loud noise.

Sometimes Brian appreciated the ability to get away from it all. The ability to dip into the middle of nowhere and find himself being his only company. Despite his ears ringing, it was a beautiful silence. A distant chatter of people within the town participating in the nightlife.

He sat by himself as he pulled his lighter out from his pocket and flicked it open, pressing his thumb rapidly against the wheel to ignite it. The lighter sparked several times before he saw a flame. There wasn't much in doing what he was doing, he had left the rest of his smoking gear inside. The lighter was all he had to briefly entertain himself.

Brian often felt different from the rest of the group. Perhaps it was their age gap? Maybe it was just the difference in their circumstances? Nothing was ever sunshine and rainbows. Nobody was perfect.

Although, being in an emo band Brian could easily put his thoughts and feelings into a song he could shout on stage. People managed to relate to his pain through music and that had always felt good. Even if they couldn't *entirely* relate.

Of course, later in the evening the band would have passed a blunt around and he was looking forward to it, even if there was an emptiness inside that getting high couldn't solve.

Being in a band was tough when most of the people who Brian claimed to like had only been there to sleep with him to add points to their popularity scale. He had been with people in the past with whom he wanted to develop relationships with, only to realise they were there for his status and not him as a person.

Sleep with the son of a famous pop singer? *Check.*

Make out with the frontman of an emo band? *Check.*

Get high with a 'famous' singer? *Check.*

Commit yourself to a relationship with the wannabe romantic? *No thanks.*

As much as he was happy to abide to their sexual desires and his frustration, he hoped one day they wouldn't just want him for...*that.*

Brian spent a moment alone with his thoughts before heading back inside to pack everything off the stage. They should have done it sooner, knowing the venue owner would already be backstage shouting at them for not cleaning up quick enough, desperate to close.

He thought the prospect of the two girls following the band across the states was a pipedream, but it was true — Max and Farah were still following the band and they *were* at the show that night. The issue was they were at the back of the venue.

Max had managed to squeeze her way through the crowd to jump around in the mosh pit, but Farah spent most of her night at the back by the bar. An inkling of desire within her wanted the man to come and speak to her again. Although, this time he didn't go anywhere near the bar. At least not from what she had seen.

Despite not being able to speak to the frontman again, she had watched him with wide eyes as he played the guitar. She had never seen anyone with so much talent before. She had played the violin for a short while as a kid, but as soon as her parents moved her onto other pursuits, it quickly became an item better suited in its case under her bed.

The music was abstract and Farah wasn't sure if over time she would have found a way to appreciate it more. She appreciated the instrumentals, but the overall tone was slightly more aggressive than what she was used to.

Farah kept trying to get the thoughts of the frontman away from her mind. It was insane to think he wanted anything to do with her. He could have been...anyone.

She desperately wanted to know more about the man, there had to be more about him than what his Wikipedia page revealed. She refused to entirely believe what had been written on an open online forum. From what she had read he had a rather tragic past, but that wasn't something she would have brought up in general conversation.

Farah had spent the whole show sipping on tap water at the back of the venue, patiently awaiting Max's return from the pit. As much as she enjoyed the show, she wasn't ready to participate in much other than holding the plastic cup with her arm and clapping awkwardly.

Farah didn't want to stand in the background forever, but for the second night, she was happy right where she was. She had visited the Liberty Bell in Philadelphia that afternoon and was happy with the photos they had taken.

"Come on!" Max held onto Farah's hand and attempted to pull her forward. Max was convinced that soon enough she would have been able to get Farah to jump around in a pit with her.

"I don't think so!" Farah chuckled, shouting over the slight intermission between the songs and shaking her head.

"You're missing out!" Max shouted back, letting go of Farah's hand and smirking.

As much as Max wanted Farah to be a part of her deep love for music, pushing her too far wouldn't have been ideal. It probably would have made Farah hate the music even more. Max had to continue to remind herself that Farah was doing her a favour by coming along on the trip.

"Maybe one day!" Farah nodded before looking back up towards the stage, the members of the band exchanging glances as they prepared for the next loud song. Farah was wearing earplugs, but they didn't help.

"Fine!" Max groaned before patting Farah on the shoulder to assure she knew she wouldn't have been too far away.

Sure, the pit looked like fun. It was a different kind of fun Farah wasn't sure she would have enjoyed at a first glance. It looked claustrophobic and sweaty.

Bruises. There were going to be bruises. Max had already shown her new collection of them appearing after the previous night. She was going to have been covered head to toe with them by the time the tour was over.

It didn't matter though, she was having fun!

Fun. The tour was going to be fun.

Farah needed to stop worrying about the little things that plagued her mind, including the idea the frontman could speak to her again.

Farah took a deep breath inward and smiled as she watched Max disappear into the crowd in front of her knowing she wouldn't have seen her again until the end of the show.

Sixteen more nights of this?

Farah knew if she wanted to get out of her comfort zone soon, she would have to dive in headfirst.

WASHINGTON, DC

The third night of the tour was interesting for both parties. Neither of them had expected to cross paths so soon.

Farah was excited, it wasn't as if she hadn't been to Washington before, but this was the first time visiting without parental guidance.

Max was happily dragged around every tourist location imaginable they could fit in with a short amount of time before the show. Unfortunately for Max, Farah was the sort of person who enjoyed reading every exhibit, especially at museums.

Although Max was also interested in the history they were discovering, her style of learning was different and considered a visual experience. Farah studied the writing as Max took slightly blurry photographs of every exhibit they visited. They were useless, even Max knew she wouldn't have done anything with the pictures. She probably wouldn't have ever looked back on them.

It didn't matter what they were doing, they were having a lot of fun not studying for college. Farah valued her time with her best friend. Max was incredibly studious and although she found herself humoured by more immature things than Farah, she was intelligent and enjoyed college just as much as Farah did.

They knew the drive they would have to embark on the next day would have been the longest yet, but it was worth the travel. Farah was starting to get used to sleeping in motel rooms and spending most of the day driving. The drives hadn't been too bad so far.

The venue Social Dropouts were playing at in Washington was going to be the largest venue they had played since the beginning of the tour. The show was yet to sell out, but they were hopeful.

Considering the large number of small bars and half-broken stages the band played on, the venue they were in that night was near to one of the fanciest places they had ever performed in. The band took full advantage of the laundry room the venue had for touring musicians. It was a godsend.

As much as Brian wanted to be excited about the fantastic venue, there was another thing on his mind.

The band had nowhere to stay that night.

They spent a lot of time looking online and seeing if there was anyone that would have taken them up on their couch. Most people were friendly and kind enough to offer, but Brian worried about it until there was a solution. He couldn't relax until he knew everyone in his band had somewhere to sleep. The last thing he wanted was for them to have to pile into the van. They had done it in the past, but Brian didn't approve. They needed somewhere safe to stay.

Brian knew that if worse came to worse he would have to dive deep into his savings to get them a motel for the night. None of them had much money aside from whatever they made from merch and the shows. It wasn't a lot, mostly just enough for gas, weed and pizza.

The *essentials*.

Brian had spent the whole day worrying until he strummed a single note on his guitar and stared up at the crowd. As the lights blasted on the large group of people in front of him in the distance, he noticed a somewhat familiar face. The face he had been thinking about more than he cared to admit the past couple of days.

He breathed heavily as the crowd screamed at him, it looked as if the sea of people went on for miles. He had never played in front of so many people. Not only were there people in front of him, but the balcony around the venue was also filled with crowds of adoring fans. He appreciated every one of them and yet the only person he could truly see was the girl from the bar.

She had come to another show. Judging from her facial expression it didn't look as if she wanted to be there. Brian suddenly felt bad about it. He wished he could have played an indie song to spark her attention, but with the show being their biggest to date he couldn't pull it off successfully without embarrassing the whole band.

As the lights projecting themselves on the crowd disappeared, so did the girl. Brian attempted to stare through the darkness to find her again but to no avail. She had disappeared like a ghost. He furrowed his eyebrows before wiping his sleeve against his forehead, everyone patiently awaiting another song.

Little did Brian know the girl had disappeared from the crowd for a particular reason, her best friend had just been kicked out of the venue.

Farah hadn't expected to see Max being escorted out of the venue near the end of the song. As she had done throughout the previous nights, Farah had spent most of her time at the back of the venue with a plastic cup of water clapping on cue. Max spent a lot of her time within the mosh pit or, well, on *top* of the mosh pit.

Security didn't like having to catch Max repeatedly when they had shouted in her ear that if she surfed again, she was going to get herself thrown out, she only assumed it was an empty threat. Little did she know the security guard who caught her as she rolled off the crowd was more than willing to escort her out of the building.

Farah noticed out of the corner of her eye, scurrying through the crowd to be with her friend who had suddenly disobeyed all the venue rules. The 'no crowd surfing' signs were there for legal reasons, Max hadn't expected security to *act* on them.

Farah pushed past everyone before finding herself at the venue exit. Like the last two nights, the stamp on her hand indicated there was no re-entry and Farah knew as soon as she stepped through the doors there was no way of getting back in.

Farah didn't mind, she was more worried about Max being left behind. The show didn't matter, it wasn't as if they weren't going to be seeing the band again. Not only that, but the band had nearly completed their set. They would have only been missing out on the encore.

"Really? Get off!" Max snatched her arm away from the security guard who let go as soon as they were outside of the door to the venue.

"Sorry, t-that's my friend." Farah politely squeezed past the abundance of security in the building. They all watched as she stepped outside to meet with Max.

"Yeah, and you can fuck off too, *baldy!*" Max lifted both of her middle fingers and pointed them towards the bald security guard standing by the other door giving her a dirty look.

Farah didn't say a word as she grabbed Max's waist with her arm and dragged her away from the heated scenario. Max had been drinking.

"You need to relax." Farah instructed, somewhat frustrated with Max as she turned around and walked beside her friend. Max adjusted the beanie on the top of her head and sighed.

"They don't know what it means to have fun."

"And you don't know what it means when security tells you to *stop.*" Farah sighed with a small chuckle.

"Fuck the police!" Max shouted aggressively before looking back at Farah and seeing her laugh. "C'mon Farah, say it! I know how much you hate cops."

Farah glanced around to check for any unsuspecting authorities in the area before cupping her hands over her mouth and shouting.

"Woo! Fuck the police!"

Max burst out laughing as they walked down the street together, the venue beside them still bursting with noise from the concert happening inside. Max was annoyed she had been kicked out of the venue but was having too much fun to care. This was what the trip was all about and some venues could be stricter than others. It was all part of the experience.

"Hey, do you want to try and sneak in the back?" Max suggested with a slight mischievous giggle.

"That sounds illegal."

"What happened to 'fuck the police' Farah? I want her back." Max shook her head as she placed her hands on her hips, disappointed her friend had suddenly changed her opinion on the matter.

"She was murdered by anxiety." Farah laughed nervously.

"See? This is why you need more alcohol in your system at all times. It would improve your life *drastically*!" Max spoke as she led Farah behind the venue.

Farah knew they weren't supposed to be in the area, but it didn't seem like Max cared. Max was going to go wherever she wanted to go.

As they walked around the building they noticed a small parking lot that would usually have housed large tour buses and vans, but instead, they noticed a couple of cars and a singular white beaten-up van that had seen better days. It didn't look like the glamorous tour bus Farah had envisioned.

Instead, it was a fifteen-year-old Volkswagen Transporter T5, a well-loved vehicle that had seen the band through multiple tours. The front bumper was a different colour from the rest of the van and there were a few other aesthetic blemishes throughout. Other than that, it was a reliable vehicle.

"That's their van! I've seen it in photographs before." Max pointed at the vehicle as she gasped. Farah felt uncomfortable being behind the venue, she was certain they would have been arrested and taken into custody for their crimes.

"That probably means we shouldn't go near it." Farah suggested as Max beelined towards the van. There was no use in trying to stop her.

"It's fine, they go near it all the time!"

"We're not them..."

"But we *wish* we were, so it's basically the same thing."

"That's— Y'know what? Nevermind." Farah sighed, unable to comprehend Max's tipsy dialogue.

Farah stood by the van and folded her arms, glancing around the back of the venue on the lookout for anyone that came within prying eyes of Max gawking at the vehicle. Max pressed her face against the window as she looked inside. It was exactly how she had expected it.

It wasn't clean. The 'van' was worn down and looked as if the interior had been ripped apart. The inside didn't look very pleasant, but Max enjoyed the aesthetic of the candy wrappers tucked between the seats and the stained carpets.

"I will ride in this car before I die..." Max whispered as she stared through the window, her breath fogging up the glass.

Suddenly, there was a loud noise coming from the back of the venue. Farah turned around in shock, her entire body shivering in fear.

They were going to jail.

"Someone's coming!" Farah gasped; Max still completely entranced by the van.

The back door to the venue swung open and Farah instantly froze, immediately wishing her fight or flight senses didn't buffer.

She wanted to run!

Nothing.

She couldn't move.

"That drum solo you smashed out tonight...*killer.*" A monotone voice spoke as they exited the door.

"Couldn't have done it without you, man." Another voice sounded.

Farah stood in shock as three people exited the building, each one of them suddenly staring up at her. She clenched her fists by her sides and swallowed hard. She was as stationary as a deer in headlights.

"What are y'all doing by our ride?" A feminine voice spoke in a firm yet friendly tone. Max's ears spiked at the noise, causing her to remove herself from the glass of the van.

"Z-Zoe!" Max gasped, noticing three members of the band by the building. Max's heart dropped; this was their chance.

This was her chance to get a ride in that van!

"What are y'all doing?" Zoe placed her hand on her hip, exchanging glances between a nervous-looking Farah and an anxiety-ridden Max.

"We got kicked out of the show." Max blurted out before pressing her lips into a thin line.

" *You* got kicked out of the show." Farah corrected as she folded her arms, not wanting to get on the bad side of the band. Max bit on her lip, curious to know if her best friend had done her a favour or not.

"Nice." Catfish commented.

"Kicked out of the show? You're not troublemakers...are you?" Zoe questioned, trying to get a better look at them. They looked like two strange college students who were way out of their depth.

An accurate description.

"Crowd surfing." Max corrected as she held a single finger up.

"Hey, I remember you!" Russ pointed over at Max, re-membering her face from the show. She found herself on the crowd more than anyone else.

"You *do*?" Max's eyes widened. She had been noticed by Russell Watkins from Social Dropouts.

"Yeah, I saw you surfing. That's rad." Russ nodded towards Max, causing her to blush. He remembered the red beanie on top of her uncontrollable hair, internally questioning the physics of how it had managed to stay on her head through the show.

"This your first Social Dropouts show?" Zoe questioned, interested to know more about the so-called fans who looked like they were about to break into their van.

"N-no, we're following you guys on tour! This is our third night." Max nodded back at them.

Two girls that were following them across the country on tour.

Brian was right.

"He was right." Russ gasped, lowering his tone.

"This better not be like Portland." Catfish threw his hands into his pockets.

"Bringing up Portland makes me feel sick, man. Stop." Russ shuddered.

Zoe stepped forward, deciding to take control of the situation as the two boys bickered.

"Since you missed part of the show, do you guys want to come and hang out with us?" Zoe asked as she held her hands

41

in the pockets of her leather jacket. Brian was right about them being cute.

Farah couldn't believe it. Was it this easy to hang out with the band? There was no way this was happening. Meanwhile, Max stood behind her ready to combust with excitement.

"Wha—" Farah was stunned. It shouldn't have been this easy. The third night? *Really?* Did Max have a secret gift? Did they have no concept of stranger danger?

"Yes! We would love to!" Max walked forward and threw her arm around Farah who was a few inches taller than her, holding onto her shoulder as she gleamed. Farah smiled awkwardly, knowing now they wouldn't get any sleep.

"Sweet." Russ commented as he watched the faces of the two women light up. One of them more so than the other.

"Security can't kick you out now. You're official crew members." Catfish pointed his finger at them both before pushing his back against the door and granting them access to the bright corridor.

"Sick!" Max squealed as she stepped past them all and into the corridor. Farah followed behind, slowly.

"So, where are you guys travelling from?" Catfish asked as he took the lead in taking them through the corridors back to the room they had accommodated for the evening.

"We both go to Duke University. North Carolina." Max laughed awkwardly as she attempted to make small talk with the band she was infatuated by. She had to be their biggest fan.

"Duke, huh? Isn't that the super fancy college for smart people?" Russ turned back as they reached a door, opening it up and revealing the inside.

"Well, not *super* smart, but—" Farah began as Max immediately cut her off with her excitement.

"Woah! You guys have everything in here!" Max gasped as she stepped into the room.

Situated around the room were several couches attached to the walls, the ceiling was painted with a fancy image in a similar styling to those in museums. There was a mini fridge filled with beer the band had already helped themselves to. Backpacks were leaning against the long couch and a bizarre colour scheme of orange and purple was slapped against the surrounding walls.

"Oh, don't get too excited. Most of the time we just get a dirty old couch and a table if we're lucky. We've never played anywhere as fancy as this before." Zoe commented as she pulled out her phone to text her sister and tell her about the show, just as she had promised. She slouched herself down on a section of the couch, Max didn't hesitate to sit beside her, far enough apart for it not to be weird.

Farah wasn't sure where to sit, so found herself sitting beside Max on the long couch. She felt awkward being there. She had no idea who anyone was.

"What are your names?" Russ asked as he found himself deflating on the couch, an evening of playing the guitar had been exhausting.

"Oh! I'm Max and this is my best friend, Farah!" Max pushed Farah's arm slightly as she smiled.

"It's nice to meet you. I'm Ru—"

"You're Russ, Catfish, Zoe and...where's *Brian*?" Max pointed to each of them, her knowledge of the band was awesome.

Although the band had been together for a while, it felt nice for someone to acknowledged each of them. For the most part, people only knew who Brian was. Each of the other band members, although a huge part of everything they did, were sometimes forgotten about.

Brian. That was the man who had spoken to Farah at the bar. Farah would have preferred to have avoided another interaction. It would have been strange now she knew he wasn't just a man at the bar.

"Brian does his own thing after the shows before joining us. He is in a world of his own." Russ leaned back on the couch before pressing his finger against his temple, a subtle hint to Brian's spiralling headspace he contended with every day.

"Do you guys want a drink?" Zoe questioned as she glanced over to them. Their expressions were opposite.

"Sure!" Max responded quickly.

"What's your jam?" Catfish asked as he pointed down at the small fridge filled with beer they knew they would have to pay for. Taking the cut from the show was worth it if they got to drink after.

"Anything that gets me drunker than I currently am." Max winked as she pointed a finger gun over to Catfish.

"Nice. Farah, was it? Cool name. You want anything?" Catfish reached into the fridge before dangerously throwing a glass beer bottle at Russ, Max and Zoe. He stared at Farah in anticipation.

"I'm good, thank you."

"Good for you. I could never resist free beer." Zoe sighed as she cracked open the top of the bottle, everyone else in the room doing the same thing. Farah felt left out as she balanced her hands on her knees.

Just as everyone, minus Farah, was about to take a sip of their beer a crashing sound erupted in the room as the door burst open like there was a police bust. Farah's heart dropped, anxious that perhaps security had found out they had been let back into the venue and they were coming to make an arrest.

Her parents would never forgive her.

Instead, a figure absorbed in his phone came through the door shouting about something the two new guests didn't understand.

"Guys! I spoke to the photographer at the show tonight and he managed to get us somewhere to stay in a place called Arlington. It's like...a ten-minute drive? He said that it's an old friend of his, he doesn't have much room, but he does have a basement we could stay in. It's not going to be fancy, but it will keep—" Brian began to explain, stressed he couldn't find anywhere for the band to stay sooner. His words were cut off as he removed his eyes from his phone and looked up to see two new faces.

It was the girl from the bar.

"*Brian Blossom...*" Max whispered his name as she stared up at him, her eyes were starry with excitement as she held the bottle of beer tightly.

Farah's eyes widened at the sight of the man, not in the same kind of wonderment as Max, but in a way that expressed shock. The stare between them lingered longer than either of them would have liked to admit, despite everyone in the room seeing Brian's gaping jaw.

"Hi, Brian! Turns out you were right about those people following us on tour. This is Max and this is Farah." Zoe pointed at them individually, smiling widely at Brian. She was happy Brian had truth in his words the other night after the show. It was hard to believe people would follow them on the tour.

Sure, going to a few shows was normal...but following them through the whole tour? That was new.

"Farah..." Brian spoke under his breath, hoping nobody in the room was able to hear him utter the name of the stranger he so desperately wanted to know. He wanted to feel what it sounded like to say her name on his lips.

Brian placed his phone in his pocket before silently brushing his fingers against his bottom lip.

"They're cool to hang out, right?" Catfish tilted his head for an answer. As much as Brian wasn't in control of them, they always felt the need to run things by him before making decisions. They probably should have turned to Zoe for guidance.

"Yeah, that's cool!" Brian responded suddenly, taking his eyes away from Farah for the first time since he had lifted his head from his phone.

Farah noticed him staring at her and unfortunately, she couldn't help but stare back. He looked much better in a brightly lit room in comparison to the dark stage she saw him playing on every night. There was no longer sweat dripping down the sides of his face and he had fixed his hair, probably with his fingers. The lower half of his face was covered in facial hair, his jawline and chin thick with prominent stubble.

This time, he was wearing a white t-shirt with an abstract print on the front and a black denim jacket. His jeans matched his jacket in colour and were ripped at the knees. He had red sneakers with a branded white line running down the side of them. They were broken and frayed from years of use.

Brian sat down on the couch opposite Farah. He was sitting far away from everyone as if he were isolating himself.

"Beer?" Catfish looked over at Brian before pointing at the fridge.

"I'm good, thanks. Otherwise, you won't get to Arlington without me." Brian smiled, taking note Farah also didn't have a drink in hand. "Besides, I'm part of the sober squad."

Farah looked up at the mention of the phrase, hearing it made her realise he was saying it to get her attention. She felt her cheeks go red at the gesture as they made eye contact from across the room. Although, it didn't last long.

"Do you want a smoke instead?" Zoe cocked an eyebrow, knowing how Brian's mind worked.

Brian didn't promote driving whilst high, but a small smoke and a few hours in between wasn't going to hurt. He had done worse in the past, unfortunately. He didn't want to admit his past mistakes.

Brian looked up at Farah, he had never felt uncomfortable smoking in front of anyone before...even his father. Yet, with the stranger on the other side of the room he was somewhat embarrassed by their hobby. She didn't look like the type to smoke, but Brian wasn't going to judge before he knew her.

"Are you sure we can even smoke in this room?" Brian glanced around the room for any smoke detectors, despite knowing from past endeavours that smoking pure marijuana wouldn't have set off any alarms. It was more of an act. An act...for Farah.

"Since when have you been nervous about smoking?" Zoe chuckled as she reached over for one of the backpacks on the floor. Brian sat in silence. He didn't have an answer that wouldn't embarrass him.

Farah watched anxiously as Zoe pulled a small bag of pre-rolled blunts from the backpack.

Farah's heart sank.

Was she going to have to smoke weed? This hadn't been on her plan of things she was going to experience on the road. Drinking was one thing, but getting *high*? Nope.

She glanced around the room nervously, eventually meeting eyes with Brian who was opposite her. He clocked onto the slight panic in her eyes.

She wasn't a smoker.

Zoe pulled one of the blunts from the bag and began to light up, everyone waiting in anticipation.

Zoe stepped over to Brian and held the blunt in front of him.

"It's got to go to the left." Zoe chuckled down at Brian who was looking confused by the tradition as if he hadn't smoked what felt like a million times before.

Brian shrugged before taking the blunt between his finger and thumb and taking a hit, this time not looking back up at Farah, embarrassed he had been part of the circle that was subjecting her to a new activity she may or may not have been on board with.

Brian passed the blunt to Catfish as it made its way around the room. Farah kept an eye on the object as it was passed around. She dug her fingernails into the skin on her knees as it inched closer, regretting not sitting further away from the middle of the room. Why did the blunt have to reach Farah *before* it got to Max? Why couldn't Max have gone first?

Russ held out the blunt for Farah, she didn't know what to do as she furrowed her eyebrows at the dangerous item between his fingers.

"It's okay. I don't smoke, thanks." Farah shook her head and smiled; the room let out a collective groan. Farah was terrified of every one of them. They were all intimidating. Even Brian.

"What!? Really?" Catfish gasped in frustration.

"Man, you broke the circle!" Russ sighed as he leaned over and passed the blunt to Max instead who took it from him without hesitation.

"It's not that bad, don't you want a go?" Max offered Farah the blunt, seeing whether she would change her mind. It wasn't going to have been that easy.

"Nope. I'm good. Thank you." Farah chuckled awkwardly, waving her hands out in front of her.

"Dudes, this isn't the first time some fancy vanilla college kid has broken the circle. Shit!" Catfish groaned, not in a particularly malicious way, but that didn't mean the words didn't sink deep inside of her.

"No respect for the tradition." Russ tutted as he shook his head.

"You can't be serious." Brian huffed under his breath, enough for Farah to hear his change in tone.

Farah had been subjected to peer pressure before. This didn't seem much different. She was riddled with anxiety at the thought.

"Farah, c'mon...it's okay. Statistically speaking it's pretty harmless." Max smiled, gritting her teeth together as she spoke in a slight whisper. Max never would have wanted to pressure Farah into anything, but she was currently in a circle with her favourite band. The last thing she wanted was for them to hate her.

Farah felt Max's boot nudge against her leg as she kicked her gently. Farah was slightly irritated Max had suddenly favoured the friendship of the band over her feelings.

Farah's mind was conflicted. With nearly everyone in the room having mentioned something about not taking part, her body temperature rose. The room felt warm. Her hands were clammy, suddenly finding themselves back on the tops of her knees.

"I can't believe you broke the circle, man. Shouldn't have wasted good weed on this. Max — pass it back." Zoe instructed, Max's heart skipping a beat as she said her name.

"This sucks." Catfish added to the pressure that was building in the room. Max timidly passed the blunt back to Zoe.

"The tour will be cursed with bad luck because of this!" Russ clenched his fists, becoming overly dramatic about the circumstance.

"Okay, last chance to save the tour and prove you're not a narc." Zoe held the blunt in front of Farah who stared at it reluctantly, her chest tightening at the sight.

"Narc!" Russ shouted as the band laughed. Everyone apart from one.

"Shit. Don't narc on us, man. Just be cool and take a hit." Catfish urged, insistence in his words.

Farah blinked at the blunt between Zoe's fingers. They were wrong to push, but she felt so alone as the walls around her became suffocating. Everyone's eyes were on her. She couldn't breathe. There was nobody to—

"She doesn't want to smoke, just leave it!" Brian snapped as he gestured to Farah who looked terrified of the situation she was in. He was irritated by his band's lack of respect for their guest.

"Jeez, Brian. What's with you? We're just messing around. It's supposed to be *fun*." Zoe's expression dropped as she pulled the blunt away from their guest whilst stepping back to face Brian.

"Not *everyone* is having fun." Brian scowled at Zoe, un-afraid to face her as he glowered. It hurt him to see the stranger so out of place that it caused him to grimace. His mood had changed dramatically upon seeing the girl so upset.

Farah noticed the disconnect in the room. It felt as if the four walls around her were collapsing. Hanging out with a band wasn't as fun as it first sounded. It was a lot of pressure and Farah wasn't sure she wanted to be a part of it.

Everyone watched as Farah stood up and exited the room, a blank expression over her face. She needed to escape.

She couldn't breathe!

Farah clenched her fists together as she paced down the corridor. She was desperate to get away from the room. She needed to take a moment to be anywhere but there.

Brian suddenly exchanged glances with Max on the other side of the room. It had been the first time he had taken note of her, having selfishly focused his attention on Farah the rest of the time. She was the friend who had dragged Farah across the states to see him play.

Brian and Max sprang into action at the same time. They were both overwhelmed with concern and although Brian hadn't known Farah for long, or at all, he was desperate to know she was okay.

The rest of the band watched as their newfound friend and frontman made their way to the exit, stumbling into one an-other as they went. As they stood in the corridor, they noticed Farah could have gone in one of two directions, narrowing their chances of finding her.

"We should split up." Brian suggested, exchanging glances between the two escape routes.

"Sure, I'll go this way." Max pointed at the corridor that led into the building.

"I'll go this way." Brian nodded in confirmation, twisting on his heel and heading towards the exit.

Brian switched his walk to a slight jog as he found himself exploring the corridors to the unknown venue. He didn't see many people around, after the show most people had already packed up and left. It wasn't as if the band had long left in the venue either.

Brian's immediate thought was to exit the building, he knew sometimes the best thing was to get some air, especially if she had just been inside of a room that reeked of pot. Brian felt guilty he had allowed his friends to put pressure on the poor girl. It wasn't fair.

Brian made his way out of a fire exit that was propped open, slowing himself down to a walk as he crept through the door, not wanting to disturb anyone on the other side if it wasn't Farah. As he pushed the door open, he noticed a figure leaning against the wall, their arms folded as their body language shouted at him desperately to leave them alone.

The young man furrowed his eyebrows as he stepped outside, watching the girl wipe away a tear that had started making its way down her face. He knew from a glance she would have rather been somewhere else.

"Hey, are you...o-okay?" Brian questioned softly, stepping as close as he could without invading her personal space. Brian was an intimate person and resisted the urge to pull her into a hug and try to make things better. He hated seeing people crying.

Farah glanced up and noticed Brian stood before her, his voice was soft and sweet. It was an incredible contrast to the screaming he had been doing throughout the night. It even sounded different to the first time they had spoken at the bar. This time, he wasn't shouting over a room full of people.

It was just them.

"Y-yeah, I'm fine." Farah looked away, wiping her eyes once more as she tried to hide her emotions.

Brian wasn't sure what to say to make her feel better. There wasn't a lot he could have said other than apologise profusely for his friend's behaviour.

"I'm sorry they did that. They can be jerks sometimes." Brian half-smiled, hoping Farah would see the sincerity in his expression. "I know it doesn't make it feel any better, but they were just teasing. They can take it a little too far sometimes a-and I'm going to tell them! They shouldn't have done that."

"It just feels like every single time I ever try to—. It's so unfair to expect—." Farah sighed heavily, trying to hold in her feelings. "I'm sorry. I didn't mean to. I wouldn't want to speak badly about your friends. They seem like really nice people, I just—."

"What? You didn't do anything wrong! You can talk about it if you want to. They can be giant assholes sometimes; I know that better than anyone." Brian gave her the space to talk if she needed to. He smiled sweetly, but Farah was too embarrassed to lift her head to see.

"It's okay." Farah sniffed, she felt bad that Brian had come out to comfort her when it should have been Max. She didn't even *know* Brian. He was just some guy in a band. Nothing more and nothing less.

"I get them too." Brian suddenly commented.

"What?"

"Panic attacks. My old therapist said you should say objects and colours around you out loud. She says that helps with keeping your focus. You have to find a...*focal* point? I think that's what it's called." Brian shrugged, providing her with useful knowledge.

Farah looked up at him, rather than just being a man in a band he suddenly became...human.

"I-I'll...remember that for next time. Thanks." Farah half-smiled, feeling grateful for the tip on mental health. She could always do with more of those.

"No problem. I just wanted to make sure you were okay, you seemed upset." Brian placed his hands in his jacket pockets and glanced away. He was genuinely concerned about her; it was in his nature to want to look out for others...even if they were strangers.

"It's fine, it's...I'm not used to any of *this* stuff. The loud music, alcohol, *weed*?!" Farah admitted with a small chuckle. She turned to look at him. "I'm pretty lame, aren't I?"

"I don't think you're lame! This lifestyle isn't for everyone and sometimes I don't even think it's for me." Brian pointed to himself, becoming more sincere with every word.

"Really? Why?"

"I don't know...it just looks like the kind of lifestyle everyone wants, but it's not. Sure, it can be fun. It's kind of tiring. Uh...I think *draining* is the word I'm looking for." Brian rubbed the back of his neck as he spoke, even after three days of being on tour he was ready to be put in a coma.

Farah had picked up on the fact Brian looked exhausted. His eyes were heavy from driving throughout the day followed by the show in the evening. Everything continued to pile on top of each other causing copious amounts of stress.

"You *do* look pretty tired..." Farah commented as she chuckled, looking away shyly.

"Shit, is it that obvious?" Brian smirked, running his hand over the top of his hair.

"Just a little bit." Farah smiled as she pinched her thumb and index finger together.

Brian placed his hands back into his pockets and grinned, shaking his head in the process. Farah wasn't sure what else to say on the subject but stood awkwardly with the man in silence for a moment before the fire exit swung open.

"There you are!" Max sighed with a smile, making her way over to Farah with her arms wide.

"Hi!" Farah waved, before she could even comprehend what was going on Max had thrown her arms around her.

Despite what may have been seen as selfish behaviour exhibited by Max, she would have always come back for Farah. As much as Farah wanted to be mad at Max for being on the side of some strangers in a band, she understood how excited Max was to be with them.

"Don't ever leave me again!" Max sniffed. Farah exchanged looks with Brian who stood smiling at her overbearing friend.

"I just went outside for some air. It was...a little too much in there."

"It was too long! I thought we'd lost you!" Max gripped Farah's shoulders and looked into her eyes. Her best friend was fine, Max, on the other hand...not so much.

Max was still tipsy from spending the night drinking and Farah wasn't sure whether she had taken a hit of the blunt, she didn't stick around long enough to find out. Farah didn't mind, it wasn't as if Max's choices were anything to do with her. As long as she was safe, that was all that mattered.

"It's okay. I'm fine." Farah smiled, pulling Max's arms down away from her.

Max turned around and saw Brian stood behind her teetering on his heels as he awaited permission to leave.

Max turned back and stared at Farah with wide eyes.

"Am I dreaming? Is *Brian Blossom* standing behind *me*?" Max gasped, moving her hands to Farah's shoulders. Brian could hear the conversation, but it wasn't as if it were an exchange he hadn't heard before.

"We were just all in the same room together." Farah furrowed her eyebrows, confused by Max's logic.

"But now he's standing right next to us and it looks like he wants something." Max threw her thumb over her shoulder before quickly glancing back at Brian to make sure he was still standing there.

"I mean, I just wanted to ask you guys if you wanted to keep hanging out with us until we get kicked out of this place? If you're...*comfortable* of course. I know my friends can be a bit pushy sometimes, but they're all nice really. You'll like them if you get to know them. They're not bad people, I promise!" Brian shrugged, directing his speech towards Farah more so Max.

"He wants us to hang out! *More*!" Max gasped.

"Yeah..." Farah smiled at Brian who responded with the same expression, completely entranced by the way she looked back at him.

"You're Brian Blossom!" Max turned around and stuck her finger out at the man. Brian glanced down at his chest where a drunk and excitable Max had pointed.

"I am."

"That's *so* cool!" Max gushed as she clenched her fists together with elation, bringing them to her chest. "*You* are so cool!" Max was unable to contain her excitement as if she were going to combust if she spent any more time with the band.

"Thanks!"

Brian and Farah chuckled at Max's behaviour. Max was great and having her around made everything a little more exciting, especially for Farah. Farah had always been thankful for Max's friendship and despite everything, they were always there for one another.

"Can I offer you a sober beverage?" Brian asked Farah as he found himself beside her, Max happily taking lead by pottering in front of them.

"Do you always offer people drinks?" Farah folded her arms as she walked beside Brian. He continued to hold his hands inside his jacket pockets as he snorted at her comment.

"Only the cute girls I want to get to know better."

There it was again. Another one of his flirtatious comments. He had called her *cute*.

Farah felt her chest tighten again, but this time it wasn't in the same way as back in the room. His words radiated through her. Why would *he* want to get to know her? She wasn't anyone special.

She didn't know how to respond, so kept quiet.

"I know you're not super into alcohol so maybe we could spice things up with a lemonade? Diet, of course." Brian questioned with a smirk, attempting to start a conversation.

She didn't want to admit he was charming, but it was hard to deny with a smile like *that*. He seemed caring and willing to help. Unfortunately, she wasn't sure if he had another motive. Either way, it was surprisingly nice to feel special if only for a moment. He had made her feel that way.

"I'll think about it." Farah tried to hide her smile.

"Sober squad, right?" Brian grinned with a small wink to accompany his expression, lying about his alcohol consumption. He had a little to drink and had taken a few hits of the blunt, he wasn't *entirely* sober. That didn't mean he wasn't going to dig around in the mini fridge for a diet soda though.

"Sober squad." Farah responded, smiling over at him as she kept her arms folded.

Farah felt good knowing she was a little more open to the experience. It wasn't so bad when the people around her began to make her feel like she could fit in with their crowd. She still stuck out in the way she dressed and her personality; she felt like the least *alternative* person any of them had ever met.

As they walked back towards the room, Farah could feel herself getting warm again. It was mostly from the anxiety she was feeling about going back into the room and facing the people who had tried to pressure her.

Although, with Brian standing beside her, it was hard to be as nervous as she once was. With Brian around, she was protected from the rest of his friends. That didn't necessarily make it any better.

"Are you okay with seeing them again?" Brian whispered as he turned back towards Farah. "We could hang out somewhere else? Maybe I could see if I can find another room for you and Max?"

His offering was kind, but not one she was willing to accept. Farah was a little concerned about the idea of Brian suggesting they could hang out elsewhere, it felt like he was pushing for them to be alone. That felt...*strange.*

Farah had little idea of who this man was, so being alone with him sounded like a bad idea.

"I...I'm okay." Farah smiled awkwardly, the last thing she wanted was for everyone to focus the attention on her. If she were to try and get away from the band, it would have only caused them to dislike her more.

Brian nodded as he opened the door to the room they were previously in. Farah suddenly felt a hand on her shoulder. Knowing it was Max, she stopped in her tracks and turned around.

"We can go if you want. Y'know...if you're not comfortable. I understand." Max nodded. Farah knew there was no way Max would have wanted to leave. Max was only saying these things because she was a *good* friend.

Farah placed her hand on top of Max's and smiled. She very much appreciated the concern.

"I'm okay with staying."

"Are you sure? We can bounce if it's too much."

"Everything's good, they all seem...nice." Farah gritted her teeth together; she wasn't used to spending her time around people like this. Perhaps she was too *uncool?*

"That wasn't very convincing."

"I know..."

"I know you're lying because you want me to hang out and be happy and I appreciate the effort, but you don't have to."

"Max..."

"I mean it, Rah. This band is super cool, but you're even cooler! We don't *have* to stay." Max encouraged with a smile, wanting nothing more than to be there for her best friend.

"I'm not cool, but thank you." Farah smiled, unable to accept the compliment. Max was ready to respond but was quickly interrupted.

"Are you guys coming? I thought I'd lost you." Brian stuck his head out the door to check on the two college students. The two best friends turned around with smiles spread across their faces.

Max nodded at Farah before turning to face the frontman of her favourite band.

"It's getting late. Farah and I are going to dip." Max gestured her thumb over her shoulder. She had put the decision in her own hands so Farah wouldn't feel bad about asking to leave.

"Really?" Farah whispered under her breath, confused by Max's action.

Farah only wanted to stay for Max's sake. It would have made her far too anxious to go back into the room after everything that happened. Speaking to Brian had made her feel better about the situation, but that didn't mean it made her feel *great.* Max had come to her rescue.

"Oh. Is everything okay?" Brian's expression dropped as he focused his attention on Farah. He couldn't help but feel as if their desire to leave had come from something he had said.

"It's cool. We're tired. It's been a long day." Max placed her hands on her hips and smiled.

"You're coming to the show tomorrow night, aren't you? Maybe we can all catch up then?" Brian offered, feeling terrible that his friends had forced Farah to feel uncomfortable. He didn't want anyone to feel that way, especially when it was his friends' fault. They hadn't meant to be so harsh.

"Yeah...that would be good." Farah piped up softly causing Brian's lips to curl.

"Sweet. Thanks for letting us chill with you guys, that was hella cool!" Max held onto Farah's arm to help pull her away as they waved to Brian.

"Anytime. J-just let me know!" Brian held onto his own hands awkwardly as he stood in the middle of the corridor alone, the two people he was excited to hang out with leaving.

It wasn't Max's grandest plan to leave, but she wasn't going to allow Farah to feel uncomfortable. She knew deep down

Farah would have done the same for her. It was only right they left the venue that night.

"Are you okay?" Farah asked as they walked back through the corridors of the venue towards the exit.

"It's cool. We'll see them again tomorrow!" Max blew air through her lips as she shrugged off the emotional turmoil that came with supporting her best friend. She wanted to hang out with the band so much, but there were more important things to worry about.

"Sure. We can hang out then." Farah pressed her lips into a thin line as she attempted a smile. She had no idea whether they would have ever had another opportunity to be in arm's length of the band. This could have been Max's only chance to meet them and Farah felt guilty for ruining it.

Not only that, but Brian's vacant expression made her feel as if he were a little deflated that she didn't want to hang out after they had a short-lived conversation. He had managed to help calm her down when there was anxiety coursing through her.

She felt as if she owed him the same courtesy.

Either way, she wasn't sure when that would have been. She may never have gotten the chance to speak to him again.

For now, they headed back to the motel ready for their drive the next day.

ASHEVILLE, NC

Farah didn't always enjoy driving, especially long distance. She had been taught how to drive by her dad after she turned sixteen and managed to obtain her license. It wasn't as if she utilised the skill much.

Part of the agreement of going on the trip was that Max and Farah would have taken it in turns to drive. Farah was starting to regret agreeing to it, considering she was the one who drove the most.

This was partially down to the heavy alcohol consumption Max found herself swimming in. Despite Farah being a better driver, Max was a much better DJ.

They had decided to take Max's car on the journey. Farah didn't own a car and simply borrowed her dad's whenever she was back in her hometown. It wasn't as if she had far to go when she was in town, mostly using it to visit the beach or see some old friends. It wasn't much but the independence felt good.

"We didn't have to leave early last night." Farah gripped onto the steering wheel a little tighter.

"I know. It just didn't seem fair to stay." Max sighed. She had given up a lot to be with her best friend and Farah appreciated it. The band meant everything to Max and for her to leave an opportunity like that was unlike her.

That was their one chance to be with the band and Farah had ruined it for Max.

"I'm sorry."

"N-no it's not your fault. I think I set my expectations too high." Max pushed her cheek against her fist as she watched the world roll by the window.

Farah was finding it hard not to feel guilty about the situation she had put them in. A part of her kept replaying the scene in the back of her mind. Would they all have been best friends now if she had just sucked up her anxiety and smoked pot? Was it *that* simple?

Farah had the entirety of the trip to make it up to Max. Whether that was trying her hardest to get the band's attention again or allowing her to pick the nerdy locations they would visit. Either way, Farah knew she owed her best friend for what she had sacrificed.

"Brian said we could hang out again. We just have to ask." Farah mentioned, trying to keep the conversation positive.

"*Brian,* huh?" Max cocked an eyebrow.

"You were there when he said it."

"I know. He just seems pretty *enamoured* by you."

"Okay, that's a strong word to use." Farah chuckled nervously, hoping that her cheeks didn't turn red at her comment.

"It rolls off the tongue. It's fun to say. Enamoured. Enamoured. *Enamoured.*" Max stared forward for a moment. "Okay, now it doesn't sound like a word anymore. Either way, I think it's a word I would use to describe how he feels about you."

"I think we've spoken twice. One of them he bought you a drink and the other I was *crying.* I don't think that's the case." Farah shook her head as she glanced at the navigation device.

She had shared a few conversations with Brian, but that didn't mean they *liked* each other. At least not in that way. She didn't. Brian seemed to be persistent on throwing hints at the idea, but that didn't mean anything.

"Okay. Okay. I'll believe you." Max didn't believe her one bit.

Max chuckled into her hand as she continued to stare out of the window, watching the road pass them by. It had been interesting to spend so many hours in the car between locations.

Driving back through North Carolina meant they were going back through the state their college was in. Despite this, their college was still over a three-hour drive to where the venue was.

Considering Farah had spent most of her life cooped up in one state, the journey gave her a different outlook on life. Farah wanted the trip to be a way of her finding herself.

She wanted to have fun!

Sure, she had turned down the advances of drugs and alcohol from the band and Max, however, she didn't need either of them to have fun. She still felt awkward about the experience. The last thing she wanted was for the band to spot her in the crowd and think poorly of her.

"You have got to be shitting me." Max abruptly sat up in her seat, turning around as she stared back at a parked van that was by the side of the road.

"What?" Farah exchanged glances between Max and the road ahead.

"That van on the side of the road!"

"What van?" Farah questioned, gripping hard onto the steering wheel as she looked at the rear view mirror.

"The band! It was the band!" Max gasped, practically jumping around in the passenger seat.

"Do you think they have Triple-A?" Farah sighed deeply. She was unsure how else to manage the situation. Stopping for the band would have meant allowing Max to bond with the band again but leaving Farah with copious amounts of anxiety.

"I don't know, but we've got to help them. What if their van is broken? What if they can't make it to the show?" Max gripped Farah's closest arm practically begging her best friend to stop. "I-I know they weren't nice last night, but this could be different. They might feel bad about it and maybe we all just got off on the wrong foot! We've been given another chance and I think we should take it. If they're a bunch of assholes I give you my full permission to *floor* it. Even if you get a ticket, I don't care!"

"I care!"

60

"You know what I mean!" Max argued with a shrug.

"It could be anyone's van!"

"It was their van. I saw Russ!" Max calmed herself down slightly, relaxing in the passenger seat.

"We're supposed to be going to Biltmore!"

"We've been there before."

"So?"

"I promise we'll go again when we're back in college. This might be our only chance to speak to them again."

Farah looked over at Max, continuing to drive in the direction of Asheville. Max had a quick change of heart the moment there was another opportunity to see the band.

"You want me to turn around and help? What knowledge do we have of cars?" Farah attempted to argue her point despite knowing she could never win.

"My brother's a mechanic."

"Can he control your mind and body from four states away?" Farah mocked in a sour tone.

"Video calling exists, genius." Max rolled her eyes.

"*Genius*? Thanks for the compliment, Max. I appreciate it." Farah spoke sarcastically as she touched her fingertips to her chest.

"You're welcome. Regardless, we're good people, Rah Rah..." Max pouted. "Even just keeping them company is considered a good deed. Please! I promise we'll leave if it's weird."

Farah knew she owed Max for the night before. Now it was Farah's time to do everything she hadn't done the previous night. She wanted to make a good impression on them. Although, that didn't mean she was going to change her ideologies on drugs for the sake of looking cool.

Farah groaned as she flicked the blinker and took the next exit. She turned the car around, heading back in the opposite direction to try and find the van parked on the side of the road. It took a while to circle back around to the opposite side of the road and take their place behind the van.

As she pulled the handbrake, she stared forward at the back of the van where she saw the band sitting outside of the vehicle on the side of the road. She gulped, breaking the circle really had given them bad luck. They probably hated her.

Max was the first one to clamber out of the car, throwing her hands out as she made eye contact with each member of the band that was sitting awaiting recovery. Farah stepped out of the car and folded her arms as she joined Max at the side of the road.

"Max! Farah!" Zoe shouted at the pair, the rest of the band perking up upon their arrival.

"Farah?" Brian stood next to the side of the van in his usual attire, cocking an eyebrow at the pair. The last people he had expected to show up were the people from the show.

"Are you guys okay?" Max asked with concern, noticing the hood of the van propped up. Farah followed closely behind, holding onto herself as she silently waved at them all. She didn't want to be around them after the previous night.

"How did these guys find us? Are they really...*following* us?" Catfish whispered over to Russ loud enough for everyone else to hear.

"Magic. Also, they just so happen to be going the same way as us. Logic depicts this was bound to happen. Probability and science." Russ shrugged as he leaned over to Catfish and responded swiftly.

"I don't know much about cars, but...no, I've got nothing. It's dead. Completely." Brian scratched the back of his neck and laughed nervously. He was stressed about the whole scenario, considering he had spent the last twenty minutes searching online for answers only to find negative results.

"The tow truck isn't going to be here for *hours*! We're worried we might not be able to make the show. It would be a bummer to disappoint any fans." Zoe sighed. It wouldn't have been the first time they would have to cancel a show due to transport issues. They were all about getting to the show no matter what and they were contemplating sticking their thumbs out in the middle of the road to get a lift from a stranger.

"We'll take you!" Max shouted without regard for the reality of the situation.

"What?" Farah's face dropped.

"Really?" Zoe's expression filled with both gratitude and shock.

"Yeah! We might have to make two journeys though..." Max turned back and counted the seats in her car.

One short.

The band members all exchanged glances. It seemed as if the fans they had been burdened with were now useful. Max believed if they helped them with this favour then there would have been no reason for them not to have all become best buds.

"If you guys go ahead, I'll wait behind for the tow truck." Brian offered. Despite being the band's van, it was Brian's pride and joy.

"Shit, are you sure? We have no idea how long they're going to be. We can't do a show without you, man." Catfish stressed.

"We've got hours until the show. I'm sure it'll be fine." Brian knew he could use the alone time.

"We can take you guys to the venue and then Farah can swing back around for Brian." Max shared her well thought out plan.

"What?" Farah's subtle attempt to get her best friend's attention was futile. This wasn't what she had expected when she had agreed to turn around.

"You guys don't go on stage until late, you have a local band playing support, right?" Max focused her attention on the band, ignoring whatever Farah had to say about the situation.

Farah realised what was happening. She had suddenly become a taxi driver for a band. Back and forth to Asheville. Max had thrown her in the deep end. Farah took a deep breath in...*it was all about the experience.* She had to remember the mantra else she may have gone insane in the presence of everyone. She had to be cool about it.

"Yes, Mister Static says it's so we don't get emotionally attached to the bands we tour with." Russ commented, briefly mentioning Brian's father. Stan Static.

"Something like that." Catfish grumbled.

"Brian's dad is hella rich and has mad connections but touring with other bands is 'too *distracting* for us'. Bullshit. That's how you get *big*!" Zoe rolled her eyes, revealing some information Farah had already assumed about Brian. It was hard not to be from a rich family when your mother was *Cherry Blossom.*

"Can we get back to discussing the situation?" Brian tried his hardest to ignore what had been said.

The last time Farah had looked on the navigation, the venue was just under an hour away. The journey between Washington and Asheville was a long one and they had been driving since the morning. Both parties were exhausted from the trip, despite the band being used to the lifestyle.

"Are you okay with waiting?" Russ asked, the remaining members of the band turned around to face Brian, voicing their concerns.

Farah raised her eyebrows, hoping she received the same courtesy from Max. That wasn't going to happen.

"Guys, it's fine — just focus on getting to the show. I'll be there!" Brian insisted, pulling out his phone and checking the amount of battery he had. It was in the high nineties after un-plugging it from the charger within the van not too long ago. Charging his phone probably hadn't helped the van situation.

"Only if you're sure. I don't like leaving you. I know that you can be fragile." Russ furrowed his eyebrows, barely visible underneath his large glasses.

"I'm not *fragile*! I'll be fine! Besides, the van is in my name and I was the one to call the tow truck. They might need me here." Brian sighed, only having a slight understanding of how everything worked. He should have just called his dad for help, but he knew that he could do it himself. Eventually.

Farah grabbed Max's sleeve and pulled her to one side.

"What the hell, Max?" Farah scowled, unsure if she un-derstood what she had volunteered her for.

"Hey, I'm giving you an opening..." Max nudged with a whisper as she gently coaxed the car keys from Farah's fingers.

"An *opening*? What for?"

"Look, I'll drive to the venue and you can drive back to pick up Brian."

"What? No way! I didn't agree to that." Farah's eyes sud-denly widened at the idea.

"Well, I'll pick him up then."

"No!"

"See, you *totally* want to pick him up. We're doing them a favour and I, my friend, am doing *you* a favour. It also means that I can chill with the band for a few hours and you can chill with Bri Bri. It's a win win!" Max pointed at Farah with a smile. She was stuck in a hard place of not wanting to be alone with the rest of the band and not admitting she would be happy to spend more time getting to know Brian.

However, allowing Max to spend the time hanging out with the band would have made up for the loss of their time together from the previous night. Max would have been grateful for it.

"This wasn't on the itinerary. Making me drive an extra two hours when I didn't need to isn't doing me any favours." Farah folded her arms once more as her eyebrows dipped into an angry expression.

"But letting you spend an hour alone with the person you want to get to know better is. We can explore Asheville anytime! *This* is a one-time event." Max smirked back, knowing that as much as Farah didn't want to admit it, she continued to hit the right chord.

Farah looked over Max's shoulder as she watched Brian take his place at the side of the road. She hoped his phone had enough battery to keep him entertained. It would have been a while before she went back to get him.

Why did everything have to be so complicated for Farah?

"Just know I'm not happy about this." Farah sighed, looking Max in the eye as she spoke.

"You're going to love it." Max spun the keys around the end of her finger before winking and turning back to the band. Max said Farah would have loved a lot of things only for her to...not. "Everyone ready?"

Max and Farah watched the band grab condensed versions of their bags from the back of the van, most of which were filled with a change of clothes for the show and an abundance of weed.

"I'm excited to set up." Russ smiled before clambering into the small car.

"If we miss a soundcheck, I'm going to be pissed." Zoe sighed, relying on a soundcheck to boost her confidence before a show.

"Are you *sure* you're okay?" Catfish turned and questioned, staring at Brian who was sitting on the grass at the side of the road.

"You guys need to stop worrying about me." Brian waved his phone at them.

"Farah will be back in a couple of hours to pick you up." Max gave Brian two very enthusiastic thumbs up.

"Farah?" Brian's face got hot as he stared up at the girl standing beside Max, trying her hardest to look away.

"Yeah? Is that a problem?" Max cocked an eyebrow as she placed her hands on her hips.

"N-No." Brian was taken aback by Max's tone.

"Good because my friend Farah is skilled in seven martial arts and could kick your ass if you ever step out of line. No funny business, I know how you band dudes can be. This scene is fucked and you know it." Max nodded towards Brian before throwing her arm around Farah in a protective stance.

"*Seven*?" Brian gulped.

"T-that's not true." Farah shook her head, embarrassed by Max's comment.

Max turned towards Farah and burst out laughing, keeping her close. Brian wasn't sure what to believe.

"Farah! You could still totally kick ass!" Max shook Farah as she rolled her eyes.

Brian sat rinsing his hands in front of them, unsure of how to respond to the exchange.

"*Your* ass, maybe." Farah mumbled under her breath as Max chuckled followed by a small cough. Max let go of Farah's arms allowing her to stand up straight.

"Anyway! My best friend will be back in the next couple of hours to pick you up and take you to the venue. If you don't bring her back in one piece I'm taking the rest of your friends hostage. Alright?" Max smiled happily as she spoke.

"*Hostage*?" Brian's eyes widened, trepidation running through his spine.

"Ignore her. I'll text you when I'm on my way." Farah gently pushed Max out of her vicinity before turning back to Brian.

"Okay, sounds like a plan!" Brian smiled up at Farah as he watched everyone pile into the car.

Farah headed to the car before stopping in her tracks and spinning around. Brian watched as she got closer and pulled out her phone.

"I...um...I don't have your number." Farah blushed before opening a new contact on her phone.

"Oh, right!" Brian laughed. "I've never had a girl as pretty as you ask for my number before."

"Sure." Farah chuckled nervously as she held her phone out for him. She very much doubted his statement but appreciated his offhanded flirtatious attempt.

"I'm serious." Brian took her phone and smiled, inputting his number into the small box. He tapped his thumbs against the screen before staring down at the keyboard. Farah furrowed her eyebrows, allowing his comment to stew whilst wondering what the delay was.

"What are you doing?" Farah questioned, curious to know why it was taking so long to input a number. Was he looking through her phone?!

"Oh, I was trying to find the guitar emoji. That way if you had any other Brians in your contacts you'd be able to tell which one is me!" Brian beamed as he pointed to the phone.

Farah hated him. A complete dork.

"I don't have any other Brians on my phone." Farah confirmed, much to Brian's newfound happiness. No other Brians?

He had a chance.

Right?

It was around this time on a tour he had already spent nearly every night with a different girl. This time, he hadn't even shot a glance at anyone. His mind was preoccupied with the girl standing in front of him.

"Well, now you have one!" Brian handed the phone back to Farah.

She glanced down at the phone and noticed the contact. He had placed a guitar emoji next to his name without any shame at all. Brian was Farah's first contact with an emoji next to it, so it wouldn't have been hard to find. Not that she had very many contacts, most of which she tried her hardest not to be in contact with.

"Are you coming?" Max shouted out the window of the car before aggressively slamming her palm against the middle of the steering wheel to make the car sound loudly. The rest of the band had already piled into the back of the car.

"Don't go anywhere!" Farah pointed her finger down at Brian as she tucked her phone into her pocket.

Brian looked up at her with a smile, slowly bringing his legs to his chest as he hugged them like a child. She hated how cute he looked. She shouldn't have been thinking that way.

"I won't!" Brian chuckled as he spoke, the seriousness in Farah's voice being a tone he adored and one he was slightly terrified of.

Farah smirked as she turned around and walked back to the car. She clambered into the passenger seat and everyone waved at Brian as they pulled away. It felt terrible to leave him behind.

The worst part about it was being stuck in a car with the three people who had caused her immense anxiety the night before. The journey was going to be a long one with them in the back.

The three passengers shuffled around for a moment to make themselves comfortable. The car was silent until Russ decided to break the awkwardness.

"Hey, Farah?" He spoke softly, both Zoe and Catfish looking towards the passenger seat where Farah was sitting.

"Yeah?" Farah turned in her seat, a little shaky at his tone. Anxiety ran through her at the thought of his next words.

"We're really sorry about last night. It was never our intention to make you feel anxious or for you to feel left out. We respect your decision." Russ nodded before adjusting his glasses. Farah chewed her lip as she looked through the two seats at the group in the back. Their expressions were genuine.

"Thanks. I—"

"Farah, I'm so sorry. Brian said how upset you were and we all—" Zoe began.

"We felt like shit, dude." Catfish finished her sentence.

"Right." Zoe nodded, giving Farah a sympathetic expression.

Farah looked over at Max who shrugged whilst still trying to keep her attention on the road. It would have been strange to be around the band, but it was nice to hear what Brian had said about them was true. It helped settle her thoughts at the very least.

"T-thanks. I'm sorry I didn't—"

"Ah! No apologising, this is on us." Zoe interrupted.

"We should probably all start again." Catfish suggested, feeling awful. They had never intended for their banter to be harmful.

"Agreed." Russ nodded.

"You guys are super cool. It would be a shame to start badly, especially since you're both kind enough to take us to this damn venue! So sweet!" Zoe smiled at Max in the rear view mirror before passing the same look to Farah who was turned around in her seat.

"We'll get you to the venue, don't sweat it!" Max commented, unsure if Farah knew how else to add to the conversation.

"Killer." Catfish clicked his fingers.

"No hard feelings?" Zoe held her hand out between the two seats. Farah was still turned as she looked in the back. Zoe was sitting in the middle between the two boys, it was easy enough for her to reach out.

Farah furrowed her eyebrows before adjusting her expression. The last thing she wanted was for her to continue to be anxious around the band. Of course, things were going to be awkward between them from the get-go. Farah wasn't going to forget what had happened. Although, that didn't mean she was going to hold it against them forever. Despite everything, they didn't seem like malicious people.

Their apology seemed genuine and Farah would have felt bad if she didn't take the time to accept it.

"No hard feelings." Farah nodded back at each of them as she held out her hand and gripped onto Zoe. Zoe smiled back as she shook her hand, happy their newfound acquaintance had accepted their apology.

The journey to the venue didn't take as long as Farah thought it would. The conversations Farah had been a part of during the trip had mostly been regarding the band. It was Max's personal question and answer session with Social Dropouts.

They asked the college students a few questions too. Each of the band members was excited to hear about what the students had to say.

Farah was interested in their answers, especially when it was about their aspirations around anything other than music. It was nice to hear some of them had a partially extended plan of what they wanted to do with their life. Being in a band wasn't what they did all their time, but it was something to fill the void between everything else.

She had learned a few interesting things about each of them.

Zoe worked in her family's bakery back home and had a twin sister. Russ was a tattoo artist who did online courses on coding. Catfish loved comic books and worked at the local movie theatre.

As soon as the band had gotten out of the car, Farah texted Brian she was on her way only for him to respond with a text message that read:

'Hope you're okay. Come quick. Very bored.'

Followed very quickly by another one that read:

'Not too quick. I wouldn't want you to get a ticket!'

And another, which was hilarious to her considering she had been the one to text first:

'This is Brian btw. Brian Blossom.'

Farah cocked an eyebrow at the messages, the quick succession in which they had come through had made her laugh. She didn't bother to respond, pulling up the navigation on her phone and starting the car.

The drive back along the highway felt longer than the one on the way to the venue. Farah didn't want to be reminded she would once again have to make the same trip on the way back.

A part of her was nervous about going to pick Brian up. It would have been the first time she would have been alone with the frontman of the band for more than a minute or so.

It was only a few days since Brian had bought her a drink at the bar, well, Max's drink. He had been nice to her since the beginning and she had taken note. She realised that she did enjoy his company and would have liked to have him as a friend. Even if it was just for the remainder of the tour.

When she pulled up to where the van had been parked previously it was no longer there. Instead, it had been replaced by Brian with headphones around his neck, sitting at the side of the road flicking through his phone. He looked bored.

Farah beeped the car horn and smiled as Brian looked up in shock. It took him a moment to clock, not recognising the car at first. As soon as he realised who it was his expression changed. He was glad to finally get away from the side of the road, his boredom quickly consuming him.

Brian waved before stepping over to the car, opening the back door, throwing his bag and skateboard in and finding his place in the passenger seat.

"One ride to Asheville, please." Brian smirked as he looked over at Farah, pulling the seat belt over his chest.

"Did the van get fixed?" Farah brought up a question of logistics, the car filling with a dull scent of what Farah could only imagine was weed from his clothing.

"It got towed, we should be able to get it fixed by tomorrow. They've taken it to a garage downtown. Something about the serpentine belt...we fucked it up. Luckily, they can fix it quickly, but it's not going to be cheap at such short notice. They roped me into getting the rest of the van checked out too." Brian confirmed, his tone more serious than the perky one he had been using when he got into the car.

"Does that happen...often?" Farah asked as she pulled onto the road and started their drive towards the venue.

"This? Nope, we've never had a problem like this before. It's usually flat tyres and a lack of care. I've got a big bill coming, but that's the price you pay for touring." Brian chuckled to himself as he pulled on his seatbelt slightly, readjusting it for comfort. "But hey, I'd rather they fixed it all now than breaking down again on the road. We cover a lot of miles."

"Right." Farah confirmed with a nod.

"Besides, getting to spend time with you kind of makes the van breaking down worth it." Brian shrugged as he hid his smile by looking out the window.

Farah held onto the steering wheel and concentrated on the road, not saying a thing as her cheeks flushed a shade of red. He must have gotten a kick out of making her feel that way. He probably did that to every woman he met.

Brian looked around the car, taking note of each little thing inside. The car was an automatic and had a few band stickers stuck on the dash. Brian noticed the CD player and the auxiliary cord hanging loosely from it towards the passenger seat. There was a small tree-shaped air freshener that hung from the rear view mirror. It was clear it wasn't Farah's car from the way she had expressed her lack of interest in the music Max listened to.

"You go to college, right? You and Max?" Brian stared out of the window as he spoke, it was going to be a long journey, he may as well have sparked up conversation.

"We do. Max and I go to Duke. It's not too far away from here." Farah was quick to answer the question to get away from his previous point.

"So, you're really pretty *and* smart?" He pushed his luck. Perhaps a little too far.

"Uh, I don't know." Farah chuckled nervously. She had never been complimented the way Brian complimented her. He was trying to be sweet and it was *working*. She hated that it was working. Her face was red.

"Did you and Max meet at college? Or were you friends before?" Brian asked to take the awkwardness off his previous comment. Farah could feel this was the beginning of an interrogation. She was happy to talk about anything that wasn't the subject of his flirtation.

"We met in college. We had to share a dorm and on the first day we made each other laugh more than I'd laughed in my entire life." Farah let out a long breath, glad to have met someone she got on so well with at college. The concept of moving to another state had been terrifying, but it was reassuring to know they were both scared. It was something they bonded over quickly.

"Laughing until you can't breathe anymore is the best feeling." Brian smiled, understanding what it was like to have been surrounded by good friends. The band was everything to him.

"Yeah! It's a great feeling."

Brian stared out the window for a moment, collecting his thoughts. Farah rinsed her hands on the steering wheel as she prepared for his next question. Maybe she should have been asking him questions instead?

"What do you study?" He quizzed before she could think of something to say.

"Me? I study sociology. Some other things too, but that's the easiest to explain."

"What's that?"

"Oh, it's the study of society. The study of people and why they act the way they do. It's pretty interesting." Farah didn't want to get too much into it, she predicted he wasn't actually interested in what she had to say about college.

"That sounds pretty cool. I never went to college; it seems like fun though." Brian shrugged. It wasn't the only thing Brian had missed out on.

"If you *had* gone to college, what would you have wanted to study?" Farah questioned, interested in what Brian had to say about the topic.

"Can you study music at college?"

"Yeah..."

"I'd study music then."

"It doesn't look like you would need to go to college for that. You seem to have it handled *without* student loans." Farah laughed; it was silly to her that Brian would have considered it. He had already pursued a career in that chosen topic, a successful one at that.

"Yeah, I guess you're right. It would have been nice to go for the social aspect though. I never went to school, so going to college would have been a blast!" Brian continued to stare out the window, his words somewhat vacant.

"You never went to school?" Farah attempted to hide her small gasp.

"Not traditionally. I was home-schooled. Sort of..." Brian's words trailed slightly into a slur.

"*Sort of?*"

"If being taught the basics by a tutor in the back of a tour bus counts as home-schooling...then sure."

"Oh." Farah wasn't sure what else to say.

As much as Brian didn't mind speaking about his past, he wasn't prepared to make Farah suffer by listening to him speak about himself for the remainder of the hour. He wanted to get to know the college student better.

"What do you want to do after college? Y'know...as a career?" Brian was interested to know more.

"I...uh...Max wants to be a lawyer. I could never be a lawyer, but she's really into the idea of helping families out. She has a big family and her mom—"

"I didn't ask about Max." Brian interrupted, realising she had avoided the question. She didn't want to speak about herself.

"Oh. I...I have a plan. I am prepared. It's just graduation's next year and I'm trying not to think about the *after* right now. I'm focusing on the present." Farah continued to avoid his query. She had a plan. Kind of.

"Sweet."

"Yeah."

Brian reached over and flicked the tree hanging from the rear view mirror. Farah watched it swing back and forth, confused by his action in the silence. He was pondering on something else to ask.

"Now you've been to a few shows, do you have a favourite song yet?" Brian swiftly changed the subject as the interrogation continued.

Farah pondered on the question, still embarrassed that despite them going to a couple of shows she still wasn't aware of the names of the songs other than the ones Max had shown her. Even then, the names were too bizarre to remember.

"I don't know the names. I'm sorry." Farah's expression dropped in embarrassment, causing her to blush slightly. She tucked a loose strand of hair behind her ear.

"N-no, it's okay! They have stupid names, anyway." Brian snorted, knowing one of his songs was a reference to something he had seen on the back of a packet of chips once. Music could be anything you wanted it to be and that was one of the many reasons why Brian enjoyed it so much.

"Like?"

"The one we play during the encore is called *'I Dropped My Ice Cream off The Roof of my Dad's Garage'*." Brian couldn't help himself but laugh at the title.

"What? *Why?*" Farah glanced over at Brian and chuckled, unable to hold it in at the utterly ridiculous title.

"That's just emo. It's what this genre does, also, we were super high." Brian gripped onto his knees as he spoke.

"That's pretty funny. I enjoy that one, it's catchy. Everyone likes it."

"It's our most popular song!" Brian was happy to be speaking to someone about his band that appreciated the work he put in, despite not knowing a whole lot about it.

As much as Brian enjoyed hanging around the merch stand after shows to meet the people who liked his music, it felt nice to speak about it with Farah in an environment that wasn't forced. An unbiased opinion on the things he had created. He wondered whether Farah would have enjoyed the different genres he had explored in the past.

It was plausible she had listened to his mother's work and enjoyed it. There was even a possibility she enjoyed a song his father had mixed at some point in his life. It was hard to find someone who hadn't heard of his mother's music. It was hard to go inside of a grocery store or turn on the radio without hearing her voice playing through the speakers. A voice of a ghost.

They had spent the past hour exchanging simple conversations about everything from college to what their favourite food was. Brian found Farah to be an interesting person to speak to and although at first glance he had been attracted by her looks, he was starting to find himself entranced by the way she spoke. She had such a way with words.

Admittedly, his pursuits at the bar had been one of a sexual nature...until he had realised, she had no idea who he was. That was...different. It had made him *feel* different. Surprisingly, it felt good she didn't know him.

Unlike the other women he had been around after a show, she had made no advances. It was strange. It was confusing.

Although, in a way, Brian liked it.

She wanted to hear what he had to say and he felt like she was seeing him as a human being and not simply a frontman with no emotional standing. He was appreciative of her and Max tagging along with them on tour and was more than happy for them to hang out around shows. He wanted that. He wanted to spend more time with Farah.

Brian never wanted to admit to anyone how many people he had slept with in the past, none of which were for reasons other than wanting to be close to someone. It wasn't Brian's fault nobody wanted to be around him for longer than a sexual favour and despite his never-ending search for someone who would stay the morning after, they never came along.

He couldn't focus on the idea of trying to be with anyone in that capacity when Farah was speaking to him about her cravings for ramen after a long day of lectures at college. He had no other motives than to *talk* to her. It made him feel a little less alone.

They arrived in Asheville around twenty minutes before needing to play. They were cutting it tight. There had been a lot of traffic. Brian instructed Farah to park around the back of the venue. Farah watched as he called Catfish to inform them they had arrived. It didn't take long for Catfish to respond.

"Thanks for the ride. We wouldn't have been able to make it to the show without you." Brian smiled as he clicked open his seatbelt. He had missed the soundcheck, but he was okay with that.

Farah turned the key in the ignition as she looked at Brian with a small smile. She had enjoyed getting to know him as they travelled. There was a lot more to him than musical talent and she was desperate to find out.

"It's not a problem." Farah smiled back, just hours ago wishing she wouldn't have to drive anymore. They had already driven so much and she was ready to fall flat on her face on a motel room bed. She would have to check for bed bugs first.

"Is there any way I can make it up to *you*?" Brian held onto the car door handle, ready to exit after he had finished speaking. "Make it up to you both...you *and* Max, I mean." He added, unable to remove his eyes from Farah.

Farah didn't have any favours to ask of the frontman. She took note of his wording.

"Max is a pretty big fan of you guys, perhaps you can invite her to hang out a few more times?" Farah gave an uneasy look, unsure if that was a reasonable request.

"Are you coming to hang out too?" Brian questioned, not wanting Farah to miss out.

"Only if you invite me too." Farah chuckled awkwardly.

"Of course we'll invite you! I just hope the guys didn't scare you off. Plus, I know you didn't get off to the right start, but they like you both! I like having you around—*both* of you! You're cool and we'd like to get to know you. The guys can get boring when you're stuck with them in a van all day. It's nice to have some new faces around." Brian grinned before diverting his eyes to Farah.

They shared a simple moment as they stared at each other in silence.

Farah wasn't sure how to feel about the man in front of her, but whatever it was...it wasn't something she had felt before. She attempted to ignore the feeling, but it kept coming back since the first time he had made eye contact with her at the bar. A feeling she couldn't shake.

"Don't you have a show to get to?" Farah's lips curled upwards as she spoke.

"Aren't you coming?"

"Yeah, just...I have a ticket. I need to line up by the doors." Farah pointed behind her, referencing the front of the venue.

"Ticket? No way! You're coming through the back with me." Brian pointed proudly to his chest.

"Are you allowed to do that?" Farah gasped as Brian opened the car door and stepped outside. She was quick to join him as he reached into the backseat and grabbed his bag and skateboard.

"Yeah, sure! Worst case scenario is they make you line up. C'mon, it'll be fine!" Brian gestured for her to follow him as he threw the bag over his shoulder.

Farah stared up at the venue, this time the building was huge and made of red bricks. There was a distant chatter coming from the front of the venue where people were lining up. The venue looked more like a warehouse; the logo painted boldly at the back of the building.

Farah locked the car as Brian began to walk towards the back of the venue, causing her anxiety until a door opened and Catfish stepped out. Farah followed closely, not wanting to be left behind. She hadn't heard from Max in a while and hoped she was doing okay.

"Dude, you're cutting it tight. Some band from Raleigh is playing." Catfish spoke as he held open the door for them to enter.

"I wouldn't have made it without Farah." Brian pointed back towards Farah who was nervously following them. Brian and Catfish may have been used to a life of making their way through the back of venues, but Farah had a feeling at the bottom of her stomach warning her she shouldn't have been there.

"You and Max are my new favourite people. Stay cool, man." Catfish nodded at Farah as she smiled back, pleased her efforts had been mentioned.

"Where's Max?" Farah questioned. She couldn't lose her. They were responsible for one another.

"Oh, she's chilling with Zoe and Russ. I'll show you guys to the room." Catfish responded, having spent the whole afternoon with Max. Enough for them to have food together, Brian and Farah were regretting not picking up any food.

Brian and Farah followed Catfish through the looping corridors in the back of the venue. Brian took the lead as they walked; Farah watched him from behind as he held the skateboard under his arm.

"Look who I found!" Catfish shouted as he pushed open the door to reveal Russ, Zoe and Max sat inside of the cramped room.

Unlike the last room Farah had been in with the band, this one was small. All it had was a couch and a horrible outdated wooden border in the middle of the wall that went around the whole room. There wasn't anywhere else to hang backstage, so the small room would have to do.

"Farah! You made it!" Max threw her arms above her head, excited to see her best friend.

"Of course we made it! Had a pretty sick driver." Brian grinned as he stepped into the room, placing his skateboard and bag down against the wall.

"You guys are late." Russ stated.

"There was a lot of traffic." Brian was quick to answer. The last thing he wanted was to raise suspicion about when he was alone with Farah.

"We haven't got long. We should get ready." Zoe reminded everyone they were there for a show.

"Sounds like a plan." Russ inputted.

"You're both staying stage side tonight, right?" Catfish asked, curious to know if that was what the rest of the band had decided. It was the least they could do for the friends after they had helped them out.

"*Stage side*? Really?" Max's face lit up at the suggestion. Farah only knew what that meant due to the self-explanatory name. It didn't mean much else to her, but Max was excited about it and that was all that mattered.

"Wouldn't have it any other way!" Brian laughed.

"Thank you! That's amazing!" Max was overly excited by the idea of being at the side of the stage.

It hadn't taken them long to try and befriend the band.

Max had never been as excited as she was in the moment when the band had told her she could stay next to them as they played. Elation ran over her as she decided it was one of the best nights of her life. The show had lived up to the expectations that had been made inside the small room.

When the band went to perform, they had taken Max and Farah with them. This time, they got to stand beside them to watch them play. It was crazy to look out past the stage and see the crowd.

"I'm going for it!" Max winked as Catfish's drums dropped a beat and Brian began to shred on his tatty red guitar, accompanying the twinkly tones with lyrics he shouted at the top of his lungs.

Farah watched as Max ran and launched herself off the stage, falling on the pit of people who held her up with ease. Farah giggled with her arms folded as she watched her best friend shout and point back at the band who were also laughing at their new friend's excitement for their music.

Brian slammed his hand against the guitar and leaned back against Russ as he played a solo. Farah watched the sweat drip from his hairline under the stage lights, a light mist spraying over the equipment as he shouted from the bottom of his lungs. A deep bellow that came out more like a growl, his teeth grazing against the microphone as he sang.

Farah noticed Brian's eyes occasionally meeting hers as he played, a small grin creeping up his face whenever they caught a glance at one another. Brian was filled with confidence as she watched him play. He was fluent in the setlist and Farah was starting to recognise the songs being played. Farah's support made the show better.

The band had made their way back to the room after packing everything up into the second van that was used to take their gear to the next location. Most small bands took their gear with them, but Brian's dad had enough money to pay someone else to do it for him.

Farah liked to think she helped by carrying some of the equipment, the band insisting they shouldn't, but Farah and Max were more than ready to work. It was fun! Max claimed they had become roadies, but Farah didn't seem to pick up on the name change.

At least it was better than being called a *groupie.*

"Oh, shit...*fuck*!" Russ suddenly gasped as they packed the last of the gear into the van and closed the doors for removal.

"What's up?" Zoe questioned. It was likely he had dropped something on his foot, but that didn't seem to be the case...this time.

"Has anyone looked for somewhere to stay?" Russ looked at everyone in the band, each of them sheepishly exchanging glances of panic.

"Um..." Brian bit down on his bottom lip. He had been...distracted.

"We don't even have the van!" Zoe gasped, the panic starting to set in.

"Guys! Don't panic, we'll find somewhere." Brian gave reassuring looks to each of them as he held his hands out, attempting to calm the situation. There had been far too much on their minds to think about accommodation.

It hadn't been the first time they had found themselves in this scenario. They had managed to get through it before.

"How about camping?" Farah suggested one of her hobbies, thinking it would be an easy solution to their problem. She would have loved to have camped at some point during their journey. It was one of her favourite things to do.

"We could, but all our shit is in the van!" Zoe groaned as she pushed the palms of her hands against her face, they had sleeping bags and sleeping mats inside the back of the van that they used when they stayed in different locations, especially people's basement floors.

"Camping does sound pretty fun regardless. Another night, maybe? When we get the van back?" Brian pondered on the idea, trying to keep the tone positive.

"Sure, but that doesn't solve tonight's issue." Zoe crossed her arms and pouted.

"Do we have enough money for a room?" Russ copied Zoe's action of folding his arms as the van full of gear disappeared down the street.

"The van repairs blew through the next few night's earnings." Brian shook his head, sorely disappointed in the situation they had found themselves in. Touring was supposed to be fun...not a headache.

"Call your dad. Stan always knows what to do. Sometimes. If not, his beefy stacks of cash will know what to do." Zoe attempted to direct Brian, the suggestion causing him to breathe deeply.

"Nope. I'm not calling my dad." Brian clenched his fists and sighed, looking away from the situation.

"Dude, he'll just send you some money. One night!" Catfish attempted to get Brian to see sense over the scenario. It didn't seem as if their frontman was going to give in that easy.

"My dad isn't my personal piggy bank. I'm not calling him." Brian countered. Asking his dad for money wasn't something he took lightly. Despite having millions to his name, Brian wasn't ever going to accept that money.

"It's a band thing, he'll give you like fifty bucks. You can pay him back!" Zoe continued to argue the point.

"Why don't you ask him? It's your band too. Better yet, you could dig into your *own* pockets." Brian threw his hands to his sides, clenching his fists with frustration in the process.

"He's *your* dad and you know I don't have shit!"

"He's *your* manager."

"Really? You're really doing this?"

"I'm not asking him."

"Ugh! It's not even that big of a deal. He's supposed to help us on tour! That's the *point!*" Zoe huffed, frustrated with Brian's behaviour.

"So why won't you call him? Ask for your fifty bucks and tell him we fucked the van. *You* won't be the one who hears about how you're irresponsible!" Brian snapped, pointing his finger at Zoe as he raised his voice.

Max and Farah stared at each other. This felt like a conversation they shouldn't have been hearing.

"Oh, grow up, Brian."

"Fuck you, Zoe—"

"Guys, stop." Russ stepped between them and raised his arms. The last thing he wanted was for them to fall out. Farah noticed Brian's disconnect as Zoe turned away and sighed.

There was a silence between them.

"Sorry. I'm sorry. I just...I can't call him. He's going to think it was my fault and—" Brian began to spiral.

"It's okay. We don't have to call him. We'll figure something out." Zoe gripped onto Brian's shoulder as they came to a verdict.

It pained Farah to see the situation play out in front of her. She felt as if she was missing half of the story, but that didn't matter. All she saw was the pain behind Brian's eyes and the fear that came with asking his father for help.

"Why don't you come and stay with me and Max in our motel room? We have one booked. It's less than five minutes from here." Farah shrugged, offering the room to them all.

"What?" Max's expression dropped.

Once again, everyone exchanged glances.

"Really?" Zoe blinked rapidly, excitement in her tone.

"Oh Farah, we couldn't acc—" Brian began, waving his hands in front of him.

"Amazing! You two cuties are *amazing*! Yes!" Zoe cut off Brian's words as she threw her arms around Farah and Max, grabbing them in quick succession.

Brian furrowed his eyebrows, becoming rather embarrassed by asking the two college students for more help than they could afford. It wasn't their job to look after the band. They had to look after themselves.

"Five minutes away?" Russ questioned, on board with the idea.

"That's fifteen on foot, maybe?" Max inputted; the car didn't have enough space for them all.

"Maybe eight on a board?" Brian sighed, finally giving in to the suggestion. It wasn't as if everyone was going to go back on the idea now it had been suggested. His skateboard was in the room, he would have used it to travel. That way he would have a few moments to clear his mind, getting fresh air as he skated down the street.

"Sounds like a plan. Let's go!" Zoe grinned. All she wanted to do was crawl in bed, no matter where that may have been. She craved sleep like an alcoholic craved a drink.

Farah wasn't keen on having the band staying with them, but she felt it was the best solution. It was a nice thing to do.

It didn't take long for the party to decide what they were doing. Brian still felt guilty about accepting Max and Farah's offer. They had done a lot for them during the day and he didn't want to take advantage.

Brian opted to use his skateboard to get to the motel. Thankfully for the rest of them, there was enough room in the car for them to all get in. Max, surprisingly, hadn't drank throughout the night and offered to drive. She had been too distracted by the band to drink.

Farah was nearly falling asleep in the passenger seat as they drove around the corner to the motel.

Max went to reception to grab the key for them all, not letting the motel owner know they were having a whole party staying in a single room that night. They would have left no trace of ever being there.

They all waited around the car in the parking lot for Max to come back. Brian skated around the corner and swiftly came to a stop, kicking the tail of the skateboard up and catching it in his hand before tucking it under his arm. Other than the skaters around the college campus, Farah had never paid attention to the sport before. It looked like a fun mode of transportation and watching Brian glide so effortlessly into the parking lot was mesmerising and made her jealous of yet another talent he held.

As Max came back with the key and instructed everyone to follow her for the room number, Farah picked her bag up from the ground and made sure Max had locked the car correctly. Upon turning around, she jumped at Brian standing directly in front of her.

"I'm sorry, by the way. I don't want it to seem like we're taking advantage of you. That's not the case. Really." Brian awkwardly scratched the back of his neck, his backpack held tight to his back and the skateboard tucked under his arm.

"Huh?" Farah was confused.

"This is the second time today that you've helped us. I just wanted to say thank you for everything. I don't know how to re-pay you and as you probably heard...money probably isn't an option, yet. I'm working on it. I mean, I could get you money for gas or whatever. J-just let me know and I can do that." Brian moved the skateboard in front of him, revealing the scratched artwork. Farah looked down at the bottom of the board; the picture was of what looked to be a pink cartoon alien abducting some cows. She appreciated the strange yet pleasing artwork, despite the number of times Brian had torn through the bottom of the board making the image barely visible.

"It's okay, I don't want your money." Farah snorted, that was the last thing she was worried about.

"Right. Yeah. Sorry. Thanks." Brian chewed the inside of his mouth.

"Thanks for letting us hang out though. Max is going to be talking about this for the rest of her life." Farah chuckled, glanc-ing over to Max who was happily leading the rest of the band to the room that they had been given.

"How are *you* though?" Brian questioned.

"Me?"

"Yeah, you seem to worry about Max a lot more than yourself. It's not a bad thing, I can be guilty of the same thing with the guys. I had to learn to look out for myself too, y'know? It's hard, I get it." Brian shrugged; a little concerned Farah had sacrificed a lot to go on the trip with Max. They were best friends and Farah was happy to do just about anything for her.

"Yeah..." Farah held onto her bag as she gave Brian a look of concern.

"Just...thanks for everything. We appreciate it." Brian smiled, attempting to get past the awkward barrier he seemed to have created between them.

"Hey, Brian and Farah, you coming?" Russ shouted across the parking lot; the door of the motel room wide open.

Brian and Farah looked at each other for a moment, a million things whizzing through each of their minds. Brian won-dered what his band thought of the time he was spending with Farah, anxious they would have been judging him for it. They knew his track record when it came to women he had decided to spend time with in the past. It never ended well for him.

Farah, on the other hand, couldn't stop thinking about the words he had spoken. He was pushing for her to look out for herself. It felt nice to have the reminder.

They made their way over to the motel room, it didn't look like the fanciest place they had ever stayed, but at least it was something. Brian shut the door behind them as they stepped inside the cramped room. After having so many people inside, they suddenly realised the room wasn't intended for more than two people to stay in at once.

"I'm calling dibs on the bed." Zoe threw her arms up in the air, splashing herself down on the bed.

"Um...are you sharing?" Max cocked an eyebrow as she placed her bag down on the floor.

"Sure, Max. Get on in here, it'll be like a sleepover!" Zoe rolled over and spoke with laughter in her tone. Max didn't hesitate to jump beside her, giggling at the gesture.

Farah had been thrown out of the equation. She didn't mind sharing a bed with Max, they had done it previously when they had stayed overnight somewhere before. They were best buds, it didn't matter. However, Farah internally sighed knowing how much Max would have wanted to spend the night beside Zoe. Farah knew she would never be able to compete and that was okay. Max was having a great time and that was all that mattered...

"Hey, do you guys want the bed?" Catfish questioned, pointing to the second and last bed that was up for grabs. He looked at Brian and Farah as he spoke.

Farah furrowed her eyebrows with confusion as she stared at Brian, he seemed to copy her actions before throwing his hands up in defence. Did they think something was going on between them? What was Catfish thinking? Why did they get offered a bed *together*? Why were they suddenly paired off with one another?

"N-no, we're good. You take it." Brian stuttered on his words, speaking for them both without realising.

"Suit yourselves." Russ shrugged, happy to have shared the bed with Catfish if they knew they would have gotten a good night's sleep.

Farah stared down at her shoes, realising what situation she had been put in. She had been paired off with Brian. It didn't matter how many times she wanted to try and avoid it, the situation kept creeping up on her. The issue was...she hadn't been trying to avoid it.

There was a part of her that wanted to be with Brian.

It was new. It was exciting. It was strange. It was...

"Looks like we've just become *floor buds*." Brian laughed nervously before staring down at the floor with a deadpan expression.

Uncomfortable.

Farah didn't say a word as she placed her bag down on a space in the middle of the floor, hoping that maybe she could have used it as a pillow throughout the night. Brian couldn't tell whether she was angry or not, but either way, he was finding it hard to read her emotions.

Brian noticed what she was doing, placing his bag down beside her as she sat down.

There was an ample amount of floor space. Why had he chosen to place his bag beside her?

Farah laid her head down on her bag, looking up at the ceiling and noticing a stain on the paint. The scratchy carpet beneath her probably had years' worth of horror stories to tell. She didn't want to think about it too much.

She had been camping plenty of times in the past to know what sleeping on the floor felt like. Years of deflating air mattresses through the night were all the experience she needed to know it wasn't going to be pleasant.

Brian hit his bag gently, attempting to make it as comfortable as possible before lying down beside her. They were still in their clothes they had worn all day and at the show. Brian knew he smelled slightly like stale sweat and probably weed, but he had blasted himself with deodorant from his bag halfway through his skateboarding session on the way to the motel.

"Uh...do you guys want a blanket or something?" Russ sat at the end of the bed and cocked an eyebrow at the pair who had simply accepted their fate of sleeping on the floor.

"Yes!" Farah piped up, afraid if she didn't accept the offer Brian would have stupidly denied it.

Russ passed the blanket to Farah before crawling back into the bed. Farah knew her best option would be to get off the matted carpet, laying the blanket down on the floor.

Disappointment spread across her face upon realising it was only big enough to cover the space by her bag.

"It's cool. You can have it." Brian stated, noticing the stale expression on her face.

Farah sighed as she laid down on her bag, shuffling around a few times on the blanket to get comfortable. It didn't help much. At all...

Catfish turned off the light, nobody was messing around, everyone wanted to go to bed immediately. The day had been more than what would have been considered exhausting.

"You should have just taken the bed." Farah grumbled under her breath, Brian moved his head on his bag and looked towards her in the dark. The only thing illuminating her face was the streetlight outside that made its way through the slits in the broken blinds.

"Sorry..." Brian apologised shyly. It was a mistake on his part to not have just accepted the bed space, whether that was with Farah or not. He had been too busy thinking about the implications of sleeping in the same bed with her and contending with potentially making her uncomfortable.

"This carpet probably hasn't been cleaned for years..." Farah laughed uneasily. If she didn't laugh, she probably would have cried. How did she get here?

"At least you have the blanket." Brian chuckled as he laid on his back, holding his hands on his chest and mimicking Farah's actions by regrettably staring up at the ceiling. He could hear everyone else in the room toss and turn to make themselves comfortable. Nobody had bothered getting changed.

"It's probably no better." Farah gritted her teeth together. She didn't want to think about it.

She could have gone to Max's car and dug around for her sleeping mat she had packed in case of an emergency, but it would have been awkward now that everyone was settling.

"Hmm, yeah..."

"If I wake up with bites from an insect or any other creature, I'm blaming you." Farah knew Brian couldn't see her smug grin in the dark, but she did it anyway.

"Oh. I'm not really into biting, but if that's what you're into then..."

"No, that's not—" Farah tried not to laugh at his inappropriate comment. Brian got a kick out of making her blush.

"Okay then, what kind of creature?" Brian smirked, suddenly invested in the conversation.

"Rats."

"*Rats?*" Brian gulped, he hoped there weren't any rats.

"All I'm saying is—"

"Can you guys either take it outside or pipe down?" Zoe groaned loudly, despite not being able to see her, they both knew she had her head buried in the middle of a pillow.

There was a moment of silence as Brian and Farah stared at one another in the darkness. They could see the outlines of their expressions, desperately pushing their lips into thin lines.

Brian began to snigger like a child, Farah quickly joining him. She covered her mouth and gestured for Brian to do the same. Brian chuckled lightly, covering his mouth before he burst into laughter and disturbed everyone. Farah let a *'shhh'* sound escape her lips as she gently whacked Brian on the arm to silence him.

They heard the creak of the bed as Zoe sat up and glared over at them in the dark.

"I will fuckin' end you both if you don't *can it* in the next thirty seconds." Zoe gritted her teeth together in anger. If she didn't manage to get some rest, they would have seen a darker side to her that wouldn't have been so pretty.

Zoe's response made everything much worse, the two of them now violently attempting to get the other to be quiet with a gentle *shhh*, childish giggles and playful touches as they tried to cover each other's mouths to silence them.

Suddenly, they got each other to stop as they laid there in the dark, their hands lifted above them, intertwining their fingers by accident. Farah could just about make out the silhouette of his face under the light coming through the blinds from the streetlight. She could tell he was looking back at her with just as much shock as she was providing him.

His hands were warm in comparison to hers. They were much larger too and aside from his rough fingertips...*soft*.

They pulled away at the same time, realising they had lingered a little too long. They both turned onto their backs and continued to stare at the darkness above them.

Farah didn't know whether what she had just experienced was awkward or not. It felt...new. She liked his touch and felt a little disappointed when he moved away.

"Goodnight." Brian whispered, furrowing his eyebrows with concern. He wasn't going to have been able to sleep. All he was going to be able to think about was that single moment.

"Goodnight." Farah's voice was barely audible, nearly choking on her words. She wasn't going to be able to stop thinking about the connection that had happened between them under the cover of darkness.

They had only known one another for a couple of days and they were already overstepping personal boundaries.

They were both filled with deep pitted feelings of guilt.

CHARLESTON, SC

Neither of them was willing to admit how little sleep they had gotten throughout the night. It wasn't as if they could see one another in the darkness, but Farah could tell from the switch in Brian's breathing he had dropped in and out of sleep several times.

Admittedly, the floor was incredibly uncomfortable, and they knew they would have woken up feeling stiff from being there all night. Farah wasn't driving to Charleston in the morning, it was Max's turn. She would have been far too tired for that.

It was late morning by the time each of them finally started to wake up. Catfish was the first one to dip into the shower and use the bathroom, knowing if he had left it any longer, he wouldn't have gotten a chance. Each of them had gotten pretty used to washing themselves in public bathrooms before shows, which wasn't a great way to live, but a lifestyle each of them welcomed.

Brian and Farah hadn't spoken much in the morning, mostly exchanging awkward glances after accidentally finding themselves a little closer than what they thought the other person was comfortable with. They didn't want to make things...*weird*.

Except it wasn't weird. At least, neither of them thought it was. They were more worried about what the other person thought of them.

Farah hated to admit she was enjoying his flirtatious comments, but she was. They made something spark inside of her. It didn't feel like this when the boys her parents suggested called her beautiful to make a good first impression. It was always so fake and forced. Brian's comments had felt genuine, even if he had other intentions.

Max had agreed to take Catfish and Brian to the garage to pick up the van as everyone else stayed in the motel room taking it in turns to use the shower.

Brian drove the van back to the motel, as good as new. The van had a new serpentine belt and whatever other repairs they had overcharged them for. He hoped now that it had been fixed they wouldn't have any more problems during their journey. It had cost enough to get it fixed so quickly; they really couldn't have afforded for it to have happened again.

After picking the band up and all piling into the van, they made their way across the state towards Charleston for their next show that evening. Max and Farah followed closely behind them in the car, they didn't seem to go out of sight the entire time along the roads.

They hadn't left Asheville until the afternoon; they hadn't gotten out of bed until late.

"I can't believe they like us." Max shook her head in disbelief as Farah slowly awoke from her gentle slumber that had made her neck stiffer than it already was from sleeping on the floor.

"They're your best friends now." Farah grinned, rubbing her eyes.

"No! They could never take that title away from you." Max gasped, holding onto the steering wheel as she glanced over to Farah. "Well, Zoe is pretty close. Did you see us? We shared a bed. Okay, maybe the best friend title can be rearranged."

"I slept on the floor." Farah groaned before staring ahead at the back of the familiar van driving in front of them. They truly were...*following* the band.

91

"*All in all, a great sacrifice, my friend.*" Max stated in a poor attempt at a British accent.

"How?"

"I got to sleep next to Zoe and you got to sleep next to Brian! That's a winner winner chicken dinner situation." Max nodded with a smirk. She had been beyond excited for the trip, but after everything that had happened, she was on a completely new level of happiness. A level of happiness that Farah hadn't even unlocked yet.

"No. No chicken dinner winners. It was..." Farah shook her head.

"What did you two talk about on the drive? Y'know, when you picked him up?"

"I don't know—*stuff?*"

"What kind of stuff?"

"It was mostly small talk. He wanted to know about college and we spoke about the band and the stupid song titles they come up with. It was nothing."

"What? Like '*I Dropped My Ice Cream Off The Roof of my Dad's Garage*'?" Max questioned, snorting at the name.

"Exactly that."

"So, nothing sexy? Nothing that would deserve a 'parental advisory' sticker?" Max was curious to know what was going on in Farah's life when they weren't together.

"No. Nothing like that. It's not—"

"You've nearly spent a full working week pining over this dude." Max shrugged, preparing for Farah's next move.

"*Pining?* I don't think so."

"Just...ask him out!"

"Ask him *out?*"

"Sure!"

"Where? A *concert?*" Farah scoffed before realising what Max was trying to get at. "It's not like that anyway, he's just...a nice guy. We get along!"

"A *nice* guy? What does *that* mean?" Max couldn't help but laugh.

"He's nice! Nice to be around? He seems like a good person!" Farah huffed in frustration, clenching her fists.

"I can see the headlines now. *Brian Blossom—Nice Guy.*" Max waved her hand out in front of her as she spoke.

"You are such a dick sometimes, you know that, right?" Farah shook her head in disbelief, a small laugh escaping her lips.

"Yeah, I know. It's cool. I own it." Max scratched the side of her face as she drove behind the van. There was a slight silence within the car before Max continued. "If you like him, you should let him know. I don't like thinking about it...but this trip is pretty short-lived. We might not have this opportunity again in our entire lives. You must seize the day. *Carp in your DMs*!"

"*Carpe diem*?"

"That's what I said. Anyway, what I'm getting at is...shoot your shot. *Pew Pew*!"

Farah briefly thought about her friend's words. Despite her not always wanting to listen to the silly things that frequently came out of Max's mouth, she also managed to speak a lot of sense. Max was right about one thing...the tour wasn't going to last forever.

Was it stupid for Farah to even consider trying to start a fling with the lead singer of a band? Would it have been worth it? Would it have been morally corrupt? She was sure people did this kind of thing all the time, but did that make it right? Would it have made her feel good?

"I'm not here to do...*that*."

"What? *Do* Brian Blossom?"

"No—"

"Now, is it so wrong for a girl to love a boy? For a girl to love a girl? For a boy to love a boy?"

"No...but, I'm not in *love*. I've known him for like...five days. You can't possibly fall in love that fast, it's stupid." Farah shook her head, there was no way she believed any of that garbage.

"Jeez girl, have you never seen a *Disney* movie? Your childhood was whack." Max audibly gasped before huffing through her teeth.

"It's not reasonable."

"You can still *like* someone though. Look, do what you want. I've seen the way he looks at you. He looks at you like you're the last woman on this godforsaken planet. You're hot, Rah Rah...you should own it!" Max gushed over her best friend, wanting to build Farah's confidence. She knew how self-conscious Farah could be.

Max wasn't wrong about one thing...Brian gave Farah a look that showed his desire in a single stare. He may not have known her for long, but he had a deep admiration for her.

"Even if I *did* end up liking Brian—"

"You admitted it!"

"I didn't! Let me finish!" Farah complained.

"Okay, sure. What is it?" Max rolled her eyes as she gripped onto the steering wheel a little tighter.

"Even if I did...which I don't, it would be impossible. What am I supposed to do? Flirt with some guy in a band and then that's it? That's so *cliché!*" Farah groaned, having read one too many books to know exactly how the story was going to end.

"I'm no love expert, but I don't think that's how it works."

"Besides, you really think anything could come of that? What the hell would my parents say? It's silly, he's just...*nice.* He's nice to be around. He's not someone I could be with." Farah defended, raising her voice at the idea of being with Brian in any capacity other than a friendship along the road. Realistically, it couldn't happen. It *shouldn't* happen.

"For a start, Brian Blossom is a much better candidate than any douchebag your parents have ever picked out for you. If that Hasan dickwad calls you whilst you're on this tour I'm going to scream." Max sighed, realising Farah's situation with her parents was a lot to handle.

Max had been in Farah's life long enough to know that her parents were picky people. Every couple of weeks they gave Farah a few options of new potential sweethearts, some of which she would have to humour to make her parents happy.

None of which made *her* happy.

"Ugh. Please don't talk about *Hasan.*" Farah buried her head into her hands and groaned. The last thing she wanted was to think about the son of her parents' friends who had been pushed as a suitor for years. He continued to try his luck and it was in Farah's best interests to put up with it. Even if that did mean accepting a phone call from him now and then.

"Look, I'll be real with you, bro. You may as well try to have some fun on this trip. Just fool around with the guy, he seems into you." Max shrugged, taking the next turn in the road, following the van.

"If my parents ever found out I went on this tour, they'll kill me. They're probably already suspicious about this *historical* road trip. I can't throw a *boy* into the mix. Especially not one with tattoos and bleached hair and a band and *drugs*! He does drugs! Weed is a drug! One that my parents are very much against the legalisation of for recreational use. Ugh, this is so stupid." Farah made sure to keep her attention on the window, watching the world pass by.

"It's not stupid, this is a trip of opportunity. It's not even a rebellion, it's just you experiencing the world for whatever you want it to be. Forget about college, forget about me, forget about your parents...you have to do what you want to do. Be selfish, think of yourself for once! What do you want?" Max repeated similar words to what Brian had mentioned the previous day.

"I don't know..."

"Use this time to find out! The band has no idea who you are, hell, you may never see them again after this tour. You have the whole trip, and you can do whatever you want. You can *be* whoever you want!" Max attempted to make sure her point got across.

Farah didn't want to admit it, but Max was right. Farah had already shown them who she was on a small scale, but they had no idea. She could have faked a persona if she wanted to, despite being unable to show anything other than herself.

They continued to follow the band until they stopped for food at a drive-through restaurant, both vehicles parking next to one another with their windows down to chat. Max aggressively threw fries through the window at Catfish as he threw them back with force. Farah pouted; the car would have ended up with fries down the side of the seat that they would regretfully discover in a couple of weeks.

Farah had found herself actively avoiding Brian throughout the night. It hadn't got anything to do with him, but her mind was telling her to stop interacting. An internal screaming that wouldn't go away.

After they had played the show in Charleston, Max had insisted on hanging out with the band again. This time, Max had decided on drinking heavily with them all in the room at the back of the venue. Brian knew they wouldn't be able to go to the person who offered to house them until later in the evening, around two in the morning. This was due to their unusual shift patterns.

Despite this, the band were grateful they had found somewhere to spend the night. It also meant they were willing to bum around the venue for as long as it took them to be kicked out.

As per usual, the show had been a good one. This time, Farah stood nearer the stage. Brian still managed to find her in the crowd and smile. It was as if he suddenly relied on her presence to get him through the show.

On a cool and breezy night, Brian was in the parking lot at the back of the music venue skating. Going on tour with a skateboard was always fun.

Farah walked to the back of the venue, a part of her hoping that was where she would find Brian. At least then she would have someone to speak to about subjects she would be more interested in. Ones she wanted to learn more about.

"Nice moves, *Blossom*." Farah smirked as she stood by the fire exit watching the man in the red flannel shirt suddenly trip on his skateboard in the middle of the parking lot.

Brian placed his hands on his hips and breathed heavily as he noticed Farah stood off to the side with a plastic cup in her hands. He could only assume it was water. Not only had he spent the last hour or so sweating under the lights of the stage, but he was now panting heavily from all the tricks he was attempting.

"Yeah? Do you want a go?" Brian wheezed as he stood up straight, kicking the board over so it stood on all four wheels under his beaten-up red skate shoes.

"Do you need some water?" Farah chuckled as she held out the cup of water from the venue.

"You didn't answer my question."

"You didn't answer mine."

"I asked first."

"I don't think you're going to get me on that board." Farah shook her head with a smile, she didn't see herself as much of a skater. Farah could have done anything if she put her mind to it, but skateboarding wasn't something she had ever considered.

"Come on. You'd be good at it!" Brian insisted, popping the board up with his foot so he could bring it closer to Farah.

It just so happened to be their first real verbal interaction since their night on a scratchy carpet. Exchanging glances throughout the day didn't count.

"I wouldn't. You would just laugh because I'd most definitely fall and break my ass." Farah snorted, holding out the plastic cup. He took the cup, allowing his fingertips to brush against hers. She shivered slightly at the touch, despite his hands being warm.

"I wouldn't laugh." Brian looked at Farah with a serious expression, keeping his eyes on her as he took a long drink of the water.

"Hmm...I don't know." Farah gave the board by his feet an uneasy look of concern. She watched him wipe his mouth on his sleeve as he passed back the cup. There wasn't much left.

"Would it help if I held you? You wouldn't fall off. I promise."

Farah was right about him being a nice guy. She could never tell whether he was flirting with her or just being a nice person.

Farah placed the plastic cup down by the door and looked back up at Brian in anticipation. Was she going to step foot on a skateboard? Was this what her life had come to? Was she punk now or just a *poser*? She had read both of those words online but was shaky on the definitions.

'Carp in her DMs'?

Brian watched carefully as she walked over to him with hesitation in her steps. Brian held the skateboard underneath his foot, making sure it didn't run away without him.

"How do you do it?" Farah pulled her messy bun a little tighter before placing her hands on her hips and staring down at the battered piece of wood on wheels, the grip tape peeling at the edges.

"Years of bruising my shins." Brian snorted, causing Farah to react in the same way.

"You're not exactly filling me with confidence."

"It's okay. I won't let you fall." Brian took a step back, holding out both of his hands and gesturing for her to step onto the board.

"Do you have health insurance?" Farah suddenly cocked an eyebrow with concern.

"Yes..."

"You're still covered if you don't wear a helmet, right?"

"I wouldn't know, I've only ever broken my ass and skaters don't tend to wear helmets there." Brian smirked, entertained by his comedy.

"You're not selling this skateboarding experience well." Farah laughed.

"Come on, it's easy!" Brian held his hands out a little further, gesturing again for her to hold on.

Farah glanced around the parking lot, there was nobody around to witness her falling. Not only that, but they wouldn't be able to see her gripping tightly onto Brian's hands. Max would never have allowed her to live it down.

Farah slotted her fingers between Brian's as she stepped onto the board. Just as she had accidently done the night before. His hands were larger than she remembered and yet her fingers still locked perfectly in place.

She suddenly found herself taller than the man, usually standing around the same height, give or take an inch. Now, she felt like she towered over him as she stood on the board.

Farah felt herself being pulled forward on the edge of the board. Enough that Brian was only inches away from her.

"No falling unless it's for me, okay?" Brian smirked, feeling his body heat up at his flirtatious comment. It had taken him a lot to say, but it was worth it as he watched Farah blink at him as he pulled away.

"Okay." Farah nodded in confirmation with a blush. She couldn't focus on his comments when she was concentrating too hard on not falling off the board.

Pushing her fingers between his was a new experience. She welcomed the warm touch and appreciated his firm grip.

He was right in saying he wouldn't let her fall. Farah trusted him.

Unlike the night before, neither of them wanted to let go. It wasn't weird...Brian was teaching her a new skill. A new skill where he got an excuse to hold her hands again.

There wasn't much skateboarding happening as she stood on the board and stared down at him, unable to loosen herself from his soft hands. She didn't want to let go.

"What now?" Farah questioned.

"Huh?" Brian had found himself in a trance looking up at her with wide eyes.

"The skateboard?" Farah laughed; Max was right. Max was very much right. He did look at her differently.

"Oh, right!" Brian chuckled awkwardly, holding onto her hands and naturally brushing his thumbs over the tops of her fingers as he spoke. She felt her breath stammer at the touch. "I'll probably just drag you along for a bit. It'll help you get used to the feeling of the board underneath you. Is that okay?"

Farah nodded as Brian tightened his grip and pulled her along the parking lot. Luckily, the asphalt below was smooth and had recently been resurfaced. It was the perfect place for skateboarding.

"Hey, this is pretty fun!" Farah smiled as Brian walked alongside her, pulling her across the parking lot with ease.

"Yeah? I'll have you popping kickflips in no time!" Brian chuckled to himself, Farah didn't know what he was talking about.

"One step at a time."

"Sure." Brian beamed up at her, unable to remove his stare as she rolled beside him. She looked down at him and noticed the emerald in his eyes, shining under the streetlights. She blinked. She hadn't realised how attractive he was. Not in *this* way.

Brian didn't realise walking sideways across a parking lot and staring up into her eyes as he pulled her along wasn't the safest activity. Suddenly, the front wheel caught itself on a small stone, causing the skateboard to come to a halt and tip forward.

Farah was thrown off by the sudden jolt, finding herself falling into the chest of Brian Blossom. Brian immediately let go of her hands to catch her. Farah placed her hands on his chest as she fell, attempting to regain her balance.

"You said you wouldn't let me fall!" Farah began to laugh as she pressed her hands against his chest, not realising his arms had fallen around her to hold her up. The last thing he wanted was for her to fall any further.

"I caught you, didn't I?" Brian held her, not clocking onto how close they were. Face to face. Inches apart. So close that Farah could feel the breath of his whisper against her lips.

"Yeah, you did. No casualties." Farah sniggered, realising he had kept his arms locked around her. As she applied pressure to his arms by leaning back, they quickly detached.

Brian gave Farah an apologetic look as they took a step back from one another. He didn't mean to let her fall and he certainly didn't mean to impose anything. There was some incredibly awkward flirting happening. Comments were one thing, but he would never touch her intentionally without permission. Even innocent touches.

Brian had always been so smooth with women and yet Farah was an enigma. Perhaps he was just smooth with other partners because they were the ones who wanted to sleep with *him*? They were willing to listen to whatever he had to say if it meant they would have sex with the frontman.

Was he always this awkward when he flirted? He didn't think so.

"Heh, I forgot to mention skateboards don't fare well with any kind of bump or rock. Rule number one." Brian laughed before scratching the back of his neck as a way of escaping the conversation.

"It would have been nice to know that before." Farah shook her head with a smile, not feeling as embarrassed as she should have about stumbling into Brian like a fool.

"Rule number two, Brian will always give you advice after you need it, never before. Be careful." Brian spoke in the third person as he kicked up the skateboard and caught it in his hand.

"I don't think I'm going to be a pro skater any time soon." Farah sighed as she folded her arms with a smile.

"Everyone starts somewhere. Plus, you sound like you're good at so many other things." Brian shrugged. Farah ran her finger against her bottom lip at the comment. She didn't know how to respond, but she appreciated his words.

Without question, they made their way towards the fire exit at the back of the venue.

Brian decided to sit down beside the door, leaning his back against the wall. Farah sat down beside him, a little closer than two people who would have called themselves friends.

Brian pulled out a small device from his back pocket, Farah wasn't sure what it was at first.

"Do you mind if I—" Brian held up the device, it looked like a vape pen. It didn't take long to clock onto the fact it probably didn't contain nicotine.

"N-No...it's fine." Farah waved her hand, assuring him it was okay to smoke.

Farah had never been a fan of smokers and had scolded the stoner kids on campus multiple times. It was the sort of thing she had been raised to be repulsed by but when Brian did it...it seemed so normal. It shouldn't have been. She knew it was wrong.

"Do you want some? It's not as harsh as a joint but it works a little faster." Brian took a puff of the device before offering it to Farah. He glanced over, not wanting to make her uncomfortable. "You don't have to if you don't want to, I'm just being polite." He chuckled.

"What does it make you feel like?" Farah questioned, genuinely curious. "Weed, I mean."

"Uh...numb? A good kind of numb." Brian shrugged, glancing down at the vape pen.

"What does that feel like?"

"It makes a black and white world a little more interesting...even if just for a while." Brian smiled at her, his words poetic with meaning and intent.

Farah looked down and picked at the skin around her fingernails. Brian noticed her disengagement, distracting himself with another puff. Farah could smell the vapour as the breeze gently swept in her direction. Unlike the other times she had been subjected to the pungent smell of weed, the vape was less intense. A much cleaner and herbal smell.

"I hate to say it, but you're selling it to me." Farah laughed. Her parents would have been disappointed if they had heard her comment.

"Yeah?"

"—But I could never." Farah came to her final decision. She wasn't going to be getting high with Brian Blossom any time soon. Ever.

"That's okay. I'd probably say the same if I were you. When I left home as a teenager, someone offered me a joint and I never looked back. I guess I was just angry at the time, I wanted to do anything and everything to not be...*me*. I understand where my mom was coming from, but I'm glad I'm not like her." Brian shrugged, taking yet another puff of the vape. He knew he would have regretted the quick succession not long after. "S-sorry, I didn't mean to spill my guts. That was weird." Brian immediately apologised.

"I-it's fine. I don't mind."

Farah watched the vapour float above her head, thinking about the mention of his mother. All the information she knew about the pop singer was from the internet. Even then, the things she had read were horrific. It wasn't something she wanted to bring up.

"Are you sure?" Brian questioned, not wanting to get too personal with the woman he knew little about. It would have been unfair to offload his lifelong problems onto her, but she didn't seem to complain. Instead, she shared her own.

"I thought when I went to college I could become someone different. I failed miserably on that one." Farah laughed, continuing to pick at the skin around her fingernails.

"It's weird how we're all so desperate to be someone else. Why can't we just be satisfied with what we've got?" Brian turned the pen in his hand, suddenly bringing his knees to his chest as he sat against the wall.

"Because humans are needy and never satisfied."

"Too right. Sounds like my family."

"Sounds like my parents." Farah snorted, looking away as she found herself relating to someone she thought she would never have anything in common with.

"What are they like?"

"Where do I start? Overbearing? *Invasive*?"

"I'm surprised you haven't rebelled yet." Brian laughed, speaking from his own experiences.

"I'm here, aren't I? They think I'm on a historical tour of the USA." Farah smirked.

"Ooo, that's good." Brian nodded, appreciating her rebellion. That was punk.

"Technically, we're doing the historical tour too. They would never talk to me again if they found out where I was. They think most pop music is drivel and rock music is too influential on young minds. I hate to think what their opinions on this would be. Unless there's an orchestra, they don't want to hear it." The young college student tittered as she pushed her glasses up the bridge of her nose.

She never wanted to disappoint them, but she wanted to be someone she could be proud of too.

"Russ uses a trumpet sometimes."

"That's not what I mean." Farah laughed, causing Brian to grin.

"Hey, there's no harm in living a little. Life is supposed to be lived; they can't keep you cooped up forever. You have to decide what you do and don't like yourself; they can't decide for you."

"You sound like Max."

"That's because Max is right."

"Don't you dare tell her you said that." Farah sniggered, pointing up at Brian to increase the threat.

"Okay! Okay! I won't!" Brian laughed as he waved his hands to defend himself.

"How about you? What's your family like?" Farah asked, hoping it would have been a casual conversation topic.

"That's a loaded question."

"You don't have to answer."

"It's cool, most of my family are just people I was raised around. I don't talk to them much. But, my dad? He's okay, mostly. I don't think he...*gets it* sometimes and we clash. Not in a bad way, maybe. It's just hard for him to see things how I see them. It's my fault for trying to distance myself, I guess. It doesn't help he always pushes me into things, things I don't want to do. I needed to go." Brian's words were somewhat broken as he shrugged his shoulders after speaking, putting his lips to the end of the vape and then deciding against taking another drag. "I just wanted to get out of that house, if you could even call it that..."

"Oh, I'm sorry." Farah spoke faintly. There was a sadness in his tone.

"After my mom died and we moved to Nashville for some permanence, my dad was always out working. Trying to be something he wasn't. It worked though. So, as a teenager I got super into skateboarding and I met Russ at a skatepark. They're all a few years older than me, but they look out for me. Russ' family looked after me when my dad was away. I mostly went home for clean clothes. Russ' mom makes great chicken pie. It's...*so* good." Brian explained with the sense of normality to his words.

"I'm sorry your dad wasn't around."

"It's okay. It's what I get for being the son of a *Flower Child*. Ugh, I hate that name so much. I know my band name sucks, but The Flower Children? It's terrible! What the *hell* was she thinking?" Brian waved his hands as he laughed, snorting slightly at the name.

"That's pretty crazy...they're always on the radio. I can't believe you're..."

"Don't. I know—*related*." Brian sighed as he finished Farah's sentence. "'*You can't choose family*' or whatever those shitty quotes you get on wall art say. Catfish's grandma has one in her kitchen."

"I was going to say 'so humble'. I probably wouldn't be able to stop talking about it." Farah shook her head, imagining what it could have been like to live in Brian's shoes.

"Sometimes you get pretty sick of talking about it when it's the only thing people see in you. You don't even feel like a real person. All you are is a product of what they once were and the expectations everyone sets for you is far beyond what you're capable of. Why can't people accept I want something different? I don't want to be like her. I want to be *me*!" Brian ranted, trying not to raise his voice. He was suddenly caught inside his emotions and sighed deeply at the end of his speech. "It's...hard." Brian added before taking a long drag of the vape pen. It wasn't working the way he wanted it to.

Farah could hear the pain and distance in his voice. They had hit a nerve when they spoke to one another, Farah had never intended for her to cause him any harm.

"I'm sorry." Farah mumbled.

"No! I'm sorry, I-I shouldn't be speaking about this. I barely even know you and I'm offloading all my baggage. I didn't mean to—" Brian became stressed by his own words, digging his fingernails into his knees as he spoke.

He unexpectedly felt a warm presence on top of his hand. Another hand. Farah's hand. Brian breathed deeply as he stopped ranting to himself, the touch calming him down almost instantly.

She knew her action was forward, but she had sent him in this spiral, she wanted to be the one to pull him out.

"It's okay. You're human...you're allowed to feel things. I may not know much about playing music, but I am good at listening. If you ever need someone to listen, I'm happy to do so." Farah gently rubbed her thumb against the top of Brian's hand causing him to turn his head and look directly at her.

"Nobody has ev—" Brian stopped his speech. Nobody had ever spoken to him the way Farah had unless they were paid to do so. "That's really nice of you."

"No problem." Farah smiled. She wanted to listen to Brian and hear what he had to say. She was interested in him as a person and not so much his music, which was the first time anyone had done that in his life.

Brian glanced back down to Farah's hand that sat so perfectly on top of his. Farah was scared he was becoming far too suggestive and pulled away, not wanting to bring any more awkward tension between them.

"Thanks for listening." Brian smiled at her sweetly, a little upset she had removed her hand.

"Anytime." Farah nodded back with little effort, happiness in her tone.

Although Farah had unsuccessfully attempted learning a new skill, there was one thing she was starting to learn more about...

Brian Blossom.

BIRMINGHAM, AL

After Brian and Farah's conversation the night before, they had quickly gone their separate ways when the rest of the band had searched for Brian. Max and Farah went back to a motel room where Farah was pleased to have the option to sleep in a bed rather than the floor.

The band were happy to know the next day of the tour was nothing more than travelling. When booking the tour, if the states in between were a longer car journey than usual they would try to extend the days between when they played. Having a night off meant they could relax throughout the evening and be ready for the next day with minimal fatigue.

Brian enjoyed it when they had a day off. It gave them time to explore whatever city they were in. It made the travel worth it.

With a free day to spare, they decided to spend their first full day away from tour travelling for as long as they possibly could. The car journey between Charleston and Birmingham was around six hours long and they were happy to take their time getting there.

This time, Max and Farah didn't manage to keep up with the band. They had slept in far later than anticipated and made their way slowly across the states. There was no need to rush.

After spending a lot of time with the band it was nice to be just the two of them.

Most of their day had been spent exploring several of the tourist locations in Atlanta. Neither of them had ever been before and spending the day touring the city was fantastic. Farah was certain she would have rated it one of the best days on the trip so far. That accounted for the days and not the nights they spent watching an emo band slam their hands against instruments and shout about their emotional hardships.

It was late in the day when Farah received a text from a familiar-looking contact who hadn't sent her any messages since they were in Asheville. The guitar emoji sat by his name as she glanced down at the unopened text, Max was beside her completely entranced by a wordy looking exhibit at the *National Center for Civil and Human Rights*. They were enjoying themselves, but there was far too much information to absorb.

"I thought we had a *no phones* rule?" Max scowled as she glanced over to Farah, taking her eyes away from the exhibit.

"It might be my parents!" Farah rolled her eyes. She had already seen the emoji on-screen and was currently in the process of unlocking her phone—it wasn't her parents.

"Are your parents more important than the extensive history of the American Civil Rights Movement?" Max shook her head as she stared at Farah who was ignoring her, too engrossed in her phone to care. "I think the *fuck* not…" Max mumbled before focusing her attention back on her reading.

Farah looked down at the text.

'We're going camping just outside of Birmingham tonight. Do you and Max want to come?'

Brian's words were simple and friendly. Farah watched as another text came through.

'I say 'camping'…I mostly just mean a blanket on the floor underneath the stars. We don't have any tents.'

And another.

'Better than the floor the other night though, right? Haha!'

And then another…

'Anyway...think you and Max can make it? Would be great to have you there.'

Farah bit the bottom of her lip as she looked down at her phone before glancing back up to Max who she could tell was slightly mad about Farah using her phone for something other than taking photographs.

"Hey, Max?"

"Wassup? The folks calling you back home? *Hasan?*"

"Do you want to go camping tonight?" Farah questioned, ignoring her comment. She had taken Max camping before.

"Did you sneak your gear in the trunk?" Max cocked an eyebrow as she placed her hands on her hips. The underneath of Farah's dorm room bed was filled with all kinds of camping gear, Max wouldn't have been surprised if some of it had made it into her trunk.

"No—" Farah replied sheepishly, not wanting to admit the bottom of one of her bags held a sleeping mat and bag she had packed for emergencies.

"How are we going camping?"

"Brian and the band asked if we—"

"Yes."

"Yes?"

"You mentioned the band. I'm in. I don't care what it involves. I'm fucking *in*. Sign me up. Where do I sign? Do you have a pen?" Max jumped towards Farah making her laugh. She swiped her phone from Max's vicinity and stepped back.

"No signing, I'll just say yes." Farah nodded, looking back down at her phone and sending a confirmation text.

Farah sensed Max's presence behind her. She could feel Max's eyes staring at the phone screen. Despite there not being anything inappropriate, Farah felt as if her privacy had been invaded. Never in her life had she felt that way, having spent all her teenage years without a lock on her phone to grant her parents' easy access.

"When did you start texting Brian?" Max purred, interested to know what the heck was going on between her best friend and the frontman of her favourite band.

"It's not what you think. It was just so I could tell him when I was on my way near Asheville." Farah sent the text before desperately scrolling up, revealing the small number of messages that had been exchanged between them. Much to Max's disappointment there was nothing of a juicy nature.

"Boring." Max sighed, removing herself from Farah as she walked off to continue her tour of the museum. Max was going to get her money's worth, even if Farah wasn't.

'Really? Cool! I can't wait to see you. I'll send you the address.' Brian texted back almost instantly. Farah's heart sank as she read the message, his words were incredibly personal and direct.

'I can't wait to see you' was such a simple phrase.

It was about her. He wanted to see *her.*

Her thoughts were stupid. He was just a nice guy with nice hair and a nice voice and nice eyes and a nice...

Farah took a deep breath and pocketed her phone. She couldn't spend her whole day thinking about a boy. After all, she had hundreds of exhibits to read.

Knowledge was power and boys were just, well...*boys.*

It didn't take Max and Farah long to get into the car and drive the remainder of the way. At that moment in time, neither of them would have passed up the opportunity to hang out with the band. They were too excited to decline the offer.

According to the weather report, there would be clear skies all night. Farah enjoyed sleeping under the stars and since college she hadn't done it enough. She missed back yard camping with her dad. An activity they used to do together when she was younger.

The journey didn't take long. Most of their time was trying to find where the band had parked their van on the edge of the large forest. Brian dropping a pin in the middle of nowhere felt like a trap. Wasn't this how every horror movie started and ended?

Eventually, the small car pulled up opposite the band's van. Farah wasn't sure if it was legal for them to be there, but she had been wild camping in the past, and it had been fine.

Everyone cheered when Max and Farah got out the car. The applause caused Max to bow in response and Farah to blush at the warm welcoming. The band were all sat around what she could have only assumed was their attempt at a campfire.

"Come and join the party, guys." Catfish insisted as he waved his arm towards them. They had managed to pull up a few broken logs towards the 'campfire' as a means of seating.

Farah stared at the middle of their makeshift seating area where an abundance of branches with leaves still attached were propped up in the centre. It seemed as if they had tried to start a fire, but it was clear to her the band had a lack of basic survival skills.

"What's *that*?" Farah unforgivingly pointed at their poor attempt.

"Uh...it's supposed to be our campfire." Catfish scratched the back of his neck as he stared down at the mess they had made.

"There's no fire." Max stated bluntly.

"We haven't gotten to that part yet." Brian chuckled.

"We tried. It wouldn't light." Zoe sighed, feeling defeated by the task.

Farah looked down at their effort once more. It was clear to her what they had done wrong.

"*How* were you lighting it?" Farah asked.

"We tried to set the leaves on fire with our lighters, it didn't work." Russ claimed with a shake of his head.

"Weed is a leaf. Those light okay." Catfish shrugged.

Farah blinked. There was no way—

"The leaves retain moisture. They're not going to light. You need *dry* wood." Farah confirmed as she picked up one of the leafy branches. The band stared at one another in disbelief. There was no way they had gotten it *this* wrong.

"Dry wood?"

"Yeah! Best wood to get is branches that have been on the floor for a long time. I-I can show you all if you like?" Farah offered. The band exchanged quick glances and shrugs. They were sceptical, but they didn't have anything to lose.

Farah loved the outdoors and being able to show people the skills she had was important. Sharing the knowledge would have been a lot of fun. Everyone agreed with the idea.

Within moments, Farah was leading the band and Max to the edge of the forest, teaching them what kind of wood they should use for their campfire. Nobody questioned it. They were happy to comply. A campfire sounded pretty cool and it would have heightened the camping experience.

Brian spent the whole time with a huge smile on his face, listening to Farah speaking about something she was interested in. He was learning a lot and was thankful she was there to help support them in their outdoor endeavours. He was impressed by both her confidence and bravery in the way she spoke. It must have taken a lot to correct them and lead a group of people who only days ago had attempted to pressure her into something she didn't want to do.

Farah felt good. It was nice to share her interest with the band. They were out of their depths in her world, just as she felt everyday with them.

Catfish placed the last dry stick on the floor beside Farah as she kneeled in the dirt by the collection of stones, arranging the sticks into a tepee formation. Naturally, she had brought her survival kit with her and showed them all her fire starter, lighting the kindling they had gathered. She gently blew on the sparks to help the fire spread before laying it down nicely at the bottom of the twigs.

"There you have it...a *fire*!" Farah smirked as she sat back from the building flames, proud of her achievement. She looked around at the smiling faces surrounding her, all impressed with what she had done.

"Holy shit, Farah! That's *so* cool! Thank you!" Zoe exclaimed, extremely impressed with their new friend.

"Fire is the greatest thing known to man, dude! One hell of a creation!" Catfish giggled excitedly as he pointed at the fire.

"Bear Grylls has nothing on *my* best friend!" Max stated loudly before throwing her arm around Farah who was in the process of standing up. Farah attempted to hide her smile from everyone, but it was hard to do so with so much praise surrounding her.

"Thanks, Farah. That's amazing!" Brian joined in with the cheering, smiling at her as he clapped along with everyone else. Her talents were impressive.

"You're welcome." Farah tucked her hair behind her ear and smirked over at Brian, nodding in confirmation at her efforts.

After the commotion with the campfire, everyone settled down as Russ brought over a case of beer for them to enjoy. They slumped themselves down around the logs and watched the campfire burn.

Max sat beside Zoe leaving the only space left beside Brian who had opted to be on his own. Farah sat down, smiling beside him. Brian smiled back, this time holding his stare a little longer than before.

"Did you guys do anything fun today?" Zoe questioned, cracking open a beer and passing it over to Max without hesitation.

"We spent the day in Atlanta. Saw like..." Max began to count on her fingers. "Three museums?"

"That's cool. Respect the arts." Russ grinned.

Brian held his hands against the log and glanced over at Farah. He had spent all day contemplating what to say to her, watching her start the fire had thrown those thoughts away. He wanted to let her know how much he appreciated that she was willing to discuss hard-hitting subjects with him.

Most of Brian's relationships consisted of sex and nothing more. It wasn't his fault. It wasn't as if he wanted that, Brian *wanted* companionship. He didn't want something that was going to make him numb, but at least the sex helped fill the void, even if it was only for a while. It wasn't the same, but it was all he had.

Brian had never slept with the same woman twice. A clear indication of their lack of romance past their first and last night together. Nobody wanted to be with Brian past ticking a box that indicated they had slept with a guy in a band. They had slept with someone that was *considered* famous. They had slept with the son of Cherry Blossom from the nineties band, The Flower Children.

The sex wasn't bad, in fact...Brian was pretty good at it. The issue was Brian came with a lot of emotional baggage that people looking for a one night stand didn't want. They didn't want to listen to him. Brian always pretended to be asleep when they left the room the morning after or even the same night. Mostly the same night. He always had to hear them leave.

It was a strange feeling knowing he was physically attracted to Farah, but they hadn't had sex. Something was different this time.

"Good trip?" Brian tilted his head back, speaking directly to Farah as Max and the others began to jeer about the alcohol they were going to consume.

"I'd say I'm getting used to all the driving, but I'm not." Farah snorted, stretching out her legs and sighing deeply.

"It doesn't get any easier. We're not particularly good at taking it in turns. By that, I mean...I'm *usually* the one driving." Brian laughed. Despite his tone, he didn't mind driving the van.

"Tell me about it. It's not even my car!" Farah shook her head.

Brian looked up, the sun was setting and they were surrounded by a beautiful hazy red sky. It wouldn't have been long before the sun set completely, leaving them in darkness with nothing but the campfire to light their faces and stain their clothes with a pungent smell.

"It's so beautiful..." Brian smirked before looking back at Farah.

"The sky?"

"Yeah, that too." Brian let a small flirtatious comment slide. He wasn't being secretive about his intentions.

Farah looked at him, a gauge within her mind ticking over at the comment. It took her a while to clock onto what he was trying to say.

He was calling her *beautiful.*

"Oh..." Farah blushed, feeling flustered by his comment. It wasn't the first time he had attempted to flirt with her, but every time he did, she felt butterflies in her stomach.

Someone as charming as Brian shouldn't have been flirting with someone like Farah.

"Does anyone want some marshmallows? Otherwise, I'm going to eat my way through this whole bag and that won't look pretty." Zoe held up a large bag of marshmallows they had bought from a gas station after deciding they would camp under the stars.

Everyone accepted joining in on roasting marshmallows around the fire.

Other than a blanket and a pillow, none of them had any *real* camping equipment. Farah didn't want to selfishly be the only one with her sleeping mat and bag, so decided to keep them at the bottom of her bag for now.

Brian's attempts at flirting felt ineffective at first. However, Farah began to respond more to the way he spoke to her. It was a different tone. One he didn't use around anyone else. He wanted her to know he was interested without saying any words to confirm it. The only way to describe his display was a comparison to a bird attempting to thrill its feathers. Brian's thrilling feathers consisted of a gravelly tone, small comments, and the recent addition of subtle touches she had taken a liking to.

Farah noticed how many times he got closer to her throughout the evening. Enough to be subtle and not uncomfortable. Farah was enjoying the attention he gave her, especially when Max was spending so much time with the others. There was little she could do other than keep Brian's company.

Brian sat on the floor beside Farah, their backs against the log they were previously sitting on. The campfire was close, crackling and burning. It was providing the only lighting they had. Farah had thrown on a hoodie branded with her college and Brian sat in his black denim jacket.

They weren't so much the sober squad anymore as Farah watched Brian leaning against the log taking a sip of a beer. He wasn't a big drinker; it was more of a social thing.

The others had already made their way through a six-pack. Farah spent most of the night sipping on diet soda, Brian joining her every time aside from his one beer.

"I convinced Max we needed to leave and I'm glad we did. Ten minutes after that the cops showed up and shut down the party. They made a lot of arrests that night and it was all anyone spoke about for weeks. Felt weird to have been a part of it."

"Woah, college parties sound pretty intense." Brian snorted before taking another sip of the beer. He leaned his elbow against the log and held his head up with his knuckles, facing Farah as she told her story.

"It was nothing, really. Max is the one who's good at that stuff. I usually sit in the corner on my phone." Farah traced her finger around the top of the soda can, her legs stretched out towards the campfire.

"What do you do on your phone? Play games?"

"No. I usually study." Farah laughed before looking up at Brian who had his head tilted. Farah would have been lying to herself if she had said she didn't find him somewhat attractive. It was an unconventional attraction, but she was finding it hard to deny after their short-lived yet deep conversations. "Ugh, that's so lame!"

"You're not lame. I think you're cool, you started a fire! With nothing! Just...*trees*!" Brian found his cheeks heating up, unsure if he was blushing or it was the heat from the campfire. Either way, Farah noticed.

"It's not that difficult."

"Nobody here knew how to do it, but *you* did. *That's* cool." Brian pointed at her with a smile, he had been impressed with her expertise.

"I'm not the *frontman of an emo band* cool!"

"If anything, that's the lamest thing I've ever heard." Brian found himself laughing as Farah copied his action.

"Okay, it is a *little* lame..." Farah teased.

"You think my band is lame?" Brian pouted, trying his hardest not to smirk under his act.

"No comment."

"Really? Is that how you're playing it? You've said it now and I'm super offended!" Brian closed his eyes and looked away, continuing to pout over her last tease.

"I never said anything about the *band*. I did hear something about the frontman though..." Farah looked back down at her soda can and smirked.

"What was it? I heard he has great hair and is super attractive." Brian shook his head as he ran his fingers through his bleach blonde hair.

"Oh, yeah? Maybe, but that's not what I heard." Farah snorted at his ego inflating comment. She didn't entirely deny his statement.

"Oh?" Brian smirked, her words giving him a boost of confidence.

"I heard the frontman was kind of lame."

"Where did you hear that?" Brian furrowed his eyebrows, desperate to find an answer to the extended flirtation technique. "Was it *The Alternative Poster*? They're *always* writing stuff about me. I don't like that website."

"I honestly wouldn't know. I don't know much about music or bands." Farah laughed at his silly comments, giving up the act, her lack of knowledge on the subject shining through.

"You must know some things now!"

"A little. I do know that a lot of work goes into touring. Seems pretty...stressful." Farah knew she wouldn't have wanted the same stress Brian had when it came to travelling across states.

"It *is* stressful."

"I'm getting that feeling already and I'm not even the one on stage every night."

"Did you *want* to come on this trip?" Brian suddenly questioned in a whisper. Even though they had been casually flirting with one another, it felt as if this was a more private conversation.

"What do you mean?" Farah turned her head at his words.

"Music isn't really your thing. You must have spent a lot on this trip." Brian didn't want to pry, but he wanted to know more about her.

Farah adjusted her seating position and let out a little sigh.

"Originally, I was going to hike part of the Pacific Crest Trail this summer."

"What's that?"

"It's a really long walk on the West Coast. From the bottom of California to the top of Washington. It usually takes people five months or more to complete. I wanted to try and experience some of it before I eventually do the whole thing."

"Why aren't you walking hundreds of miles right now?"

"Because Max isn't much of a hiker and I didn't want to go alone." Farah admitted, feeling a little embarrassed by her words. It felt silly she had sacrificed something she wanted to do for herself by coming on the trip with Max instead.

"You're telling me you'd rather be dragged across the country to follow a band you don't even like just so you don't have to be *alone?*" Brian's tone dropped as he spoke; Farah feared his judgement on the topic.

"Yeah...that's right." Farah looked down at her fingernails. "You must think that's stupid, right?" She snorted, unable to look at him as her anxiety took over.

It was usually at this point people always had something to say. Inspirational bullshit about living however you want to without the input of others. It didn't work that way for Farah. She was a loyal friend and was more than willing to sacrifice what she wanted for Max. Selfishly, for her own mental wellbeing and security too.

"No. I don't think it's stupid." Brian shook his head as he continued to lean against the log. "It makes a lot of sense."

"It does?"

"Yeah. I wouldn't want to be alone either." Brian half-smiled at Farah as she took in his words. She was unsure if he was being genuine or if he was trying to flirt again. Either way, she respected his outlook.

Brian took a sip of his drink as Farah looked at the campfire, watching Max and the band laugh at stories they were telling through the flames. She knew she had made the right choice. She wouldn't have changed her experience so far. It wasn't what she was expecting, but that was okay.

"It must have been scary to go on such a long trip away from home. Especially doing something you're not super interested in." Brian commented, trying to continue the conversation.

"It's..."

"Really brave. I—"

"You do this all the time."

"That's different. You're going completely out of your comfort zone. You should be really *proud* of yourself for that." Brian tapped the top of the bottle before looking over at Farah with a smile. His words were sweet and so was he.

Farah didn't know if she agreed with what he was saying, but it felt nice to hear.

The band chatted around the campfire for the better part of the evening, falling into the early hours of the morning as they decided to put the fire out and unroll their blankets on the floor. Farah placed her sleeping mat near Max, still wearing the oversized hoodie she had put on earlier. She had given Max the sleeping bag as a trade for being comfortable on the mat.

Max wouldn't have admitted she was tipsy after having a couple of beers, but she needed to sleep whatever was in her system off. It didn't take her long to fall asleep.

Farah thought she would have been excited about sleeping under the stars like she had done in the past, but she couldn't do it. Despite staring up at the open night sky for as long as she could remember.

She had been having fun with the band, especially after the rocky start they had together. The lifestyle they led was one of interest, but it wasn't ever something Farah wanted to participate in herself. It was a niche adventure and one Max thrived on.

Farah had been lying there for hours, unsure if she had drifted in and out of a poor night's sleep. Farah stared up at the stars as she noticed a sweet sound, one that was melodic and amiable. She laid there and listened to it for a while, not questioning its source. It was beautiful. A distant sound of a guitar accompanied by the steady breaths of every bandmate as they slept. Farah was intrigued to know where the sound was coming from as she stood up and searched for the noise.

The sound was coming from the edge of the woodland area opposite where they had set up camp. It was surprising that the sound hadn't woken anyone up, it was loud amongst the silence of the night.

She stepped over to the edge of where the treeline began and noticed a figure sat on a fallen tree, a guitar in their hand as they faced away from the rest of the camp. Farah didn't want to disturb or scare them, so decided on making herself seen as she stepped around the woodland debris to sit beside them.

"Hey." Brian looked up at Farah as he spoke, taking his attention away from the acoustic guitar he was holding. He held his stare for a moment, noticing it was the first time he had ever seen her with her hair down. It flowed so naturally past her shoulders as it sat on the hoodie.

"Can't sleep?"

"No, you?"

"Nope." Farah confirmed, sighing heavily. It was the early hours of the morning and they had both been up for too long. They desperately needed sleep.

"I hope it wasn't my guitar that disturbed you." Brian attempted to hide the fact he lamented as he removed the guitar away from his body and propped it against the fallen tree beside him.

"No, no! You play beautifully, I wish I could play like that." Farah insisted, it was never her intention to offend him. His guitar playing was gorgeous and she was jealous of his talents.

"Have you ever tried?" Brian looked over at Farah and smirked.

"Not really."

"Do you want to try? I can show you..." Brian picked the guitar up by the neck and held it out for Farah. She took the instrument from him, still thinking about the words he had spoken earlier on in the evening about his relation to loneliness and the flirtatious comments he had made.

"Is the first lesson free?" Farah chuckled as she held the guitar.

The acoustic guitar was moderately heavy, although the weight felt good in her hands. She placed it on her lap and held it as Brian had done so a moment ago. It felt large in her lap and she had no idea how Brian was able to play so well.

She looked down at the frets, the paint underneath several strings having been rubbed away after years of use. The neck of the guitar was beautiful, gorgeous mahogany that still held a sweet earthy smell to it. The body was large and uncomfortable against her chest, she could still feel the warmth from where Brian had been holding it.

"The first lesson is always free." Brian smiled.

"I'm glad. I still haven't paid you for your skateboarding lesson." Farah laughed, gently running her thumb against the strings and allowing the guitar to strum lightly.

"Next time I'm charging."

"So, how do I become a rockstar?" Farah cocked an eyebrow, teasing him as she held the guitar tightly.

"You should probably know some basic chords first. Let's try...C! Okay, so... the first finger, first fret, second string. The second finger, second fret, fourth string. The third finger, third fret, fifth string." Brian quickly explained, the words going straight over her head.

"What?" Farah laughed, tapping her fingers against the strings. She was out of her depth.

"Here, let me show you." Brian insisted as he stood up and walked behind Farah who was still sitting on the fallen tree. She half expected him to take the guitar from her, but he had other things in mind. He wasn't sure how Farah liked to learn, so teaching her visually was the best way to do it.

Farah didn't expect the man to come right up behind her, she felt his body heat within her presence. He didn't hesitate as he kneeled on the floor, his hand meeting hers by the fretboard. She welcomed the warm touch of his calloused fingertips as he attempted to reposition her fingers into the correct places.

"How do you stretch your fingers this far?" Farah chuckled as he gently pulled her fingers over the fretboard.

"Practice."

"Am I doing it?" Farah fingers were touching the frets in a pattern that would supposedly form a chord.

"Perfect, now..."

Farah noticed his body getting closer, he had practically wrapped himself around her as he moved enough to get his hand into position to strum the guitar. She felt his chest against her back, they had never found themselves so close before.

Nobody had been this close to Farah before. Not like *this*.

The longing stares and the time they had spent together on tour the past week had been building tension within them both. It was as if the other person were all they could think about.

From the moment they had seen one another at the bar, all they ever wanted to do was get to know each other.

Most girls were happy to sleep with Brian after thirty seconds of knowing his name...Farah was different. He didn't want to sleep with Farah. Well, he didn't want it to cross his mind just yet. He wanted to *know* her and unlike the other times, it had finally become an option.

Unlike the other girls, she wasn't there for sex. She wasn't there to tick a box. She hadn't even known who he was before her friend had dragged her on the trip. He wanted to turn his charm on to find out if she felt the same way. Now was a perfect time to see if she was starting to like him back.

He found himself unable to sleep. Something was on his mind.

Someone was on his mind.

Farah.

They were alone.

"Should I strum?" Farah questioned, his body heat and lingering presence were especially distracting.

"Yeah, just like this." Brian strummed the guitar, Farah feeling his chest push into her back gently as he leaned forward. Farah strummed the guitar in response, creating her first chord. She felt herself tense at his touch.

"Can you show me more?"

"Slow down, Hendrix. One chord at a time." Brian chuckled; he was so close to her that if she were to turn slightly they would have been facing one another.

A satisfying shiver travelled down her spine as she felt his warm breath against her neck.

"What's next?"

"A minor. You do that by doing this." Brian moved her fingers on the fretboard once more.

Farah strummed the guitar.

"D is pretty easy. Here."

Farah strummed the guitar, the tips of her fingers hurting from the pressure.

"Um...G is a good one too." Brian instructed as she passively allowed him to rearrange the placement of her fingers. She welcomed his touch, a sudden physical attraction that she couldn't explain.

"I don't think my fingers can stretch that far." Farah chuckled, unable to form the chord, finding her finger arrangement difficult.

"It's okay, you'll get it eventually. You can join my band when you do." Brian teased, his words almost a whisper as Farah felt his breath graze against her hair.

"Yeah? I don't think I'd be any good..." Farah couldn't resist turning to see his face above her shoulder. They were so close.

Brian backed away, unravelling himself from the girl as he repositioned himself to sit down beside her. They were both facing opposite directions on the fallen tree, Brian balanced himself as he held his hands out either side of him, shuffling as close to Farah as possible.

"I think you would be perfect..." Brian purred as he gazed at Farah, unable to focus on anything other than her eyes under the moonlight. She was stunning.

Farah slowly placed the guitar beside her, leaning it up against the fallen tree they were perched upon. Her mind reared with anticipation for what could happen.

"That's really nice of you to say." Farah shyly pushed her glasses up the bridge of her nose before finally meeting his eyes again. This time he was closer. As close as two people could be without suggestion.

"You'd be amazing." Brian chewed his bottom lip.

"I don't think—"

"*You're* amazing." Brian corrected as he found himself flirting with the girl who had fallen into his life at the beginning of the tour.

Farah was speechless, her body feeling a comfortable rise in temperature as she blushed. He was looking at her in a way that nobody else had ever looked at her before. His eyes were mesmerising, she couldn't find herself looking anywhere else. He was very attractive and Farah was finding it hard to concentrate.

She hadn't expected any of this when she had agreed to go on tour with Max. She hadn't expected to be hanging out with the band themselves. She also hadn't expected to be in a position where she wanted to...kiss him.

Farah wanted to *kiss* him.

"I'm not. I'm—" Farah began to fluster, feeling as if Brian had complimented her too much. She didn't have the highest self-esteem and although Brian felt the same way about himself, he couldn't bear to see Farah's self-deprecation.

She felt guilty for her thoughts. Brian wouldn't want to kiss someone like her.

Would he?

"You're so smart and brave and fun to be around. Don't ever say otherwise." Brian smiled, his feelings building within.

"You're too nice to me." Farah chuckled.

"And you're too mean to yourself." Brian snorted, desperately wanting to hold her hands for reassurance.

Farah thought about their short time together. Brian had always been so kind to her no matter what they did and where they went. There was never a dull moment with him around.

"I hope you're willing to teach me more guitar." Farah cocked an eyebrow, still teasing him with a slight whisper.

"I w-will, but not right now."

"Why not?"

"Because right now...I want to kiss you." Brian chuckled nervously, scratching the back of his neck as he glanced away. He had never been embarrassed about flirting with someone before, he usually did it so easily. So smoothly. Yet in front of Farah...he was a mess.

"You want to—"

He wanted to *kiss* her.

"If you're okay with it. I wouldn't want to—" Before Brian could finish his sentence Farah's lips had crashed against his.

Brian stumbled back in shock but was quick to balance himself as he closed his eyes and followed through with the kiss.

She had kissed him.

It wasn't the first time either of them had kissed someone. Brian, for one, had kissed copious amounts of people, some of which he still felt guilt over for not remembering their names.

Farah, on the other hand, had kissed a boy in high school once and made out with a guy her parents pushed on her to date a couple of times who also happened to be an adjunct professor. Her experience didn't go past that, but Brian's ability stretched far beyond, allowing him to lead the kiss with ease.

Farah gripped his shoulders as Brian shuffled closer towards her. He hesitated slightly at putting his hands on her hips and settled nicely for slightly above to not impose anything further.

There was a comfortable silence at the edge of the woodland as they held each other tightly, unable to remove themselves from the kiss. Brian was drunk on her affection, completely head over heels for the pressure he felt against his lips.

Farah had made the conscious decision to kiss him and refused to think about any regrets she may have had. She was kissing the frontman from Social Dropouts. The sweetheart who was beginning to win her over with his authenticity.

It was nearly three in the morning and with everyone else in their party asleep, it felt like they were teenagers sneaking away to be together. Brian moved his leg over the fallen tree to be closer to her, refusing to let go of her lips as he changed position.

They moved together, perfectly in sync with each other's actions. They found themselves desperate to hold onto the kiss for as long as the other person would allow.

Farah slowly shifted her hands from his shoulders to the back of his neck, providing him with a pleasurable shiver as she brushed her fingers on the back of his short hair. His scruffy blonde hair on top felt soft between her fingers, encouraging her to stay as she gently massaged the back of his head with her fingertips.

Brian had kissed people in the past, but nothing ever felt like this made him feel. His adoration for the feeling was unmatchable as if sparks were flying inside of him.

Farah was afraid the others would have woken up at any moment and witnessed the kiss. The people they were with should have noticed their attraction to one another, Max *had*...multiple times. The constant gazes and hints pointed in that direction. Wasn't it obvious? They wanted this more than they would have previously wanted to admit.

Brian brought his hand to the side of Farah's face, continuing to guide her softly through the kiss. Their movements were so fluent Brian found it difficult to unlatch his lips, even when he did, he kept going back for more. Slow and sensual as if they were running out of energy to do much more.

They finally pressed their lips together for the last time, keeping close as they caught their breath.

Farah had just kissed Brian Blossom. According to alternative rock magazines, that was probably a big deal.

Brian brushed Farah's long hair away from her face, gently placing it behind her ear. It was a short attempt at keeping them close, craving the touch.

Farah gradually moved away from him, not in the sense of not wanting to be close, but she wanted to look at him. She had to see the glistening eyes looking at her as if she were the most important person in the world. As she pulled away, Brian opened his eyes revealing what she had been expecting. He was marvelling at her.

With only the moonlight to lead them, Farah could just about make out each of his features.

She cupped his cheek in her hand, his bristly stubble grazing against her palm. He melted at her touch, practically nuzzling his cheek into her hand. Farah couldn't deny the fact he was gorgeous, from his perfectly rounded face to his dishevelled hair. He was undeniably attractive in the most unconventional ways and he knew it.

He owned it.

"You're so beautiful." Brian gushed as he looked towards her with wide eyes. He was so caught up in the moment, unable to control whatever came out of his mouth.

Despite being high a lot of the time, nothing compared to the high he had gotten after connecting lips with Farah. No drug in the world could make him feel that way.

As much as Farah wanted to argue his words, she knew she couldn't win. Farah didn't want to believe she was beautiful, but how Brian looked at her heightened her confidence. Even if she didn't believe she was beautiful...Brian saw otherwise.

"You're so...handsome." Farah spoke softly as she stared into his eyes, continuing to cup the side of his face. Brian blushed at her comment.

Her words felt sincere, unlike the social media comments that noticed his looks and left copious amounts of emotes or posts saying how 'hot' he was. In a way, it felt degrading. His band wasn't big, but after his mother's success, he was always looked down on for that. Always compared to her no matter where he went.

Farah's comment felt so honest. So adorable. So...

Brian kissed her once more, this time a lot less frantic. It was slow yet meaningful. The slow kiss didn't last as long as the last, despite it feeling as if it meant more. A reassurance that this was what they wanted. An attraction to one another.

Brian smiled on her lips before pulling away, causing her to let out an adorable giggle that melted his heart. She opened her eyes to see him smiling back at her, his hands balancing on her waist. She appreciated the touch.

"I could kiss you all night." Brian spoke in a husky whisper causing Farah's entire body to internally react to the words. She would have been thinking about this moment for weeks.

"Yeah?"

"Yeah..." His voice was deep and raspy.

Farah pulled a sharp gasp of air through her teeth, attempting to prepare herself to be kissed again. All she wanted to do was to spend the night with the man on the outskirts of the forest.

Just as Brian was about to go in for another kiss, there was a sudden flash of light that caused both Brian and Farah to gasp. They were both quick to frantically face the light. For some reason, Brian half expected it to be a police officer. It wouldn't have been the first time he had been caught with a girl by the law.

Although, unsurprisingly, it was a member of their party holding their phone up with the flashlight shining on the back.

"Um...hi." Catfish exchanged glances between the pair.

They sat together awkwardly on the fallen tree, smiling up at Catfish casually.

"What's up? Nice weather we're having." Brian chuckled nervously, sweat suddenly dripping down the side of his face. He couldn't be caught out by one of his bandmates, it would be all they would speak about until the end of time.

Farah looked over to Brian with her eyebrows dipped, watching him desperately try and keep his cool under pressure. There was no way they would have gotten out of this one.

"Clear skies at three? I dig that." Catfish shrugged.

"So, what brings you to this side of town? Tree place. Town? *Tree town?*" Brian continued to laugh with anxiety in his tone. Farah desperately wanted to slam the palm of her hand against her forehead. Why did she have to kiss him? He was such a dork.

"Looking for a cool place to pee. Do you know any good spots?"

"Ha! Oh boy, you bet. See that tree over there? Quality location...you can't beat it." Brian was serious in his tone, wanting to get rid of Catfish so he could focus his energy on kissing Farah.

"Alright, man. If you say so. What are you two doing out here so late anyway?" Catfish cocked an eyebrow as he pointed the flashlight at them both.

"Smoking!" Farah was quick to answer with something that was somewhat believable, although her word was quickly overshadowed by Brian's shouting.

"Bird watching!"

Farah shot him a stare of confusion as she internalised her screams.

"*Bird watching*...at three in the morning?" Catfish was incredibly confused.

"Sleeping birds. We're watching them sleep. It's a thing. They do it on those nature shows, the one with the British dude with the accent! Yeah! Big fan. Big fan." Brian chuckled, wiping the sweat from his brow as he spoke. He didn't want to see Farah's expression of sheer disbelief.

"That's rad, man. Mad respect for sleeping birds." Catfish nodded with a smile, either high or half asleep. Possibly both.

"Yeah! Real cool." Brian grinned, casually leaning back on the tree trunk he was sitting on as much as possible without falling off.

"I'll leave you to it. Don't stay up too late."

"Ha. We won't!" Brian waved as Catfish turned and made his way over to the tree he had suggested.

Brian let out a deep sigh of relief. He couldn't have been caught with Farah; it would have only raised more questions about what their relationship may have held.

"Sleeping...birds? You've got to be kidding me." Farah exhaled, in disbelief at how ridiculous his remarks were.

"It's fine. It's believable."

"No, it's not."

"Catfish would believe it. Plus, it's kind of neat." Brian shrugged, trying his hardest not to laugh.

Farah thought for a moment, what she had done sank into her mind. She had kissed Brian Blossom. What had she done? What would Max say if she found out? What if her parents found out? If Farah was kissing boys her parents would never have expected it to be a weed-smoking emo boy.

Farah sighed as she buried her head into her hands and groaned, pushing her glasses up the bridge of her nose. Brian's expression switched at the response, terrified he may have done something wrong by kissing her. He never wanted to make her feel uncomfortable, it felt as if she was into him at the time.

"Sorry, did I—"

"N-no, you're really nice!" Farah instantly pulled her head away from her hands, looking up and smiling back at him.

"Oh." He had heard that one before. Perhaps a little too often.

Farah reached over and gripped the hand he had balanced on his lap. She allowed their fingers to intertwine as they had done a few days before. Nobody had ever held Brian's hand the way Farah did.

"You're really sweet, Brian." Farah whispered under her breath, looking at him with a smile. He had shown her kindness she had never experienced with a man before.

"But?" Brian waited in anticipation.

"Huh?"

"You're really sweet...*but*..." Brian repeated, waiting for her to finish her sentence. It was coming. He knew it. He would never have been able to mentally prepare for rejection, but he was used to it.

"Nothing. No buts." Farah laughed, noticing the panicked expression on his face. It made her heart ache seeing he was no stranger to rejection.

"Oh..." Brian was filled with confusion. How was it possible for him to kiss a girl and not receive any kind of backlash for his actions? Why was she not *leaving*?

"I'd like to kiss you again...it's just late and..."

"The others might wake up?" Brian caught onto her anxiety. He understood. It wasn't as if he wanted his band to find out about his fling with the girl who had been following them on tour.

"Exactly."

"We should probably try to sleep." Brian smirked before looking down at her hand that was balancing on his. His palms were clammy, but she didn't notice.

After her time with Brian, Farah wasn't sure whether it would have helped her sleep or hindered her mind more. She was still in shock she had pressed her lips against his. It was all she could think about.

"We should..." Farah looked over at Brian with a small smile creeping up the corners of her lips. There was a moment of silence shared between them as Brian leaned in for another kiss.

She wanted to kiss him again. Why wouldn't she have wanted to kiss him? She desperately wanted to press her lips against his to savour the touch. What if she never got to do it again?

What had made him so attractive? She knew it wasn't the blunt smell of weed that stuck to his denim jacket like glue. It was his sweet mind and soul, his talent, his kindness and the longing looks he had given her repeatedly. He wouldn't leave her mind no matter how far they travelled.

This time, as they kissed, Brian took a deep breath through his nose. Farah wasn't like the other girls. She wasn't drunk or high and certainly wasn't begging him for it. This was a new experience for him and Brian had to learn to be patient.

He was a lover at heart and as much as he wanted to hold her waist or pull her onto his lap to be closer, he didn't want to rush into anything. This was a kiss. Nothing more and nothing less.

Just moments ago, Farah was afraid of being caught by Max and the others, even though Catfish was probably still stumbling around in the trees beside them she kept kissing him.

"Okay." Farah pressed her forehead against Brian's and breathed deeply. "Really." Farah spoke between his kisses. "We have to drive a long way tomorrow." Farah pushed his chest gently as he planted kisses along her jawline. The act was forward, but one she accepted.

This was *new*.

"Maybe someone else can drive? We can make out on the backseat of the van." Brian spoke in a slur as he whispered into her ear after pushing gentle kisses along her jaw. Nobody had ever kissed Farah like that before. Brian was more than good at it...he was fantastic.

"Brian!" Farah began to blush as she chuckled at his flirtatious words. She hadn't expected to say his name as an amorous slur. "I don't think Max would be happy about that."

"Neither would the band, but *I'd* be pretty happy with that." Brian pulled away, wanting to get a better look at her. She was just as beautiful as he had remembered from the last time he had looked at her around thirty seconds ago.

"I can tell..." Farah giggled, drunk off his presence.

They wanted to kiss all night, but they were sensible enough to realise they needed to go to sleep.

"Maybe we could do this again sometime? If you're around?" Brian picked up his guitar and stood up from the fallen tree, reaching out his hand for Farah to hold onto. Farah took the offer and allowed him to pull her to her feet.

"I don't know...I'm pretty busy." Farah chuckled, looking away with a shy smile.

"Could you at least pencil me in?" Brian cocked an eyebrow, trying his hardest to entertain her flirting.

"I can do that." Farah agreed as he pulled her closer. They hadn't known one another long, but long enough for Farah to decide she liked him enough for them to kiss.

Brian used one hand to hold his guitar and the other to pull Farah closer, planting a short kiss on her lips.

"Goodnight." He whispered. Farah felt a little silly about feeling shy. He had kissed her...multiple times.

"Goodnight." She responded softly as he let go of her hand and waved as he walked back towards the camp.

Farah knew to wait, if anyone was awake they may have suspected something.

She watched Brian from a distance putting his guitar into the van, trying to be quiet as he stepped around his sleeping band members. He closed the van door carefully and watched as Farah walked back to camp and laid down on her mat by the extinguished campfire, the only thing illuminating their faces was the moon.

Brian smiled, waving at her, unable to stop looking. Farah found it impossible not to smirk at him and return his wave, a million things flooding through her mind about the boy. Brian went to the other side of the van and slumped himself down on his blanket.

Despite being on opposite sides of the van they both looked up at the stars and smiled. They were happy with their choices that night. All they wanted was to kiss, finally watering the seed that had been planted the first night of the tour.

They both fell asleep with each other on their minds.

When departing their campsite the following morning Brian and Farah had spent a lot of time giving each other little glances and smirks. It was fun to share a secret. Nobody needed to know they had kissed. Several times.

"So, what happened?" Max leaned her elbows on the roof of the car as Farah opened the back door and threw her bag inside.

"What?" Farah looked over the top of the car and furrowed her eyebrows, confused by what Max could have been referring to.

Did she know?

"You can't stop looking at each other."

"Who?"

"Don't play stupid with me, Farah. Y'know who I mean. Mr. Lover Boy back there who has spent the past hour at breakfast unable to take his eyes off you." Max leaned further on the roof, dropping the volume of her voice.

"Nothing. Nothing happened." Farah shook her head as she clambered into the car.

Max followed, finding herself in the passenger seat and watching as Farah pulled out her phone and began to look for their next destination.

"Did you sleep with him?" Max questioned.

"No!"

"Okay, well... I'm just checking. Zoe is convinced you guys are screwing. Traffic in Asheville? Yeah right, we got through fine." Max added casually.

"There *was* traffic! We left at different times!"

"Yeah, okay. Sure."

"Nothing happened, she's wrong."

"Is she though?" Max teased.

"Yes! She is. Can we drop this?" Farah groaned, feeling as if she was never going to get away from being teased about Brian.

"Fine. You're no fun."

Farah snorted, continuing to flick through her navigation app as Max watched the band pack their makeshift camp away.

The two parties decided on travelling separately, agreeing to meet at the show in the evening. Farah and Max had spent the day travelling to local historical sites and taking photos of themselves outside exhibits to send to Farah's parents.

Not long after, Farah was standing in the crowd staring up at Brian as if he were the only one on the stage.

Brian was humble at heart, but he did enjoy gloating when he was good at something. He knew Farah was watching and did everything he could do to flex his skills. The crowd loved feeding off their energy.

The show had been a lot of fun and Max had nearly gotten herself in trouble with security again. Luckily, she managed to avoid them after the warning she had gotten.

The evening after the show was mostly filled with hanging out in one of the back rooms, the band invited Farah and Max into the back as if it were to be expected.

Farah had her mind locked on someone else as she spent her time with her legs crossed and her finger and thumb pinching her bottom lip as she stared across the room at Brian Blossom. Max was beside her, talking to Russ and Catfish as she pretended to listen. She was distracted by the man on the other side of the room. Brian continued to chat with Zoe, his elbows leaning against the back of the couch, a red flannel with the sleeves rolled up draped over his t-shirt. His hair was damp from the show and with his arms exposed she could see his unusual tattoos.

She watched him laugh at something Zoe had said before turning towards her. Their eyes met from opposite sides of the room as she returned his sweet smile.

Brian reached into his pocket as his phone buzzed, taking his attention off Farah and unlocking the device. He stared down at the screen. His expression dropped at the message he had received.

132

'Hey bud, you're in Nashville tomorrow. Any chance you want to pal around with your old man when you're back home? Let me know if you're free!'

Brian glanced back up at Farah who had now focused her attention elsewhere. He looked back at his phone and sighed.

It was his dad.

NASHVILLE, TN

Brian had woken up on the couch of a stranger's house. It wasn't unusual. It happened frequently whilst touring.

He sat up and looked around noticing the rest of his band in the room. Zoe had taken the other couch and Catfish and Russ were on opposite ends of a coffee table on sleeping mats.

Brian knew with everyone asleep it was his only chance to use the bathroom and shower.

It didn't take him long to hop in and take advantage of the hot water their host had graciously provided. Brian had brought his bag of toiletries through and made a start at shampooing the blonde locks he barely tamed. It felt refreshing to have finally cleaned himself somewhere that wasn't a public bathroom that held more germs on the sink than there were on the toilet seat.

After stepping out of the shower he wiped his hand across the mirror, exposing a blurry version of his face he had created through the swift swipe of condensation. He reached into his bag and pulled out a razor. He never allowed his adequate amount of stubble to grow into a full beard, usually leaving hair to grow around his jawline and chin. That was how he liked it and the most he would do to impress his father was to tidy it with a trim.

He dried his face and hair with a towel. Without running styling gel through his hair, it was a scruffy mess. Brian knew he should have taken a page from Russ' book and worn a hat.

He pulled what he assumed to be a clean t-shirt over his head before throwing on a clean flannel, covering his tattooed arms. A cactus, a group of stickmen skateboarding, an astronaut with a boombox, a retro television, a female figure smoking a cigarette and someone in skateboarding shoes dressed as a ghost. He liked his random selection of tattoos, but that didn't mean everyone else did.

Brian stared into the mirror and forced a smile as he ran his fingers through his hair to fix it neatly into place.

He was going to be seeing his dad today. He wasn't sure what that would entail. He knew his relationship with his father hadn't always been the best. It wasn't as if they had ever been on bad terms, but that didn't stop Brian from feeling awkward around him.

He had tidied himself to look presentable. Brian needed his father to know he could look after himself and he was doing fine on tour without him. Admittedly, some of his effort to look good came with knowing he would see the girl he was interested in sometime in the evening.

Despite knowing he would have to spend time with his father, he felt good. It was hard for him not to be happy after the previous night.

If he could just get through one day with his dad he could have continued the tour with ease. Besides, there was one thing to look forward to after the show.

Farah.

He couldn't believe they had kissed. He hadn't experienced a kiss like *that* before. Girls only usually made out with him because they wanted something, but Farah didn't want anything. She wanted to kiss. That was it.

She had no ulterior motive, at least he didn't think she did. A part of him worried the tour was nothing more than a rebellious streak for her. Was Brian part of a phase? Phases could come and go.

Brian was a hopeless romantic and that was using the word *hopeless* kindly. It was a shame nobody would give him a chance.

He didn't want to think too deeply into it. He could already feel himself spiralling into a pit of depression fearing she wouldn't want permanence. He was afraid of rejection. A fear pitted within him from years of seeking romantic companionship.

It was impossible. Yet, the stories he had been fed about his parents were the only things he could think about when it came to love. Not that their relationship was ever perfect outside of news headlines.

All he saw as a child was how much love his parents shared. He didn't see the issues that came leading up to his mother's death. He didn't see the struggles that they faced. He didn't see the heartbreak that came with loving Cherry Blossom.

He didn't see any of it until she died.

The pain his father felt when she had passed away was pain that wasn't comparable, even to a physical wound. The emotional pain was so bad for his father that he probably would have preferred physical pain. It had stuck him in a rut he was unable to get out of, the only thing saving him from himself had been Brian.

If his father had managed to find the love of his life whilst on tour, Brian was convinced he would have been able to do the same.

Nothing was stopping him.

There was still hope yet.

The band left Birmingham after shovelling granola bars in their mouths they had gotten from a gas station. They knew they had been overcharged but they needed to eat. There wasn't much choice.

The drive wasn't particularly long and gave Brian enough time to ponder on his thoughts. He also knew the sooner he got to Nashville the sooner he could have blasted himself with weed before seeing his father. He wanted to be as numb as possible for that conversation.

Brian's relationship with his father was complicated and could have been considered one-sided in some aspects. His father tried his hardest and Brian wasn't always up to the challenge of accepting his praise. Not only that, but it didn't help that his father enjoyed pushing Brian to be the best he possibly could. Brian wasn't like his mother and he didn't want to be anything like his father. It was hard to get away from the life he was destined to have.

Brian's father, Stan Static, had made his way into the music industry when he was a teenager. He had started as a roadie for small-time bands playing in local venues, eventually finding himself managing bands and his own record label in recent years.

A beautiful story of both love and disaster came to mind whenever anyone thought about the man.

Stan had been a roadie for the famous pop group The Flower Children in the early nineties. That was where he had met the lead singer, Cherry Blossom and had fallen in love with her bubbly personality. Except, he wasn't the only person who had fallen for her.

The whole world loved her.

The Flower Children flew up the international music charts with several hit records. With plenty of tours and love in the back of her mind, Cherry decided the roadie who saw them through several tours was the person she wanted to spend the rest of her life with. At least, who she wanted to spend her time with when it suited her.

Cherry gave everything to Stan he desired. Mostly apologies for the horrible things she did outside of their relationship. Including sleeping with several people who weren't Stan throughout their time together. He knew, but her beautifully long pink hair, curvy pale figure and loving eyes were hard to deny. It wasn't worth giving all of that up for the sake of his own emotions.

It was late '96 when Cherry had discovered she was pregnant with the roadie's baby. It was going to be fine. Cherry had agreed with Stan they would raise the baby together, even if that meant raising a baby on tour. She wasn't going to drop her career for a baby; besides, it would have been fun to raise a child amongst it. Everything would have been perfect.

Except...it wasn't.

Brian still had memories of his mother. Her long pink hair she dyed frequently and silly faces she would pull to make him laugh. The way she would hold him tightly when he was upset or the way both her and Stan would read him bedtime stories together. He remembered the soft touch of her fingers as they wrapped around his small hand, dragging him away from whatever childish exploits he was interested in. He remembered her singing. The angelic voice hummed through the large house, loud enough to be heard in any room.

She would sit him on her lap in front of the grand piano that filled a large space in the corner of their living room. At first, his tiny hands could barely press the keys, until eventually his index finger copied Cherry's every movement. His favourite thing was when she let him run his hand across all the keys, a noise that made them laugh.

Cherry taught Brian that music could be fun, even if it wasn't *good*.

He remembered her being there and then...he doesn't. As if one moment she was there and the next she was gone. Someone had flicked the switch and caused all the colour in the world to flood away, only leaving black and white.

Little did he know the world had always been black and white. His parents had done everything they could to let him see the world differently. Brian didn't need to see his mother's addiction and his father's issues with his crumbling dreams.

He remembered the tour bus. The bus his father decided to use to look after him. Stan had enough money to house them thirty times or more if he wanted, but he wasn't going to. Stan was determined to keep his career on track even after Cherry's death and Brian wasn't going to be the one to stop him.

So, everywhere that Stan went for work, Brian was destined to follow.

He remembered the—

"Hey, *Rockstar*! Get over here!" Stan immediately pulled Brian in for a huge hug. Brian stood still, awkwardly looking at his band as a cry for help.

"Dad..." Brian kept his hands to his sides as his dad held him tightly. Even if Brian wanted to hug him back, Stan had trapped him in such a way that made it impossible to do so.

"Hey, Mister Static!" Catfish threw his hands in the air and shouted as they approached the outside of a large music studio.

Stan loosened his grip around Brian as Catfish spoke. He held his arm around Brian as they turned to face the rest of the band. Brian didn't argue with his affection, as much as he didn't feel deserving of the love his father gave him, he was still willing to allow the connection.

Usually, when things got tough Stan was someone Brian could turn to. Unless it was related to the band and money...

"Hey, if it isn't my favourite band! How are you all doing?" Stan grinned as the band made their way towards him.

Stan Static was just over average height and build, but with time on the road, he had developed a beer belly. In recent years with all his success, he didn't always dress as if he had a decent amount of money. *Decent* meaning millions of dollars. What little hair he had left was grey, thin and scruffy. Wearing a white buttoned-up shirt tucked into some blue jeans and a pair of pointed boots, he was exactly as Brian remembered after a few weeks of not seeing him. Not a lot ever changed with his father.

"As cool as ever. Good to see you, Mister S." Russ smiled, the band were always happy to see Stan Static. He always supported them through their endeavours. Stan was the one who organised everything for them and if it wasn't for him then they wouldn't have been on tour.

Stan was a living legend and the band held a great admiration for him. He wasn't the kind of legend to have been noticed on the street by a passer-by, but he was distinguishable by someone who was into their music.

"Thriving." Zoe gleamed before staring back down at her phone.

"That's great! It's so good to see you all, how's the tour going? Making the big bucks? Got fans clawing at your feet?" Stan questioned. His comments made Brian want to crawl into a hole and never leave.

"We have groupies!" Catfish cheered before pumping his fist in the air. Brian's eyes widened at the comment, that wasn't something he wanted to discuss in front of his father.

They weren't groupies. They were...Brian didn't know how to define them. He couldn't call Farah a fan when she wasn't exactly there for their music. Max was. He could have mentioned that.

"You wha—"

"There's a few fans that are following us on tour." Brian butted in before his father could question it.

"Hold on, you have *groupies*?" Stan laughed nervously.

"Yeah! Pretty cool, right?" Catfish was confident in his words.

"They're *not* groupies!" Brian clenched his fists together and raised his voice, embarrassed by the situation playing out in front of his dad.

"Max is totally a wannabe groupie, but she's awesome, so I'm not complaining." Zoe snorted, much to Brian's horror.

"They're *fans*. Fans who are following us on tour. Not groupies. Groupies want drugs and free merch a-and *sex*!" Brian stumbled on his words, arguing his point.

"I'm certain Farah wants one of those things from you and it isn't free merch..." Zoe chuckled before hiding behind her phone.

"It's not like that, I—" Brian raised a finger, ready to defend himself against them all. He was frustrated with their teasing.

"Woah, Bri. Settle it down, big guy." Stan began to laugh, Brian's mood calming as he felt his father's hand fall on his shoulder. His grip was gentle yet firm, enough for Brian to take a deep breath and mentally step back from the situation. "Sounds like you guys have had a pretty eventful tour!"

Stan didn't want to press, it was a topic Brian didn't want to discuss and one he didn't want to know more about. Brian was happy to talk about a lot of topics in front of his dad but it would have been weird to have that conversation in front of his friends. That wasn't the kind of awkwardness he needed in his life.

"It's been pretty sick." Russ smirked, ecstatic over how well everything had gone so far.

"We had some trouble with the van, but it got fixed." Catfish added, informing Stan of the situation they had been in a few days ago. Brian hadn't told him what happened, knowing Stan would have overreacted and offered to pay for the repairs if he knew how much they had cost them. He didn't want to seem irresponsible.

"Trouble with the van? You didn't tell me there was anything wrong with the van." Stan sighed, still holding onto Brian's shoulder as he spoke. Perhaps a little too hard. Brian grimaced at his comment, there was no way he was going to get out of it.

"It's fine. We got it fixed." Brian assured as he pressed his lips into a thin line.

"What happened?"

"Dad, it's cool. We fixed it. It was just a small engine issue or something." Brian huffed, trying to throw his dad off the trail that the fault with the van was close to causing them to cancel a show.

"You should have called." Stan's expression dropped as he turned to his son.

"We solved it ourselves. We didn't need to." Brian stated bluntly. There was no reason for him to call his dad for every difficult situation they found themselves in. They didn't need his help.

"Right." Stan nodded, squeezing Brian's shoulder. It felt as if the conversation wasn't over yet. Stan still had more to add, but it wasn't something he was going to speak to his son about until they were alone.

"Hey Stan, did you break down a lot on tour? It's always so annoying." Zoe snorted, Brian was thankful she hadn't mentioned catching a ride with Farah and Max.

"Oh, it happened all the time. You'd think that with a huge band like The Flower Children they would have decent vehicles. Not for us roadies. Cherry was sitting in that fancy tour bus with the rest of them and I was stuck in an old van carrying sound equipment. You'd think they'd want something nicer, beats me. Cherry's management was bad. There was this one time that Cherry and I—" Stan began to extensively tell one of his many stories about him and his adventures with the loveable Cherry Blossom.

"Hey Dad, didn't you say we were going to hang out?" Brian interrupted. He didn't want to be rude, but he also didn't want to hear a story about his mother and father for the millionth time. Not today.

That was the one thing he always wanted to avoid whenever he visited his dad. A conversation about his mom. He could never escape the thoughts of his mother when his father was around.

"Right! Sorry guys, story time with your uncle Stanley will have to resume another day!" Stan grinned awkwardly, realising he had overstayed his welcome.

Brian used to enjoy the stories his father told him. He would sit and listen to the same story over and over, his father even putting his words into lyrics as he strummed his guitar in the back of the tour bus. Brian enjoyed hearing his stories, but something about hearing them now filled him with a disconnect he wished he didn't have.

"Bummer. Anyway, we're going to see Catfish's grandma because she's agreed to feed us before we all stop home quick. See you later, Brian." Zoe waved her hand towards them both.

"Catch you later, Mister Static! I'll bring you some leftovers." Catfish waved.

"Goodbye, Mister Static. We'll text you, dude." Russ nodded at Brian.

"Sure. Sounds good." Brian sighed with an awkward thumbs up. He would have much preferred to have visited Catfish's grandma. She was so nice and it was always fun to hear her laugh whenever anyone mentioned her grandson's nickname.

"See you later, guys!" Stan waved energetically before turning back to Brian as everyone else departed.

"Did you have anything in mind?" Brian shyly questioned as he took a slight step away from Stan to regain his personal space.

"Do you want to grab some food? How about a burger at *Mabel's*? We haven't been there in a while!" Stan scratched the side of his face as he spoke, mentioning the diner frequented when they were both home.

Stan was always worried Brian hadn't been looking after himself when he was on tour. Taking him out for food was a sure way to know he would get a decent meal. He knew his son smoked recreationally; except he also knew he frequently relied on it to get through the day. After experiencing heartbreak through drug abuse, he never wanted his son to follow the same path. Weed was fine, but as soon as Stan was aware of him overstepping that line he would have been there to put a stop to it.

Brian wasn't stupid. He knew what he was doing. There was no way he would have swallowed pills or injected anything harmful into his body. Weed was where he drew the line.

"That would be good, I just—I don't think I have enough for anything fancy." Brian shrugged through his words; he couldn't help but feel a little sad he was in his dad's presence without being able to stomach a happy face. His dad reminded him of his mom and his mom reminded him of...

Disaster.

"Brian, money isn't an issue. You know you can—"

"It's okay. I have money. I just don't want anything too fancy." Brian pushed his hands into his jacket pockets and looked away, the last thing he wanted was his dad to pressure him into opening up about his financial situation.

"You'd tell me if you were struggling, right? I wouldn't want my number one Rockstar going hungry!" Stan placed his hand back on Brian's shoulder...again. Stan had more money than he knew what to do with and as much as he was willing to support Brian, it was hard to provide for him when he didn't want to accept it.

"Dad, really...it's fine. I've got money." Brian was embarrassed and he knew his father was happy to give him everything he needed to get by, but Brian didn't want that. Brian wanted to provide for himself with the money he had earned, not a cash injection from his father and the never-ending flow of money that came from a percentage of his mother's music sales. He didn't want that. It wasn't his to take.

"I'll cover everything today. How does that sound?" Stan asked, desperately trying to help his son where possible.

Brian didn't know what to say to his father. Maybe he would have been able to afford it if he hadn't blown so much on weed in the morning. It wasn't just that, it was the van too.

Brian knew he was a disappointment.

"Thanks." Brian half-smiled at Stan, feeling awkward over the offer. Brian was an embarrassment to his father and he knew it. If it wasn't for his musical talent, Stan would have cut ties with his son years ago.

He could have scraped something together but spending fifteen dollars or more on a meal compared to the fifty-cent ramen he had in his apartment was a lot different.

Stan led him to the diner, it wasn't a long walk over to the establishment and their conversation fell flat several times. Stan explained a lot of things that had happened in the business recently, Brian was compliant enough to hold his hands in his pockets and listen. His dad always had something to say.

The best part about working in the studio was that his father was only there a couple of times a week. The best part about touring was that his dad never came. He had bigger bands to manage. They had plenty of space apart from one another.

Although, the time he did have to spend with his father always felt like a chore.

Brian pushed the fries around his plate as he stared down at the food, his appetite had diminished the moment he sat down. He would have much rather been with the band or at the back of a venue hanging out with Farah. He had debated on whether to text her and see what she was doing or wait until the evening.

Either way, she was on his mind. Only a couple of nights ago she had pushed her lips against his. Lots. They had kissed and he savoured every moment.

A slight smile crept up his face at the thought which was immediately ruined by his father's voice.

"Not hungry?" Stan asked as he looked over at his son who hadn't looked happy their entire time together. Stan had gotten used to Brian's distance; he knew it wasn't something he could have solved.

After his mother died it had always been them against the world. He never wanted his dad to feel as if he had failed as a parent. Brian just wanted to do something with his life that was his own choice rather than something his family decided for him.

Except when Brian did want to do something, his dad always felt the need to be involved. Music had been fun until his dad had insisted on being his band's manager. Sure, touring was fun...but Brian would have liked to work hard on his own accord. Having his dad's connections helped a little too much.

"Not really." Brian sighed, placing a fry back on the plate and exhaling deeply.

"What's up, Bud? Is there something going on?" Stan's expression dropped, a genuine concern for his son.

"It's nothing."

"It doesn't look like nothing."

"I'm just...I'm tired." Brian sighed as he pushed his fingers against his forehead.

"Are you staying at home tonight?"

"I haven't thought about it."

"Maybe you should. You can't just do everything on a whim all the time. It's a little irresponsible, Kiddo." Stan grumbled, his words trailing off slightly.

"I don't do everything on a *whim*." Brian perked up, feeling offence over his father's words.

Stan was unsure how to respond. He knew his son could be standoffish when it came down to him nit-picking his lifestyle. Stan was ready to support his music and his choices, if he was ready to show him respect for everything he had done.

"I'm out of town after the show tonight. You and the band can crash at my penthouse for a night. It's bigger than your apartment and you'll be able to stick together." Stan offered as he reached into his pocket and pulled out a set of keys before placing them on the table in front of him.

Taking his dad's offer was his only way of keeping the band comfortable without forcing them all back home.

"Thanks." Brian regretfully reached across the table and picked up the set of keys.

"Tour can be a killer, but I'm sure you rock that stage every night. You're okay with me coming tonight, right?" Stan respectfully asked as if Brian would have ever denied his dad the ability to see him play. He took a quiet sip of his soda.

"Yeah! Of course I am!" Brian looked up and forced a smile at Stan. He was grateful for his dad's support, regardless of what form it came in.

"Alright. Just wondering. I wouldn't want to embarrass you or anything." Stan nodded, not entirely convinced by his son's words.

Brian smiled down at his plate before eating one of the fries. It was pretty good.

"Thanks for setting up the tour, it means a lot." Brian showed his appreciation for his father's input into the band's wellbeing. Stan always made sure to look after them. He had a bias with them being his son's band.

"I can get you more shows, all you have to do is ask."

"Maybe we could tour with another band one day? That would be cool." Brian perked up at the idea. Stan had never let Social Dropouts *tour* with any support or with a bigger band. It was unheard of, but something Stan insisted on.

"A lot of the bands that want to tour with you now are worthless. They're just a bunch of wannabe rockers doing *drugs*. You can't get distracted by that. Do I currently trust you to tour with any of the bands on my label? No way! It's not so much I don't trust *you*, but these bands are unpredictable. You're not ready for that yet, but you will be! Soon. Best to stick to local college bands until you're touring stadiums." Stan licked his fingers as he spoke, balancing on the line between a client or his son sitting in front of him.

"I don't know about anything bigger, Dad...we seem to be doing fine."

"Think of the bigger picture, Brian! You're a person with substance and that's what they all love about you. You have a face built for the cover of *Rolling Stone*. Literally. Your mom was on there once, it's in your blood!" Stan continued to shovel food into his mouth as he spoke.

"I don't think that's how it works." Brian gritted his teeth together at the thought. He didn't push his music because he didn't want it to be popular amongst the masses. He didn't want it to lose its authenticity.

"It's my job to promote you. We're going to have you playing stadiums in no time! People will be falling at your feet as you walk in the footsteps of legends. You'll be a goddamn Rockstar!" Stan laughed before practically throwing a handful of fries into his mouth. Brian grimaced at the sight, his dad tended to get ahead of himself.

"Yeah, but—"

"How about a European tour? Next year!" Stan suddenly inputted, as if it were something he had been thinking about for a while. Stan watched as Brian's face filled with confusion. "I say *European...*I mean the UK. I don't know what the whole visa situation is going to be. I'll figure it out!"

"I don't think the band could afford that." Brian's face dropped with concern. He knew there were plenty of Social Dropouts fans across the pond but touring abroad sounded expensive.

"That's my problem to deal with. I'll get you all to the UK. Then it's onto a *world* tour! You may have to change your sound though; the whole emo thing is a bit too niche for stadiums. How about pop-punk? Maybe we could get Travis Barker on a track? The sad kids love it *and* it sells!" Stan pointed at his son. "You could always change your band name. Social Dropouts is okay, but people are really into inanimate object band names right now. How about that band named after a vagina? Now that *sells!*"

"Dad..." Brian sighed again, he was grateful for his dad, but he had lived independently for a lot of his life. With Stan unsure of how to support his son in the long run, he tried his hardest to support him in his current pursuits. Except, Stan didn't always have the best motivation for his suggestions.

It didn't feel as if Brian was ever listened to when it came to his music.

"It's just a suggestion, you don't have to go if you don't want to. When your mother and I used to go on tour overseas it was so much fun! You get to see parts of the world that you otherwise wouldn't see. It's a huge adventure." Stan attempted to sell the dream of playing shows abroad. Brian didn't have that in mind yet.

"Thanks." Brian didn't bother to smile as he ate another fry. Slowly but surely he was going to have made his way through that meal.

Stan stared out the window for a few seconds, pondering on other questions he could have quizzed his son on. He liked it when they got an opportunity to hang out, Brian mostly spent his time alone in his small apartment. Although, sometimes when things got a little too much for Brian on his own and his dad was home he would go to Stan's penthouse and spend the night in his room there. Brian was free to stay whenever he wanted.

"When are you going to tell me about this girl you mentioned?" Stan brought up as if it were an acceptable subject to speak about.

"What girl?" Brian played dumb. He had spoken to his dad in the past about some of the women he had been with. Mostly claiming how hurt he had felt after they didn't want anything to do with him, skimming over the whole section that contained them sleeping together. Stan knew Brian well enough to know his search for partnership didn't come from holding hands.

"Y'know...the one who's a grou—"

"She's not a groupie. She doesn't even like our music. Her friend is super into the band and she's just...being dragged along for the ride. It's nothing." Brian put up his shield of defence. Stan instantly took note of his tone.

"*Nothing?* You're *not* into her?" Stan questioned, unsure if Brian had even attempted to pursue the girl.

"I like her." Brian looked down at the table as he scratched his finger against the surface. He didn't want to meet eyes with his father. "I like her a lot."

"Does she like you back?" Stan pressed, asking Brian a question he didn't know the answer to.

"I don't know." Brian shrugged.

"Oh."

"We kissed. T-that was...amazing." Brian found it hard to get his words out, nervous about what his dad may have thought of him. He happily welcomed being able to speak about mundane things with his father. Anything that wasn't music.

"Yeah?" Stan raised his eyebrows; he had never heard Brian talk so positively about a girl he was pursuing. Most of the conversations Stan had with Brian about women had mostly been consoling him after someone had rejected his romantic interest.

This didn't sound like any of the other times.

"I've never met anyone like her before. I don't want to...mess it up." Brian exhaled before running his fingers through his hair.

"She kissed you back, didn't she?"

Brian nodded. His dad had made that sound weirder than it was.

"She's probably interested in you too." Stan smiled, the realisation hitting Brian a little harder than the conclusion he had drawn in his mind. It felt more powerful coming from someone else.

"Maybe?" Brian's eyes lit up slightly, hearing the words from his father were impactful.

"How could she not be interested in you? Look at you! You're so handsome! A Rockstar!" Stan complimented Brian the best he could as he pointed across the table.

"Dad, come on!" Brian groaned, slightly embarrassed. He held his head in his hands before running his fingers back through his hair. He placed his hands on his neck before smiling up at his father.

"You've got your mother's smile." Stan grinned, unable to help himself from commenting. It wasn't the first time Brian had heard the phrase and although the mention of his mother often dampened the mood, this time it didn't.

"You say that all the time." Brian smirked shyly, Stan seeing that same smile Cherry used to give him.

"That's because it's true."

Brian brushed his fingers against his bottom lip, realising how intensely his father was looking at him. It hurt him knowing how much pain his father held after losing his mother.

Stan's love for her stretched further than what Brian could ever imagine. Even if things weren't perfect.

"Dad?"

"Yeah?"

"You *are* coming to the show tonight, right?" Brian asked, unsure what he wanted his answer to be. On one hand, he was excited to have his dad at the show and the other half of him was less inclined, knowing he would want to put on the best show possible.

There had been a time in the past where Stan didn't turn up to the show he had agreed to go to. As invested as Stan was in Social Dropouts...they weren't always his top priority.

"I cleared everything for this. I even set up the tour dates based on this one show! I do have to fly out of Nashville after you play, but I'll be there." Stan assured with a small nod.

"Okay. Good. It's been a long time since you've seen me play...that's all." Brian felt sad knowing his dad hadn't even

come to see them practice before they went on the tour this
time. Even Russ' mom had come to see them practice once.
Zoe's sister had come too.

"I get to see you tonight, don't I?" Stan shrugged. Seeing
Brian play would have been the best way to show he cared. Not
only that, but he would have been there to see how much pro-
gress his son was making with his band. It would be a good opportunity for him to study the crowd's engagement.

Brian spent the rest of the day with his father as opposed
to the rest of the band. It was a small home comfort he needed.

He still would have preferred to have been with the band.
With Farah.

He would have been happier to spend time with him
when his father wasn't pushing the ideology of him being a famous Rockstar. Brian couldn't help but feel as if his father's futile attempts were ones he wanted for himself when he was
younger, but never got the chance to do. Some people were naturally talented when it came to music, others not so much.

Stan fell into the latter, finding himself being a roadie
when he was younger followed by music management as he
progressed through the ranks. He had a good ear for sound,
but he couldn't make it himself.

No matter what, Brian would have always been forced to
fill the shoes of his parents. Even the shoes they never stepped
in, but always owned.

Before the show, the band went outside to smoke, Max and
Farah found their way around the building to join them on their
natural pre-show warmup. It felt weird for Brian and Farah to
be close to one another knowing that not too long ago they had
been exploring each other's mouths.

Brian chewed his bottom lip whenever she was around,
anxiety passing over him as he noted the fact his dad was inside
the venue. He would have two people cheering him on that
night and that would have felt good. There was so much that
went through his head when he was on stage and yet with them
there it would have only tripled his thoughts.

"We're about to go on the longest leg of our tour. Do you know how much driving we have to do? It looks horrible!" Zoe groaned as she pushed her back against the wall of the venue, venting her frustrations to the people surrounding her.

"We've done it before." Russ shrugged; he didn't want to spend the next couple of days cooped up in the back of the van but he had things planned for the ride. He had audiobooks to catch up on and would have liked the free time to listen whilst filling copious sketchbooks with peculiar doodles.

"How are you guys finding the drive?" Catfish asked the two girls that were standing opposite them, not participating in the same smoking activities as the band.

"Exhausting." Farah folded her arms and chuckled. Despite her first interaction with the band, things had been going well between them. Her anxiety had calmed when they were around.

"Hey, we take it in turns!" Max argued.

"That doesn't make it any less exhausting!" Farah shook her head at her best friend.

"I zone out when I drive. I sometimes forget I'm driving and then I'm just...there." Brian inputted, the people around him mistaking his words for something different.

"Brian...that's worrying. I don't think we should let you drive anymore." Zoe furrowed her eyebrows with concern, shocked by Brian's comment.

"N-no, that's not what I—"

"No, I get it!" Farah added, causing Brian to smirk at her defensive nature. "It's called unconscious competence. It's when skills become second nature to you, so you complete tasks without thought. In this case...driving. It's pretty common." Farah shrugged as she spoke, trying to make sense of his words.

"Yeah! *That*!" Brian pointed with a smile, impressed with her knowledge.

"Okay, well, that still sounds terrifying." Zoe shook her head.

"This conversation is making me unconsciously incompetent." Max nodded towards Zoe, wanting to flex her knowledge on the same psychological model Farah knew.

Farah rolled her eyes before catching Brian's stare with the small smirk that was creeping up the side of his face. He would have given anything to kiss her again. It wasn't like all the times before. Even his dad had mentioned how likely it was that she liked him back.

This was a *romantic* kiss.

It had to be.

The back door of the venue opened and a man with unkempt hair revealed himself, glancing over at the band and the two new additions they had made.

"Do you always go on this late? You've had all night to smoke whatever shit you're smoking!" Stan ran the palm of his hand across the top of his head as he raised his voice out of desperation. "You kids are killing me, you're on in two minutes."

The band had done fine without Stan making them a schedule. Although, it was nicer for someone they knew to shout at them for being late rather than a venue owner.

"We'll be right there, Dad!" Brian shouted.

Farah looked over to the door and took note of the man before he disappeared. Farah didn't know what she was expecting his father to look like, but she hadn't expected him to look exactly as the pages on the internet had depicted.

Stan Static. Once a roadie on tour with The Flower Children only to fall in love with the lead singer, Cherry Blossom. When Farah read the articles, it sounded like something from a cheesy movie.

Stan was a rich band manager and music producer; he had even worked with a few musicians Farah would have recognised the names of if she dug deeper. She even listened to one of them frequently, a folk-pop singer who went by the name Bailey Craig.

It had never occurred to Farah how *famous* Brian's family were. Brian didn't grow up in the prying eyes of the public, meaning he had been allowed a somewhat private life. It still wasn't great, but at least he was able to go to a supermarket without being bothered. Usually.

"We might have to catch you guys at the next show. It's the start of a long drive tomorrow." Catfish stood up straight as he stretched his arms. It was going to be another night of drumming.

"We can hang out in between, right? They're part of the band!" Brian suddenly threw in his opinion. Of course, he wanted to make sure that throughout the next couple of days they would have spent time together. After Austin, it was another long journey to Scottsdale. It would have taken them a few days and luckily the tour had been set up in such a way to allow the long travelling times. Despite this, they would still have to spend a lot of their days driving.

"Oh yeah, we're not leaving these cuties behind." Zoe pouted towards the three boys in her band. Russ and Catfish exchanged shrugs.

"I'm not leaving the band behind." Max shot finger guns at them all. "Wait, don't you guys live here? Are you staying at home tonight?"

"We were going to—"

"I got the keys to my dad's penthouse." Brian folded his arms and sighed, not too happy about the situation.

"Fuckin' A!" Catfish snapped his fingers.

"That place has a mini-bar!" Zoe laughed, turning to Russ and high fiving him quickly.

"The view from the penthouse is bewildering. You can see all of Nashville from there." Russ commented, having been in the penthouse a few times in the past.

"Yeah, it's pretty cool." Brian chewed his bottom lip as he nodded. It was *much* better than his apartment.

"You're inviting my dudes, right?" Zoe pointed over to both Farah and Max who stood there awkwardly placed inside of the conversation.

"Oh, we already have—" Farah began.

"Count us in! That sounds *great!*" Max clicked her fingers back at Zoe with a wink and an uncomfortable smile. Farah let out a heavy sigh as she allowed her shoulders to sag.

"Cool. I'm sure dad won't mind." Brian shrugged. His father probably would have encouraged it.

Farah bit her tongue. As much as she wanted to fight against Max's decision, it sounded fun hanging out in a penthouse. Farah knew she would have internal irritation at what would have probably been the poor materialistic choices of the rich. The penthouse was likely to be white and boring, just like most millionaires' residences.

"Sounds like a plan. We've got to go, but we'll catch you guys after the show!" Zoe held out her hand for Max to high five. Max had no problem in accepting the gesture and Farah happily lifted her hand so Zoe could do the same to her. Farah smiled awkwardly at the touch.

The group dispersed. Making their way onto the stage as Max and Farah went into the crowd. Once again, Farah stood at the back of the venue and watched. There was nothing she found more interesting than the way Brian's fingers slid up and down the neck of the guitar with such little effort.

Brian believed he would have been nervous about playing in front of his father, but Stan stood at the side of the stage clapping and cheering his son whenever he hit the right notes. Stan had always been supportive...in his own way.

There was no denying how talented Brian was and regardless of what song he played, everyone enjoyed it. That didn't mean Stan wouldn't stop trying to push Brian into one of the more mainstream genres to help boost his popularity.

Stan eagerly watched the show, extraordinarily proud of his son and the effort he put into building the hype around the shows and the lyrics he sang. If Stan were to listen deeper into Brian's lyrics he may have found a larger meaning and understanding to what Brian felt. Stan knew Brian was going to sing about whatever came from the heart and unfortunately, Brian had experienced a lot of pain there.

"I'm so proud of you! My very own *Rockstar*!" Stan threw his arm around Brian and ruffled the top of his sweaty hair, messing it up completely as he stood to the side of the stage.

"Dad!" Brian groaned, attempting to swat his father off. Brian stood up straight in front of his dad as the sound of the music system began to play a generic song to help flood the crowd out of the building.

"You're all so good! You crushed it and *everyone* loves you!" Stan was over the moon with excitement. The band had blown him away. They were more comfortable on stage than they were back when Stan had last seen them perform.

"Really?"

"What do you mean 'really'? Did you not hear them shouting?" Stan laughed, pushing Brian gently in the shoulder.

Brian looked down at where his father had made contact, bringing his hand up to touch the same location.

"They do shout pretty loud..." Brian blushed, not wanting to gloat about the number of fans who were excited to see them play.

"Next year. Social Dropouts. Brand new album. UK tour. What do you think?" Stan asked as he pulled Brian in for yet another half-hug.

Brian thought about his words. He wasn't sure if the band was ready just yet. Either way, Stan would have guilted him into doing whatever he wanted. It was no use making an argument out of it.

"Yeah?" Brian shrugged.

"We'll talk about it when you're ready. We can drink some beers and you can teach me those guitar skills of yours. I never taught you how to shred like *that*!" Stan laughed, Brian had surpassed all of his father's skills when it came to music.

"I was taught by the best." Brian grinned, Stan beaming in response to his words. Stan had taught him a lot of musical knowledge, but it was Brian who was talented enough to pursue that interest into a career.

Stan helped Brian pack away some of the gear off the stage and move it into the second van that was ready to take it to their next location.

The band had helped them to start with and then disappeared into the back. Stan convinced them he and Brian could pack the rest away. Stan didn't get to pack away sets the same as he did when he was younger, so doing the task gave him a rush.

As Stan and Brian stepped through the back of the venue they made their way to the room the band had been provided. When Brian entered with Stan, it was nearly empty, except for one person sitting on an old beaten up couch flicking through their phone.

"Where is everyone?" Brian questioned, it hadn't been long since he had seen them.

"Oh, they went to smoke and get more alcohol." Farah looked up at Brian and Stan in the doorway, exchanging glances between them. She still couldn't believe she had kissed Brian Blossom. They hadn't spoken about it. Were they supposed to? "D-do you want me to go?" Farah pointed to the door, not wanting to intrude on the relationship Brian had with his father.

"No, no—stay!" Brian insisted. He didn't want to kick Farah from the room.

"Okay..." Farah felt awkward being in the presence of Brian and his father. All she had done was kiss him...was it already time to meet the parents? She hoped not. Her parents wouldn't have warmed up well to Brian.

"Oh, Dad...*this* is Farah!" Brian gestured towards the girl sitting on the couch as she put her phone on her lap, adjusted her glasses and smiled politely. She added a little wave to her greeting. Stan smiled back, connecting the dots in his mind regarding his previous conversation with his son.

"Stan Static. It's nice to meet you." Stan smiled as he walked over to the couch and held out his hand. The college student reached up and shook his hand, noticing where Brian got his intense body heat from.

"It's nice to meet you too, Mister Static." Farah nodded politely.

"Um...Farah is touring with us. Her and her friend Max." Brian made his way into the room, scratching the back of his neck as he repeated why Max and Farah were there. As long as his dad didn't think they were groupies then everything would have been fine.

"Ever thought of a career as a roadie?" Stan questioned with a smile, relating her current adventure to a future career. Brian felt embarrassed by his father.

"Not...really." Farah admitted, chuckling lightly.

"Farah is super smart, Dad. She's not going to be a *roadie.*"

"Hey! What do you mean by that?" Stan turned and laughed, embarrassing Brian further as he realised what he had said to cause offence.

"Farah could be a doctor or astronaut if she wanted. She's smart. *Really* smart." Brian attempted to explain. After spending time with Farah he had discovered how dedicated she was to her college education. That and her well thought out and logical answers to everything.

"*Astronaut* is a bit of a stretch." Farah tittered as she pinched her thumb and index finger together, looking up at

Stan. Farah did, however, appreciate the compliments Brian was giving her.

"Astronaut or not, are you enjoying the shows?" Stan decided his best option was small talk.

"Yeah! They're fun. It wasn't my kind of music to begin with, but I'm warming up to the sound."

Stan got a little closer to Farah and used his hand to poorly hide his words from Brian.

"Oh, I don't understand the *emo* thing either. I just let him do whatever he wants. He's 'too good' for the *mainstream*. Some underground hipster bullshit if you ask me. This kid could be the next Angus Young and he's hiding it from the world." Stan complained to Farah loud enough for Brian to hear. She only half knew what he was talking about.

Brian pinched the bridge of his nose, trying to ignore his father's comments. Farah observed the relationship between the two men, one that over time had become one of passive-aggressive support.

"He does play very well." Farah nodded, an uncomfortable yet polite smile spread across her face.

It wasn't very often Stan got to meet a girl Brian was interested in. Stan had met a few in the past, but none of them stuck around long enough for Stan to take note. Meaning, he nor Brian ever saw them after that night. None of them had greeted Stan in the way Farah had.

Farah was different and Stan could immediately see why Brian had become smitten over her. Although Brian had never intended to go for the 'party-girl' types, they were the sort of women he used to attract. Farah was well-spoken and reserved. She was sweet.

"I've got to go. I've got a flight to catch in the next hour and I think my ride's here. It was great to see you, Kiddo." Stan tapped his watch, noticing the time. It was likely he had a meeting somewhere in the morning. Brian wasn't interested enough to ask further.

Farah saw that Stan didn't want to stick around for any longer than need be. He was too preoccupied with his own business to care about what Brian was doing. It didn't seem to phase him that he wasn't sticking around for another couple of minutes to wish his son goodbye.

"You can't stay *any* longer?" Brian tried not to pout. Before he could even think further on the subject, his father had wrapped his arms around him. Brian half-smiled at Farah over his shoulder, she could only seem to muster up a sympathetic smile.

"Amazing deal for the label is inbound. If I snap this up, your dad will be in the big leagues!" Stan held onto Brian's shoulders a little tighter than expected.

"You're already in the big leagues."

"Bigger! This one is up and coming *and* British. Everyone's going to love him."

"Sounds good..."

"Have fun partying at the penthouse. Don't do anything stupid, but have a good time. You can leave the keys in the lobby when you go. You can sleep in my bed, just make sure that's *all* you do." Stan patted Brian's shoulders and laughed, followed by a wink. Brian knew what his suggestion included.

"Right. Yeah. Sure." Brian nodded.

"Later, Kiddo. I'll say goodbye to your band buds on the way out. See you after the tour and good luck!" Stan patted Brian on the shoulder a little harder than he had anticipated before turning back towards Farah and nodding. "Look after my boy, Sara. It was nice to meet you."

"It's *Farah*." Farah corrected with a snappy tone. She hadn't meant to come across as rude.

"Right. *Farah*." Stan furrowed his eyebrows at her attitude. Brian watched as Farah stood up to his dad in a way he never felt he could.

"S-sorry. It was nice to meet you." Farah quickly apologised, feeling bad about snapping at Brian's father. That wasn't her intention.

"No worries, Darling. I'll see you sometime in the future." Stan avoided using her name. With yet another pat on Brian's shoulder, Stan exited the room. He was on the verge of missing his flight.

Brian placed his hands in his pockets and teetered on his heels before looking over at Farah with his lips pressed into a line. He felt embarrassed.

"I'm sorry about that. That wasn't okay. He can be a little too much and I didn't mean to impose anything. I didn't even think you were—" Brian began to apologise profusely for his father's actions.

"N-no! It's fine. I'm more interested to know if *you're* okay." Farah placed her hands on either side of the couch, ready to stand up if the moment called for it.

Brian stood in silence for a moment, taking in her words. It felt strange that someone was willing to show how much they cared. Not even the rest of his band checked on him in that same way. He turned around towards the door to make sure his father had gone.

"Yeah, we just have an interesting dynamic. That's all. He's a good guy when he wants to be." Brian shrugged, far too used to his father's behaviour.

Farah didn't have a great relationship with either of her parents anymore and yet it still felt as if they would have stuck around for longer than Stan did. Stan only stayed as long as it was convenient for him.

Before Farah got the chance to respond, the rest of the band began to walk back into the room. That also meant Max followed. Farah was happy for Max getting to spend a lot of time with her newfound friends, especially if it meant she could spend more time with Brian.

She was never going to admit that out loud.

"Just saw Stan head out, are we going to the penthouse now?" Zoe folded her arms, Max standing close sporting a quick nod of agreement.

"Yeah, sounds like a plan." Brian confirmed, the one thing on his mind was getting out of the venue as quickly as possible.

It didn't take long for the band to get into their van and make their way to the penthouse that belonged to Stan Static. It was something he had purchased when he moved to Nashville and kept ever since. A luxury apartment situated in the middle of the city.

Brian had spent a lot of his early teenage years there. It was strange going back, taking note of the fact his room there was still the same as he remembered when he was younger. Nothing had changed. It wasn't as if his dad was going to bother redecorating.

When Brian felt alone he would often stay with his dad. Even if it was only for a few nights and sometimes even if he knew Stan wasn't going to be there. It was nice to have gotten out of his cramped apartment and have a bit of luxury for a few days. Even if that was just when his apartment building lacked hot water for a shower.

Farah didn't know what to expect when she entered the penthouse. The band had been there before and Max had her own expectations.

Brian flicked the light on as they entered, they all held their bags for the night. The band were planning to go home for the night but with the prospect of staying in luxury without having to grab a ride to the other side of town, it was perfect.

The entirety of the penthouse lit up to reveal a huge open plan kitchen and living area. It wasn't as big and lavish as Farah had expected, but even still, it didn't look cheap. The entirety of the wall in front of them was made up of windows, some of which were doors leading out to a balcony overlooking the city.

The penthouse snaked around itself, with hardwood flooring, white walls and doors leading to different sections that she could only assume were a selection of bedrooms and bathrooms.

There was a huge television stuck to the wall in front of a long couch. There was a stale smell of cigarettes in the air and an ashtray sat in the middle of the coffee table. The kitchen was practically empty aside from a few take-out boxes that were balanced on the side. It was clear someone was living there, but if they did, it didn't look as if they did very often. It didn't look like a *home*.

Brian was quick to direct each of them into a particular bedroom, claiming he would sleep in his dad's room. He gave up his old bedroom to Russ and Catfish. Zoe took one of the guest bedrooms for herself and Max and Farah took the other.

The party wanted to stay up all night and spend the early hours of the morning drinking and watching weird videos on the large television. However, they knew they needed to rest before their drive tomorrow.

"I can't believe we're sleeping in Stan Static's penthouse. This is *insane*." Max looked around the room as she sat at the end of the double bed. Max and Farah were going to share the bed, but it wasn't the end of the world. As long as Max didn't accidentally kick Farah the same way she had done the last time they had slept in the same bed together.

"Pretty weird, huh?" Farah looked over at the windows that took up the entirety of the wall. From the floor to the ceiling. She could see so much of Nashville below.

"Hella weird. When I said this was going to be a great experience, I didn't mean any of this! I thought maybe giving them a high five at the end of the show would have been cool enough. This is next-level." Max nodded, falling on her back in the middle of the bed and staring up at the ceiling.

Farah wanted to admit she had kissed Brian. That would have added to the list of things that were super cool about the journey. It was something she had thought about repeatedly throughout the day. It was hard to concentrate on anything else.

The feminist inside of her was mad at herself for not being able to stop thinking about a man all day. She couldn't help it. He was the one constant on her mind since the moment their lips met.

They had been on tour for little over a week and it felt as if things had only just begun.

Farah had been kicked three times by Max throughout the night and that was enough for her to move to the couch. As much as she loved Max, she was never going to get to sleep in the same bed.

Her first port of call would have been to trail into the kitchen at four in the morning and retrieve a glass of water. She silently padded around the kitchen barefoot in nothing more than her college hoodie and a pair of short shorts she opted to wear in bed.

The last thing she wanted to do was snoop through Stan Static's cupboards, so made educated guesses where he held his glasses. If she didn't find them soon enough, she would have to lean over the sink with an open mouth. There weren't very many options.

Luckily, after a couple of attempts, she managed to find the cupboard that was filled to the brim with all kinds of drinking glasses.

She filled the glass with water and took a few large gulps, finally feeling refreshed enough to figure out what she wanted to do about her sleeping situation.

She felt a cool summer breeze that encouraged her to turn around and notice the doors to the balcony were open. It was only then she saw somebody smoking on the balcony.

It was Brian.

Farah knew she had two options. One of them was to ignore that she had seen the man on the balcony alone. Option two was to approach the man with whom she was developing a new relationship with.

Anxiety was one thing, but her curiosity was stronger.

Option two it was.

Farah gently stepped over to the open door, wanting to do everything she could to not scare Brian. Even though he had what looked to be a cigarette in his hand, he wasn't smoking it. His entire back hunched on the edge of the balcony, one of his hands held on the top of his head as he stared down into nothingness.

He was only wearing a red long-sleeve flannel and a pair of tight black boxers. Farah noticed the cigarette had nearly burned through, leaving a large section of ash yet to flick off the end. She didn't want to make him jump but she knew she wasn't going to get his attention without doing so.

"Can't sleep?" Farah questioned softly as she held her hands inside the front pocket of her hoodie.

Just as she had predicted, Brian practically jumped out of his skin at the sound of her voice. He had been completely entranced by his thoughts that the wake-up call to reality was enough to shake him. He immediately spun around with a look of shock on his face, his blonde hair dishevelled from where he had been aggressively pulling at it in frustration. His flannel shirt was open at the front, revealing his bare chest to Farah. She averted her eyes, he had been caught in a moment of vulnerability.

"F-Farah! Oh wow, you scared me! I'm just smoking. No. I mean, I don't really smoke. I do. Not really. Not this kind of smoking! Smoking is bad. B-bad for your lungs and stuff. It's my dads'. They're my dad's cigarettes." Brian blabbered as he placed the cigarette between his lips so he could button up his shirt, trying to make himself somewhat presentable under the night sky.

"Oh. Right." Farah nodded, she didn't know how to feel about his bad habit.

As soon as his shirt was buttoned, he pressed the cigarette out against the balcony railing before placing it in a small ashtray his father had for outside.

"I'm really sorry. I never do that. It's nice. It's nice out! Look!"

Farah knew that Brian was fumbling his words to make her divert her attention away from him. It wasn't working until he had mentioned the view. Farah stepped out on the balcony and looked around, the cool breeze brushing through her long hair she had allowed to fall past her shoulders. She took a deep breath in as she looked around at the city below, holding onto the balcony with both hands.

"Woah. It's beautiful." Farah's mouth fell slightly ajar as she stared out at the city surrounding her. She wondered what it was like to live somewhere where you could wake up to a view as pretty every morning.

Even though it was still dark out, the sun was rising in the distance. It wasn't showing itself much yet, but just enough to know the sun was on its way to light up the day.

"It sure is." Brian nodded, focusing his attention on Farah.

With them above the illuminated city lights, he could see all her facial features. From her beauty marks to the way her lips curled. It was obvious she had also made her way out of bed to be on the balcony. It wasn't as if she wore much makeup beforehand, but she wasn't wearing any now.

"We should probably stop meeting at early hours of the morning." Farah chuckled as she turned towards Brian, taking note he had been standing there staring at her the entire time. She brushed her hair over her shoulder as she placed her elbows on the edge of the balcony and balanced her chin on her hand.

"We should probably learn how to sleep through the night." Brian smirked as he pushed himself forward on the balcony and looked at the city below.

"It's a mixture of new places and anxiety." Farah confirmed.

"What are you anxious about?" Brian asked, giving her the option to share what was on her mind. "I-If you don't mind me asking."

"Everything. All the time. It's nothing." Farah had no idea if Brian was the right person to be speaking to, but he was someone willing to listen. That's all she needed.

Brian shuffled a little closer to Farah on the balcony.

"I know I might look like a judgemental asshole, but I'm not. You can talk to me about anything." Brian nudged her elbow. His touch was gentle, but one Farah found herself desiring.

"You don't look like a judgemental asshole." Farah argued with a smile, brushing her hair back with her fingers. Despite this, she still wasn't sure if telling her secrets to Brian Blossom would solve any of her issues. It may have been a good start.

"Good. I'm glad to hear it."

"Good." Farah nodded, trying to hide her smile. She looked back at the city below, listening to the gentle whoosh of the occasional car.

With Brian standing beside her copying her stance she could feel him wanting to ask a question. So, she waited. It took a few moments of awkward shuffling for him to finally pipe up.

"So...that uh...*thing* we did. The guitar in the woods thing. The thing. Y'know..." Brian began to choke on his words.

"Kiss?" Farah raised her eyebrows. She was much more composed than the nervous man beside her.

She hated the thought, but his flustering was...*cute*.

"Y-yeah, that's the one. *Kissing*. It's a strange word." Brian laughed through his shaky tone. Most of the time he was able to flirt with people with ease, but Farah didn't make it easy for him. She was the type of girl to make his palms sweat and his heart race.

"It sure is." Farah turned back to the city landscape, trying to ignore how awkward he was being. It would have only given her more anxiety.

164

She stared at the city with a level of intensity. Farah adored the outdoors, but city landscapes gave her a feeling of comfort. A reminder that even in such a big world, she was always surrounded by people. That didn't mean she didn't often feel alone.

Brian noticed her looking away, a sadness swept over him at her disconnect. He felt embarrassed. Maybe it was the way he had presented himself or perhaps it was because he was currently standing in his boxers? Either way, he was sure he had messed up.

"Do you still have me pencilled in?" Brian asked softly with a glum expression. Farah turned to look at him, realising what he was referring to.

"I do."

"Okay, just checking." Brian swallowed hard as he looked down at his feet before leaning back on the balcony. "The best thing about pencils is they're not permanent. So, y'know...if you don't want to do something ever again you don't have to. Especially if it's giving you anxiety. You can just be *friends* with the pencil if it helps or...never speak to the pencil again. It's up to you."

Farah smiled at his words, noticing how nervous he was about kissing her. The reality was, she had been the one to kiss him first...he had just *asked* first. She appreciated his concerns, but he didn't need to worry. Her pent-up anxiety and inability to sleep wasn't about him.

"Wait. Are you the pencil?" Farah snorted as she tilted her head and faced him.

"Uhh...maybe?" Brian scratched his head. He had already forgotten the awful analogy for his scenario. "I don't know. I'm just worried that you wouldn't want to hang out after we kissed."

In Brian's case, this was a genuine concern. Nobody had ever really hung out with Brian after a kiss unless it was for meaningless sex. Brian always wanted to be the man to make his sexual partners coffee the morning after and yet it had never gotten to that point.

There had never been a *morning after.*

There had never been anything *after.*

"I like hanging out with you." Farah admitted. It was something she hadn't thought about at first. However, hanging out with the band for the past week had been...fun.

"I like hanging out with you too." Brian grinned as he pushed himself a little harder against the railing of the balcony, shuffling closer to Farah so their elbows were touching.

"That means we should probably hang out more, huh?" Farah smirked, feeling her confidence around the man grow. She was starting to feel as if she could be herself around him.

"Yeah! Totally! We should hang out more!" Brian let out a small excitable chuckle as he straightened his back. "—But we should probably try and get some sleep." Brian made the sensible suggestion, despite wanting to spend the rest of the night outside with Farah.

"And miss the sunrise?" Farah cocked an eyebrow at the idea.

"Oh. We can do that..."

"I'm joking. We really should try and sleep some more, the drive to Texas is long."

"We have to leave soon." Brian groaned, allowing his head to drop slightly with exhaustion. Another night of not being able to sleep as much as his body desired.

"Max is driving. I'm sleeping." Farah proudly stated as she pushed her thumb against her chest. There was no way she was going to play any part in driving for the first couple of hours.

"Sounds like a plan. I think I'll ask Zoe to drive for a while." Brian took a deep breath, knowing that the rest of the band were probably going to have woken up any minute so they could get ready to leave. They were running on a tight schedule with two days to get to Texas. The thirteen-hour drive would have to be split in two for their own sake.

"Hey, maybe we could hang out in Austin?" Farah suggested, taking Brian by surprise. Farah was surprised she had asked.

"Y-yeah. That would be cool." Brian nodded in agreement as he stood up straight and brushed the front of his shirt.

"*Cool.*" Farah folded her arms in the oversized hoodie as she stepped away from the railing. There was no use in her hiding her smile.

"Are you going to miss me? Y'know...o-over the next few days." Brian queried, showing little shame standing so casually in his boxers.

Farah faltered at his words. The tone of his voice shouted for validation. He needed to know she would be thinking about him during their days apart. She knew she would be thinking about him.

The image of him standing in his boxers on the balcony would forever be engrained in her mind. That wasn't such a bad thing...

"Sure, but I hope you'll miss me too." Farah bit on the inside of her lips to stop herself from grinning. It didn't work.

"It would be impossible not to." Brian smiled sweetly.

He was going to miss her. That was enough to make her heart beat a little faster.

He was blocking the exit, as if he were expecting something before she left. She watched him stare down at the floor before looking back up at her with a smile. He was...handsome. She wanted to kiss him again, but it didn't feel like the right time.

"C-Can I text you?" Brian clapped his hands together softly.

"That would be...nice."

"Awesome. Cool. I'll uh...yeah...I'll text."

"Sounds great." Farah beamed, holding her hands inside the front of the hoodie. He was adorable.

He knew he couldn't hold her attention for much longer.

"So, uh..."

"Sleep."

"Yeah! Yeah, we should sleep."

"We should." Farah chuckled at their awkward conversation, it was clear he wanted to spend more time with her.

"Yep!" Despite his confirmation, he didn't seem willing to put the plan into action. Farah decided to put matters into her own hands.

"Goodnight, Brian." Farah gave him a little wave before stepping forward to go back inside.

"Goodnight, Farah." Brian pulled on his shirt as he spoke with a sweet smile on his lips.

He stepped out of her way as she walked past him. He watched as she disappeared inside.

Farah walked away from the balcony feeling butterflies in her stomach. Nothing compared to spending any amount of time with Brian.

After treating themselves to a few hours of sleep it was time for them to head to the next location on the tour.

Austin, Texas.

AUSTIN, TX

There were over eight hundred miles between Nashville and Austin.

Luckily, there was a day between their show in Nashville and their show in Austin.

It allowed Brian and Farah to get caught in conversations over text as their counterparts took the wheel. They also managed to catch up on some sleep.

Max and Farah had spent the day between the shows trying to visit locations with cultural significance. Farah's parents were still asking for pictures to confirm her whereabouts. She hoped they would never suspect her of doing something different.

Pining over a stranger who she had little understanding of? Her parents wouldn't have approved of that even if they *were* on a historic road trip.

Farah was stressed about her feelings over the man. A warm gooey feeling inside of her that she hadn't felt about anyone else. She felt different around him and she had even noticed her temperature rise frequently in his presence. She wasn't sure what she was experiencing, but she didn't want her crush to go too far.

He was kind and handsome, kissing him had been a new experience. She was all for experiencing different things on the trip, but that didn't include trying to get with the frontman of a band.

It wasn't as if she was going out of her way to woo the boy. That wasn't her intention. Although, the way he looked back at her was mesmerising. The way his lips had tasted earthy and minty all at the same time. The way his hair had felt between her fingers. The way he—

"Earth to Farah. *Wakey wakey*! The guys said they would meet us here so we could hang out." Max snapped her fingers as she leaned across the car towards Farah.

Farah broke from her daze; she had been sitting inside the car for a long time and had gotten lost in her mind. A full day had gone to travel.

Now they were in Austin and they would have been able to see Social Dropouts at the small venue. There was so much Farah wanted to see and do in Texas but couldn't due to travel times.

"We're here?" Farah blinked rapidly, unsure of her surroundings. Her mind had its focus elsewhere.

"We're not at the venue yet, we wanted to explore Austin. Remember?" Max pulled into a parking lot that looked to be attached to some sort of diner.

Farah noticed a wall with the words *'Smile! Even if You Don't Want to'* written on it. Her eyebrows dipped at the sight of the passive-aggressive sign.

"Where are we?"

"We're getting pizza with the band!"

"*Pizza*? Do they eat anything else?" Farah rubbed her eyes, groaning at the idea of eating pizza *again*. She wished the band opted for a more varied diet.

"Farah, they're an emo band...it's *all* they eat." Max sighed, finding it strange Farah hadn't caught onto the tropes of the genre yet.

"I thought you told me pizza was pop-punk."

"Similar culture. Fewer khaki shorts."

Farah noticed the band's van in the parking lot as Max pulled in. She hadn't seen them since Nashville, not even crossing paths on the road. The band had grown attached to the two people who were travelling across the country with them. They enjoyed Max and Farah's company.

Max and Farah didn't have to go far before they saw the band sitting in the outside dining area of the restaurant waving frantically for them to come over.

"You made it!" Zoe cheered as she stood up and gestured for them to join. Naturally, there were two seats free between Brian and Zoe they had saved.

"We sure did! *Welcome to Texas. Yee-haw*!" Max did a terrible Texan accent as she sat beside Zoe. Farah sat next to her, finding herself between Max and Brian.

"This place is *too* hot." Zoe complained, picking up a menu and fanning it towards her.

"Texas is pretty prone to tornadoes. Let's hope we don't encounter one." Russ stared across the table at the two guests, Farah feeling concerned by his comment.

"Nature is terrifying. Let's not go camping here." Catfish suggested, not wanting to be engulfed by a wild animal or tornado.

"Have you guys seen those videos of those crazy killer hornets? They eat bees. It's *insane*." Max got involved in the conversation.

"No. Bees must be protected at all costs." Russ barely showed his internal outrage, unable to manifest more than a deadpan expression. Farah silently nodded in agreement, wanting to take part in the conversation about bees, but feeling too nervous to do so.

"They can eat fifty a day."

"That's *so* gross!" Zoe shook her head as Max began to exchange further disgusting nature facts, the band were invested in what she had to say.

"Hi." Brian whispered as he nudged Farah with his elbow to get her attention, making sure they still looked somewhat like part of the conversation.

"Hi." Farah whispered back, smirking as she glanced over at Brian, they both sat close to one another despite being on separate chairs.

"How was the drive?"

"Hot." Farah attempted not to snort her answer, still trying to keep their conversation private.

"That's because you were in the car." Brian nudged her with a wink. His dorky flirtatious comment made her smile.

"Sure..."

"The next three days are worse." Brian sighed, realising how long the journey they had between Austin and Scottsdale was.

"Will we see you guys during that time?"

"We can always meet up. If you want to see me—" Brian bit his lip, realising the words he had allowed to pass through his lips. "If you want to see *us*." He quickly corrected, Farah still taking note of his mistake.

"That would be nice." Farah smirked, noticing his phrasing. Brian placed his hands on his knees underneath the table and flushed a shade of red.

"What does everyone want to order?" Zoe quickly passed the menus around the table.

Farah had a quick look at the menu to notice most of the items were either pizza or pie. She had consumed more than her fair share of pizza on the tour. Her parents would never have approved of her awful diet of saturated fats.

The band and their two additions quickly ordered food, they still wanted to spend what they had left of their day walking the streets of Austin. They had to go to the venue soon, but they wanted to take their time in the heat. The state capital was worth exploring.

Brian had decided on ordering a cold beer to help offset the heat, even offering a sip to Farah. Farah tilted her head slightly at the suggestion. His question wasn't forceful and didn't pose to make her feel uncomfortable. Farah hesitantly took a sip of the beer, knowing she wouldn't have enjoyed it. She was right.

Despite this, she took a couple more sips from Brian's glass bottle. Nobody questioned a thing.

After finishing their pizza and pies, the band decided on walking through Austin to see what there was to discover. Russ was thrilled to have been in Austin, wanting to study the street art around the city. If the band had let him out of their sight, he would have currently been scaling a wall with some spray paint.

The band walked down the street together, Catfish explaining to Russ what he had previously read online about

Austin's street art only to be corrected. Max had occupied herself by speaking to Zoe about what Farah overheard to be...frogs? She didn't question it.

Brian and Farah trailed behind the group, everyone too caught up in their own world to notice the two of them paired off a lot. If Farah didn't enjoy Brian's company it would have been an incredibly awkward experience.

Brian wished he had enough confidence to thread his fingers through Farah's hand as they walked down the street. He had never held hands with anyone before, not romantically anyway. He would have liked to have shared that moment with Farah. He didn't want to make her uncomfortable in front of all their friends.

Was it time for them to hold hands? They had only kissed once and there was a special kind of intimacy that came with hand-holding. Brian was unsure of the rules. It was hard to grasp without the sex part.

"Oh, guys! Check this one out. It's pretty iconic." Catfish pointed to the opposite side of the street towards a café with the words *'I love you so much'* sprayed in red paint on the side of the green wall.

It was simplistic and yet something about it held meaning.

"Is this the one you were talking about with the story of the cute chick with her girlfriend?" Zoe questioned as they stood on the opposite side of the street and stared at the art from afar.

"That's the one. They had a gnarly fight and then one of them wrote this on the side of their building to remind them of their love. Pretty sweet, huh?" Catfish nodded towards the sight.

Max pulled out her phone and snapped a quick picture.

"The passion isn't within the art itself, it's the act. It's beautiful." Russ commented, feeling compelled by the painted wall.

Brian stared across the street with starry eyes, blinking at the words in wonderment.

"Despite everything, love came through. They were romantics. They loved one another more than whatever they were fighting about." Brian whispered under his breath. It was amazing and Brian appreciated the street art more than he would have wanted to admit.

"Save it, *Casanova*. It's just paint." Zoe snorted as she pointed over at the wall.

"But the story has a powerful meaning! Think about the meaning *behind* the paint!" Catfish groaned, understanding the message Brian was trying to get across.

Farah looked over at Brian and saw him staring at the writing on the wall. It was sweet, but it wasn't something Farah was head over heels for. She couldn't have said the same about Brian, she had never seen him stare at something so intensely. He was enamoured by the simplistic romantic gesture.

The band continued to make their way through the streets before they had to set up for the show. There wasn't time to do much else throughout the day, but they tried to fill the void the best they could.

Farah and Max stood outside in line for the show, not wanting to always take advantage of the privileges that came with getting to know the band. They had paid good money for the tickets that it often felt wrong to go in through the back with the band.

Despite having to wait outside, Max was glad for the opportunity. The band needed to set up for their show that evening and Max wanted to speak to Farah about something important.

"Farah, I don't ask very much of you...but I need your help." Max leaned against the wall at the front of the venue, Farah stood next to her with her arms folded.

"I don't like the sound of this already."

"It's nothing *bad*."

"I hate this even more now."

"Look, it's just a simple favour. No biggie." Max shrugged; Farah couldn't even hazard a guess at what she would ask for. It could have been anything.

Anything.

"What do you want?" Farah sighed.

Max stood up straight and looked over at Farah. Max looked around nervously before pushing her fingers together.

"Rumour has it that the band is staying in a hotel tonight. I think it's the one across the street from ours..." Max began to explain. "Well, it's not *really* a rumour...Russ told me."

"I already don't like where this is going."

"Listen. It's not weird or anything, it's just a really simple favour."

"What is it?" Farah was desperate to know what it was her best friend wanted from her. If it was that simple then why was it taking so long for her to talk about it?

"I need you to distract Brian for...*maybe* an hour or two?" Max bit her bottom lip nervously, attempting to gauge her friend's reaction.

"Wait, what?" Farah's expression dropped, incredibly confused by Max's request.

"Catfish and Russ are probably going to hit a local night-club and I doubt Brian will join them. I just...I want to hang out with Zoe." Max pressed her lips into a thin line. "Alone."

"Oh no. Nope. No way." Farah shook her head quickly.

"C'mon...it's not *weird*! I promise! Neither of you will come back into your rooms with anything questionable. It's—"

"Nope."

"Brian usually ends up in a room with Zoe out of the process of elimination, they'll probably hang out together if Russ and Catfish go elsewhere. Brian goes on that strange 'alone time' thing a lot, just catch him then!" Max attempted to make the situation sound pleasant.

"What the hell am I supposed to do with Brian for *two hours*?" Farah argued back in an aggressive whisper, making sure nobody else in the line could hear.

"There is one thing, but I doubt he'd last *that* long."

"Oh my god..."

"You were in the car with him for a long time to Asheville. Just do whatever you did then that you're not telling me about!" Max argued, a million things shooting through her mind, mostly inappropriate.

"We just *talked*!"

"Talk again!"

"Max!"

"J-just...go and get ice cream. I don't know!" Max shrugged.

"At...one in the morning?" Farah huffed, unsure how Max's plan could work out.

"I'm sure I saw a twenty-four-hour store down the street." Max pondered for a moment.

"Wow..."

"Look, it's one night. Two hours. Don't give me any of that bullshit with you saying you don't want to hang out with him. I know you do."

"I don't." Farah shook her head.

She did.

"Deny it all you want, but I *know* something is going on between you two." Max squinted at Farah before pointing a finger to her friend's chest.

Farah felt a little nervous about Max pointing fingers. Did she know about the kiss? Had she seen them the other night?

There was no way.

"You're wrong."

"Hmm, I don't think so, but I'll let you keep lying to yourself if it makes you feel better." Max shook her head slowly as Farah sighed in frustration.

"If I somehow manage to get him away from you both, you owe me *big* time." Farah pointed back.

"Yeah yeah, add it to the tab." Max rolled her eyes before leaning back against the wall. She looked up at Farah and smirked. "Thanks though. You're the best."

Farah, although frustrated, glanced over at Max and smiled back.

"Yeah...I know."

Farah was nervous. Would Brian even accept her offer of hanging out late at night? With the infatuation he had with her she found it hard to imagine him rejecting the offer unless something swayed him otherwise.

Max had somehow predicted correctly about Catfish and Russ burning off more energy by going into nightclubs. They enjoyed a good drum and bass night until the early hours of the morning after a show.

It was mostly for the drugs.

This left Max, Zoe, Farah and Brian to their own devices.

The band had already parked the van at the hotel they were staying in, catching a ride over to the venue so they could drink. It wasn't very often they got to stay somewhere that wasn't someone's floor, but after the long drive, they knew they deserved a real bed regardless of cost.

Farah drove them all back to the hotel in Max's car, having been the only one who hadn't consumed above the legal limit of alcohol or smoked weed that night. Max and Zoe sat in the backseat laughing about things they saw on each other's phones. Brian sat in the passenger seat and stared up at the swinging air freshener shaped like a small tree.

The car journey was less than ten minutes back to the hotel and everyone quickly stumbled out the car. Max and Zoe weren't waiting for anyone as they ignored Brian and Farah who had once again been left to themselves.

Farah shook her head at Brian as he smiled, seeing both Max and Zoe giggling to one another as they walked away, far too high and drunk to comprehend much other than the hilarious videos Max had found on the internet.

"They look like they're having fun." Brian continued to smile as he looked at Farah over the roof of the car, slowly moving out of the way of the door and shutting it closed.

"It's a little worrying." Farah snorted at the sight of them, locking the car once the doors were shut.

"They can look after themselves." Brian shrugged, stepping around the front of the car and awaiting Farah to join him.

She looked over at him, the only thing illuminating them was the streetlight above and the moonlight of the clear sky.

They had been incredibly thankful for the weather throughout the tour. The only time they had encountered rain had been whilst driving and that wasn't so bad.

Despite having just played a show, he was wearing a long sleeve red and black flannel shirt he had worn throughout the day thrown over his white ringer t-shirt with a red collar.

Luckily, the men's bathroom at the venue had some spare deodorant on the side otherwise his presence would have been a little more unwelcoming. Sure, using a random bottle of spray deodorant in a bathroom he had found wasn't one of his finest hours, but he wasn't willing to wait until his shower back at the hotel to clean up. He was willing to risk the random bathroom deodorant if it meant not smelling bad around Farah.

Farah had been given a mission by Max that she had agreed to. She needed to make sure it was a plan Brian was willing to agree with too. Brian watched her carefully, her body language giving him mixed signals as they stood in silence for a moment, her fingers running across the car keys she was holding.

"D-do you want to hang out?" Farah popped the question, worried to hear his answer. She had already proposed the idea of hanging out back in Nashville.

"Now?" Brian's eyes widened. Farah was a little taken back by his expression, feeling nervous about the question.

"I mean, it is pretty late. We can alwa—" Farah began to panic. It was one in the morning. Why would he have wanted to hang out with her now? That was ridiculous.

"N-no. I'm free now. If you want to." Brian interrupted her speech, feeling a little awkward. He couldn't think of anything he would want more in the world than to hang out with Farah.

Alone. Was it a *date?* A *mini-date?*

He had never been on one of those before.

"Yeah! I'm free now too."

"Good. What do you want to do?" Brian asked, intrigued with where her plan was going to take them.

She didn't have a plan.

"Where do *you* want to go?"

"You asked me to hang out. You have to decide." Brian countered. Farah felt put on the spot and was unsure what she could have suggested without sounding lame.

"Maybe we could walk around? We might see something to do? Something that's still open?" Farah shrugged her shoulders; she knew bars and nightclubs would have been the only things open at that time of night. Either way, if Brian wanted to go inside of one of them, she probably would have followed.

She felt safe within his presence.

"Sure. That sounds like a plan. Are you ready?" Brian pointed his thumb over his shoulder towards the centre of the city where they had previously been walking around aimlessly.

He was ready to do that again, but this time with Farah. Alone.

"Yeah!" Farah stepped over, standing beside him as they made their way into the town. Brian knew Farah had no idea what they were going to do with their evening, but he was appreciative of Farah asking him to hang out.

They were still contending with the fact only a few days ago they had kissed. It was the one thing that was on both of their minds.

"Do you usually explore new places after midnight?" Brian smirked at Farah as he slid his hands in his jean pockets, making their way down the street together.

"I'm usually in bed by ten." Farah laughed.

"Oh. Sensible."

"College is really demanding. You'd think with the amount of money you pay you wouldn't have to work so hard." Farah chuckled as Brian listened contently to what she had to say. He had very little knowledge of what college was like.

"The money should go towards paying someone else to do your work."

"Exactly! Oh, it's all a big corporate scam. Don't get me started. We pay all this money to go to college and some of the facilities haven't been updated in years. It's disgusting. How can they expect us to pay such a large sum of money when half of the stuff we need to graduate is inadequate? I go to a pretty fancy school and even sometimes they slack in their teaching abilities. I had this professor last year who spent most of the lectures on his phone. You *bet* I reported him." Farah huffed, suddenly realising their simple conversation had turned into an excessive rant. "I'm sorry, I didn't mean to rant."

"No, it's okay. I like it when you talk about things you're passionate about." Brian grinned, it didn't matter what she was talking about, he just wanted to listen.

"Why don't you talk to me about music?" Farah suggested.

"Music? But you hear me play every night. Are you not sick of it yet?"

"If I was that sick of it I would have driven home already." Farah laughed, making sure to tease him whenever the time was right. She was starting to realise it was the best option to getting under his skin in a subtle yet flirtatious way.

"Yeah? Well, I'm glad you stuck around." Brian smiled, pushing the conversation back onto them.

"Even if I wanted to...Max wouldn't let me leave."

"That's true." Brian chuckled, beginning to understand how attached her friend was to the band and Farah.

They continued to walk down a singular street a little further until they reached an area that felt familiar. It was different in the dark, the sidewalk lit up by streetlights. A few people were walking around, but this side of town didn't appear to be the one that contained a lot of nightlife. The street was mostly littered with cafés and independent stores.

"Hey, isn't that the café with the writing on the side?" Farah pointed over to the café she remembered from earlier during the day.

"Yeah, I think so." Brian confirmed as they continued to step closer.

The outside of the café was no longer littered with tourists. They stood on the correct side of the street, right beside the words painted in red against the green building. Brian and Farah stood beside one another as they turned around and stared at the writing.

"*I love you so much...*" Brian read out loud, his eyes grazing over the text on the wall. Farah listened to the words falling from his lips.

"It's cute." Farah smiled at the writing; the backstory they had been given earlier made the whole thing far better than just words on a wall.

"Super cute. Imagine waking up in the morning, believing the person you love doesn't love you anymore and then you go outside and see *that*! It's...incredible." Brian pointed to the wall, excited about the story that had been told about the words. He was a romantic and loved the gesture and the deeper meaning.

"You really *love* love, huh?" Farah chuckled, looking over at him continuing to stare up at the wall in front of them.

Her words bounced within Brian's mind before he turned his head to face her.

"Y-yeah. I do. It's sweet." He confirmed. He *loved* love; he had been surrounded by people telling him how wonderful it was his entire life. Except, he was yet to experience it himself.

Farah found it sweet that the boy was a romantic. She could tell by the way he acted around her he was a kind and respectful individual. Although he had flirted with her numerous times, she knew he would stop if anything made her uncomfortable. He had even asked permission before kissing her. He tried his hardest to be a romantic *and* a gentleman.

"Have you...ever been in love?" Farah looked away as she spoke, unsure why she would have asked such a question.

"I...I don't think so. Heh, I probably thought I was a few times in the past. I-I'm not very *good* at it." Brian scratched the top of his head, curious to know the reasoning behind Farah asking the question.

"Good at what?"

"Love." Brian laughed.

"Oh. What makes you think that?" Farah tilted her head, suddenly far more invested in the conversation than she would have liked to admit. She didn't want to pry too deep into his private life, but the conversation topic had come up suddenly. It was hard not to ask questions.

Brian wasn't sure if he should have revealed his past to Farah. Would it have ruined his chances with her? Was this the kind of thing that had pushed other people away?

"People don't really like emotional attachment." Brian shrugged, not wanting to give too much away about his past 're-lationships'.

"Oh." Farah stared back up at the writing on the wall, Brian was quick to do the same. It was clear it was a conversation topic he didn't want to speak about any further. A sensitive subject that made Brian squirm with anxiety...especially around Farah.

"I hope people consider this art. I think it deserves that title at the very least." Brian sighed as he placed his hands into his jean pockets and continued to look up at the wall.

"Russ considers it art and that's the highest of merits." Farah tried her hardest to lighten up the mood with a slight chuckle.

"Russ would consider anything art. I once dropped a coffee on the floor of the van and he spent hours replicating the stain on a napkin."

"That's modern art."

"It had become an antique by the time he'd finished." Brian snorted, clenching his fists the best he could in his pockets.

Farah felt bad bringing up the subject of love, although it wasn't entirely her fault considering the mural they were currently standing in front of. The words came with a million different meanings. She held her arm, feeling awkward as she thought about how she could bring up the one thing that had been on her mind the past couple of days. She had to do it.

"I've been thinking a lot about the other night..." Farah began to speak. Although there had been a couple of nights between them, Brian automatically knew what night she was referring to. It couldn't be about Nashville. It had to be the kiss.

"Yeah?" Brian turned towards her...she was going to reject him. Tell him that she never wanted anything to do with him again. He had blown it. He was wrong about her...it was going to be just like all the times before.

Farah didn't want anything to do with him.

It was over.

"I still can't believe we *kissed*..." Farah placed her fingers by her bottom lips to stop herself from smiling, her face flushing red. It felt strange to finally have the confidence to say it out loud.

"I-is that a bad thing?" Brian's eyebrows dipped as he stared at her with concern. He had felt this rejection time and time again. She had told him in Nashville she would be willing to kiss again. What could have changed?

"N-no! It's not a bad thing. It's just...I'd never kissed anyone like *that* before." Farah chuckled nervously. No encounter she had ever had when kissing had felt like that. It was different in so many ways.

"Oh. I'm...*sorry?*" Brian bit his bottom lip, unsure what Farah was trying to tell him.

Farah felt the pain in his expression, instantly stepping forward and placing her hands on either side of his arms, his hands still tucked in his pockets.

"You don't have to be sorry! I told you, I-I liked kissing you." Farah laughed, feeling as if she had an unexpected burst of confidence.

Brian felt her touch on either side of his arms, removing his hands from his pockets and placing them on her arms in return. They stood for a moment, exchanging a small stare between them. One of their many longing looks they did in the presence of others. This time the only company they had was the occasional passer-by and the odd car driving down the street.

They were practically alone.

"I liked kissing you too." He whispered.

"Maybe we should—"

"Kiss again?" Brian cut her off before realising he had spoken his mind. "O-only if you want to. I-I wouldn't want to double book you. You pencilled me in—"

"It's okay. I used pen." Farah nodded. A part of her wishing she had enough confidence to kiss him on the balcony in Nashville.

"Oh." Brian's lips parted as he took note of her mental gesture of permanence.

She felt one of his hands move slowly from her arm to the side of her face, giving her enough time to reject his advances if she didn't want to pursue them.

He took a step closer into her personal space as she moved her hands to his chest, no longer able to put them on his arms. Farah looked at him again, his eyes a hazy colour under the light above them. He slowly ran his thumb against her cheek before he tilted her head slightly and leaned in for a kiss.

Farah welcomed the connection, allowing his lips to press against hers in the same way they had done a couple of nights ago. Although they were in what was a busy tourist location throughout the day, it didn't seem to bother her that the occasional person would walk past them. She was too lost in the moment to care.

He was an expert in guiding the kiss which helped boost Farah's confidence. Brian was worried about overstaying his welcome, releasing himself from the long kiss before planting a few shorter kisses against her lips.

Before Brian could pull away, Farah took him back for another slow kiss. This time she removed her lips as slowly as possible, making sure they could feel each other's smiles. Their noses were pushed together, Farah's hands now wrapped around the back of Brian's neck.

"We're getting pretty good at that..." Brian hummed as he continued to hold her, the confidence in his words slowly returning.

"You were already pretty good." Farah practically slurred against his lips, he felt her breath against him.

"We should probably keep practising to make sure we're both caught up. Making up for lost time or something." Brian smiled, his eyes still closed as he cupped her cheek with his hand. He was incredibly alluring and Farah was finding it hard to resist his charm. This was all she had been thinking about the past couple of days. The only thing on her mind.

Farah laughed, gently putting her lips on top of his for a further kiss. This time deepening it a little further, enough to be considered romantic and not cause any turmoil in public. As they found themselves lost within each other's lips a car horn loudly sounded behind them, making them both jump.

They practically knocked their teeth together as they jumped, the car getting a kick out of startling the couple. The noise made them laugh as they quickly pulled away from the kiss. They were nervous about being caught in the act. Although, nobody in the area cared.

They stood and giggled together for a moment, the writing on the wall beside them being an aesthetically pleasing backdrop for their pursuits.

"Do you want to go and get ice cream?" Farah asked, following Max's advice for some unknown reason.

"What? Where are we going to get ice cream at this time of night?" Brian chuckled, still unable to control himself after only just stopping his giggle.

"Max said there was a store down the street."

"I mean, that sounds...*good?*" Brian shrugged, a little perplexed by Farah's plan.

"We don't have to—"

"You can't offer me ice cream and then go back on it." The young man in front of Farah smiled sweetly with a small shake of his head.

"Right." Farah nodded.

They began to walk along the sidewalk again, leaving the words on the side of the building for tourists to enjoy the next morning. Brian couldn't believe he had kissed the girl *again*, his attraction for her rising.

Neither of them hid the fact they were giddy as they walked with huge grins spread across their faces, happy with the kisses. Brian decided he wanted to shoot his shot and make his romantic fantasies a reality.

Farah glanced down at the palm of his hand as he held it out in front of her whilst they walked. His hand was open in such a way that if she desired, she could have slotted her fingers between his...so she did. Her fingers fell so gently into place as they allowed their hands to slowly drop to their sides intertwined together.

They were holding hands.

That only made them smile more.

Max was right in her brief knowledge of the area and they made their way into the convenience store. There was a lot they could have bought there, but they stuck to what they had originally gone in to buy.

Ice cream.

Other than when Brian had quickly pushed his card against the contactless machine before Farah got a chance, they hadn't disconnected their hands. Farah liked the warm hold of his hand and he felt the same way about her.

With a small tub of ice cream and a branded plastic bag that Farah had reluctantly taken, they made their way back to the hotel. They decided not to go back to the room much to Farah's pleasant surprise. She was concerned what kind of suggestion doing that could have brought on.

Instead, they sat by the Colorado River that ran through Austin. A small bench overlooked the water and the lights that surrounded the city.

"We don't have a spoon." Farah suddenly realised as Brian sat with the tub of ice cream on his lap. Brian stared down at the ice cream and started laughing.

"Oh...we'll just have to use our hands." Brian continued to laugh, the whole situation was hilarious to him.

"No! That's gross." Farah began to chuckle with him, struggling to get their words in.

Brian pulled off the lid to the ice cream. It was cookie dough flavoured, Brian's choice. Farah's eyes widened as he went to dip his finger into the top of the tub, she leaned forward and grabbed onto his wrist.

"What are you *doing*? When did you last wash your hands?" Farah gasped, disgusted by his potential behaviour. Brian looked up, her hand gripping tightly on his wrist.

"Um...the venue."

"What have you *touched* since then?" Farah furrowed her eyebrows in disgust. Brian glanced off to the side attempting to recall his night. A small smile crept up the side of his face.

"You..."

Farah gave him a stern expression, shook her head and used her hand holding his wrists to push his finger into the top of the ice cream. Brian gasped at the sudden change in temperature, his knuckles brushing against the ice cream. Farah smirked, realising she had ruined her chance of eating any. She didn't like being wasteful, but this had been worth it.

Brian removed his finger from the tub, hooking it around and taking a large amount of ice cream with it.

"Want some?" Brian held out his finger, offering the ice cream to Farah. She moved backwards and grimaced.

"I'm okay, thanks."

"Are you sure? There's plenty!" Brian teased as he held his finger closer to Farah, only causing her to back away further in disgust. She grabbed his wrist and pushed it back towards him, she knew he was stronger than her, but he didn't put up much of a fight.

"Nope!"

Brian opened his mouth and ate the ice cream that had been dangerously balancing on the end of his finger. His mouth made a popping sound as he removed his finger and Farah watched in slight disbelief. Just as he went to grab some more ice cream with his finger Farah shuffled closer to stop him.

"Wait!"

"What?"

"You're putting your *spit* in that ice cream! What if I want to have some? Can't you admit that's a *little* gross?" Farah shook her head with concern, releasing her grip from his wrist once again.

Brian shrugged before dipping his finger in the ice cream much to Farah's horror.

"Brian!" Farah gasped as she watched him devour the ice cream for a second time. She covered her eyes in disgust.

"Spit isn't gross when we're kissing, but it is in your ice cream?" Brian laughed, causing Farah to question her logic as she removed her hands from her face. It didn't make any sense.

"I—"

"Do you want some?" Brian smirked, persistent in trying to get Farah to take some of the ice cream.

"Yes, but I'm not eating it from your finger." Farah snatched the tub of ice cream from Brian. He didn't argue, letting her take it as he placed his elbow against the back of the bench and balanced his head on his knuckles.

Farah couldn't look down at the ice cream when all she could concentrate on was Brian's flirtatious stare from the opposite side of the bench. He was incredibly attractive and she felt a little self-conscious with him constantly looking at her as if she was the most important person in the universe. She gently pushed her hair away from her face, worried he was picking out her imperfections.

He wasn't. He was too entranced by her. Everything about her was *perfect*. The slight discrepancies in her hair from where she hadn't brushed it since the morning or the zit that was growing beside her right eyebrow that hadn't come through yet. It didn't matter. None of it mattered. They all added to her beauty.

"You're incredible..." Brian spoke under his breath, unable to remove his eyes from her.

Farah held the ice cream and smiled back at him, both sat opposite on the bench.

"Says the *Rockstar*." Farah scoffed with a smirk.

"Not exactly." Brian winked, blushing slightly at her comment. It felt wrong when his dad called him that, but it was different when she said it.

Farah reluctantly dipped her finger into the ice cream and took a bite. Brian watched her every move, a stupid smile on his face the entire time.

"Y'know...this is pretty good. Good choice with the cookie dough." Farah nodded her head in confirmation.

"I'm a professional ice cream taster."

"Oh, yeah?"

"Not quite, I just *really* like ice cream."

"Me too..." Farah smiled, looking at him with wonderment and realising at that moment that perhaps spending her time with Brian Blossom wouldn't have been such a bad thing.

The tour had become less about the music and more about the people who made it.

More about Brian Blossom.

The pair almost finished the tub of ice cream as they sat by the river. They spoke about all kinds of things as they spent the early hours of the morning together, the same as they had done before.

Farah enjoyed his stories and listened to them all without fuss. He was sweet and his stories were fascinating. She wanted to hear what he had to say.

She had concluded she just enjoyed hearing him talk. His voice was charming and one she could swoon over. She understood now why whenever he spoke at shows he always received screams of excitement back.

After a few hours spent together, they finally decided it was time for them to go to bed. Brian walked Farah to the lobby of the hotel she was staying in. They held hands until they were somewhere they could be spotted before saying goodnight to one another.

Farah stared into the mirror inside the elevator to her room, fixing her hair casually and waiting for it to go up. As soon as the doors closed behind her she let out a little squeal of excitement.

Brian walked back to his hotel room that night with a huge smile across his face.

SCOTTSDALE, AZ

"What did you two do last night?" Max questioned as she stared at Farah who was first to drive on their three-day trip to Scottsdale.

"We went and got ice cream, as per your suggestion." Farah told nothing but the truth, lifting a single hand off the steering wheel as she spoke.

"Wait, really?"

"Yes. You suggested it, did you not?" Farah cocked an eyebrow as she drove.

"Well, yeah. I just...I didn't expect you to *actually* get ice cream. That's way more innocent than I assumed. Huh." Max stared out of the window and pondered on Farah's words, curious to know if there was more going on between her best friend and Brian Blossom.

"I'm assuming what happened between you and Zoe was *less* innocent then?"

"Even if it was...I don't remember." Max sighed.

"Wait, what?" Farah was confused.

"Oh yeah, I have no idea what happened. I think I had too much to drink at that pizza place. Not only that, but I'm telling you now...there was something weird in that weed last night." Max shook her head, still attempting to get rid of the headache she had been burdened with since she had rolled out of bed in the morning.

"Oh."

"Did you see us doing anything...weird?"

"Last time I saw you both you were laughing over a video of a cat meowing underwater. Then you were passed out in your bed when I returned to the hotel. That's it. That's all I know of your crazy night." Farah sighed.

"Weird. I guess we'll never know the truth."

"Y'know what? That's probably for the best." Farah was glad Max hadn't pressed further into what she had spent her night doing with Brian.

She didn't want to push Farah on the questions. Max had noticed whenever Farah hadn't been driving she had been spending an awful lot of time texting on her phone. Farah had never been the sort of person to spend copious amounts of time on her phone, so seeing her using it for much else other than studying, writing passionate movie reviews, or watching videos on outdoor equipment seemed odd to Max.

Farah had been exchanging text messages with Brian whenever they hadn't been driving. Their text messages were a mixture of friendly chatter and slight flirtation. Farah had never texted anyone the same way she had texted the contact on her phone with the small guitar emoji beside their name.

Over the past day, she had been receiving a lot more text messages from someone who she hadn't heard from much throughout the trip.

She half expected a text from Brian to come through when suddenly—

'Hi Farah! I hope you're having a great time on your trip across the states. I find it compelling you would take the time out of your summer to do something so extraordinary. I have started reading more about that hike you wanted to do. Did you know that it's 2,650 miles? Obviously. You're not stupid and this is your calling! Of course you knew that. You're the smart one. Although, I wouldn't say that trying to move up the ladder in my father's highly successful company is a form of idiocy on my part. I guess you have to factor your personal definition of the word. Either way, let me know how you are. We should

totally catch up over dinner when you're home. I'd love to hear all about your adventures!'

Hasan, the suitor her parents approved of had been texting her frequently since they had left Austin. Farah rolled her eyes at the message, texting back with a simple *'cool'.* All she had to do was text him back with one-word answers to keep her parents happy. The only person she was interested in texting was Brian.

'I wish it snowed more in Tennessee. What's your favourite thing about winter?'

Brian had been texting her about much more interesting things. Getting to know one another over text was great when they couldn't be together.

'It doesn't snow much in Delaware or North Carolina either, but I like warm blankets, hot cocoa and cosy sweaters. They're the best!'

'You must run cold...you're always in sweaters. They're cute though.'

'Thanks! I get cold a lot.'

'I can keep you warm without the sweaters.'

Farah stared at his text with a smile, another text from Hasan flashing on the screen. She swiped it away to get back to her conversation with Brian.

'Oh, yeah? How?'

'You could take my jacket, or we could cuddle. If not, I know plenty of other ways for us to keep warm...'

Farah blinked at the message, noticing it came accompanied by a winking emoji. It was a little more suggestive than what he had sent in the past. Her cheeks went red as she glanced up to see Max tapping her hands against the steering wheel of the car to the beat of the song on the radio.

She wasn't paying enough attention to see how much Farah was blushing about the text.

It would have been a lie to say things of a not-so-innocent nature about Brian hadn't crossed her mind the past couple of days, but she had tried her best to push those feelings aside. With his flirtatious words, it felt as if he was granting her permission to those thoughts and she was happy to oblige.

She texted him back a few emojis before holding her phone to her chest and taking a deep breath.

The first day without seeing the band went quickly. Max had texted Zoe to see how the band was doing on the drive. They had been on tours before and knew what it was like to travel across states. Farah was still anxious about bothering the band, but it had passed that. At this point, they would have considered themselves friends.

Farah had made her way as more than a friend to Brian and that felt strange. She feared the idea of anything more. She liked him, but how soon was *too* soon? How did people figure out if they *liked* someone? It felt foreign to her.

Brian had stretched himself unsafely across the back of the van. He stared at his phone, awaiting the next text message from Farah. It wasn't as if they were being particularly flirty, simply sharing their opinions on their favourite types of pasta and other fun things. It was a simplistic conversation, but one that allowed them to know more about each other.

"We'd be pretty bummed if you get sucked into that phone, man." Russ turned in his seat, voicing his concern over Brian's newfound devotion to his phone, absorbing as much blue light as humanly possible.

"It's cool. I'm just texting." Brian sat up, refusing to remove his eyes from his phone.

"*Ooo* is loverboy texting *again?*" Zoe teased as she looked up into the rear view mirror and stared at Brian who was sitting in the back seat.

"Hey, you're always on your phone!" Brian countered.

"Not right now."

"You're driving!" Brian sighed as he put down his phone and threw his hand out towards the front of the van.

"So, like...are you and Farah a *thing* now?" Catfish asked as he turned around in the seat beside Russ. Was everyone going to keep asking him these questions no matter what he said to get them to stop?

"N-no! We're just...we're *friends!*" Brian wasn't sure how to get them off his back. He had to say something.

"You haven't slept—"

192

"No! It's not like that. This is...different." Brian looked back down at his phone to check for another text.

Sure, Brian had been sexually active with the people he had been interested in previously. It was strange to Brian to have spent so long with Farah *without* sleeping with her. It wasn't as if that was his usual pursuit, but that was all women ever wanted from him. Farah wanted to be there to kiss him and make his heart skip beats.

Was that normal? Was that how it was supposed to feel when you *liked* someone? Brian was interested in her and he would have liked to eventually have been with her in other ways, but that was on *her* terms. He didn't want to rush anything...not this time.

"Wait. You *haven't* slept with her?" Zoe's eyes widened as Brian noticed her face appear in the rear view mirror again.

"No, I haven't." Brian gritted his teeth together, growing frustrated with the fact his friends believed his only relationships with women had been strictly sexual.

They were right.

He was sure they didn't believe him.

"You're a real cutie, but ain't nobody chasing you for nearly two weeks just to get in your pants. She's after something else." Zoe inputted the slightly offensive comment. Brian tried not to let it get to him.

"Woah. An *emotional* groupie. Rad." Catfish nodded.

"They're not groupies!"

"Is this going to be like Portland?" Catfish asked, bringing up the fateful day he had previously mentioned.

"No!" Brian laughed awkwardly as he unlocked and locked his phone, still awaiting a text back.

"We're just looking out for you, man. We don't want you to get hurt. You're our favourite frontman." Russ grinned as he spoke.

"Look, guys, I appreciate the concern. I do. It's not like that. Farah is a wonderful person and I respect her a lot. We've grown close this past week or so and that's *okay*. Zoe has gotten close to Max; I don't see anyone bothering her about that." Brian chuckled, trying his hardest to get the conversation away from himself.

"That's because I don't usually spend the tour trying to fuck my way into a relationship with a stranger, *Brian*." Zoe sighed, emphasizing his name as she spoke.

Brian felt a little hurt by the comment. It was the truth. He usually did try and fuck his way through a tour and normally, it worked. Although, on this tour, he hadn't slept with anyone. Instead, he had been focusing his efforts on the girl he thought he may have been romantically interested in.

He didn't have to have sex with her to realise he liked her. This was different.

He liked Farah. He liked her far more than he had liked anyone before, and they hadn't even slept together. They didn't *need* to and that was an important thing for him to remember.

Russ and Catfish exchanged a look of concern, not wanting to hear how the rest of the argument played out. Although, there wasn't going to have been an argument. Brian didn't have the energy to fight anyone.

"Whatever. It's fine. It's not like that. This is *different*." Brian huffed, assuring them this wasn't like the other tours they had been on where he had spent his time attempting to find love.

It wasn't his fault nobody wanted to love him as much as he was willing to love them back. How was he supposed to know if someone was only there for sex and nothing else?

"I'm not digging you out of a mess if you can't handle it. Don't do anything stupid." Zoe scowled up into the rear view mirror, catching Brian's eye.

"You sound like my dad." Brian sighed, unhappy with the way he was being spoken to. Zoe was always there to look out for him, even if it didn't feel like it. She would forever treat him like a little brother.

"That's probably not a bad thing." Zoe sighed, focusing her attention back on the road. Brian looked back down at his phone and smiled at a new notification from Farah.

The second day of travelling to Scottsdale came around quickly. This time, the band managed to catch up with Max and Farah. They crossed paths one evening when they decided to stop over in a motel, once again pouring some cash into some-where to stay. Even though they were still paying for the repairs on the van, the last couple of shows they had managed to sell a lot of merchandise.

Farah was beginning to get impatient. They had finally crossed paths again and yet it was getting hard for her to catch a break with Brian. All the sneaking around they had been doing didn't seem healthy, but they both enjoyed the rush of hiding their small romance from their party.

They had been texting every moment they got, most of which had little substance. Farah had never been so attached to her phone in her entire life. In a way, it was beginning to worry her. She didn't want to look at her screen time, it would have concerned her with how big the number was going to be.

Max flicked through the channels on the beaten-up televi-sion, she was surprised it even worked. As much as they wanted to hang with the band, they had agreed to hang out once in Scottsdale. It felt as if they had been stuck in Texas for years with the amount of travel they had done.

"Ugh, I'm so bored." Max groaned, her head hanging off the bed as she laid the wrong way and got an upside-down view of the television.

"Nothing on?" Farah questioned as she looked up from her phone for just a second, watching the three dots on the screen bounce. Another text from Brian. She felt like a teen-ager.

"Nothing worth watching. The first time I get a chance to sit down and watch TV and it's terrible! Worthless!" Max sighed as she threw the remote on the bed, flopped out her arms on either side of her and stared up at the ceiling.

"Why don't you just watch something on your phone?"

"Because then I wouldn't have anything to complain about!"

Farah saw another text coming through, her heart skipping slightly at the message.

'*Want to hang out?*'

She wasn't sure how to take the message. What did he mean? They were in a motel on the side of a highway with nothing in its vicinity.

'*Where?*' Farah texted back with confusion.

'Outside? I'll tell the guys I'm smoking.'
'What do I tell Max?'
It took a little while for Brian to reply before...
'I think I saw a vending machine downstairs. Say you're getting snacks.'
'Meet you outside in 5?'
'Okay x'
Farah took direct note of the kiss at the end of his message. He had been sending them frequently. As a gesture of goodwill, she tried to send some back. It wasn't her style of texting, but she had been trying to make an effort for him.

"I'm going to grab some snacks. Want anything?" Farah asked as she swung her legs off the bed and went to stand up, butterflies in her stomach over how she would once again be able to spend a short amount of time with Brian.

"Chips. Every flavour in the machine."

"Don't watch anything too interesting without me."

"Oh, I'll be lucky to get anything more than a soap commercial." Max grumbled, not even bothering to look over to Farah as she slipped on her shoes.

Farah didn't know what he had planned in the amount of time it took for her to get snacks and for him to smoke. Were they just going to say 'hello' and then leave each other to their own business?

Farah had felt so special when he kissed her for the second time in Austin. It was different from the time they kissed before, it felt nice. It was a new feeling Farah hadn't gotten used to and yet there she was with her hand gripped around the handle of the motel room door hoping she could kiss him again.

She *wanted* to kiss him again.

Even the act of them holding hands whilst walking down the streets of Austin had been one of intimacy. Perhaps a little more so than a kiss.

That was the missing piece when travelling. It had been Brian. Why was it that whenever they had gotten closer to one another the earth was destined to curse her by forcing them apart? Did the world know that she...*liked* him?

No. That inner turmoil kept Farah up late at night along with everything else. Did she *like* Brian Blossom? Sure, she liked him. She wasn't sure yet if she *liked* him.

It was an internal conflict she was yet to get over. She had to admit in her mind she was both mentally and physically attracted to him. As soon as she could have admitted that everything would have been so much better.

Farah stepped out of the motel room, glancing over to the parking lot below at both the band's van and Max's car. As she closed the door she turned to her left and saw Brian on the opposite side of the motel step out of a room. He looked up and smiled.

He was wearing a white ringer t-shirt with red around the neck and his black denim jacket. Brian ran his fingers through his scruffy blonde hair and adjusted his jacket as he began to walk along the second floor of the motel to meet her.

"After you." Brian bowed and gestured towards the stairs. The stairs weren't big enough for two people to have gone down at once. A poor design.

"Thank you." Farah smirked as she watched him bend over with a smirk, she stepped past him and made her way down the steps. It took a second for Brian to notice she had passed, quickly catching up to the step behind her.

"What brings you here this fine evening?" Brian kept exactly one step behind her as they made their way down the stairs.

"Chips."

"Chips?"

"That's what Max was after. What are you here for?" Farah turned with a grin, knowing his answer would have been one of two things.

"A girl." Brian ran his hand against the railing as they both reached the bottom of the stairs.

Farah turned around and folded her arms, noticing Brian was directly behind her providing very little personal space.

"A *girl*? I don't see any around here." Farah jokingly pushed Brian out of the way to look behind him. Brian chuckled at the game she was happy to play.

Brian gave Farah enough confidence to be goofy around him. Enough confidence to tease him.

"Aw, she must have stood me up." Brian scratched the back of his neck and blushed, the words hitting a little too close to home. Something he had said in the past without it being a joke. He had been stood-up before. Maybe too many times to have counted on one hand.

"Why would anyone do that?" Farah shook her head with a frown, upset with the mystery girl and the idea someone would stand Brian up. He was far too sweet for that.

"I'm not sure, but it doesn't matter anymore."

"Why not?"

"Because you're here instead and you're much prettier." Brian smirked, unable to stop his lips from curling. He held onto either side of his jacket and rocked on his heels.

Farah stared at him, matching his expression almost instantly. She noticed him biting the inside of his lip as he stared back, just like the previous nights there was an internal desire for them to be closer. A desire that neither of them could hold down for much longer.

Farah had never been a forward person and yet at that moment, there was a spur of confidence she had never felt before. She glanced behind her and noticed the vending machine under the stairs, by a few different rooms.

It had been a hard couple of days without the physical touch they craved.

From the constant text messages, they knew how they valued one another. Brian's every thought was swamped by thoughts of Farah. He desperately wanted to be with her.

All she could think about was his large hands on her waist and the taste of his lips. Things she greatly desired. Clean thoughts had been plagued by lustful ones and all of them included Brian Blossom. He made her think of things she had never considered before.

Farah reached out and grabbed the front of Brian's denim jacket, just above where his hands were holding on. He looked up at Farah with wide eyes as she slowly stepped backwards, pulling Brian along with her. Brian wasn't sure what was happening...but he was loving every second of it.

He could feel the warmth of her hands, the pressure that pulling his jacket had on his back and the look of determination as she pulled him along. He was completely locked under whatever spell she had cast on him.

Farah pulled Brian over to the side of the vending machine, causing him to give her a look of confusion as they stood in the poorly lit and open area where the machine sat. Brian allowed himself to be pulled wherever Farah wanted him.

"Where are we going?" Brian laughed nervously; he felt his back gently press against the side of the vending machine.

Farah refused to move her eyes from his. She wanted this. She wanted him. She had never had the same desire for anyone before, but his presence was like a drug.

Days of waiting for him to be beside her. Days since they had eaten ice cream and gotten a little too close in Austin. The text messages weren't enough to nurse the yearning she had developed for the man. What were her parents going to say if they ever found out?

The trip hadn't been what she was expecting, but she was finally learning to enjoy every second.

Farah made her move as she leaned in for a kiss as if it had become second nature to do so. Brian welcomed the connection, closing his eyes and moving his hands to her waist as he held her close. Farah fell into him as she moved her hands to his chest before sliding them to the back of his head, desperate to feel his soft hair between her fingers like the first time they had kissed.

Despite having kissed before, they had never matched their current level of intimacy. Their first kiss had been on a fallen tree trunk and Brian had insisted on keeping his hands to himself. Their second kiss, although in an aesthetically pleasing location was sweet and soft.

This time, as Farah pressed into his lips, she wedged him between her body and the vending machine. It hadn't been her original intention, but the way their bodies slotted so perfectly together was enough for her mind to drift elsewhere. She shamelessly let her mind wander to places that had never involved Brian before, but welcomed him without question.

Brian had wanted to believe he had always been the one in control in any sexual situation. That was untrue. Although he had practice and experience in these departments, it wasn't that often he got to take control. He had previously been the one to take control of their kiss, but this time he was willing to see what Farah wanted.

It was a little more than he had expected. It was a little more than Farah had expected too.

As they furthered their kiss, Farah got as close to him as she could. She wanted to be near him and everything inside of her was flagging inappropriate feelings she was shocked at herself for thinking. She pushed aside the anxiety that came with her unchaste desires.

Farah felt his chest press against hers as he pulled her closer, his hands respectfully placed just above her hips. His hands were noticeably warm, and she could smell his usual cologne on his clothes, sweet and overpowering. Enough to make her recognise it was him. The man she couldn't stop thinking about.

Brian could feel her thighs against his, practically on the cusp of grinding as Farah tugged on his hair, his hands now half an inch lower than they were previously. It hadn't changed much, but Farah noticed.

Brian was worried if they had gone any further or made any more suggestions things would have turned out as they had done in the past. Everyone he had been with always wanted one thing and as soon as they got what they wanted, they didn't bother acknowledging Brian's existence.

Farah pushed him a little harder against the vending machine, his lips just as soft as she remembered. She had thought about it a lot. She had thought about *them* a lot.

Farah smiled on his lips as their frantic kiss slowed down. She wanted to be there all night with him. She wanted to sleep beside him, she could already tell he was a great hugger. He was a sweetheart and he needed to know.

"How long do you think we have until they come looking for us?" Farah didn't bother to open her eyes as she breathed softly against his lips, her voice a slight whisper in the dark.

"Long enough." Brian purred, his internal yearning outgrowing the thought in his mind that said he was going to allow Farah to take the lead.

He knew she was a little out of her depth, but all the signs she had given him were shouting for something a little more personal and Brian was happy to provide. He kissed her lips slowly before brushing her hair over her shoulder, pecking her jawline softly and keenly bringing his lips to the crook of her neck.

Farah held onto the back of his head as he buried himself in her neck wanting nothing more than to satisfy. She had never been kissed so affectionately in her entire life and the experience was bringing her to a new level of euphoria. She made sure to close her eyes as she felt his soft skin against hers, his hands travelling up her back.

He had made flirtatious suggestions over text and as she felt his lips against her that was all she could think about. Was this it? Was this the time those suggestions became a reality?

Farah hadn't expected him to be so *intimate*, but she couldn't complain when it felt so good to be in his arms with his lips on her skin.

"*Brian...*" The way she cooed his name came out unintentionally pornographic causing Farah to gasp, so involved in his touch.

Brian pulled away, looking at her with wonderment in his eyes. His ego was boosted by the noise that passed her lips. As much as she wanted to spend all night against the vending machine, she knew she couldn't when Max was waiting on her return.

Max was nearly as bad as Farah's parents. It wouldn't have been long until she was making her way down the stairs with the kettle from the motel room, swinging the cord above her head, ready to attack anyone who may have captured her best friend.

"Are you okay?" Brian questioned, concerned he had taken things too far.

Farah didn't know what to do. Flirting over text with sexual undertones was a very different experience to...*this*. As much as she wanted to pursue, now wasn't the right time. However, that was the thing she was starting to realise...she *wanted* it to happen.

"Y-yeah, I'm fine. Really. I'm just worried we're going to get caught. It's uh...a little open." Farah sighed, disappointed she had to break the kiss amongst other things. It was going so well, and Farah's anxiety had to ruin it all. Why would it have mattered if she was caught with Brian? Was it embarrassing?

Yes. Not because of him, but her nerves told her it was something people would have questioned. She didn't have the emotional capacity to answer.

"Oh right. Yeah." Brian gave her a sad look to express his disappointment.

"I'll see you tomorrow, at the show?"

"We were going to ask if you and Max wanted to hang out." Brian pulled Farah closer as she balanced her hands on his chest.

"What were your plans? We're on track for the Griffith Observatory when we get to LA and I'll be extremely disappointed if I don't get to go." Farah snorted, inches away from Brian's face, still finding herself leaning her entire body against his.

"It's not that exciting. We were going to go to the mall tomorrow for more clothes."

"For a show?"

"No, for a party we've been invited to in LA. My dad wants us to go to this party and make connections or whatever. I'm just going there to make him happy. It's not even as if he's going to be there, he just wants me to show my face." Brian explained, reaching up and brushing a loose strand of hair away from her face so he could get a better look at her eyes.

"A party? For famous people?"

"Parties are for everyone. He wouldn't have invited us if it were just for famous people. My dad's always trying to get us to do something radical so we get our names out there. It's like he wishes we were Mötley Crüe *without* the drugs." Brian scoffed with half a smile.

When booking the tour, Stan had agreed to let them play in LA as long as they attended the party as planned. Everyone was excited about the party aside from Brian. He was your average party pooper and wasn't looking forward to going.

"Oh. That doesn't sound fun."

"You and Max should come. You'll make the party worthwhile."

"You want us to go to a fancy rich person's party?" Farah cocked an eyebrow. Never in a million years would she have expected something like that to have been asked of her.

"I mean, you don't *have* to come. It might be intense. I'll be there though and...you can always stick with me." Brian smiled, giving her his reassurance.

"I'm not exactly a party person."

"What if I sweeten the deal?" Brian smirked; Farah felt the touch of his finger circling her lower back.

"How?" Farah held herself against him as he spoke.

"My dad has a house in LA. It has loads of bedrooms, a big TV and there's even a pool! He said we could all stay there. It would be pretty cool if you could come too." Brian suggested with an innocent smile.

"I don't know about the party..." Farah looked away, anxiety sweeping over her. Brian's family wealth didn't bother her as much as she thought it would, but she wasn't holding her breath, she hadn't seen the house yet.

"You should still come and stay at the house even if you don't go to the party. It'll be fun."

"Uhhh..." Farah felt put on the spot. Something about his suggestion felt like the one thing she had on her mind. He was inviting her over to his dad's house to *stay the night*. Sure, that had happened before...but things felt different now. An offer like that didn't come *without* suggestion after everything between them.

"You can think about it."

"Max is going to want to go to that party."

"Maybe if we do go we could stand in the corner together?" Brian suggested, keeping his hands looped around her. He could hear hesitation in her tone, enough for him to know she would only attend for her friend's happiness. The party aspect didn't interest her in the slightest.

"I'd like that." Farah kissed his lips as she kept her arms rested on his shoulders.

A party? Max was going to freak out about it. There were no two ways about it. Attending a fancy party in LA with her favourite band?

They had to go. She had no choice. Standing in the corner of the room with Brian and observing what was going on would have been fine. She felt comfortable around him. It would be a scary experience but being with Brian would have helped. She knew Max wouldn't have stuck by her side for long.

"Don't you have to get snacks?" Brian asked with a smug grin, noticing his speech was delaying Farah's return.

"Yeah, I do. You keep distracting me."

"Do I?" Brian gave her a look of innocence, making him far cuter than he was before. Farah wanted him to stop, but the look on his face was adorable. She couldn't resist his charm.

Farah rolled her eyes before pulling away from him and standing in front of the vending machine. Brian felt deflated, in a good way. He was incredibly relaxed, feeding off the high he got from Farah and not the drugs he usually consumed to reach that same level. He placed his hands in the pockets of his black denim jacket before taking a deep breath and smiling, keeping his back against the vending machine as he heard Farah tap numbers in the keypad.

He turned, his head remaining against the machine as he stared over at Farah who was concentrating on making sure she got the correct snacks. It was hard to concentrate with Brian leaning against the machine giving her a flirtatious stare.

"If I politely asked for a chocolate bar, how much would it cost me?" Brian kept his head against the side of the machine, not bothering to look for himself.

"Two dollars and sixty-three cents."

"Huh. That seems expensive."

"We're in a motel in the middle of nowhere, Brian. These machines are here for our convenience, they're a corporate scam designed to bleed money from the avid traveller when faced with desperation." Farah spoke casually as she typed in yet another number into the keypad.

"Can I pay you back for the chocolate?" Brian smirked as he shuffled closer along the side of the vending machine.

"Yes. You can pay me back for the chocolate."

"What kind of payment plans are available?"

Farah looked over at Brian and tilted her head slightly. If he was struggling *that* much for money then she would have happily bought him a chocolate bar.

"For two dollars sixty-three?"

"I don't know, *maybe*...you'd want your payment in the form of another currency?" Brian raised one of his hands to his mouth and chewed slightly around his thumb as she watched in anticipation. He looked back at her and shrugged. "I heard kisses are worth investing in just as much as some cryptocurrencies."

"Do you know how bad cryptocurrencies are for the environment?"

"No...but I'm sure kissing can save turtles or something." Brian shrugged. He was trying.

"Kisses do produce fewer carbon emissions, so I guess that's a benefit." Farah nodded in approval. Brian was happy to listen.

"Cool. I like the idea of kissing to save the planet."

Farah desperately tried to stop herself from smiling at his silly way of flirting. She shook her head before deciding what else she wanted from the machine. She hadn't been concentrating on snacks.

Brian watched as Farah reached into the bottom of the vending machine, pulling out the goods she had bought. She had an armful of different snacks that she and Max would eventually get through.

"One incredibly sugary chocolate bar." Farah handed Brian the chocolate bar, holding the rest of the food in her arms to make sure they didn't fall. Brian gently took the chocolate from her fingers.

"How much do I owe you? One kiss? Two? I'm unsure on the conversion rate from dollars."

"You really are a dork, aren't you?" Farah sniggered, finding herself completely smitten with the man.

"Uh...if that's a good thing, then *yes*." Brian shrugged as he placed the bar of chocolate in his jacket pocket and stepped forward. Farah allowed him to move within her space as he leaned forward and planted a small kiss on her lips.

If Farah wasn't holding an armful of snacks, she would have kissed him more.

"I'll see you soon."

"Let me know about LA! It'll be fun!" Brian raised his voice as she began to walk away.

"I'll think about it!" Farah spoke from the steps before walking back to her room.

Brian stood by the vending machine and smiled as Farah disappeared. He touched his bottom lip where she had kissed him and smiled. He was completely blown away by her.

Farah grinned the whole way back up the stairs, opening the hotel room door with her elbow to grant her access. Max hadn't moved an inch since she had been gone.

"Did you go to the store by campus? What took you so long?" Max sat up on the bed and watched as Farah dropped the armful of snacks on the bed beside her.

"The machine didn't work." Farah lied through her teeth.

"It didn't look like it was broken."

"It *was*."

"Okay, well, were they out of chips too?" Max pointed down at the pile of food, expectant of something more than what Farah had provided.

Farah stared down at the pile of snacks. No chips.

"They were out of stock." Farah lied again; she was terrible at it. She had been far too distracted by Brian to think about the kind of snacks she was getting. She had one job. Chips.

"Someone must really like chips because there were loads of them earlier." Max glanced to the side as she spoke, a little perplexed by the lack of salty snacks. "I bet it was Catfish. Greedy bast—"

"You'll be happy to know we've been invited to a party."

"Whose party?"

"A famous person's party in LA. I don't know *which* famous person, but a famous person nonetheless." Farah explained, trying to get the subject of snacks off Max's mind.

"Wait, what? A party in LA? We don't know any famous pe—" Max's eyes lit up. "D-Did the band invite us to a party? How do *you* know?"

"Um, when I went outside for snacks Brian was there too. I caught up with him. He was...*smoking*." Farah tried her hardest to keep to the lie they had created. Max smirked up at Farah and laughed.

"Oh, you just so happened to see Brian? Isn't that *interesting*?" Max gave Farah a smug expression.

"Yes. It's a small motel. The chances of us running into one another are pretty high."

"*The chances of us running into one another are pretty high*." Max mocked.

"Do you want me to take those snacks away?" Farah cocked an eyebrow.

"Don't touch my snacks. I will *end* you." Max pointed up towards Farah with an aggressive tone, defending the pile of food she had accumulated. "Now, tell me more about this party..."

Farah briefly explained everything she knew about the party as she crawled into bed and texted Brian goodnight. She enjoyed the time they had spent together.

The band members didn't question Brian's disappearance like Max. They were much more forgiving when it came to Brian disappearing. On every other tour he usually disappeared somewhere with a girl for a short period, it was a common occurrence and they never wanted to ask.

They managed to make their way into Scottsdale the next day and had agreed to go shopping together. The band were excited about the party and so was Max. Farah was nervous but was getting used to the idea.

Everyone in the band had found something to wear, even if some of the choices were begrudgingly made. They still had two shows and a whole day of travel before they got to showing off their outfits.

Farah hadn't spoken to Brian much throughout the trip other than their meeting outside the vending machine. After their back-and-forth texts and numerous kisses, it would have been hard to deny their attraction.

Once playing the show in Scottsdale that evening, the band had decided to part ways with their new friends for the night a little earlier than usual as they made their way straight to LA. They would have gotten enough opportunity to spend time with one another at the party.

Max and Farah made their way to a motel on the edge of a highway, curious to know what stranger's house the band had ended up in that night. Farah texted Brian goodnight and went to bed with their next location in mind.

They called it the City of Angels.

LOS ANGELES, CA

Everyone was excited for the show in Los Angeles...even Farah. It wasn't just about playing a show in LA, it was everything that surrounded it. From the lights to the people, LA was different from anywhere they had visited so far.

Not only that, but after being in California they had a day to relax before heading to Denver for the next show. That meant that spending leisurely time in California was acceptable. There was so much they wanted to see and do!

The show they had played that night in LA had been great. The energy that came from the crowd was outstanding and the band fed off it like a drug. It helped them stay focused when all they could think about was the party.

Max was convinced that getting drunk before the party was the best option. This meant she spent the entirety of the show chugging as many drinks as possible. She wanted to be drunk enough to barely remember a thing and sober enough to still have the ability to walk. Farah wasn't impressed with her drunken behaviour but had spent most of the show standing at the side of the stage watching the band play.

Watching *Brian* play.

He had occasionally looked back after songs and smiled at her as she waved. He felt supported, knowing she was there beside him every show.

Max was thrown around in the mosh pit all night and although Farah still wasn't confident enough to join her, she enjoyed having the advantage of being at the side of the stage to keep an eye on her friend's status. Not that Farah would have been able to save her, but it was the thought that counted.

Stan had agreed to let the band stay in his house in LA. It wasn't the same house Brian remembered when he was younger. Stan couldn't stand to be in the house where he had lost his wife, so the best option had been to move. He mostly used it for when he had work in LA and needed somewhere to stay. Admittedly, it was far too large for that purpose.

Brian allowed Max and Farah to stay in the house through their time there. They had no idea what to expect.

"Dude, this place is huge! This is some Hollywood star in the hills bullshit! Wow!" Max whispered inside of the room Brian had directed her into. Farah sat on the end of the bed as Max paced back and forth in excitement. Farah had also been given her own room to stay in.

When Farah had first stepped into the property she was met with the white walls of a lavish lifestyle. There was a lack of tasteful décor and upon entering her bedroom for the night she was struck with the feeling of emptiness. Nothing about the house shouted it was a *home*.

"It's pretty big, isn't it?" Farah gripped onto the bedsheets as she looked around the room. If this was the size of one of the *guest* bedrooms she was curious to know what Stan's room looked like.

The house was more like a villa.

"We're in Stan Static's house. I don't think you understand how *cool* this is! We're in a famous dude's house, Farah! This is awesome!" Max giggled with excitement as she continued to pace around the room. It was the first time in the evening Farah had seen her best friend without a drink in her hand.

"Don't we have to get ready for a party?" Farah questioned, still a little unsure if she wanted to go or not. It was already so late.

"A party! Farah we're going to party! Go and get ready. I want to see that sexy outfit of yours!" Max held out her hands and encouraged Farah to stand, she hesitantly obliged.

"It's not—"

"Go on! I'll meet you downstairs!" Max got behind Farah and pushed her out the door of the bedroom, an encouragement for her to get ready.

She trailed back into the room she had been given and grabbed her bag. On the way to the bathroom she heard the sound of the band laughing downstairs together along with the clinking of glass bottles. She knew she would have to face them all soon.

The bathroom was large, but it gave her enough space to get ready, but not enough space from her thoughts. Thoughts of Brian. She wanted to look good for the party because she wanted to *feel* good, but also there was something subconscious about impressing Brian that hammered in her head. She felt silly for making the extra effort for a *boy*.

Farah had opted for a new combination of outfits. A pair of high waisted skinny jeans that fitted her figure perfectly, a black strapped top with a clear sheer to drape over her shoulders and her usual pair of comfortable black slip-on shoes. She had put her long hair down for the event, allowing it to roll off her shoulders.

She hadn't felt the need to bother with much makeup, but just enough to help fuel her confidence.

Farah stared at herself in the bathroom mirror. The outfit was different, but it was different because it gave her confidence. Something she wasn't used to. She took a few deep breaths as she clenched her fists.

It was nerve-wracking and as she felt her chest tighten and body heat up, she began to name the colours she saw around the room, just as Brian had suggested when they first met. The only way to combat an upcoming panic attack.

White. White. Black. Blue. White. White. Red. White. White. White...she really hated poor interior design.

The distraction had given her enough confidence to carefully step down the stairs, listening to the cacophony of chatter in the large living room. She knew everyone was going to look at her as soon as she entered and nothing would have been able to prepare her for that moment.

As she stepped into the room everyone stopped to stare. She didn't say a thing as they all looked back at her, excited to see her in the outfit. Other than the wave of small cheers, the one thing she focused her attention on was Brian's eyes.

Although he was a reserved man and had nothing but respect for the people around him, if Farah knew how much effort it took Brian not to look at her in the outfit then she would have been provided with copious amounts of unsung confidence. How could he have ignored the fitted jeans and the vast amount of exposed skin above her chest?

She was gorgeous.

" *Wow...*" Brian's not-so-subtle audible reaction was rectified by brushing his hand against his growing facial hair. It didn't help, it only made Farah's attraction for him heighten.

Farah stared back and noticed his slight outfit adjustment. Brian had switched out his usual t-shirt for a new dark red button-up shirt and put his black denim jacket over the top. He continued to wear his ripped black jeans and beaten-up skate shoes. There was only so far he could go with making an effort to look somewhat presentable. Besides, only one person's opinion mattered to him.

"Farah! You look *amazing*!" Zoe complimented, Farah drawing her attention away from Brian for just a moment. It felt nice to be fed the compliment when only moments ago she was filled with anxiety.

"Thanks." Farah spoke shyly as she held onto her own arm.

She looked back up to Brian once more and smiled. Neither of them were hiding their secret well.

She wanted to tell him how good he looked in the red shirt, but it was within seconds after she entered the room, they were all being directed to the front of the property so they wouldn't miss their ride to the party.

Farah sat between Max and Brian in the back of the large car they had hailed on a ride app. It was hard to concentrate on anything when the back of the car was suffocating in the smell of Brian's overpowering aftershave.

The car was small and Farah's leg was pressed tightly against Brian's. It had been around fifteen minutes of sitting uncomfortably before the subject of the city came up.

"They call this place '*The City of Angels*'." Russ whispered through his teeth as he stared out the window, the lights of the city skyline passing them by and reflecting off his glasses.

"That's sweet." Zoe commented.

"Why do they call it that?" Brian asked, out of the loop when it came to everyday trivia.

"Los Angeles. It's '*The Angels*' in Spanish." Farah shared her useless fact with the rest of the car.

"You speak *Spanish*?" Brian raised his eyebrows as he looked over at the woman beside him.

"N-no, I don't. I just know the fact." Farah sniggered at his excitement.

"If we do see any angels I'll be sure to say *halo*." Max snorted with drunk laughter at her pun.

Everyone let out a long groan.

"What's everyone's plan?" Brian questioned. He knew it would have been different from any party they may have attended in the past.

"Russ and I are going to see how many big-shot music producers we can speak to." Catfish leaned back in his seat. "The sober ones. If not, it's going to be the biggest business card pickpocketing scheme of all time."

"It's about *who* you know, not *what* you know." Russ confirmed their plan, still not completely convinced of their potential success rate.

"Oh, and *drugs*! I want to be able to hear colours." Catfish winked at Russ who was quick to nod in agreement.

"We could see sounds! That would be dope." Russ clenched his fists together with excitement, his voice still monotone.

"Please don't do anything stupid." Brian mumbled under his breath, desperate to make sure his bandmates were safe. Drugs or not. Farah was the only one in the car that heard him, but took note of his caring nature.

"Are you girls coming with me to get smashed?" Zoe asked as she looked at Max and Farah.

"Are you sure she should keep drinking?" Farah gestured towards Max who was regretfully staring out of the window. She had to look away, if she continued to view the motion she was going to have made herself sick. The shots they had taken before they left didn't do her any favours.

"I'm fine. Fine. Absolutely. I got you, girl. We're going to have so much fun!" Max pointed her finger towards Zoe with a drunk wink to follow. Zoe wasn't sure how to respond, simply giving her a thumbs up.

"What's your plan, man?" Catfish asked the frontman. Brian placed his arm on the edge of the window and looked out at the city passing them before catching Farah out of the corner of his eye. He didn't entirely know how Farah felt about being at the party. It was going to be an interesting night, especially if they got to spend it together when everyone inevitably left them alone.

"I have no idea." Brian shrugged, all he wanted to do with his night was sit and speak to Farah. They had agreed on hanging out in the corner, right?

"Farah?" Catfish tilted his head.

"I'll probably just latch onto one of you. I'm not big on parties." Farah smiled nervously.

Farah was hoping Brian would have kept his word about spending the time at the party with her. It didn't seem like much, but otherwise, she would have been on her own and she was terrified. She was twenty-one in the middle of Los Angeles, hundreds of miles away from home with her drunk best friend who was ready to run off in a heartbeat. She didn't want to be alone and Brian was the next best thing to a home comfort at this point.

Besides, being with Brian wasn't a bad thing.

The band had never been anywhere so fancy before, so pulling up in a car outside the mansion after their show was a completely new experience. The car dropped them outside of the large pearly gates where they could immediately hear the drumming of loud music coming from the overly large house.

Loud music was something they were used to, but this wasn't the noise of a live band. Instead, it was an aesthetic hum of drum and bass that came from what looked to be the busiest party in LA.

It wasn't going to be a party with cake and balloons. This was the sort of party with drugs and strippers.

Brian hesitantly took the lead, stepping over to the security guard and showing him something on his phone before pointing to the rest of his party. The guard didn't say a thing as he pressed his finger against a button and granted them access to the mansion.

Brian whispered 'thanks' as he passed the security.

A house within the hills, large enough to house a couple hundred people with ease. Leading up to the property there was a vast amount of outdoor decoration, including, but not limited to sculpted fountains splashing water into beautifully lit ponds.

Russ' lips mouthed the word 'wow' as they walked, unable to comprehend the scale of the building they were approaching.

Going from playing at a music venue that had a problem with rats in their parking lot to be at the huge party was quite the contrast.

They were a shitty emo band. There was no way they should have been allowed access to such a large party.

As the band walked into the building they realised what it was they had found themselves caught up in. A *huge* party.

It ranged from alcohol being tipped into people's mouths, colourful pills being swallowed, loud music, flashing lights, shouting, people with little to no clothes on and even someone emptying the contents of their stomach into the pot of a houseplant. It was absolute chaos, and it was only an hour past midnight.

"Woah..." Russ adjusted his glasses to get a better look at the sights in front of him. It wasn't dark inside the room, but the ceiling was so tall that the lights sat above them high enough to make the room dim.

Max, Farah and the band stood in the doorway with their mouths slightly ajar.

"This looks fuckin' sick!" Max shouted as she gestured for them to step inside the room.

"Max *has* got a point." Zoe lifted her shoulders as she looked back at the rest of the group.

"Whatever forever. It's time to party, boys." Max grinned.

Russ and Catfish glanced at each other before following the direction of a simple shrug. Sure, the party was crazy...but it was going to be the *good* kind of crazy. One they would have remembered for years to come.

Brian looked at Farah as she stared back with a worried expression. He noticed her anxiety and held his hand out by his waist, his palm facing her. Farah glanced down at his open palm, unsure of what he was suggesting before realising the comfort he was attempting to provide.

As much as Brian was worried about the band commenting on his gesture, he didn't believe any of them would have noticed amongst the mayhem the room was providing. Brian holding hands with Farah was nothing in comparison to the man in the middle of the room attempting to front flip off a glass table.

Farah lifted her hand to meet his, their fingers gently interlocking.

Suddenly, Farah didn't feel so alone in the house full of strangers she didn't ever want to have the pleasure of meeting.

She felt a sense of security as she held onto Brian's hand.

"We're going to speak to all the people in suits and then the people with pills. Meet you guys back at the house?" Catfish came up with the plan as he referred to himself and Russ.

"I don't know if I can handle this cute one all on my own." Zoe joked as she threw her arm around Max and rustled the top of her uncontrollably frizzy head of hair no longer controlled by the beanie.

"No, you!" Max laughed, pushing Zoe off her with a giggle.

"Just...don't get hurt." Farah touched Max's shoulder with her free hand, causing her to stop. Max turned around and smiled.

"Me? Hurt? Never! Pain and parties are *punk*!" Max snorted, not noticing Brian and Farah's obvious handholding she would have picked up on if she was sober.

"Getting hurt isn't punk."

"Yes, it is." Max argued.

"Don't."

"It's fine, Rah Rah. I got this. I am skilled in the *arty of the party*."

"Be careful." Farah reiterated.

"Yes, *Mom.*" Max smirked as Farah smiled back, happy to hear how much she cared.

Farah watched as Zoe grabbed Max's jacket and dragged her away into what would undoubtedly be an unforgettable night.

As soon as Russ and Catfish walked in the opposite direction to find new connections within the industry, Brian and Farah found themselves staring into the dark abyss that was the party surrounding them. Farah felt Brian's thumb rub gently against the top of her hand.

Farah felt uncomfortable in the room and so did Brian. He was internally praying nobody recognised him. It was unlikely, but something he had considered.

"Want to try and find something to drink?" Brian leaned towards Farah as he spoke, speaking over the loud music that was dominating his eardrums. His ears were still ringing from the show he had just performed.

"You'd drink something from *here*?" Farah questioned as she looked at Brian with confusion in her expression.

"It would *have* to be sealed." Brian grinned. She was worried about her drink getting spiked, it was a genuine concern.

"That's sensible." Farah nodded, firmly agreeing with Brian's sentiment.

Brian led Farah through the party, refusing to let go of her hand as they walked. The party was busy, although it wasn't as compact as one of Brian's shows.

The mansion was poorly decorated, most of their walls and flooring were painted plain white. Farah always wondered why rich people were so boring with their interior design. She had even noticed it in both of Stan Static's homes. Paying someone thousands of dollars to decorate their houses and yet the only thing they ever seemed to come up with was marble flooring and plain walls. It was stupid.

This hadn't been the first time Brian had been inside of a mansion. Perhaps not one this exact size but growing up around people who earned millions from platinum records meant he spent a lot of time as a kid exploring the labyrinths of various mansions.

Nowhere was closed off to the public at the party and anyone could have gotten into any of the rooms. It felt as if there was no way someone could have lived in the mansion, simply using the building for extravagant parties. It wouldn't have surprised Brian if that was the case.

Brian wasn't sure where he was taking Farah. Farah looked around as they walked, taking note of the different activities that were happening. She was sure she witnessed someone scratching their name on a table with a penknife. It was insanity and after every sight, Farah held onto Brian's hand tighter.

What had Stan roped them into?

Brian stopped in the overcrowded kitchen, positioned in the corner was a large icebox with hundreds of bottles of all different kinds of beverages. It probably wasn't the only place in the mansion that had a vast amount of booze, but it was one of them.

"Do you still want to be a part of the sober squad?" Brian asked as he turned back to Farah and squeezed her hand as he spoke. Farah hadn't drank much on the tour, but Brian felt rude to not offer. He needed to have a drink if he was going to have made it through the night at the hellscape of the party.

"This party is making me feel otherwise."

"You want to drink?"

"Not a lot, but—" Farah admitted. Sure, she had drank in the past, but it wasn't copious amounts like Max consumed. Perhaps getting a little tipsy with Brian wouldn't have been such a bad thing? It would have been a good way to forget everything she had already seen at the party.

"I'm just offering. I don't want to—"

"Maybe we could share one? Like Austin? I don't want to get *drunk*." Farah shrugged, referring back to Brian's beer she had sips of at the restaurant.

"I can do that." Brian nodded, more than able to accommodate her request.

They stepped closer to the icebox when Brian spotted a bottle of wine. It looked fancy for what it was.

"How about a big bottle? What are your opinions on grapes?" Brian smirked as he picked up the green bottle that was wrapped in a fancy label, the bottle itself probably costing more than what Brian currently had in his bank account. Farah didn't allow him to let go of her hand as he picked up the bottle by the neck and showed it to her.

Farah had wine with meals before, but never as a way of getting her drunk. Although wine was the one alcoholic beverage Farah felt as if she could stomach better than any kind of beer or spirit. If she wanted to get tipsy with Brian, this was the best way to do it.

"I wouldn't exactly say I'm a *fan*."

"Oh, so you're a *grape groupie* then?" Brian snorted. Farah's expression dropped at the comment.

"Brian..." Farah groaned, unable to stop herself from smiling.

Brian used the corkscrew attached to the large icebox to open the bottle; the pop causing people in the room to cheer.

Brian and Farah both chuckled as he took a sniff of the top of the bottle before gesturing for Farah to do the same. She pouted her bottom lip before nodding. It wasn't as if she would have been able to tell a good wine from a bad one.

Grapes were grapes.

"Should we explore this huge house together?" Brian asked before taking a sip from the large bottle. The wine was unlike anything he had ever tasted before.

"Don't you have to speak to important people whilst you're here?" Farah questioned, showing genuine concern.

He passed the bottle over to Farah who took a sip of the beverage and decided she *did* enjoy wine. It wasn't bad. Brian watched with a smile, formulating a response in his mind.

"I'm already speaking to the most important person here." He grinned, causing Farah to chuckle as she ran her index finger across her bottom lip.

"If we get caught sneaking around, I'm blaming you." Farah shrugged, feeling bad about invading the privacy of the mansion. However, with someone this rich, they were just asking for people to look at their possessions.

"Cool, I'm okay with that." Brian smiled, continuing to hold both her hand and the bottle of wine she had just passed back.

Farah didn't mind consuming the alcohol, but she knew her tolerance was low. She didn't drink very often and could get drunk quickly without realising. It had only happened a few times at parties in the past. Max had attempted to get her to drink when she was at the shows, but she wasn't going to break out of her habits. A plastic cup filled with tap water was all she needed.

When it came to alcohol, Brian, on the other hand, could drink like a fish before breaking through to his tolerance. Getting high was a much more pleasurable experience and valued it greatly over anything alcohol could have done to his body.

Brian opened a door that led off from the kitchen. He was half expecting it to lead to nothing, but instead, it was an empty corridor. The fact the corridor was empty only meant good things to them both, finally they could escape from the humdrum of the party.

"Hey, this is peaceful." Brian commented as they walked through the dimly lit corridor, the marble flooring changing to a spongy cream carpet. Brian consciously attempted not to spill the wine, knowing how much damage it could do to the carpet.

"Quite the contrast." Farah sniggered as Brian passed the bottle back over to her, he didn't want to be in complete control of the alcohol. They were supposed to be sharing.

She was comfortable enough in his presence to let her guard down. He had noticed the behaviours she had when they were together in comparison to when they were with others.

She had always been shy around the band, he stuck that down to how they had treated her when they met.

They walked slowly, noticing different doors leading to all kinds of new adventures. In a way, the corridor felt like a hotel.

At the end of the corridor, they walked up some empty steps to another floor. There wasn't anywhere else for them to go.

Farah felt some anxiety about snooping around in someone else's home and in a way, Brian did too. It was a little intrusive. However, they were intrigued by what the mansion held within.

"You're surprisingly good at navigating this place. Does your lavish Rockstar lifestyle give you frequent access to mansions?" Farah questioned as they walked up the steps together.

"No, not really. I mean, my old house in LA was pretty big. It wasn't *this* big, but it was enough to show that my mom earned more money than sense. She wasn't very materialistic and I think my dad enjoyed adopting that mind-set when she passed. He mostly spends his money on his business now."

Brian chewed his lip as he walked alongside Farah, continuing to hold onto her hand. Farah was the first person in a long time he trusted enough to open up about all the things that had happened within his life. He was grateful for her listening.

"It's nice that your dad supports you and the band." Farah inputted, unsure if she was overstepping any boundaries.

"He's just squeezing the one thing out of me that I know, but I'm good at it and I *know* I'm good at it. It's hard not to like music when it's the only thing you know. Even if I wanted to, I couldn't do anything else."

"That's not true. You could do anything if you put your mind to it."

"I was raised on a tour bus, Farah. It's all I know." Brian snorted, Farah suddenly feeling privileged for her lifestyle. Sure, Brian had been raised around money, but that didn't mean it was a life he had chosen.

"Music doesn't have to be everything." Farah furrowed her eyebrows as they walked. Brian reached over to grab the wine, taking a few long swigs of the bottle. Farah watched him out the corner of her eye, not wanting to stare at him for too long.

"Hey, I wonder what that room is for!" Brian was quick to change the conversation as he pointed towards a room at the end of the corridor with a red light sat on top of it. Farah noted his diverted attention as he changed the subject.

It was a topic he didn't want to discuss further, and Farah respected that.

"A fallout shelter?" Farah laughed as Brian quickened his pace towards the room with the unlit red light.

"Oh no, it's going to be much better!" Brian pulled Farah along to the entrance of the room.

"Two fallout shelters?" Farah joked, realising her humour had been wasted on Brian who was distracted by the red light on the top of the door.

Brian let go of Farah's hand for the first time since they had gotten there and passed her back the bottle. He leapt towards the door, tugging down on the handle and sighing miserably.

"It's locked." He pouted before making his way to a room opposite. Farah watched as he pushed down on the handle and entered the unlabelled room. This one was open and as soon as he stepped through he was granted access to a beautiful sight.

Farah watched as Brian audibly gasped when he entered the room, Farah followed close behind using both hands to grip the wine. As they walked into the room they were greeted with a sight that was to behold, even Farah was mesmerised by the contents.

Inside was a vast collection of instruments, ranging from a large white grand piano to different styles of guitars hanging on the walls. There was even a collection of tambourines and other types of percussion in the corner of the room. The sight was beautiful and Brian had never been in the presence of such state of the art equipment, the instruments ranged from classics to modern-day wonders. Brian had spent a lot of money on his setup, but nothing compared to the amount he imagined was spent on lining the room with the instruments.

"Whoever lives here sure does like guitars." Farah shut the door behind them as Brian's wide eyes reminded her of a kid in a candy shop. She hadn't seen him so excited before. Farah took a sip of the wine.

"I like guitars too!" Brian commented as he paced up and down the red wall with the guitars hanging up, each one lit up by an individual spotlight for presentation.

"*Really*?" Farah sarcastically commented on his dorky remark.

"Do you know how expensive these are?"

"We're in a rich person's house...everything is expensive." Farah laughed, unable to contain herself over Brian's excitement.

"I know, but...I *really* want to play one." Brian stared up at the guitar in wonderment, his eyes practically in the shape of stars as he got the deep desire to play the instruments. His actions were childlike and Farah was loving every moment.

He didn't look like the frontman of an emo band, instead, a grown man expressing his passion for something he adored. If music was truly everything he had, Farah knew how much it would have meant to him to play the guitar.

"Do it. I won't look." Farah smiled, tucking the bottle under her arm and covering her eyes.

Brian looked over, noticing she had covered her eyes in an attempt to make him feel better about wanting to play one of the expensive guitars. Sure, he felt intrusive, but also—*guitars!*

"Are you sure you won't tell anyone?" Brian smirked, realising she couldn't see the flirtatious face he was pulling.

"I won't tell a soul." Farah used one hand to cover her eyes and the other to press her finger against her lips, whispering as she tried not to drop the bottle.

Despite not being able to see his expression, he smiled before choosing a guitar he wanted to treat himself to playing. The guitar he chose was a beautiful Martin model, it was similar to the one his dad used to play, but Brian knew it was a lot more expensive. He held the guitar to his chest and took a deep breath.

With a rosewood back and sides and an ivory-bound neck and body, it was hard to deny the value of the guitar. It wasn't in the prettiest condition, but that didn't matter. It was a collector's item.

He pushed his thumbs down the strings to make sure it was in tune. Just like a dream, it was.

Farah was hit by his musical talent as he began to perfectly pluck at the strings. Unlike the harsh yet dreamy sound of the Telecaster he played on stage, the acoustic Martin reverberated with fluid melodic tones. Each pluck and strum provided Farah with shivers that ran down her spine.

The guitar sounded beautiful and the person playing was beyond talented. Farah couldn't believe how well he played the acoustic guitar after spending the past couple of weeks hearing him slamming his hand against the strings of the Telecaster. It sounded so clean without the beautiful tones being dampened by the pedals he used.

Brian began to hum along to the song in his head. Farah wanted to melt at the sound of his angelic voice as even his hums had been kept in tune with the guitar.

"*I've got nothing left, stolen words in my every breath. I'm teetering on the ledge and I'm about to fade away...*" Brian sang softly as if he was caught in the moment without a care in the world. He was so used to playing in front of people that singing to Farah in the small room wasn't as daunting as it should have been.

222

Farah expected the song to be longer, closing her eyes behind her hands and listening to him sing. His voice was heavenly, and she suddenly wondered why he spent so much time shouting into a microphone when he had a voice like *that*.

Farah listened as she heard the body of the acoustic guitar slide away from his torso as it ran against the buttons on his denim jacket.

"That was a new song I've been working on. It's a little different, huh?" Brian chuckled as he placed the guitar back up in its original position.

Farah gently removed her hands from her eyes and looked towards Brian with a smile spread across her face.

"Your voice..." Farah couldn't believe it.

"Shouting is more fun." Brian shrugged, knowing exactly what Farah was going to comment on.

Brian watched as Farah took another sip of the wine, it seemed as if she was getting a little too used to the bottle. After seeing Farah being so against most things such as getting high and drinking, it came as a shock to Brian to see her so happily accept the beverage.

He smiled before making his way over to the grand piano, he debated whether he should have played depending on the noise levels it produced. It was likely it would have alerted people they were currently messing around in their instrument room. Brian looked around and noticed the sound absorption stuck to the red walls that would have captured most of the noise. Regardless, they probably wouldn't have been able to hear much with the music blasting downstairs.

It didn't matter. Brian *really* wanted to play the piano.

He stepped over to the stool and took his seat before shuffling over and tapping it gently, gesturing for Farah to join him. Farah hesitated for a moment before swallowing her anxiety and making her way over to Brian.

"You know how to play the piano too?" Farah snorted, blown away by his talent.

"I also know the triangle." Brian smirked as he stretched his hands so his fingers could find the keys.

"Impressive."

"My mom taught me how to play when I was younger. My dad knows how to play too, so, when she...*passed*, he taught me instead. He wasn't as good, but he knew enough for me to learn the basics. We had one like this, except it was black. Dad switched it out for an electric keyboard when we moved into the van, but he still kept it. I guess its only purpose is gathering dust now." Brian spoke casually as he mentioned his past.

Farah watched as Brian's fingers slowly pressed the keys in such a pattern to create a divine sound. Farah couldn't comprehend the talent the young man held. Frankly, it was attractive and she suddenly understood why so many girls found themselves trying to get with guys in bands. It all made sense.

The way his fingers moved was mesmerising. Farah didn't know how his brain could keep up with the succession of keys each of his fingers was playing in a different order. He had such a brilliant skill set and she couldn't help but stare intensely at his fingers as he played a beautiful piece of music. She was unsure if it was an original song or not, but regardless, it was *gorgeous*.

Brian knew he was showing off, but at that very moment, it didn't matter. He wanted to play the instruments.

As they sat on the stool together, Farah could feel the warmth of his body beside her. It wasn't as if the stool was very long. Sure, it could have easily fit two people, but that didn't mean it wasn't going to be a tight squeeze.

"Do you want a go?" Brian questioned as he allowed his fingers to slide off the keys, stopping the elegant music from playing as the piano hummed.

"I have no idea how to play."

"That doesn't matter. Just press a bunch of keys. Run your fingers down it, it makes a cool noise!" Brian instructed as he reached over and took the wine bottle. It was his turn to drink.

The bottle was a lot lighter from when he had last held it, internally questioning how much of the wine Farah had consumed.

Brian watched as Farah tapped a single finger against the keys making it ring out loudly. Brian nodded as he took a sip, Farah suddenly running her fingers over the keys.

"Okay, that is fun!" Farah laughed as she did it again. Brian copied her actions, running his fingers in the opposite direction to meet her in the middle.

Brian accidentally found his hand brushing against Farah's as they chuckled, running their fingers against the keys of the piano making a racket. It didn't sound like music, but it didn't matter. As long as they were having fun music didn't have to sound *good*.

As they laughed, they caught themselves staring into each other's eyes.

It was strange the party made them feel awkward around one another. As if every time in the past was void.

They had kissed three times now. Passionately. Birmingham. Austin. A couple of hours away from Scottsdale. Every time was just as amazing as the last.

Farah wasn't like any of the girls he had been with. She was caring, fun, honest, brave, and enthusiastic about the things she cared for. She wasn't like anyone Brian had ever met before.

She wasn't there to check a box or score some weed. If Farah had kissed Brian, he knew it was because she wanted to, not because she wanted something. Farah didn't have an ulterior motive.

Brian leaned in closer to Farah, feeling his presence becoming more prominent. His aftershave was overpowering yet satisfying. She couldn't stop looking at him as she watched the young man bite the bottom of his lip flirtatiously.

"So, uhhh...when I convince you to join my band do you know what instrument you want to play?" Brian slurred, interested to know her opinion.

"I'd like to give the triangle a try." Farah raised her eyebrows as she tilted her head, watching as Brian's hand made its way to her thigh.

"Yeah? I'd be willing to give you lessons." Brian rested his hand on the top of her knee, using his thumb to circle her jeans.

"You're going to give me lessons on the triangle?" Farah snorted slightly, noticing Brian's intimate touch causing her to blush.

"Mmmhmm. The triangle." Brian smirked, trapped in a daze. All he could think about was how beautiful she looked sitting beside him.

His mind wandered to some not-so-innocent thoughts.

Farah stared back at Brian to see his adorable lop-sided smile. She knew he wanted to kiss her. His eyes practically pleading his desire for her.

Farah noticed the collar of his shirt had curled and reached over to adjust it. Brian sat still as she moved his collar to make it neater. If she had allowed Brian to touch her, she wanted to have returned the favour.

"We should find the key to that room. I want to know what's in there." Farah stated, desperately wanting to have an adventure with Brian.

"I have a feeling I know what's in there."

"What?"

"Two fallout shelters." Brian smirked, as Farah realised he had been listening to her joke but hadn't acknowledged it.

"Dork." Farah chuckled as she confidently brushed his hand from her thigh and stood up. She took the wine bottle with her.

She wasn't sure if it was the wine getting to her, but her face was flushing a shade of red. His touch has been intimate and suggestive. It wasn't something she was used to.

"Key. Let's find the key." Brian nodded in confirmation as he stood up.

"It's got to be in here somewhere."

"It seems pretty silly for it to be in the room next door." Brian laughed as he glanced around the room for somewhere the key could have been hiding.

"Yeah, well...rich people are *stupid*." Farah commented as she also looked around the room.

"What if *you* were rich?" Brian asked as he held either side of his jacket and waddled around the room.

"What do you mean?"

"If you were rich, I wouldn't think you would be stupid."

Farah took a drink from the bottle.

"Maybe you should." Farah looked away for a moment, realising she was about to go off on a tangent if she continued. "Uh...I'm sorry. I don't want to get into it."

"Why not? I'll listen." Brian shrugged.

"I don't know...I have a lot of opinions on things and people don't usually want to listen. Unless it's an online forum or debate club." Farah pondered on the thought.

"I'm right here and I want to listen! Just say what needs to be said!" Brian chuckled at her comment, lifting his arms as he took his hands from his pockets and shrugged.

"Are you sure?"

"I'm sure."

"Okay, well, I wanted to say that perhaps the rich aren't *stupid*. At the end of the day, you've got to be pretty smart to earn success. Self-ascribed success? That's bullshit. People should have to earn their success, it shouldn't just be handed to people on a silver platter." Farah began to speak about something she was passionate about.

"Okay! Okay! That's good. I like it. What else?" Brian excitedly punched his hand into his fist, happy for Farah to continue her rant.

"Okay. Uh...*you're* a perfect example of someone who could have used their self-ascribed status to gain success, but you didn't! You work hard and disconnected yourself from that handout. I respect that. You're doing things the right way. The way that everyone should do it. You're passionate about music!" Farah nodded, her words becoming a little more confident.

"What are you *passionate* about, Farah?" Brian smirked, feeling the energy in the room radiate. Farah stared down at the top of the glass bottle, guilt spreading through her at the idea of speaking up.

"I don't want to bore you with this. It's just—"

"Farah! I shout my feelings to a crowd of people who probably don't care every single night and it feels *good*! You have to try it." Brian clenched his fists together.

"Uh..."

"Come on! What pisses you off about the *stupid* rich? Tell me!" Brian shook with exhilaration. Farah took a deep breath, collecting her thoughts in her mind.

"Do you know how many poor people are in this country? We have such a poverty issue and yet if these greedy individuals with too much money decided to give everyone a slice of pie, that issue would be resolved!" Farah took another sip from the bottle as she paced. The task of looking for the keys slipping their minds.

"Yeah! What kind of pie?" Brian cocked an eyebrow.

"It's not about the pie, Brian." Farah shook her head.

"Okay, but...pie..." Brian held his hands together. "I'm thinking apple..."

"It's not about the pie!"

"So, tell me what it *is* about? Come on!" Brian had a fire inside of him. Farah fed off his energy, noticing how excited he was becoming with her powerful words.

"All I'm saying is we have such a lack grasp on humanity. Nobody *really* knows what it's like to be human because we're so caught up in our own selfishness. It's terrible. If we distributed the wealth of the billionaires on this planet a lot of our money situations would be solved and they would *still* be rich! The world's collective of billionaires has over thirty times the amount needed to end extreme poverty every single year. Imagine earning over two thousand dollars a *second* and thinking there isn't anything remotely wrong with that. Selfish. It's selfish. Our stance on this as a society is disgusting and things have to change!" Farah didn't stop pacing, continuing to find the bottle on the edge of her lips between her sentences.

Brian listened to her rant as he looked at the guitars on the wall, picking the same guitar as he had done earlier. He pushed the guitar against his chest and turned back as she allowed the alcohol she had consumed to overtake her thoughts.

"Go on! This is *music*!" Brian grinned through his encouragement, noticing Farah gain more confidence through every word. He used his ability to strum hard and fast on the acoustic guitar.

Music was passionate and so was Farah.

"Sure, every billionaire should dedicate their life to philanthropy. It's the only way this world is going to be able to get remotely better. If money makes the world go round and four billion of the poorest people couldn't hold their own financially against eight of the world's richest people, then how are we supposed to live in this society without an obscene amount of guilt?" Farah ranted towards Brian, feeling pumped as the music he played flowed through her. The sound of the guitar was loud, only causing her to shout her opinions louder.

"That's pretty punk, I might have to write this down." Brian complimented with a smile, strumming a little harder.

228

"How is it fair that this fancy man with all this materialistic stuff gets to live such a lavish lifestyle when only blocks away from his house there's a homeless problem? That's not fair! That's outrageous! I'm *so* mad!" Farah clenched her fists together and shouted.

"Farah! You're making music!" Brian cooed with a wide grin spread across his face, the guitar copied her tone as he strummed, matching her stance of pacing up and down. She was so attractive when she spoke enthusiastically. Her speeches were academically pleasing for the ears.

"Do you want to know the worst thing? Nobody cares! If a rich person does something, then they'll always get a free pass. Someone struggling? They'll be thrown in jail! Why is it that society gets to depict who is better based on wealth? It's not a sensible hierarchy system and destroys the good people have put into this world for hundreds of years. Thousands of years. Oppression of the working man. A disgusting act that the United States of America and the corporations run by men in indestructible boxes of wealth across the world abide by day in and day out. We're pawns to society. Puppets for these *fucking* billionaires who think they're better than us! It's an insane system that I can't seem to get my hea—"

"Farah!" Brian shouted slightly louder over her speech. He stopped playing the guitar as the room fell to a comfortable silence.

"*What?*" Farah stopped in her tracks and snapped, enraged by her own words.

"I like it when you're passionate about..." Brian looked away for a second, trying to articulate the correct word for what she had been talking about. "...*things.*"

"You do?" Farah looked over to the man on the opposite side of the room who was chewing on his bottom lip amorously.

She watched his eyes as they found themselves drifting from her head down to her body.

"It's...hot. *Really* hot..." Brian purred as he tightened his grip on the guitar. Standing there with the instrument, she could have said the same thing about him. From his crooked smile to the red shirt, everything about him was attractive.

Farah stood still, unable to tell whether or not it was the alcohol or Brian that had made her stomach drop. Nobody had ever said anything like that to her before. She had never considered herself '*hot*'.

"I shouldn't have—"

"No! You should! It's good to talk about the things you care about in any capacity!" Brian argued as he placed the guitar back on the wall where it belonged. Much to his disappointment, he couldn't take it home. "It made you feel good though, right?"

Farah thought hard on his question, it had felt good to get it out of her system. Her parents would often disapprove of her opinions, meaning she had learned to hold back to avoid confrontation. It felt nice for someone other than Max listening to what she had to say, often feeling as if she was speaking to the void.

"It did feel pretty good." Farah admitted with a smile, blushing at her open opinions.

As Farah became distracted by herself and her confidence, Brian noticed a lockbox on the opposite side of the room. Farah was right about the rich being stupid in many capacities. Brian could vouch for his own family being in that category. It didn't make them all humble. Money made people selfish, or perhaps they always were selfish, Brian couldn't tell with the people around him. It was all he knew.

"It's good to shout about your feelings. I like to do it. For me, it's like...it's therapy you get paid to go to. Plus, it's a hell of a lot of fun." Brian walked over to the lockbox and flicked through the keys, waiting to find one with an obvious label.

"I don't think I could shout like that."

"You don't have to shout. Song writing is a form of poetry, better yet, *poetry* can be a form of song. Spoken word! I think you'd be good at it." Brian began a mini tangent. A way to keep the conversation flowing as he picked up the key labelled 'Recording Studio'.

The red light above the door? It made sense.

Farah was interested in his words, taking another sip of the wine. Nothing compelled her more than the liquid courage and the boost of confidence she had from Brian.

Everything in the room was heating up, including the undeniable chemistry between them.

"You found it..." Farah nodded towards the key spinning on Brian's finger as he stepped towards her.

"Want to check it out?"

"I think we should."

"Sure." Brian smiled, not wanting to be hurt if she hadn't caught onto his previous flirting. He needed to learn to back away. There was a possibility it could have been making her feel uncomfortable.

Just as Brian spun on his heel to exit the room he felt a sudden tug on his jacket causing him to spin back. He stopped in his tracks as Farah pulled him closer, this time they stood in the middle of the room...face to face. Brian noticed she had opted to place the bottle of wine on a surface to the side as she grabbed him.

"I really want to..." Farah whispered softly, this time her breath brushing against Brian's lips as she spoke. Confidence from within channelling her every thought.

"Check out the room? Yeah, we have the key!" Brian repeated with a smile before holding up the key again.

He was such an adorable idiot. An attractive dork who played in an emo band and Farah couldn't resist him. He was making her feel a way she had never felt about anyone before. She wanted to do things with Brian she had never done before.

Everything about the trip was a new experience.

Farah moved her hands to either side of his jacket and held on tightly before looking into his emerald eyes. Brian knew that look. The same look she had given him every time they had kissed. A look of desire.

"I..." Farah found herself lost for words. The fast consumption of alcohol had made her tipsy enough to stumble on her words. It was either that or she had become drunk on Brian Blossom.

"You're so beautiful." Brian whispered as he gazed into her eyes.

"You always say that..."

Brian slowly pushed Farah's hair away from her face and tucked it behind her ear. His fingers gently brushed against her neck causing her to shudder with exhilaration. She watched as Brian took a step closer and slowly leaned towards her, his breath brushing against her skin.

"What if I called you *sexy* instead?" Brian cooed quietly with intent in his tone, his voice barely a husky whisper.

Nobody had ever called her *sexy* before. Nobody.

Nobody apart from Brian...

Her skin was warm, his words sending a euphoric shiver through her body. She had never looked at anyone the same way she had looked at Brian.

She felt powerless as his hands looped around her back. Her knees were weak at his touch. She wanted him to hold her.

He too was incredibly...

"Y-you..." Farah couldn't communicate. Brian cupped her cheek with his hand, realising his words had incapacitated her ability to speak.

Brian used his thumb to stroke the top of her cheek, looking her in the eyes as she lifted her hands to place them on his chest. Instead of formulating words, she softly pressed her lips against his.

The kiss started slow, Farah gripping onto both sides of his denim jacket as if her life depended on it, pulling him as close to her as possible. Farah found herself melting into the moment as if the only thing in the world that mattered was Brian Blossom.

Brian held her closely before boldly removing himself from the kiss, his eyes still closed as he caught his breath.

"D-do you still want to check that room out?" Brian smiled on her lips.

"S-sure." Farah tittered before going in for another kiss. Brian responded with a small chuckle against her lips, moving his hands to the bottom of her back and stepping backwards, their kisses becoming a lot sloppier and desperate. Brian didn't bother looking as he opened the door with his hand and pushed it open with his foot, continuing to keep himself locked in the kiss.

They both stumbled into the corridor, nearly tripping on one another.

They needed to get to the recording studio, but they found it difficult as Brian's back crashed into the wall, Farah falling into him as they continued to kiss in the open. Each kiss was uncoordinated yet loving, Brian was unable to keep his hands off her as they held one another close.

Farah had taken to threading her fingers through the hair at the back of Brian's head. Brian held onto either side of her waist, slowly making their way further down with every frantic kiss.

Brian was determined to get them inside the studio, gently pushing his back off the wall as Farah caught sight of what he was doing. They shuffled over to the door, their lips not disconnecting as they wobbled over to gain access. Brian attempted to place the key into the lock blind, refusing to let go.

Out of sheer frustration, both sexually and now suddenly with the lock, he disconnected their bodies as he jammed the key into the hole. He wanted to open the door as fast as possible. Farah couldn't help herself, stroking his hair as he battled with the lock.

"Come on!" Brian mumbled under his breath as he attempted to grant them access to the room. Farah waited impatiently, glancing back down the corridor to see if anyone was coming. Just as before, it was empty. A distant hum of music from the floor below and Brian's grunts of frustration were the only things she could hear.

The door clicked abruptly, suddenly granting them both access to the new room. Brian stood up straight and looked back towards Farah who was still invading his personal space by brushing his unruly hair with her fingers. She was infatuated with him.

"Turns out it's not a fallout shelter." Brian pointed at the recording studio door.

"I guess not." Farah chuckled sweetly.

They smiled at one another before Brian wrapped his arms around her waist and pulled her close, instantly putting pressure back on her lips. He used his elbow to press on the handle, forcing his back against the heavy door and granting them access.

Brian slapped his hand violently against the wall to switch on some lighting. Farah continued to keep her eyes closed, noticing the change in brightness within the room. What they hadn't seen yet was the ambient purple lighting that dominated the recording studio.

Their kisses proceeded to grow more desperate as Farah rustled the back of his hair with her fingers, her fingernails scratching his scalp. She felt his hands in all the places she didn't think anyone but herself would touch. Everywhere was more sensitive to his hands, each time he touched her sent her into a spiral of physical intoxication.

Brian accidentally pushed Farah against what seemed to be a wooden cabinet by the wall, probably filled with music equipment. She didn't mind the force, but his body was hot and she could feel the difference in weight in his pursuit to pin her into an unnatural position.

"Sorry..." Brian whispered, removing his lips, unsure if he had hurt her with his strength. Farah didn't mind as Brian moved his kisses to the crook of her neck.

Farah had never been in the current position of pleasure before, her unsung confidence coming from her respect for Brian and the slight intoxication from the wine as it started to overtake her mind with drunken horny thoughts. Although, she probably would have thought them whilst sober too.

As daring as it was, she was determined to exchange the favour. Farah moved her head back enough for his pursuit of kisses to stop. Brian's mouth was slightly ajar as he stared at her, unsure of the issue. There wasn't an issue...she just wanted to look at him. To see his facial features under the purple hue.

She went to kiss him again, this time she wanted to be the one in control as she felt her lips against his stubble. She had never been so confident, but Brian was welcoming to the new experience. He felt a sense of elation as her lips touched his neck, causing him to pull her even closer.

Despite having numerous sexual partners in the past, he had never desired someone so much. Not like *this*.

Brian pushed himself forward as his hands made their way downwards from her waist to her butt.

Farah sucked in a short breath of air as she noticed the touch. Brian looked up at her, checking in to make sure she was okay with his movements.

"Is this...okay?" Brian attempted to catch the breath he had lost during his frantic kisses.

Farah nodded shyly as she held her hands against his chest, bunching up some of his red shirt and holding it tightly.

Brian gently pushed his hips towards her, this time having complete control of Farah's direction. Farah had never been sexually attracted to anyone as much as she was to Brian.

They forced their lips back together with ambition, a kiss that continued to deepen with every breath. Farah moved her hands back to his cheeks, catching his stubble against her palms. There was no time for much consideration for anything.

There was something else on their minds.

Something was alluring enough to attract them to the current conclusion of their next move:

Sex.

Brian liked to see himself as a seasoned expert when it came to sex, yet his skills seemed somewhat sloppy in the presence of Farah.

He was nervous.

He had never been nervous about having sex before.

For Brian, the kind of interaction he was having with Farah was the kind of thing he found himself caught up in many times before. The difference being that with Farah he had spent the past week or so getting to know her. Getting to understand her. Feeling an intense need for her to be closer.

He wanted her to stay with him, not for the sex...for *him.*

"Do you..." Brian unlatched their lips and began to ask the question, staring directly into her eyes to ask for consent.

Farah had never been in this position before. She had never had anyone ask the question, nowhere in the same capacity as she felt his hands hold her enough to stop her shaky knees from causing her to collapse. Being with someone like this was scary and yet Farah didn't feel that same fear she had in the past.

She was nervous, but that was okay.

She had never had sex before.

"Yes." Farah pressed their foreheads together as he kissed her lips again. She knew what he was going to ask and had already decided her answer.

"We've had a little to drink, I don't want you to—" Brian was all for making sure his partner could verbally consent.

"I'm okay, Brian. I'm saying *yes.*"

"Okay."

"I want this." Farah smiled as she slowly ran her hand against the side of his face where his bristly stubble sat. "I want you..."

"You want to have *sex* with me?" Brian questioned, asking one last time for confirmation.

"Yes! I want to have *sex* with you." Farah breathed heavily with a smile, feeling Brian push closer towards her as she gave him permission to continue.

"I *really* want to have sex with you too..."

Verbal confirmation was all Brian needed to continue his pursuit of desire. It wouldn't have been the first time he had sex with a girl somewhere other than a bed. A recording studio in a mansion didn't even make it on the list of weirdest places.

Farah, on the other hand, didn't have any previous experience to compare to her time inside of the recording studio with the frontman of Social Dropouts.

She felt like a cliché. She wanted to be mad at herself for falling for Brian Blossom. Being uncomfortably pushed against the equipment in the studio was something she never would have predicted for the trip.

Their time together had been sloppy and not Brian's proudest moment in that department. However, it didn't matter. They were having a great, yet sometimes awkward time together and that was all they cared about.

Farah was inexperienced, but Brian was happy to guide her so she could get the most from the pleasurable experience. Not in a million years would she have expected her first time to have been anything like...*that.*

Farah attempted to straighten the straps of her top as Brian locked the door behind them, testing the handle to make sure it was closed.

Brian didn't want to be smug about his time with Farah, but there was a happiness that swept through him, unlike any other time he had been with anyone. A pit at the bottom of his stomach told him that maybe sleeping with Farah was a bad idea...considering every time he did sleep with someone they had a horrible habit of leaving.

"We should have figured out how to turn on the light, huh?" Brian grinned as he pointed up at the recording studio light that was sitting above the door. Farah didn't immediately find humour in his joke, a little embarrassed by the act they had committed.

If Max ever found out about this, she would never have let her live it down. There was no way Farah could share this with anyone.

Brian noticed her disconnect as he darted into the opposite room to put the keys back in the lockbox. Nobody needed to know what acts they had committed inside of the stranger's house.

"Would it be rude if we didn't stay at the party?" Farah asked, folding her arms over her chest. Despite being dressed, she still felt exposed and a little tipsy from the wine and their time together.

"Where do you want to go?" Brian held his hands in his jacket pockets as he stepped out in the corridor beside her. Admittedly, he would have been willing to go anywhere with her.

"Back to the house? I'm a little partied out." Farah chewed her bottom lip, nervous to admit how she felt about being there.

"What about the band?" Brian innocently questioned, worried they would have left them behind. "And Max!"

"They said they'd meet us at the house. We can get a ride. I'll text Max." Farah nodded, ignoring the elephant in the room. Her flustering anxiety continued to tell her to be embarrassed by it.

Brian watched as she pulled her phone from her pocket and sent a text to Max. He swayed on his heels, wishing she would say something about the time they had spent together.

Anything.

Something to tell Brian that having sex was the right thing to do and it wasn't going to have ruined anything between them.

When Farah glanced up from her phone, she noticed Brian was staring at her. He was standing in his party attire, his red collar that Farah had previously fixed was curling again.

The buttons of his shirt were done up incorrectly. She

knew she should have told him, but something about it was cute.

"Hey...do you want to hold hands again?" Brian smiled innocently, holding his hand out. He said it as if holding hands was a more intimate act than sex. Farah gave him a small smile, the butterflies in her stomach started flapping again.

She reached out and allowed their fingers to slip together.

Brian thought his heart was going to explode. The idea she would have accepted his touch after they had sex was beyond him. Nobody had ever been this way with him before. People usually didn't even want to *look* at him after sex.

Farah nodded, feeling the soft touch of his fingers between hers. She had gotten used to his touch, enough that she craved it. There was a silence between them as they walked hand in hand down the corridor, trying to find an escape from the large building that didn't force them back through the party.

The last thing they wanted to do was to see if that guy had successfully flipped off the glass table.

As they made their way through the mansion, they came to a door that led them into a garage underneath the house.

They were surprised to have been the only people down there, surrounded by riches that were in the form of sports cars as far as their eyes could see.

Farah noticed the spring in Brian's step as he kept glancing over at her every couple of seconds. She had to admit, she had spent a lot of time fixing her hair to impress him, despite only moments ago seeing her in an impure position with her glasses skewed on her nose.

As they walked through the garage, other than a few longing looks, it was hard for either of them to find the words to say despite them having a million things on their mind. Farah wasn't sure if it was acceptable to talk about sex after it happened or if it was just something they would never speak about ever again.

They approached the outside of the building and made their way past the gate. Brian texted Russ to confirm he was still alive. It had only been a couple of hours, but he was worried about their wellbeing. Farah booked the car to take them back and anxiously awaited Max's response.

The pair sat together outside the gated mansion, Farah clung onto his arm for warmth, realising that going out without an additional layer was a mistake. Cuddling up to Brian felt strange, but nowhere near as strange as their time in the recording studio.

"So..." Brian tapped on his knees as he felt Farah's hands around his arm, her cheek gently resting on his shoulder.

"So?" Farah responded in a slur, drunk on her own emotions.

"How was it?" Brian looked forward, his lips curling at the edges as he dug his nails deep into his ripped jeans, nervous for an answer.

"How was what?" Farah questioned, oblivious to his ask.

"Y'know...the sex?" Brian nudged her slightly as he attempted to retrieve an answer, his skin feeling hot at the ask.

"Oh..."

"Oh?"

"Well..."

"Well?"

"It was good." Farah sat up, nodding the first chance she got. Apparently, it was normal to speak about sex afterwards. "Really good." She continued shyly.

"Yeah?" Brian's eyes lit up; the immediate ego boost felt nice. He naturally adjusted his posture to sit a little straighter.

"I've never really...that was my first...I don't know what—" Farah trailed off, afraid to admit her inexperience. The way she had allowed Brian to guide her through, it was clear she hadn't participated in the act with anyone before.

"It's okay!" Brian was quick to defend her, worried she may have felt self-conscious thoughts about her first time. If anything, he had made it his goal to make sure she was as comfortable as she could be. "It was really good!"

As Brian complimented her, she noticed his hand fall to the middle of her thigh, gently tracing a circle on the jeans he had previously struggled to help her out of. She noticed his newfound flirting technique; one he had also exhibited when they sat at the piano together. One she found hard to resist.

"Oh! I didn't think I—"

"It was amazing." Brian whispered as he noticed they were face to face again. There was no denying the chemistry they shared.

"I wouldn't say—" Farah found herself blushing, struggling to accept the compliments on something she had no skill in.

"It was the *most* amazing." Brian purred the compliment, leaning forward as he prepared himself to kiss her. Just as he moved forward, he felt her phone buzz inside her pocket.

Farah smiled despite realising she had missed out on an opportunity. Regardless, she needed to see if Max had responded.

Brian predicted the contents of the text as he noticed the notification on her lock screen. He chose to look away to respect her privacy.

"Oh. Max and Zoe are hanging out for longer, but they're both alive. That's good." Farah let out a sigh of relief, happy their friends were safe and preoccupied.

"I hope we can say the same for Russ and Catfish." Brian chuckled.

Much to Farah's disappointment, Brian didn't kiss her. They waited outside the mansion together. Passer-by's may have mistaken them for a couple who had spent years together. Their closeness was unmatched.

Farah huddled beside him in the back of the car, basking in his radiant warmth that served to comfort her. As cliché and archaic as it may have been, Brian offered her his jacket. A romantic gesture that Farah accepted.

She snuggled up in his jacket on the way back to Stan's house as she traced her finger over the tattoo of the silly little ghost on his forearm. Brian stared out the window and watched the city go by as he hummed the tune of the song on the radio.

The worst part about the trip back to the house was having to get out at the end.

"What's your email? I'll send you the money for the ride." Brian was the first to speak as they stood on the driveway of his father's house.

"I'll cover it." Farah insisted.

"Please." Brian fluttered his eyelashes as they made their way to the front door, Farah held his denim jacket around herself.

"No, it's okay. Really." Farah asserted; he probably wasn't going to have given up on trying to pay her back for the ride.

"Is there anything I can do? Other than let you keep my jacket for a little longer?" Brian made sure to hold open the front door after unlocking it so she could be the first one to step inside.

"You can have your jacket back if you like—"

"You can keep it for now. It looks good on you." Brian smiled, closing the door and inputting a code on the house alarm.

"Thanks." Farah smiled shyly, despite being with him all night she was still giddy.

Brian flicked on the light to the large house. Farah hadn't paid much attention to it beforehand when they dropped off their things. She had focused all her attention on getting ready for the party.

Just like the mansion, the walls were plain, and the décor was boring. It didn't feel as if the house was being lived in. Admittedly, that was correct. Stan came out to the house frequently for business, but other than that, it didn't see much use.

It was a big place for one person.

Farah silently followed Brian through the house, looking into each room as she passed. Her attention was caught on the grand piano in one of the rooms, what she could have only assumed was the one Brian had mentioned. Other rooms were filled with generic furniture. It wouldn't have surprised Farah if the house came furnished and Stan had never bothered to change it.

"Rich people are so bad at interior design." Farah sighed as she followed Brian into the kitchen. He stood on the opposite side of the island and began to laugh. This time, she didn't apologise for her words.

"I can't argue with that. This house doesn't feel like a home. It never has." Brian spun on his heel as he pulled open one of the cupboards and grabbed a glass. "Do you want anything to drink?"

"I'm okay, thank you." Farah denied the offer as she looked around the kitchen. She focused her attention on the sliding doors on the other end of the room, seeing the outdoor pool through the glass.

"Let me know if you want anything." Brian filled his glass with water and took a few large gulps. He placed it back down on the counter and wiped his mouth before looking over at Farah who had become entranced by the doors. "Do you want to see the pool? The lights are super pretty at night."

"It does look nice." Farah smiled as she held her own hands, still draped in his oversized jacket.

"*You* look nice." Brian countered, stepping towards the doors and twisting the key as he smirked back at her. Farah was never going to get used to his flirtatious comments.

"Brian..." Farah practically sighed his name.

"*Farah...*" Brian mocked in return as he pulled open the door. "Come on, the others won't be home for hours. Let's have fun!"

"Do you have something in mind?" Farah followed with her arms folded as Brian stepped into the yard. She had something in mind. The taste of his lips, the smell of his strong cologne, his hands on her body, the way her name sounded as it rolled off his tongue...

Brian turned with a smile.

"Ever been swimming wearing all your clothes?"

"What?"

"Oh, it's when someone throws you into a pool."

"I can't throw you in a pool..." Farah snorted, logistically speaking she was correct.

"I could throw you in though." Brian smirked, feeling cocky in his pursuits. Farah shook her head the moment she realised what he was referring to.

"No. That's not happening."

"Are you sure?" Brian took a few steps forward, causing Farah to take a few steps back. Realistically, she could outrun him. Sprinting in the opposite direction was an option that was currently ticking in her mind.

"You wouldn't." Farah chuckled nervously as she held out her hands, terrified he would grab her.

Unluckily for Farah, she couldn't put up much of a fight as Brian pounced on the opportunity. Farah screamed in excitement at the touch as he picked her up around the waist with a singular arm. He was strong and the thought of his masculinity made her heart flutter.

"Got you!" He laughed loudly.

"Brian, if you put me in that pool I will never forgive you!" Farah spoke through giggles, unable to get back on her feet as Brian carried her over to the edge of the pool. The light from the bottom of the pool shining on them both.

She screamed as he jokingly pretended to throw her in the pool before spinning her around in circles a few times and allowing her to stand on her own two feet. They attempted to control their laughter as they stood face to face and caught their breath.

"I would never." Brian shook his head with a smile.

Farah went to push him in the chest to return the favour, but his quick reactions caught her wrists before she was able to make the connection. Brian held her wrists gently as they concentrated on one another.

They had slept together. They had been together in a capacity Farah had never experienced before. They had been together in a capacity Brian had never experienced before.

"Want to sit by the pool?" Farah smiled sweetly, suggesting their next activity.

"Whatever you want to do." Brian shrugged as he let go of her wrists and watched her walk around the side of the pool in his denim jacket and take a seat. She was beautiful.

Brian adjusted his shirt as he went to join her, still not noticing the misaligned buttons. He sat down by the edge of the pool beside her, the only light coming from the house and the pool reflecting on their faces with a blue tint.

They sat in silence as they stared at the bottom of the pool. The water waved gently with the breath-like breeze. It was nice to share the moment as their minds flooded with things to say. Most of which were things they were desperate for the other to know.

He noticed she was silent, a fear pushing through Brian at the thought of doing something wrong. She had looked away from him. Enough for Brian to panic.

Brian held his hands together as he sighed. This was all so new. It felt amazing, but good things never lasted. Especially when it came to Brian.

"Everything okay?" Farah questioned, noticing his deflation.

Brian was a little lost for words. He didn't want to make the situation weird and he didn't want to drive Farah away. It had already been the most amount of time he had ever spent with anyone after sex. He was terrified of it changing.

"I'm sorry. For, y'know—" Brian began.

"What for?"

"We had a lot of that wine...I'm sorry if you regret anything that happened between us." Brian spoke softly, there was no way it could be perfect. It had never been like this before.

"I don't regret it!" Farah defended.

"You don't?"

"No...it was a little intense. B-but it was fine!" Farah reached out and placed her hand against his shoulder before rubbing sympathetically.

"Oh. I hope I didn't hurt you. I—" That crushing feeling came to Brian once more. He rubbed his hand against his arm for warmth, the summer breeze was a lot colder than he had expected.

"You didn't hurt me."

"Oh."

"You're sweet, Brian. It's just...you know what you're doing. I don't." Farah allowed her hand to fall to his. "It wasn't what I expected."

"It wasn't what I expected either."

"It wasn't?"

"It was nothing like any of the other times."

Farah couldn't help but feel offended by his words. She furrowed her eyebrows and removed her hand from his. He was experienced in this department and she was not.

"Oh."

"What?" Brian's expression sank to one of dread. He clocked onto her meaning as quickly as he could, practically turning his whole body to face her. "Wait, that's not what I mean! It's not like that! It was great. Everything was amazing!"

Farah didn't want to look at him and yet she couldn't help herself. It was clear she had misinterpreted his words. Brian sighed heavily, stressfully running his fingers through his hair.

"Shit. I didn't mean that. What I meant is that it felt different with you. Not like the other times. This is weird for me! It must be really weird for you too. It was incredible, but it's not what I'm used to." Brian shuffled a little closer to defuse the situation. He reached out to tuck her hair behind her ear, luckily, she allowed him to do so.

"Oh..."

"This is different too. I've never spent time with someone after having sex. They usually just tick a box and leave. It's nice that you're here..." Brian pressed his lips into a thin line, trying to force a smile through his sadness. Farah noticed the pain in his expression, placing her hand on the side of his face.

"I wouldn't want to be anywhere else." Farah smiled, she could see the amount of pain that came from Brian's past experiences. There were things she didn't know about the man, but from what she did know it sounded like his previous partners had been cruel in how he was treated.

Farah noticed his lips part from a smile as she went to kiss him for what felt like the hundredth time that evening. Even if it was, she had enjoyed it every time. They connected with a kiss, one they held onto. It wasn't as frantic as the kiss in the mansion. This time was slow and sweet.

Brian wouldn't have wanted it any other way. He wanted to be with her in any capacity. He was unsure where the kiss would take them or what would finally stop them from being together that evening, but he never wanted it to end.

Farah softly unlatched her lips, brushing the palm of her hand against the bristles on his jawline. The sense of euphoria that ran through her from her night was beyond anything she had felt before. She was tired but fuelled by the adrenaline of being with the man.

"Want to hang out somewhere a little warmer?" Brian chuckled, the hair on his arms sticking up from the temperature. It was cool enough to constitute a jacket, but his only jacket was currently being worn by Farah.

"Do you want your jacket back?"

"No, then you'll be cold!"

"Is that a pool house?" Farah questioned as she looked behind Brian and noticed the small house separate from the rest of the property. Stan had too much money.

"Oh, yeah. My dad uses it as a guest house. Not that he ever really has any guests..." Brian snorted, keeping his hands out as Farah held onto him.

"Can we see it?" Curiosity got the best of her as she gestured towards the pool house.

"Yeah! Come on." Brian stood up and helped pull Farah to her feet.

Farah felt herself being led around the pool towards the house that overlooked the water. She looked back to the house and internally questioned when the others would get back. Max could hold her own, but that didn't mean she wouldn't worry.

Brian unthreaded his fingers from the girl he was infatuated by so he could unlock the doors to the pool house. Farah watched as he dropped the keys—twice. His nerves had started to get to him.

Eventually, Brian pushed the door open with his shoulder, granting them both access to the pool house.

The first thing Farah saw when Brian turned on the lights was the made-up bed in the centre of the room with cute baby blue bedside tables. The only lighting was the ambient yellow lights from the bedside lamps, creating a warm yet dim environment. The interior was a little more colourful than the main property, with two-tone walls, blue on the bottom and white on top. It felt like a human being had overseen the décor, not a lifeless robot. There was a bathroom at the back of the property and a small kitchenette accessible by a single step.

"This is pretty." She smiled as she studied the designs. It had more personality than the house.

Farah glanced up at the clock on the wall at the back of the room, only assuming it was correct.

Four. It wouldn't have been long before the sun came up. She was exhausted.

She tried to hide her yawn, but Brian noticed. As much as he wanted to, he knew they couldn't stay awake together forever.

"If you want to stay here tonight instead of the room, you're welcome to do so. Nobody's staying in here and I'm the only one with a key." Brian placed his hands in his jean pockets as he stood beside her with a smile.

Farah slowly slipped off the denim jacket and neatly hung it over a small wooden chair by the door, making the conscious decision to not give it back to Brian. All her clothes were in the other room, the only fault with her new plan.

"We should stay here. It's nice." Farah felt exposed without the jacket, Brian unable to keep his eyes away from her as he digested her words.

" *We?*"

"I thought you were staying." The words fell from Farah's lips with a hint of concern, as if she was afraid of him leaving.

"Y-you want me to stay?" Brian turned to her, blinking from disbelief at the ask. Nobody had *ever* asked him to stay.

"Do you *want* to stay? I was thinking we should probably try to get some sleep." Farah held her hands together nervously. She too had never slept in the same bed as a romantic partner before. This was new for her too.

"That would be...nice." It was weird for Brian to feel so anxious when not long ago they were having sex. An incomparable intimate act.

Farah was lost on what to do next. It was hard for her to know how much she should undress for bed with Brian in her presence. He had practically seen her naked...so what was the problem?

She decided on kicking off her shoes and unbuttoning her high-waisted jeans. Brian turned away the moment she lifted her head, but Farah had already suspected he was watching from the opposite side of the room. As soon as she noticed him watching she could hear him frantically fiddling with his belt buckle to copy her action.

She wanted him to sleep in the same bed as her. She wanted to spend the whole night with him.

It wasn't about checking a box. It wasn't about drugs or money. It wasn't about his status. It wasn't about the sex.

It was about them.

Farah kept her strapped top on as her jeans dropped to the floor. She wanted to be as quick as possible to climb into the bed, avoiding any awkwardness that came from him being able to see her. The faster she was under the covers the better.

She found it hard not to watch as Brian unbuttoned his shirt and turned around. She had seen his chest before, but it didn't stop him from being nervous.

She stared at the ceiling and waited patiently for him to get into bed beside her. She heard the sound of him stumble as he pulled the skinny jeans over his ankles before his belt buckle hit the wooden flooring.

She didn't look as he crawled under the sheets beside her, she knew he was just in his boxers. His body heat immediately warmed up the bed and as she turned all she could see was his bare chest half covered by the sheets.

Brian noticed her turn away, feeling a little self-conscious at her decision to do so. Just a moment ago she was into the idea of him staying with her and now it didn't seem as if that was the case.

"I can go if you want. I know this might be weird." Brian turned on his side and half-smiled, he was ready to be asked to leave.

"N-no, it's fine. It's not weird. We slept together. T-this is okay." Farah shifted to match his position.

"You would let me know if you weren't comfortable with this, right?"

"Of course."

"Are you sure?"

"Brian...I'm sure." Farah chuckled as a smile appeared on his lips. He had been conscious of her comfort the whole time.

There was no mistaking the respect he held for her.

He looked up at her with wide eyes as he placed his hand on top of hers and shuffled closer under the covers. Farah kept eye contact as she accepted the touch, his hand moving to the side of her face. She didn't flinch as he reached out and held the frames of her glasses, slowly pulling them away from her face. He folded the glasses and placed them on the bedside table closest to him before turning back to focus his attention on Farah.

He let out a little sigh of relief. Happy to be there at that moment as he placed his hand on her cheek. She put her hand on his as they got closer.

"You're so beautiful." Brian smirked, running his thumb against her cheek.

He had said it before. It wasn't that the words that rolled from his tongue were foreign to her anymore, it was that she was starting to *believe* them. She knew he wanted to be with her and she wasn't willing to play any games to make it happen.

She was never going to forget their night together. For better or worse, this had been part of her time in the City of Angels and there was no changing it now.

She didn't *want* to change it.

Silence filled the space between them as Farah moved forward to close the gap, being the one to initiate a kiss. It was slow and sensual. Loving and hot. Coordinated. A kiss that permitted them to intertwine their bodies under the sheets. It was a kiss that connected them both, two people encapsulated by loneliness for different reasons.

Farah pulled away, enough for their lips to brush together.

Brian listened to her breath as he waited on confirmation to continue.

"I-I really liked having sex with you." She whispered, her words grazing his lips. Farah could feel his smile against her skin as he let out a small chuckle.

"Yeah. Me too." He pushed his nose against hers as he responded with another tender kiss. Slow. Just like before.

Farah laughed as she moved her head backwards to unlock the kiss, he didn't hesitate to chase her for more. Brian took the hint as she moved his hands away from the side of her face. He opened his eyes at the action, causing Farah to stare back in wonderment. They held their gaze for a moment as Farah built up enough courage to ask the question.

"Do you want to have sex again?" Farah swallowed hard at her words, feeling herself blush.

Brian blinked rapidly, nodding his head as he found himself speechless at the ask. She tittered before pulling him back into yet another intimate kiss.

Brian had never had sex with the same person twice and as much as he wanted to tell Farah, he knew it wouldn't have been appropriate. On the other hand, Farah wanted to strengthen their connection with whatever ounce of confidence she had.

Unlike the desperate act that took place in the recording studio of the mansion, this time was slow. There was enough time to explore their bodies. Their desires and dislikes.

It was intimate. Special. *Passionate.*

It was everything they wanted.

The blinds in the pool house were parted just enough to allow light to shine through. Farah's eyes were practically glued together as she attempted to open them. She had no concept of time as she stared at the ceiling, realising she wasn't alone in the bed.

Her pillow wasn't a cotton blend either...it was Brian.

She looked upwards, realising she had been cuddling up to him for as long as she could remember. It must have been all night. Or at least...all morning. They returned to the house at nearly four in the morning.

"Afternoon, Sleepyhead." Brian mumbled, adopting the pet name for Farah. She would have hated it if anyone but Brian had said it.

Farah stretched, removing herself from his chest and reaching over to grab her glasses from the nightstand. Brian noticed her struggle, taking the glasses off the side and unfolding them for her.

Brian went to place them over her eyes, before he could get any closer, she had taken them from him and pushed them up her nose.

Farah fell beside Brian, his arm remaining underneath her. She remembered only hours ago he had been taking the glasses from her, a strangely intimate experience.

Farah wasn't sure if it was exhaustion or alcohol, but she couldn't remember all the events that occurred the previous night. She remembered the mansion, the wine, the instruments, Brian's lips and...the *sex*.

Oh, boy...the sex.

They had sex.

"We..." Farah's voice was raspy as she looked over at Brian.

"Yeah..." Brian smirked, knowing what she was referring to.

"At the party..."

"And here..." Brian added, confident in his words. They had spent an unforgettable night together.

Not only had they had sloppy sex at the party, but they had also been intimate with one another a second time that evening in a pool house. They hadn't expected it to happen twice, but neither of them was complaining.

The memories flooded back to Farah, remembering the sheer pleasure she had experienced through the night.

"Wow." Farah placed her hand on his stomach as she nuzzled into his chest. It would have been nice if she never had to leave the bed.

"It was amazing." Brian sighed, twirling her hair through his fingers.

"I hope the others are okay." Farah exhaled as her mind went elsewhere, thinking about Max and the band. She hoped they had made it back to the house.

Farah thought about the wellbeing of them all, especially Max. The last time she had seen her was at the beginning of the party when Zoe had dragged her away. She wondered if Max had a wild night too, Farah's certainly beat her average nights being stuck in her dorm room with her head inside of a text-book.

"I'm sure they can look after themselves. I think I heard people in the house a few hours ago." Brian slurred, too caught in the moment with Farah to have considered thinking about where the heck the rest of his band were.

Farah groaned before pulling the covers around herself, she had forgotten her nudity. The strapped top hadn't stuck around for long after getting into bed that night. Within moments, Brian had been pulling it over her head between placing gentle kisses along her jawline.

Brian watched as she sat up, dragging the sheets with her and revealing her back. Brian shamelessly ran his eyes across her figure, it was perfect in every way.

Farah glanced around the room; their clothes scattered on the wooden flooring of the pool house. They hadn't been tidy in their decision making.

"I need a shower." Farah sighed, running her fingers through her hair. She kept her other arm close to her body, holding the sheets to cover herself. She was hot and sweaty, her body dominated by the stench of sex.

Brian scratched the hair on his chin before tilting his head against the headboard, reaching over and drawing a small circle at the bottom of Farah's back with his finger. She felt a slight shiver through her spine at the touch.

"You can use the shower in the back." Brian suggested, keeping his focus on drawing lines in her skin.

"Thanks." Farah turned back to see him lying in the bed.

There he was, lying back on the headboard with his usual adorable yet sexy expression. He hadn't attempted to shave yet, stubble poking through his cheeks more than usual, giving the bottom half of his face a much darker complexion. His hair didn't look as styled as it had in the past, his auburn roots beginning to show amongst the bleach blonde.

His chest was bare, exposing enough hair to show off his masculinity. Everything waist down was covered by the sheets, but Farah didn't need to use her imagination to know what was underneath. He was muscular but wasn't ashamed of his gut and broad shoulders that attributed to his hugging abilities.

Farah watched as he smiled up at her, placing one of his hands behind his head, suddenly showing off more of his body hair and the ridiculous tattoos that trailed around his arms. Farah smiled back, being that attractive should have been illegal.

"Has anyone ever told you how beautiful you are?" Brian tried his hardest to flirt, using similar words with her previously and succeeding.

"Only you...*frequently*." Farah admitted with a small smile.

"Only me? There's no way that's true!" Brian scoffed, upset by her comment. Why wouldn't anyone else have called Farah beautiful? It was clear as day.

"Maybe my parents..."

"That doesn't count. What about all those college guys?"

"What *college guys*?"

"I don't know...the guys at your college?" Brian shrugged, not grasping the concept of education and the harsh social scale that came with it.

"I don't get out much. I'm more of a 'pen and paper' girl." Farah snorted, realising how boring her life must have sounded to Brian. The man in an exciting band touring the states.

"You make it sound like that's a bad thing." Brian smirked.

"These have been the most exciting two weeks of my entire life." Farah laughed.

"This is just the start of something different. Something new and exciting! Hey, maybe you'll be inspired by your trip! You could write a book about it or make a podcast!" Brian shrugged. The trip was all about finding yourself.

"I don't know..."

"You can be whoever you want to be." Brian had gone from what Farah believed to be the sexiest man alive to being just like many pre-recorded motivational seminars she watched late at night.

Brian's tone irked her, but that didn't mean it wasn't one she appreciated.

Farah laid down on her back, bringing the covers with her. She didn't feel like responding with anything positive. There wasn't much she could have said that would have done much for her low self-esteem.

She was having an internal crisis that she couldn't share with anyone.

She had just lost her virginity to the frontman of Social Dropouts.

She promised herself she would get up, get showered and consume some food to fill her empty stomach. Her motivation for any of those things was nil, certain Brian had voided her of any existence past cuddling him in bed.

Farah turned and watched as the young man sat up and shuffled himself over to the edge of the mattress. Just as he had viewed her back, Farah now got a full-length view of his body. She had never seen his back before, but there on his right shoulder blade was a tattoo, one that made her chuckle.

Permanently embedded on his skin was a tattoo of a cartoon chameleon climbing a small branch whilst wearing a backpack.

"I like the chameleon." Farah laughed as Brian looked over his shoulder to try and see the tattoo he often forgot about.

"Oh, that little guy? Russ did it for me when I used to stay at his house a lot. Cool, right?" Brian smirked, happy to share the sentiment of one of his favourite tattoos. Farah made the connection between the chameleon with a backpack and the desire to change on his travels. She felt a relation to the art.

"Very cool." Farah nodded with a smile. Maybe Brian just thought it was cool?

She watched him grab his black boxers from the floor and put them on before trailing around the room to pick up his clothes. It didn't take long to return to his position on the edge of the bed. He held up his jeans and went to put them on, the belt buckle clinking as he pulled them up each leg.

He grabbed his red button-up shirt and threw it on, not bothering to do each of the buttons up before turning back to Farah who was now staring up at him with wide eyes, comfortably tucked underneath the covers.

"You drink coffee, right?" Brian asked as he began to buckle the belt on the front of his jeans, practically standing over her.

"I'm a college student, Brian." Farah mumbled into the covers she had pulled to her mouth.

"Just double-checking." Brian smiled, fiddling with his belt a little more than he should have.

"Where are you going?" Farah didn't want him to leave her in the pool house alone.

"I was going to get us coffee."

"Can I have a *big* coffee, please?" Farah mumbled into the sheets again.

"I'll make you a big coffee. I'll be sure to use the biggest mug we have!" Brian grinned as he buttoned his shirt, starting from the top and making his way down. Farah took note of him buttoning them correctly, unlike the night before.

Brian debated whether or not to lean over and kiss her again. He had never been with a girl like this and was unsure of where to draw the line of romance.

Farah watched him as he picked up his shoes and slid them on, not bothering with the battered shoelaces as he tucked them inside. He stepped over to a mirror by the bed and fixed his hair with his fingers, restoring it to its usual fluffy mess of blonde.

"Brian?" Farah spoke in a whisper.

"*Mmmhmm?*" Brian turned away from the mirror to face her as she spoke, his fingers still running through his hair. Farah wished she could have been the one to brush her fingers through his hair.

"Are you going to tell the others about this? About...*us?*" Farah brought up her concerns, worried he may have seen them and mentioned that *yes,* he had *fucked* the groupie. The idea pained her to think about.

Brian's expression dropped. He didn't tell his band all his escapades when it came to women. Sure, a few of them came up in conversation, but they were his family and they supported him through his choices. Farah was different and he wouldn't have been embarrassed to admit what they had done together. He really liked her.

"I wasn't...planning on it. Do you *want* me to?" Brian let out a small yet nervous laugh.

"No! It's okay, I was just curious to know. I don't want Max to—"

"It can be our little secret..." Brian smiled before heading to the door, still running his fingers through his hair as he spoke.

Brian stood by the door for a moment, debating his next move. Farah stared in confusion until she watched him spin on his heel and walk back towards her.

"What are yo—" Before Farah could question his hesitation his lips had been pushed against hers.

Brian used his finger to hold her chin, repeatedly kissing her softly on the lips. Farah allowed him to kiss her as she propped herself up with her elbow in the bed. Brian slowly unlatched their lips, pressing his nose against hers as he let out a long breath.

"You're still going to be here when I get back?" Brian questioned, desperate for verbal confirmation.

"I'm not going anywhere."

"Right." Brian couldn't help the small blush that filled his cheeks. He was over the moon. He had never felt this way before.

Farah waved at Brian and watched him exit the pool house. As soon as the door had closed behind him, Farah laid flat on her back and stared at the ceiling. A sense of impurity causing her to fold her arms across her chest and sigh heavily.

She had *slept* with Brian Blossom; the lead singer of Social Dropouts and she had *enjoyed* it. She had slept with him twice. In one night.

She had gone on the trip to explore lots of things. Mostly historical sites and potentially even herself. The last thing she had expected to discover was her sexual desires. They were new to emerge to the surface, but like a shipwreck they had been hidden for years.

However, last night she had lost her virginity. An unmatched exploit and one of sheer escapism. She didn't know when it would have happened, but twenty-one and inside of a recording studio with someone who had a Wikipedia page? That hadn't ever crossed her mind.

She had been dirty enough to commit to the act *twice*. In the spur of the moment, both times had been her idea and she was finding it hard to comprehend. Lying half-naked and staring up at the ceiling of a famous band manager's pool house had left her in a dream-like state. There was no way it could be real.

...But it was.

Farah groaned, finally dragging herself out of bed and to the shower. She felt disgusting, regardless of how many times Brian had assured her she looked beautiful. That didn't matter when crawling out of bed had been a chore.

In Farah's mind, there was always some kind of romantic integrity that came with the thought of losing her virginity. Except now her first time was ingrained within her mind. The purple lighting of the recording studio and the dimly lit pool house. A contrast in their intimacy. Desperation and desire.

Had she made a mistake?

Brian looked around the yard as he stepped out of the pool house, his mind drowning in emotions. Most of his thoughts were scenes within his mind, replaying the things that had happened between him and Farah through the night. The feel of her skin against his, the way she cooed his name, the temporary indentations of her nails in his back, the way he felt inside of—

He pulled open the sliding glass doors into the kitchen and stepped inside. It was his mission to make coffee and that was what he was going to do. He tried to be as quiet as possible as he closed the door behind him.

At first glance, it didn't look as if the kitchen had been touched. The first thing he spotted was the glass he had left on the side from the night before. The house was quiet. He wasn't sure if everyone had made it back to the house, but he selfishly had other things on his mind.

He checked through the house to see if anyone was downstairs before using the bathroom to somewhat freshen himself up before his return. It didn't look as if anything had been touched and his party resided upstairs. That meant he could take his time in making the perfect coffee.

He turned on the coffee machine upon his return to the kitchen and searched the cupboards for the biggest mugs he could find. His stomach rumbled at the thought of food as he searched through the fridge and cupboards. His dad hadn't left anything edible from his last visit.

Brian found himself humming from happiness as he practically skipped around the kitchen trying to make the perfect coffee the morning after.

Afternoon. It was the afternoon.

He was glad they didn't have to play a show that night.

Brian wasn't sure how Farah liked her coffee, but he made a good guess. It was likely to be wrong but he was sure she would have appreciated his efforts regardless.

He poured the coffee into the mugs, keeping the remainder of the pot to the side if anyone else wanted some. If they woke up soon enough. He hummed cheerfully as he gripped onto the mugs and turned around—

"Brian."

"Russ!" Brian practically yelped his name, a little coffee spilling over the edges of the mugs. Luckily, none of it went onto his hands.

"Dude, you seem super shaky. Everything good?" Russ stared at him with his usual deadpan expression. It was weird for Brian to see him without his backwards baseball cap or white denim overalls. Instead, he was sporting a plain black t-shirt and baggy grey shorts.

"Good. Everything's good. You just...you scared the shit out of me, man." Brian took a deep breath.

"Sorry. I mastered the art of stealth one summer and that's not a skill you can simply forget. One day the United States military will be able to harness the power of invisibility. They use cloaking materials already through the tap water we drink. Allows them to see things the average American can't." Russ began to explain.

"Oh?" Brian stood there awkwardly holding the two coffee mugs, hoping the conversation would end soon.

"Extracting genes from the humble chameleon and putting them into militant technology means that one day we could achieve human cloaking without the need for the colour green. *Game changer.*" Russ pinched his finger and thumb together before adjusting his glasses.

"It's too early for this."

"It's nearly fifteen hundred hours."

"Too *early.*" Brian groaned. He just wanted to get back to Farah.

Brian couldn't move, he had been trapped by Russell and he wasn't returning anytime soon.

Brian stood in the kitchen with his best friend, anxiously gripping onto the two coffee mugs as they began to hurt his hands. Russ didn't talk a lot, but when he was on a tangent there was no stopping him.

"This sounds like a good story to save for the van." Brian smiled politely, the last thing he wanted was to offend his friend.

"Yeah, you're right. Zoe would appreciate this one too." Russ scratched his goatee, it was likely he was still high from whatever drugs he had consumed the previous night.

"Good. I'm going to go now." Brian turned towards the door leading outside.

"Hey, Brian?" Russ caught his attention.

"Yeah?"

"Why do you have two coffees?" Russ' question caused Brian's heart to sink. He stared down at the coffee mugs, then back to Russ, then back to the mugs.

"*Two hands?*" Brian squinted, before realising he could get away with it. "Because I have *two hands!*"

Russ contemplated his answer as he stared down at his own two hands and realised their potential.

"I never thought about it like that."

"It changed my life."

"Yeah?"

"Oh yeah."

Russ stared at the floor for a few seconds, taking in the new information. Brian gritted his teeth together. He was lucky he hadn't run into Zoe.

"I hope you enjoy your caffeinated beverages, dude." Russ nodded before tapping his chest twice with a closed fist.

"Thanks." Brian grinned as he pushed open the sliding door with his foot and stepped outside.

His encounter with Russ had been close. Too close. He walked past the pool with the two coffees in hand before opening the door to the pool house with his elbow.

Upon entering, Farah was sat on the edge of the bed in front of the standing mirror she had angled so she could sit down and dry her hair. Her shower had been *quick*, but she was nervous and didn't want to stay in there for too long.

He placed the mugs on the bedside table beside Farah as he noticed she had her phone held up to her ear. Farah didn't say a word as she listened contently to what her parents had to say, mostly bickering about something she hadn't entirely been listening to. She was holding her hairbrush in the other hand, halfway through the task and distracted by the phone call.

Brian sat down beside her before looking over, a stressed expression on her face. He wasn't sure who she was talking to.

"It's been amazing so far." Farah responded to the conversation on her phone, hoping Brian would understand that being quiet was his best option.

Farah looked over at the large coffee that was sitting on the table and Brian took the hint. He passed her one of the large mugs. He was a sucker for chivalry and took the hairbrush from her hand and replaced it with the coffee. She mouthed the words 'thank you' as she took a sip of the much-needed beverage.

Brian, with all the wisdom in the world, crawled behind her with the hairbrush in hand. Farah watched him in the mirror as he shuffled close. He stretched his legs around her and moved closer to her back so she could practically feel him against her.

Farah noticed he was still wearing shoes, feeling uncomfortable he had put them on the bed sheets.

Much to Farah's surprise, Brian took a sudden interest in her hair. He ran it through his fingers before holding it gently and pulling it through with the brush to make sure there weren't any tangles. As much as Farah was trying to listen to her parent's conversation on the phone, all she could concentrate on was Brian.

"We're trying to take as many pictures as possible." Farah commented on her phone call as she turned back to Brian and smirked.

As Farah turned it exposed her neck, causing Brian to rid the area of any loose hairs with the brush before deciding to use his hand instead. Farah quivered as she felt his lips plant soft kisses against the crook of her neck just as they had done the night before. She prayed her parents wouldn't have been able to hear his smooches against her skin.

This was not a good plan.

Farah reached up to swat him away before realising she was trapped with both the phone and the coffee in her hands. If she wanted to get him off she was going to have to move and yet she felt paralysed, the feeling of his lips so perfect against her skin. She was overly aware of where his hands were starting to travel, underneath her arms and towards her chest.

This was a risky game and as much as she wanted to be mad at Brian for his persistence, it didn't feel as if she could be. She was so caught up in the feeling of him against her. She craved more.

"We're in Los Angeles. We're travelling to Denver tomorrow." Farah looked up in the mirror as she spoke, Brian still showering her with kisses that weren't completely innocent. She watched as his hands made their way around her waist, teasing at the hem. She knew what he wanted and she wasn't going to let him get it.

Not on a phone call with her *parents*!

Farah pushed her elbow against his arm the best she could with the coffee still in her hand, it was getting hot now and she was unable to put it back on the desk. Brian looked up at the touch, resting his chin on her shoulder and looking up in the mirror at them both. She was gorgeous and Brian smirked as she shook her head to inform him that now was not the time.

Farah noticed he had wrapped his arms around her and kept his chin on her shoulder, holding her tightly with his legs on either side of her. She felt safe in his grip and the view in the mirror was one she wasn't used to.

Farah noticed how good they looked together.

His heart was warm as he held her, wanting nothing more than to cuddle with her all day.

"We're currently exploring California. It's...different." Farah couldn't take her eyes off his reflection, looking like a photograph she wanted to savour forever.

"The best kind of different..." Brian purred into her ear causing Farah's eyes to widen. Brian hadn't paid any attention to what Farah had been saying on the phone until that point.

"Oh nothing, *Mom*! It's just Max messing around. Y'know, being Max and all!" Farah chuckled nervously before turning around and scowling at Brian. He let go of her and sat back.

There was a slight pause.

"Okay, I'll talk to you tomorrow? Alright. Bye." Farah was desperate to get off the call now Brian had made things awkward.

She was twenty-one and could do whatever she wanted and yet no matter what she did, she always felt as if her parents were watching overhead.

Farah took a long sip of the coffee and ended the call with her mother before shaking her head at Brian.

"*Really?*" Farah snorted, unable to control herself. He was sitting on the bed with his hands out behind him holding him up with his feet still hanging off the end of the bed.

"I didn't expect it to be your mom."

"I didn't expect you to...come in and do whatever it was you did." Farah sighed.

"Kiss you?"

"Yeah..."

"It's hard not to." Brian groaned with a smile.

"Try harder." Farah insisted as she smirked, standing up and taking another sip of the coffee. "Thanks for the coffee, by the way." Farah held the large cup in the air.

"It's a *real big* coffee." Brian laughed at the sheer size of the mug he had chosen. She wasn't sure if she would have been able to finish it, but she did ask for a big coffee.

"Real big coffee." Farah sighed with a smile, looking down at him with an affectionate expression. He was so handsome, holding himself up with his elbows. The red shirt he had bought for the party was creased. The top buttons were undone and the collar arched at the edges.

Just as Farah found herself getting lost in his eyes, there was a familiar voice heard through the walls of the pool house.

"Farah?" A muffled voice shouted without direction.

Farah's eyes widened at the sound, staring at Brian in horror.

Max.

Realistically, Farah knew she wouldn't have been able to keep it a secret from her best friend for long. Right now, she didn't want anyone to know about her escapades with the frontman.

They couldn't know she slept in the pool house with him. She had to make it back to the house as if she never left.

"Crap! What do we do?" Farah placed the coffee on the bedside table and stood up frantically. She couldn't be caught in the same room as Brian Blossom. Especially not by Max!

"Uh...I'll make a distraction!" Brian scrambled to his feet. He was on the same train of thought as Farah.

"You want me to sneak past?" Farah noticed her hands beginning to shake from anxiety.

"Y-yeah! That'll work." Brian gave her a toothy grin as he gripped onto her shoulders and pulled her forward to kiss her forehead. "I'll see you soon."

She couldn't believe her night with the man was finally over. She collected her thoughts and made sure she had her phone. It was time for their very sloppy plan to start. One that had little strategy attached.

She watched as Brian exited the room with a small wink. She too had to get ready to make it from the pool house to the house and hope nobody was waiting in the kitchen to spot her.

Brian closed the pool house door behind him, turning around to see Max on the opposite end of the pool.

"Hey Brian, have you seen Farah?" Max was quick to hop on the questioning, taking Brian by surprise.

"Who's Farah?" The words slipped from his mouth. He had only realised how stupid he looked after he had said it.

"Uhhh...y'know...*Farah.* My best friend. We've been following you on tour for weeks, dude." Max dipped her eyebrows in confusion.

"*Farah*! Yes! I know Farah. *Mmhmm.*" Brian nodded as he held his hands on his hips.

"Do you know where she is?"

"Not here. She's uhhh...Farah. Farah-way. Far away!" Brian stepped away from the door to the pool house and made his way over to Max.

"Okay, I'll just—"

"Wait! No!"

"No? Bro, do you know where she is or not?" Max cocked an eyebrow as she snapped. He wasn't going to be able to get anywhere until he found a way to make sure she was distracted.

There had to be something to hold her attention...

"Shows...music...*music*!" Brian gasped as his hands shook in front of his chest. He had cracked the code.

"Woo! Music!" Max shook her fist excitedly as Brian stepped closer.

"I need to ask your opinion on a new song! It's very important and I'm keeping it a secret!" He watched her eyes light up at the request.

"*Me*?" Max blinked rapidly as her dreams came true. Brian Blossom was asking for her input on a song!

"You're the band's number one fan, aren't you? I have to run it by you!" Brian gripped onto her arms and spun her around so she was no longer facing the pool house. Max was mesmerised by his ask.

Max swallowed her anxieties as she looked him in the eyes. This was everything she wanted.

"I have to admit to you now that my room back home has cut-outs of your face stuck to the wall. I got them from a magazine years ago."

"What?"

"Never mind. What's the song about?" Max got back on track. Brian looked past her shoulder to see Farah sneaking out of the pool house, carefully closing the door behind her.

"*Sneaking*!" Brian looked around to find something less suspicious. "Grass!"

"*Sneaking grass?* Okay...uh...is there a metaphor behind it?" Max was confused and she wasn't afraid to show it in her expression.

"Max, you don't understand, this is going to be the best song I've ever written. The grass is the metaphor for grass and green and weed. Weed is green. Yeah! Good job! We did it!" Brian gripped a little harder onto Max's arms as he watched Farah slide the door open to the kitchen and gave Brian a thumbs up. She had made it.

"That's...profound. I don't know if it's because I'm a little— a lot hungover or this idea is beyond me, but it's a little hard to make sense of. Is this always your creative process? It's freaking me out a little." Max gritted her teeth together as she attempted to move away from Brian. He let her go without question.

"Thanks for your input, Max. It's going to be a great help." Brian grinned as he waved and made his way towards the house. Max pulled out her phone as she watched him disappear, puzzled by her encounter with the man.

Farah had darted through the house towards the room upstairs she had been told she could stay in. As she entered she noticed the bedding hadn't been touched and her bag was still in the same place she left it. Luckily, she hadn't come across any of the band whilst sneaking through the house and making her way to the bathroom.

Once in the bathroom, she retrieved a new change of clothes. It wouldn't have been long before Max started looking a little harder into her disappearance. Farah wished Max didn't have to be so quick, having left the coffee Brian had made her on the bedside table in the pool house.

She pulled her phone from her jeans and noticed a text from Max.

'Where are you? This house is too big.'

Farah had to push every thought of Brian from her mind as she pulled open the bathroom door only to be greeted by her best friend.

264

"Hey! There you are! I've been looking everywhere for you." Max groaned.

"Oh, I just took a shower." It wasn't *technically* a lie. She held her bag and walked back into the room she was supposed to stay in, Max followed. Farah sat down on the edge of the bed, finally messing up the perfectly made sheets.

Max bounced on her heels for a moment, clasping her hands together. Farah knew she had something to say.

"Strange night, huh?" Max denied eye contact as Farah held onto her knees. She was nervous about Max finding out about her time with Brian, but this didn't feel like the start of that conversation.

"Yeah...pretty strange." Farah wasn't sure what she was referring to.

"I was pretty sick in the back of our ride home. I'm surprised I'm standing upright." Max began to laugh.

"Are you okay?" Her best friend was resilient and even if she was suffering tried to stay quiet about it. They were similar in that respect.

"I feel like there's a tiny construction site happening in my head, but other than that...I'm fine." Max shrugged. "Brian didn't seem fine though. He was acting super weird; did you see him take any *drugs*?" Max's question came with a tone of concern.

Farah clenched her fists at the sound of his name, anxiety was causing her to fluster.

"I'm sure he's just tired." Farah smiled before pushing her lips together.

"You were with him at the party, weren't you?" Max tilted her head with curiosity. This was it. This was the moment Farah was busted.

"Y-yeah, we were at the party together. We got back pretty early." Farah didn't feel as if she could lie about it. She made sure she was telling the truth.

"*Together?*"

"Together."

"Huh."

"Yeah."

"Did you—"

"No."

"Okay."

"Okay."

Farah chewed her bottom lip, keeping her hands on her knees. It felt as if Max wanted to ask but was afraid of the outcome. Farah wasn't willing to admit anything just yet, even if there was suspicion.

"I just saw him out by the pool. He started asking me questions about music. It was pretty random." Max snorted, reliving the memory of his shaking her shoulders.

"That's weird."

"He's a weird dude."

"He's just...different." Farah smiled as she held her hands together.

There was a comfortable silence between the two friends, mentally deciding on what they could discuss next before they packed their bags for the next location. Max sucked cool air through her teeth before clapping her hands together.

It was probably best for them not to discuss the events of last night. Neither of them needed to know what they had been up to. That was a conversation for the car...

Farah let out a small sigh of relief. She was in the clear...for now. Everyone was preoccupied with their own thoughts to care what she was doing with Brian.

With the evening off in LA, it gave them all an opportunity to explore the city. Farah was desperate in her desire to see some of the famous movie filming locations scattered across the city. Apparently, so was Catfish. They didn't get time for very many, but Farah was happy with what she had seen.

Zoe suggested visiting the Santa Monica pier in the evening.

Once they arrived in Santa Monica everyone apart from Max and Farah took to their boards at one of the many local skateparks.

Farah would have taken up Brian on the opportunity to skateboard again but didn't want to get on the board in front of everyone. For the most part, Farah and Brian avoided anything other than casual group conversation.

They ate street food on the pier before making their way over to the beach to watch the sunset. Farah sat beside Max and stared up at the pier overlooking the rest of the beach, the lights illuminating down on the ocean. It was gorgeous and they felt the need to snap a few pictures with one another in front of the sight.

"Come on, get on in here!" Zoe insisted as the band stood in front of Max and Farah who had been directing a band photoshoot without realising.

Max half-buried an old soda can into the sand before leaning her phone against it, setting a timer and running over to the band, gesturing for Farah to do the same. Farah laughed as she tried to run in the sand, her shoes drowning in uncomfortable grains. She quickly took her glasses off and tucked them in her back pocket for the photo. Farah stood next to Brian and smiled widely, she watched as he threw his arm around Catfish and tucked his hand neatly around her waist to pull her closer into the photograph, the pier in the background. Catfish and Russ fist bumped as Max threw her arm around Zoe before flipping off the camera. Zoe threw an El Diablo hand gesture in the air. Farah kept her hands to her sides.

Farah didn't mind the touch; it was nothing more than a friendly gesture and she hoped the picture hadn't picked up on him holding her so closely.

"Oh! I think that was a good one!" Max grinned as she sprung over to her phone to check the picture.

Farah looked back and smiled at Brian as he gently removed his hand, realising he had touched her without permission. It had become such a natural occurrence throughout the night.

When they all went back to the house to sleep the second night it wasn't as crazy as it had been before. This time, they all went back to their designated rooms.

It wasn't a bad thing, but it didn't help that Farah and Brian had spent a few hours after they claimed to have been sleeping texting.

After hours of blue light emitting from their phones, they finally decided to get some rest, knowing they would have to drive to Denver the next day.

Their memories in the City of Angels were ones they would never forget.

DENVER, CO

Max, Farah and the band had two days to get from California to Colorado and they knew they would have to spend the whole time travelling. It was going to take fifteen hours to get across the states. They should have left sooner.

Either way, Max and Farah would be taking the journey separately.

'Hi Farah. You didn't reply to my other text. I just want to make sure you're doing okay. How's the trip going? Seen anything fun? I'd love to join you on your adventures one—'

Farah swiped the notification off her screen, she didn't have the mental capacity to read any more of Hasan's desperate pleas for her attention. She would have to think of something to send him later to keep her parents off her back, but for now, she had other things in mind.

Brian.

It was hard for her not to think about him when she had experienced one of the best nights of her life with him in Los Angeles. She had texted him a few times, but none of them had been about their time together. It felt as if it was something they shouldn't have brought up over text.

The days travelling apart gave both parties time to spend with their friends. Catching up with Max had been great and Farah had enjoyed every moment, even if her mind was elsewhere.

"We could meet up with the band in Vegas. Wouldn't that be cool?" Farah asked as they drove along the highway, making their way to the next location. It was nice to have spent a day in Los Angeles hanging out.

Plus, she had gotten her wish of going to the Griffith Observatory before they left which was great.

"That sounds like the sickest idea ever, but we can't come off as *needy*. We need to give them some breathing room and they should do the same. Besides, the band have their little bonding days together. We can't get in the way of that." It pained Max to say the words. She wanted nothing more than to hang with the band but holding off was the best option.

"Oh, that makes sense."

Admittedly, Brian had texted Farah the same thing, claiming the band were having a day to themselves. A day where they didn't do anything that wasn't related to the band and the friendship they held. Brian had said they would see them at the Denver show, but other than that, there wasn't a chance for them to see one another in-between.

As much as Farah wanted to speak about everything that had happened, she didn't think the space was a bad thing. She needed the time to process the last couple of days.

Farah wanted to catch up on taking photographs she could send to her parents. After the slip up on the phone to her parents when Brian was in the room, she couldn't help but worry they were suspicious. Plenty of pictures with Max would have cleared the air.

To the Vishwakarma parents, Maxine Kayori was an incredibly talented college student who enjoyed socialising with Farah by spending their time studying together or visiting educational locations. There was nothing there to hint that wasn't entirely the case, considering Max was fairly good at putting on a mask whenever her parents did come around.

Farah was just happy she got to be with Max. She was the one person who had always been willing to drag Farah out of her tough shell and experience the world for what it was. Farah deserved that at the very least and Max was going to be the one to help provide it.

That being said...she wasn't sure if telling Max about Brian was a good idea.

"What made you so interested in the band, huh?" Max smirked as she focused her attention on Farah, holding her hands on the steering wheel.

"They're pretty fun to be around." Farah shrugged. It had been two weeks; she had gotten used to their company.

"You mean *Brian* is pretty fun to be around." Max rolled her eyes, noticing how little her best friend was willing to give away on the subject. It was fun to watch Farah become defensive over it.

"You're with Zoe the same amount of time!" Farah countered, trying her hardest to push the attention away from herself.

"At least I'm not trying to *screw* Zoe." Max pushed a little further.

"You're not?"

"No! Well...not *anymore*! I don't know, man. We've gotten too friendly with one another and I'd rather it stuck that way. You know I'm not exactly one for a *relationship*, so the last thing I'd want is that. Even a casual hook-up would feel weird. I like being friends with Zoe, she's super cool and I wouldn't want to ruin that." Max explained, her preferences shining through. Farah very much respected Max and her decisions and only hoped Max would do the same if she were to ever find out about her and Brian.

"I'm glad you're having a good time."

"You're having a good time too, right?" Max pondered, worried that dragging her friend across the states would cause them to fall apart.

"At this point, anything is better than studying."

"You like studying!"

"Sometimes."

"*Always.* Nerd." Max huffed.

"You're a nerd too!" Farah complained. They were incredibly smart and talented in their chosen subjects. It was how they managed to get into an Ivy League school and Max was still pushing on staying there for further education after graduation.

"You didn't answer my question."

"Yes. I'm having a great time. I'm glad you asked me to come." Farah nodded as she looked out the window.

"And I'm glad you accepted. Road tripping with my best friend? Couldn't have asked for anything better." Max remarked with a grin before her expression dropped. "I'm sorry you didn't get to go on your hiking trip."

"It's okay. I've got my whole life to do it." Farah shrugged, finally in a different mindset about the trail. It would have been an experience of a lifetime and one she wouldn't want to miss out on, but her trip with Max had been so much fun she wouldn't want it any other way.

"As long as you're sure."

"I'm sure."

Just as Farah was about to look out the window and day-dream, her phone began to ring. Farah picked her phone off her lap and spun it around. Her facial expression dropped at the sight of the contact flashing at the top of her screen.

"Oh no." Farah groaned as she turned down the car radio.

"Parents?"

"Hasan."

"Ugh. Just ignore it!" Max grumbled.

Farah slid her finger across the screen to reject the call. With Brian on her mind, the last thing she wanted was to accept a call from the man her parents were insistent on her getting to know a little better. It had been years; couldn't he take a *hint*? Couldn't *they* take a hint?

"I'll text him something later." Farah sighed, placing her phone back on her lap and focusing on the scenery passing them by.

Max furrowed her eyebrows at the momentary silence. She knew all too well that Hasan didn't just call *once* and that always left Farah in an awkward position. Mostly due to her inability to resist the second time out of politeness.

Once again, the phone began to ring.

"Don't—" Max began, before she could finish her sentence it was already too late. Farah had the phone to her ear and coming through the speaker was the *supposed* man of her dreams.

"Hi, Hasan...No—...Sorry, I've been super busy with school and—yeah, it's summer...N-no, I'm still away from home. Still on my trip...Colorado...No, I take something else...Just...classes. Hmm...Sure, sounds good...Probably a couple of weeks, maybe more—...I-I wouldn't, no... *Wow*, so interesting—you'll have to tell me more another time...Ah, yes—...Well, I hate to cut you short and I don't want to be rude, but I wouldn't want to ignore this wonderful tour guide...Yes...No, that's not a radio, it's an exhibit...Sure—...Speak to you soon, bye!" Farah rambled on the phone, causing Max to facepalm with every word.

"Five minutes. Imagine living five minutes without him in your life. If you open a dictionary and flick to the word 'desperate', the definition is his name." Max tutted, growing more frustrated with the man who continued to bother her best friend.

"I really don't need him contacting me right now. It's ridiculous. I didn't ask—"

"Brian."

"What?" Farah practically gasped as she placed her phone back on her lap, trying to get the call away from her mind. She was living through so many nice memories in Los Angeles, the last thing she wanted was Hasan calling her.   Again.

"Just focus on Brian. Nice guy and you dig him. Way more than Hasan, anyway." Max had continued to be infuriated by the man who called. It wasn't as if it was something that had only just started occurring, Hasan *always* called.

"I don't—"

"Nuh-uh, I'm having this one."

Farah sighed, her phone vibrating in her lap. As she turned it around, she expected it to be Hasan, yet her heart skipped a beat at the sight of a text message from the contact with the guitar emoji beside the name.

It was comforting to know that despite her parents trying their hardest to set her up with the smarmy family friend, there was nothing more satisfying than getting to know Brian. He was everything that Hasan wasn't and that was comforting. Even still, Farah didn't want to be with Brian to defy her parent's ruling. She wanted to be with Brian because she *liked* him.

This was how it was supposed to be.

Even if she did feel comfortable around Brian, it was going to be hard getting used to being around him after the night they had together. Nobody could simply let that thought pass. She was going to think about their time together every time they saw one another. It would have been impossible not to.

Farah wasn't sure if that was a good thing or not.

Days the band spent together were always nice. A day they could spend together without the interruptions of fans or other forces. A day they could use to recuperate halfway through the tour. A day to relax.

For Brian, being stuck with the members of his band was difficult when the only person he could think about wasn't there. Instead, she was miles away because they had stupidly told them to continue driving without them. Brian regretted his decision, but he knew he couldn't force Max and Farah to stay with them all the time. It also wouldn't have been fair on the band.

"Hey, Brian? You okay, dude?" Russ squeezed Brian's shoulder enough to make him jump out of the trance he had been put in. His thoughts drifted to another place. He didn't know where, but anywhere Farah may have been.

"Y-yeah, I'm fine. Everything's good!" Brian smiled as he placed his hands inside of his jacket pocket. The same jacket that was draped over Farah's shoulders a few nights ago.

"You look spacey. Do you need me to call a medical professional?" Russ questioned with concern.

"The boy's lovesick. That's the only illness he has." Zoe laughed as she closed the trunk of the van, overhearing both Russ and Brian's conversation as they stood together overlooking the parking lot they were in.

Brian squinted and turned to stare at Zoe, slightly angered by her comment. She might have been right, but he didn't need it calling out for him.

"I'm *not*!"

"Who have you been texting? Grinning at your phone in the back of the van like a little kid who got told a dirty joke." Zoe scoffed with a laugh, straightening her leather jacket before placing her hands on her hips. Russ snorted, causing Brian to shoot him a glare.

"I was watching a movie!"

"Movies don't require you to tap on the screen with your stubby little thumbs, dingus."

"It was interactive!"

"What was the movie called?"

"Uh..." Brian suddenly flushed red. He scratched the back of his neck trying to look for an escape from the situation. "I can't remember. It wasn't good."

"What or *who* had you smiling so much, *loverboy*?" Zoe smirked as she walked over to Brian and began brushing his shoulders. Brian allowed her to for a moment before realising what she was doing and quickly swatting her away. He looked away, biting the inside of his mouth as he held his tongue.

He wanted to tell Zoe. He wanted to tell Russ...he even wanted to tell Catfish, despite him being currently in the van taking a nap. He couldn't. Out of respect for Farah, he had no right to tell his friends. They would only judge him for his actions. Although, by now when he was usually on tour he would have been with a couple of women and the band wouldn't be supportive of his pursuits, but they would be accepting of them. Just as they didn't judge him for his choices, he wouldn't judge them for theirs.

He hadn't even texted her much and even then, they had avoided a conversation about sex.

"I thought we were going zip-lining? Or are we not doing that anymore?" Brian tried to divert the attention away from himself. The last thing he wanted was for them all to continue to question him about the newfound relationship he shared with Farah.

"Nice save. I'll give you that one." Zoe winked as she flicked Brian on the shoulder, causing him to flinch. He held his shoulder with a pout. He knew Zoe loved him like a little brother, but she sure did have a funny way of showing it.

The activity the band had chosen to do was zip-lining which they had booked months in advance. As soon as they knew they would get a chance to stop in Denver, it was something they all wanted to do. It didn't matter that Brian was a little frightened of heights, they would do it anyway.

After a day spent with one another they all had the opportunity to laugh. Brian valued having the band around. He wished other than when they played together on stage, he got more time to spend with them. They truly were like the siblings he never had and each of them was important to him in similar yet different ways.

It had been great spending time with the band off stage, but that didn't last forever. It wasn't long before they would be playing on stage.

Despite being in contact with Brian the entire time, Farah had taken a step back and knew her best option was to do what Max had instructed her to do.

As much as Max wanted to hang out with the band after the show, she knew the safest thing for them all to do was to arrange something for the next day instead. She didn't want to bother them, especially on the day they had planned to spend together.

When they finally showed up in Denver they didn't see the band again until they were on the stage. Brian quickly scanned the audience for them, Farah had been the only thing on his mind for the past couple of days. Sure, spending time with the band was nice...but seeing Farah again was nicer.

A part of him was terrified she would have been afraid after what had happened between them. The last thing he wanted was to have made things awkward. They were going to be on the road together, so being close was something they had to put up with. Whether that was weird or not.

She looked up at the stage and watched him play just like the previous nights she had heard the same songs. However, this time felt different.

She felt as if she knew the person behind the voice. All she could imagine was his sexy slurs and his calloused fingers that slid so well up and down the guitar touching her body everywhere usually hidden by clothing.

She enjoyed watching him play...

OMAHA, NE

Straight after the show in Denver, Max and Farah had decided on travelling ahead. Setting off for their next location late at night when the show had ended. They stopped halfway to Omaha to stay the night before continuing the rest of their journey in the morning.

If the band got a day dedicated to their time together, it was about time Max and Farah hung out without the band. A day Farah could try and free her mind from the thoughts of Brian Blossom.

She hadn't spoken to Brian much other than over text since their last time together. It had made things difficult. For them both.

Farah was having thoughts about how her time with Brian could have affected their trip. How sleeping with the frontman of Social Dropouts was something she didn't regret, but something she couldn't stop debating in her mind.

Farah focused her attention on Max for their day in Omaha. They would have the opportunity to see the band in the evening. Perhaps she could have spoken to Brian then?

Max. Today was her day with Max and *Max only*. She had to focus her attention on something else.

Max had always been someone Farah could rely on no matter what. She felt guilty she hadn't spoken to Max about eve- rything that had happened on tour between her and Brian. Max had been having far too much fun with the rest of the band that it was hard to get her to escape from whatever chaos they were causing.

It was difficult for Max pretending she wore her mask well every day. Underneath the façade she wore, Max was just as anxious as Farah, maybe more.

Farah appreciated everything Max had done for her over the years. They looked out for one another and that was one of the biggest parts of why their relationship worked so well. They were different in lots of ways, yet deep down they could relate to one another on a personal level nobody else could reach.

"I can't believe we haven't been to a zoo yet." Max held onto the straps of her backpack as they walked through the con- crete grounds of the crowded zoo. It was a hot spot for tourists.

"The band probably would have liked to come..." Farah sighed, feeling a little bad they had left everyone out. They had gotten so used to the band tagging along that it was starting to feel weird without them. Things had been a little more distant since LA. Farah put herself to blame.

"Even if they did, I wouldn't let them come."

"How come?"

"This is Max and Farah day, remember?" Max pushed Farah in her shoulder slightly making her laugh at the touch. It was great to hang out with Max. "Besides, we'll see them at the show later."

"Time to have *Max*-imum fun." Farah brushed her shoul- der where Max had pushed her.

"Hey, it's only funny when I say it."

"But you didn't say it."

"Shut up. Look at those red pandas, aren't they cute? They're like little red cats." Max removed one hand from her backpack and pointed up towards the small creatures that were sitting in the trees opposite them, dipping in and out of a slum- ber. A large metal cage capturing them.

Farah had mixed feelings about zoos. Mostly political opinions about the welfare of the animals. Most zoos were serious about protecting animals and Farah was all for them existing. Other zoos treated animals poorly and that sickened her. Animals deserved to be free, not stuck in a cage for the entirety of their life.

"They're not like cats at all." Farah snorted.

"Do you think they would notice if I took one back to our dorm?"

"*I* would notice!"

"Yeah, but that's fine. Why wouldn't you want a red panda as a pet?"

"It would probably rip your face off."

"Y'know what? *Worth it.*" Max grinned, still pondering on ideas of how she could kidnap one of the adorable creatures without anyone noticing.

It was refreshing to be themselves without having to put on any kind of front for anyone else. It wasn't that either of them was pretending to be something they weren't but being their dorky selves all day was nice.

They walked around and saw every animal inside the zoo. It was a fun day. They both needed the release that hanging with the band couldn't provide them.

Farah texted Brian in the morning and told him she and Max were spending the day together and she wouldn't be able to text him. Farah wanted to make sure her full attention was on Max, feeling as if she had been neglecting her best friend duties when Brian was around. She couldn't think about him *all* the time. She needed to have time to process what had happened.

"This little guy *needs* a home." Max held up a plushie lion inside the gift shop they had decided to explore before heading back.

"Do you know how overpriced this store is?" Farah huffed, looking around the gift shop that was filled with everything from fridge magnets shaped as elephants to novelty beach towels with animal prints.

"I read on the door they put ten percent of every sale back into the park's upkeep." Max cocked an eyebrow, now holding the front legs of the plushie. She wanted nothing more than for the fluffy stuffed lion to have joined them on the rest of their trip.

"That's a lot."

"That means we should probably rescue more of them." Max turned towards the display of plushies and began to cradle an armful of lions, picking more of them up as Farah stared at her with wide eyes.

"What are you doing?" Farah questioned as she held out both of her hands, urging Max to stop as her body filled with trepidation. She didn't want to get kicked out of a zoo gift store.

"Saving an endangered species."

"Lions aren't endangered."

"Not anymore they're not."

"You can't buy a basket of overpriced stuffed animals."

"Farah, how could you say that? Just look at its face!" Max struggled to hold up one of the plushie lions to Farah's face. The plushie was somewhat inaccurate for the price point. Farah couldn't help but stare into its misaligned dead black eyes, causing her to pull an uncomfortable expression.

"Yeah, no."

"*Farah, please. I do not want to live out the rest of my life in a gift shop. Please buy me, I am very quiet, and I will live in the back of the car. My existence is pain, but you and Max will make my life better. Wouldn't you want that, Farah?*" Max spoke in a squeaky voice out the side of her mouth as she moved the stuffed animal in front of Farah's face.

"Not for—" Farah checked the tags. "*Thirty-five dollars?!*"

"Oh fuck, really?" Max immediately dropped the plushies back into the large plastic tub, still holding onto the one she was previously voicing and had started a personal bond with.

"Yikes."

Max turned the plushie lion around and stared into its eyes, the black beads looking back at her with vacancy. It didn't matter what anyone else thought. She wanted that lion.

"I *love* him. I will empty my bank account for this fluffy being. I shall name my new son *Bryan Dande-Lion*!" Max raised the lion above her head as a passer-by gave her a strange look.

"*What?*" Farah's expression dropped at the name, folding her arms over in the process.

"Don't worry, this Bryan is spelt with a 'ry'." Max rolled her eyes as she tucked the plushie under her arm.

"Really?" Farah shook her head; Max was taunting her.

"Hell yeah!" Max smirked as she held the plushie tightly. There was no way the stuffed animal *wasn't* going home with her.

Max swiftly purchased the toy, refusing to put it in her bag as she happily paraded it around under her arm as they walked around the park. Farah found it hilarious she didn't want to put the small lion anywhere that wasn't in her direct sight. She was convinced Max was going to take it to the show in the evening.

As it got closer to the time of the show, Max and Farah found themselves buying an iced coffee each at the café that was situated within the park. They had both decided on caramel frappes that were caked with sugar. They both needed the energy after travelling in the morning and spending the day exploring the park.

They sat together on a bench in the middle of the park, drinking their iced coffees and people-watching amongst the crowds. It was entertaining to do so until Farah thought about how much she wanted to check in on Max and make sure everything was okay.

Although Max hadn't been vacant, it felt as if Farah hadn't had the opportunity to reconnect in a while. She didn't want Max to feel left out of anything she was feeling and experiencing. They both loved one another regardless. They were best friends!

Farah desperately wanted to tell Max about her time with Brian, but admittedly, she was embarrassed. Anxiety told her it was a bad idea, despite knowing Max would have been okay with it. Would she? Farah had no idea.

"How are you finding it? The trip, I mean." Farah asked, looking over at Max who had placed Bryan Dande-Lion between them on the bench as if he was their newly adopted child.

Max had already asked the question of Farah the previous day, but now it was her time to host the interrogation.

"Don't you think that sometimes in these drinks they never break the ice up enough? It sits in the bottom and blocks the straw. It's pretty ass." Max poked the straw to the bottom of the plastic cup, trying her hardest to break the large blocks of ice that laid dormant.

"Max?"

"They put a stupid amount of syrup in to bury their mistakes, but I see them. The mermaid lady coffee shop does the same thing and it only serves to piss me off. Why can't they just make the ice smaller? It makes no sense!"

"*Max?*"

"Yeah?"

"Are you okay?"

"No. They need to blend their damn ice more." Max stared at her drink with frustration.

"That's not what I meant. I'm asking if you're okay, y'know, with the whole trip. You're having fun?" Farah sometimes found it hard to tell if Max was being genuine with her emotions. It felt as if Max had asked Farah about the trip a lot and yet Farah hadn't given her the same luxury.

"Farah, I'm having the time of my life. I have never been more satisfied with my existence than I am in this moment right here." Max smiled as she petted the mane on the head of the plushie lion.

"You're happy hanging with the band all the time, right?"

"Of course I am! I love them all so much. Zoe is super awesome, and we have loads of fun together. We're similar in a lot of ways and that's lit. Russ is hard to read, but he's a lot of fun! Catfish always has the best suggestions for everything. Plus, his name is Catfish and that's hilarious. Brian? Well, Brian is...he's cool. Weird, but cool. It's Brian Blossom!" Max expressed her love for each of them, never realising how little she knew about Brian. It wasn't as if she spent much time around him when he was always with Farah...

"That's amazing, Max. I'm glad you're having fun."

"Wait, you're having fun too? Aren't you? You said you were, but...I can't tell." Max questioned before taking a sip of the iced coffee and looking over at Farah awaiting an answer. It felt as if Max asked for this same reassurance every day.

"Yeah! We've been to so many cool places! I didn't think I'd enjoy the music, but here we are. I guess I'm emo now." Farah grinned, overly excited to have been sharing the trip with her best friend.

"Never say that again until you can name *one* Midwest emo band from the mid-nineties!" Max pointed towards her friend with a smirk.

This was the real test.

"*Sunny Day Real Estate*!" Farah blurted out without thinking.

Max's eyes lit up as her jaw dropped. She held both her hands above her head, trying not to drop the coffee.

"Yes! Fuck yeah, Farah! Fuck! *Yes*!" Max shouted a little too loudly as Farah laughed, hoping there were no children in their vicinity. "Where the hell did you learn that? Have you been *studying*?"

"Oh, you've mentioned them before. I *listen*!" Farah scoffed, she was happy with the knowledge she held on the subject after weeks of being around the people who lived and breathed the genre.

"That's rad, man. I love you." Max grinned, elated that her best friend had taken enough interest in the thing she loved.

"You're not too bad yourself." Farah chuckled, bunching her fist and gently pushing Max in the shoulder.

Max smiled, flicking the straw in the top of her cup as she looked down. Farah took a deep breath and looked around the park, it was a beautiful day.

"It was a bit scary at first."

"What?"

"Meeting the band." Max admitted with a small smile, Farah felt sympathy for Max as she spoke so suddenly. She knew social interaction could be hard for Max, but anything that included her interests made all that easier. That didn't mean it wouldn't have been exhausting.

"Really?"

"I'm just glad I was a little drunk."

"A *little*?"

"A *lot* drunk." Max corrected, shaking her head in the process.

282

"It's okay now though, you guys are all best buds. Isn't that cool?" Farah took a sip of her iced coffee, trying not to make a slurping noise as she pulled it through the straw.

"It's hella cool. I'm hoping that I've made some friends for life, but we'll see how that goes after the tour. I'm not looking forward to going back home." Max sighed, pushing the ice around at the bottom of her drink.

"How come? I thought you and your family were super close?"

"We are. Just...if I go home we won't be able to hang out!"

"Okay, that's adorable. However, we've lived together for years, and we still have a year to go. I'm sure you'll survive a couple of weeks without me."

"Will I though? You don't know what it's like to live with Dylan." Max grumbled, mentioning her youngest brother who spent most of his time hauled up in his bedroom gaming.

"I can make an educated guess."

"Dad said you can come and stay whenever you want."

"Max, I love you, but I've spent more time with you these past couple of months than I have myself." Farah snorted loudly; Max copied her action. Farah knew how Max usually reacted to change and a switch in routine. For the most part, not well, but Farah still needed time alone.

"Okay, okay, I should probably leave you alone for a while. You're going to miss me though."

"Yeah, probably." Farah smiled.

They sat there in silence for a moment, the stuffed animal sitting between them with lopsided eyes and a mess of yellow fluff. The perfect plushie lion. At least, that's what Max believed.

Farah wanted to speak about her time with Brian and how she felt. Anxiety had been burning away at her for the past couple of days. It hurt not telling anyone and the lack of being able to speak about it with Brian also didn't do her any favours.

It festered in her mind as her worries grew larger. Farah wasn't good with secrets. She told Max everything and she felt guilty for not sharing how she felt about Brian with her best friend. That's what best friends were for!

Max was always willing to speak about things with Farah and she had been selfish enough to ignore she could have been speaking about how she felt this whole time without feeling guilty. Brian wouldn't have minded, right? It was only Max.

It took a lot of guts to think of what to say. The words replayed in Farah's mind for a few moments as they sat in silence. She just had to say it.

"Hey, Max...can I tell you something?" Farah didn't bother to look up as she moved the straw around the cup, copying Max's action of trying to break up the ice at the bottom of the drink.

"What is it, Homeslice?"

"I haven't told anyone yet."

"I'm listening." Max assured, focusing all her attention on Farah.

Farah balanced the cup on her leg, finding the right words to speak without Max's judgement. There was going to have been some backlash to her words. She knew they would shock Max to the very core of her being. How was she going to cope?

"I've been spending a lot of time with Brian recently. We kind of just...end up together a lot." Farah tucked her loose hair behind her ear as she spoke, a little embarrassed by her speech.

"Oh yeah, *total accident.*" Max whispered under her breath, Farah choosing not to hear her words.

"He's really sweet. I don't think I've ever met a guy like him before. I think...I think I really like him." Farah opened her heart out to Max, speaking softly as she spoke so fondly of Brian.

"Oh yeah, we all knew that." Max shrugged before slurping on her iced coffee.

"What?" Farah gave Max a look of sheer distaste.

"We just leave you to it because you're totally into one another. It's pretty sickening seeing you guys doing subtle little gestures that *everyone* can see. Oh god, the *looks*. It's like you're both incapable of paying attention to anyone else. I have never seen you pine over someone so bad, Rah. It's actually kind of adorable." Max rolled her eyes with a small smirk, Farah's jaw becoming slack.

"So, you all just...*know?*" Farah could feel her face heating up. It was embarrassing, to say the least.

"You probably shouldn't have made it so *obvious.*" Max winked before sipping on the coffee.

"Does everyone know we had sex...?" Farah's eyes widened, her thoughts slipping from her mouth.

Max's face dropped before choking on the drink, aggressively coughing into her arm as Farah watched in horror.

"W-What?! Y-you had *sex!?*" Max gasped in shock, barely making her speech through little coughs to regain her breath.

"Wait. Isn't that what you meant? You didn't *know?*" Farah suddenly placed the drink to the side of the bench, beginning to run her fingers through her hair as she spoke. The panic had set in.

"No! I was thinking more along the lines of a crush, not— *Farah!*" Max groaned, completely in shock with her best friend for a couple of reasons. The first being her friend's inability to tell her what she was doing with the frontman of her favourite band. The second being—*what the fuck, Farah?*

"What? I-It just happened! We had been spending a lot of time together and—"

" *When?* When in the *fuck* did this happen?"

"The first time was—"

"The *first* time?" Max raised her eyebrows, unable to comprehend what Farah was telling her.

"Oh no, this is bad." Farah pushed her glasses away from her face as she covered her eyes in embarrassment.

"How many *times* have you had *sex* with *Brian Blossom?*" Max shuffled closer to Farah and practically whispered his name. It didn't sound right.

"What's considered a *not-so-great* answer?"

"Anything above zero."

"Two? I mean, it was twice in one night. Does that count as one or two?"

"Two, Farah. That counts as two." Max pressed her lips into a thin line as she attempted to fathom what her best friend had been doing when she wasn't around. She was more than expectant of Farah perhaps having kissed Brian a few times, maybe even fooled around, but having *sex*? That was a whole new level.

Farah was beyond embarrassed. This certainly wasn't something she wanted to admit to Max, especially not so soon. She felt stupid to have misinterpreted what Max was trying to get across.

"Max...what have I done?" Farah whimpered, unable to look back at her best friend the same way she did before the awkward conversation. Max laughed; unsure what Farah was talking about.

"What do you mean?" Max chuckled, picking up Bryan Dande-Lion from between them and sitting him down on her lap so she could comfort her best friend.

"Did I mess up? What if my parents find out? Is this going to get me kicked out of college? He's *famous*, right? What if I end up in a magazine and my parents see it in the store? Television? Do MTV still report on this stuff? Did they *ever* report on this stuff? What if—" Farah began to spiral. There were so many things that ran through her head.

What would people think of her if they found out what she had done?

"Woah! Slow down! Did you commit arson too? Because that's what it sounds like!" Max attempted to calm Farah the best she could.

"N-no!"

"What's the problem? You just said you *liked* him!"

"I do like him, but you were just acting like this is a terrible thing!" Farah breathed deeply, intensely confused by Max's display of various emotions.

"Sorry, I was just shocked that my *best friend* is sleeping with the frontman of my *favourite* band. Y'know...*Brian fuckin' Blossom.*" Max gasped once again, impressed by Farah's efforts. She hadn't expected this to come from the trip.

"Don't say his name like that." Farah groaned, burying her head in her hands again.

"Why? You don't like it when I put the word 'fucking' and 'Brian Blossom' in a sentence together? Go figure." Max snorted, unable to control herself.

"Oh, come on! Max!"

"Sorry, you totally walked into that one. Look, all I'm saying is this isn't a bad thing. If you like one another, then what's the problem? Who gives a shit if it's Brian Blossom or some dude from our building? But not Trevor—fuck Trevor. Y'know what I mean, though! As long as you're happy!" Max was confused why Farah was so concerned about sleeping with the frontman of the band. Sure, it was a bit different from what she had been used to, but it was hard to deny how much they liked one another.

It was Farah's fault for being so awkward about it.

Farah held her hands in her lap, beginning to pick at the corners of her fingernails to get herself out of the situation. There was a lot on her mind when it came to Brian Blossom that it was near impossible to concentrate on anything else.

Max had heard rumours about Brian's experience with women, then again, she had heard a *lot* of rumours about Brian Blossom. People always had something to say or unnecessarily complain about.

"I think he wants to hang out more." Farah shrugged.

"Like...go on dates?"

"We hung out in Austin together and that was super sweet."

"Please don't tell me you slept together in my car." Max crossed her fingers and scrunched her eyes together.

"No! We did go and get ice cream. It was really...nice. I liked being with him."

"Aw man, my best friend Farah, sleeping with the frontman of Social Dropouts. Man, I love you. You're so cool." Max grinned; pleased Farah had warmed up to the band. It wasn't in the way Max had expected.

"I'm not—"

"Give me a rating. A solid five? You should leave an online review for Brian Blossom's peen."

"Max..." Farah grumbled at Max's inappropriate comment.

"What's the score?"

"I don't have anything to compare it to." Farah blushed as she looked away. The trip was turning out to have been a lot more intense than she had expected.

"Oh, right."

"Yeah..."

"But..."

"It was good." Farah spoke quickly, turning away from Max. She had successfully managed to pry it from her.

"That's what I wanted to hear. Get in there, Brian." Max giggled as Farah suddenly regretted even opening her mouth.

"You can't tell them." Farah shook her head, anxiety flooding through her at the thought of the band finding out. Even if they already thought they knew, she didn't want them to have any confirmation on the subject.

"I won't tell them, but they already know." Max shook her head.

"They don't *know*."

"You guys thought you were slick, but Brian's a huge *flirt*. He's not very subtle about much and neither are you with your hair adjustments and red cheeks." Max bluntly confirmed, shocking Farah slightly with her deadpan expression.

"Oh."

"I don't know if they really *know*, but I'd be surprised if they didn't."

"You can't tell Brian either. I haven't spoken to him about it."

"Dude, I never even get a chance to talk to the man. He's always with you and now I know *why*." Max tipped her cup of coffee up to Farah, gesturing for them to tap their drinks together. Farah didn't latch onto the suggestion.

"Right..." Farah sighed.

"It's okay, dude. Your secret is safe with me." Max placed her hand on Farah's shoulder with a smile.

Farah looked over at her best friend and returned the expression.

Farah felt as if a sudden burden had been lifted. As much as she was worried about telling Max, it didn't feel as if it had changed much.

In the back of Farah's mind, she was convinced the kind of relationship she had been developing with Brian was the sort that didn't last much past tour. It made her upset to think about, she didn't want to have developed all these feelings to have them thrown away. That wasn't fair on either of them.

Farah hoped she wasn't going to have been treated like a phase. Brian had been convincing in telling her she had been a new experience. She still wasn't sure what that meant for her.

Max was pleased to have spent the whole day hanging out with Farah at the zoo. It was wholesome fun and Max was pleased to have made a new friend. Bryan Dande-Lion took his place in the backseat of Max's car. She secured him into the seat, tightening his seatbelt and making sure he stuck to the health and safety regulations of driving. Farah rolled her eyes at the sight.

They had adopted a furry son together. Farah knew the plushie would without a doubt live in the car for the rest of the tour and beyond.

With Bryan Dande-Lion happily strapped in the back of the car, they made their way to the venue. They wondered what the band had been up to throughout the day, but Farah wasn't sure as she had kept to her non-texting ban when it came to Brian.

"When are you going to come and mosh with me?" Max questioned as they stood at the back of the venue. Max swung her arms back and forth as she asked, excited for the show.

"When you can get enough alcohol in me that I won't notice being stuck inside of a human pinball machine." Farah scoffed.

"You drank in LA, right?"

"A little bit."

"Enough to sleep with Brian though, huh?"

"I wasn't drunk in my decision making!" Farah scowled.

"Okay! Okay!" Max laughed, finding out it was a sensitive subject to tease her about.

Max continued to swing her arms back and forth, looking around the room. The venue was average size and just under one thousand capacity. There weren't that many people there yet, it wasn't very often they sold out their shows.

Farah glanced behind her at the merch stand. She had never looked at everything the band had on sale. From the t-shirts Brian wore or the CDs and vinyl records that were available to purchase. There was a little bit of everything for anyone who wanted it.

"I can't believe you haven't bought everything on their merch table yet." Farah shook her head as she looked at the merchandise they were selling. The band relied on the sales a lot and if a member of the band wasn't behind the stand selling it all it was either a worker from the venue or someone Stan had hired for a few hours to give them a hand. Either way, Farah always saw people walking out of the venue with new Social Dropouts t-shirts or records.

"I've been eyeing up the tour t-shirt the whole time." Max pointed towards the incredibly simplistic design of the band's initials on the left side of the chest and on the flip side of the t-shirt, there was a list of all the dates on the tour. It would have been a nice item to have as a memory of their travels.

"I like the hoodie." Farah pointed up at the Social Dropouts branded hoodie. Once again, a simplistic design of a black hoodie, the initials of their band name on the left side of the chest and their 2020 tour dates on the back.

"You should ask your *boyfriend* and see if he'll get it for you."

"Max..." Farah gritted her teeth together and grumbled.

"I'm kidding. Just use one of his." Max shrugged, continuing to tease. It was too easy.

"I'm regretting telling you." Farah admitted, looking towards Max with an expression of concern.

"No, you're not. You like the comic relief."

"I think I'm going to buy a hoodie." Farah decided, wanting nothing more than to think about purchasing the overpriced clothing. She knew if any of the band had seen her buy it, it would have been likely for them to have just given it to her, but she didn't want that. She was willing to support the band.

"Good choice." Max confirmed, watching Farah step over to the merch stand. It was currently being run by someone she didn't recognise, likely they were someone from the venue.

Farah purchased the black Social Dropouts hoodie and threw it over her head. It was slightly oversized, but not by much. It was comfortable to wear and reminded her a lot of her college hoodie, except this one was a lot cooler to be in at the show. At least until Max told her about the assholes that disagreed with wearing merchandise from the band you were seeing to their shows.

As the band played and the venue filled, the room got hotter and Farah regretted buying the hoodie at the beginning of the show and not the end. Either way, it was comfortable and she was willing to have made the sacrifice to wear it. She could have taken it off, but the commitment was already there.

Farah and Max stuck around for as long as they were allowed to until security came to talk to them. It wasn't long before the band came out of hiding and found their way down from the stage to meet their friends and fans. Max immediately skipped over to the band to tell them about their time at the zoo.

"Nice hoodie." Brian winked as he noticed Farah in the Social Dropouts merchandise.

It was Brian Blossom with the bleach blonde hair and distracting green eyes. He was standing in front of her in a closed short-sleeved red flannel shirt, showing off the tattoos on his arms. He shook his head to shuffle the placement of his hair on his forehead.

He looked just as good as he had done in the bed beside her in LA.

"Oh, yeah, I don't like the band that much. The design was cool though." Farah teased as she pointed towards the band logo on the front of her new hoodie.

"Oh really? That's a bold fashion statement. Shame it doesn't have a yellow smiley face with crosses for eyes. All the kids dig that design despite never listening to the band." Brian laughed at his poor joke; Farah had no idea what he was referring to but decided to play along. He noticed Farah's lack of laughter before continuing. "I could have just given that to you..."

"I wanted to support you and the band." Farah pulled on the bottom of the hoodie, showing off the design.

Brian didn't want to admit he only received eighteen dollars from the sale of the hoodie and even then, that would have been split between four people.

It had been the first time since LA they had been in the vicinity of one another. It felt weird not mentioning it, but why would they have brought that up in casual conversation? That didn't seem like the right thing to do. Even Farah knew that.

"Thanks. I'm sure I'll make it up to you soon." Brian kept his hands in his jean pockets as he grinned, trying not to blush as he kicked his feet underneath him.

Max and Farah had no plans to stay with the band that evening. They had agreed to spend the remainder of their evening in their motel room watching a trashy movie they had found online. It sounded like a great plan and the best way to finalise a Max and Farah day.

Farah was happy to stick to that, despite how much she may have wanted to spend time with Brian. She just wanted to...*talk.*

Max knew about them. It would have been hard to hide how often she wanted to spend time with him now she knew. She had to talk to him about it, but today wasn't that day.

"Dude, we've got to head back so we can fall asleep watching that shitty movie." Max threw her arm around Farah unexpectedly, causing her to jump after being mesmerised by Brian.

Max exchanged glances with Brian, he was still convinced she was put off by the way he acted in LA by the pool. Thinking back on it, he had been a little *weird.* Farah was worried Max may have said something about their relationship before she was ready, but she chose to stay quiet.

"Yeah! I'm sorry we can't hang out tonight." Farah sighed as she held up her hand to wave. She was going to be dragged away by Max any second.

"It's cool. We should all do something tomorrow though. Text us some ideas!" Brian suggested. It had been a few days since they had spent time together and it would have been ideal with the tour ending.

"Oh, Bri Bri, I have *so many* ideas!" Max laughed as she pulled Farah a little closer. Farah gritted her teeth.

"We'll see you tomorrow!" Farah waved as Max led her away from the conversation.

"Bye." Brian half-smiled and waved as he watched them both leave the venue. It had been a short interaction, but one he felt he needed.

He could feel the disconnect between him and Farah already. This was his worst nightmare. He didn't want things to be weird between them and his past experiences told him that sex never solved these issues. It wasn't a sure thing to get someone closer.

Brian clenched his fists in his pockets and sighed, the venue feeling a little more suffocating than usual. He was sure he had messed things up. It was all he ever seemed to do. It felt as if she didn't want him to be around and that made...sense.

He didn't want things to be awkward with her, but that was exactly what he had done.

He thought about whether he should have texted her. Something. Anything. He didn't want to come across as desperate, but he needed to know if she still wanted to be with him in any capacity.

It was going to play on his mind all night and day until he finally got the chance to speak to her again. Even then, he wasn't sure what he was going to say.

He hoped his big mouth wouldn't spill his guts and say something stupid.

He just wanted to be with her.

DES MOINES, IA

"Woah, this one is so...*cool*." Catfish pointed up to the black and white quilted blanket hanging from the ceiling in such a way to present its beauty.

"Whose idea was it to go here?" Zoe leaned over to Max and whispered loud enough for everyone else to hear.

"Who the hell wouldn't want to go to a quilt museum?" Max shrugged as she glanced over to Zoe with a small pout.

"We travelled an hour in the opposite direction for...*this*."

Nobody wanted to go to a quilt museum and yet there they all were...at the International Museum of Quilts. A world-wide selection of quilts from a vast variety of cultures.

It was a suggestion from Catfish. It hadn't been one anyone had taken seriously until they were at the front of the building buying tickets to the most immersive experience of their entire life. They thought it would have been a funny trip to take, but the joke had quickly worn off.

"I appreciate this." Russ pointed up to one of the quilts on the wall. A bizarre stitching of a cow that nobody thought looked like a cow, that was just what the sign said.

Brian and Farah stood by one another behind everyone else. Farah was in a weird headspace and the quilts weren't helping. As much as she was enjoying being with everyone, there were still so many things that had happened over the last couple of days that were hard to comprehend.

The feeling was starting to sink in. She had slept with Brian Blossom and everything felt...strange.

Neither Farah nor Brian wanted to be awkward around one another. They were trying their hardest to break through that barrier. They had to talk about it. A conversation they thought they had already been through and yet things weren't any less difficult to grasp.

Brian stood beside Farah with his hands in the pockets of his black denim jacket as per usual, rocking slowly on his heels as he dramatically looked around the room at all the quilts that were both on the walls and hanging from the ceiling.

"I thought you liked museums."

"Yeah, I do." Farah sighed as she held tightly onto a bottle of water.

"What's wrong with this one?"

"When I say I like museums, I'm talking about museums that extensively express the ins and outs of culture and history." Farah folded her arms and looked around the room.

"This is culture *and* history."

"Yeah...but they're quilts."

"Oh." Brian was confused.

Brian was desperate to speak to Farah about the events of the party. Sure, they had brief conversations with one another, but they hadn't mentioned what they had done. They had slept together.

Twice.

Farah was still a little torn. Despite it being one of the best nights she had ever experienced, that didn't mean she wasn't feeling embarrassed about being with Brian in any casual capacity afterwards. How was she able to hold a conversation with him that didn't revolve around the one thing she couldn't stop thinking about?

It made her feel insecure about herself. Something inside of her was telling her that being with Brian was a bad idea. What if *he* was the one ticking the boxes?

She knew she couldn't think that way.

"Next!" Catfish steered everyone into the next room, a little too enthusiastic about the quilts.

Farah didn't even bother to go through to the other room to follow everyone, slumping herself down on one of the benches and looking around at the exhibits in front of her. They were just as boring sitting down as they were standing up. It annoyed Farah how culturally informative everything in the museum was, but for some reason, she couldn't get over the barrier of them being attached to quilts that excelled her boredom into something near intolerable.

"Do you want to go and see the quilts in the other room?" Brian asked the question, seeing how uninterested Farah was in the museum. It didn't seem like the sort of thing that would have made Farah bored, but it wasn't holding her interest today.

That or it was *him* that was cause for her disengagement.

"Can I say no?" Farah laughed as she looked up at Brian. He kept his hands inside his jacket pocket as he shrugged and sat down beside her. He was also a firm believer in the museum being just as boring sitting down as it was standing up.

"Sure. Just don't say it too loudly...the quilts might hear." Brian whispered with a small wink, causing Farah to react with a titter.

"You're right. I wouldn't want to hurt their feelings."

They sat beside one another as the moment passed. After spending a night so intimately, it felt strange to Brian to have been in contact with the person he had slept with.

Farah had just lost her virginity to a man she barely knew. Yet, she *did* know him. She knew him more than any other guy she had been with, despite only being around him for a little over two weeks.

It wasn't as if she had been with many other guys, unlike Brian and his vast amount of 'experience' with other women.

He had no experience in *this* though. He had no experience in what came with blushing over a partner. Allowing him to stay until the morning after. Cuddling. Kissing. Holding hands. This was so different to what he was used to and every second of the day his heart ached for more. He craved the feeling of the connection he had made with Farah.

He couldn't stop thinking about *her*. She was intelligent, brave, witty and beautiful. He adored her smile and the way she giggled. He felt as if he could tell her anything, even his darkest secrets and she wouldn't judge him. He wanted to listen to her rant about her strong opinions and hobbies all day because he yearned for the sound of her voice and the knowledge on her passions. He wanted to know her better. She made him feel safe with her compassion and hints of aspiration of permanence. Their situations were vastly different and yet they could relate to one another on a personal level he had never reached with anyone before. She was perfect in every way in Brian's eyes, and he knew after the tour he would be at a loss without her. He couldn't ruin that.

"Are you okay?" Brian looked around the room in the museum before focusing his attention back onto Farah. He held his hands on his knees and tapped his fingers against the holes in his jeans.

"Yeah, why wouldn't I be?" Farah smiled at Brian. He wasn't convinced it was genuine, but he couldn't tell. Brian didn't know how to respond; he didn't want to make things any more awkward between them both.

"You've been kind of quiet since LA and I'm wor—"

"It's fine."

"You can tell me if it isn't." Brian bit his lip.

Farah held the water bottle between her legs, casually flicking the top open with her thumb and then closing it repeatedly. It was the only satisfaction she had away from the spot she had been put on.

She felt the anxiety rise within herself. A deep fear she would hurt Brian if she wasn't careful.

"I feel weird."

"Oh." Brian felt his chest tighten.

"It's just...n-new." Farah wasn't sure what she was trying to say as she stuttered.

Brian had been amazing in everything he had done and that to her was *new*. It was a weird experience, but one she was welcoming. Even if she was finding it hard to get her head around.

"Is 'new' bad?" Brian's began to nervously play with his hands.

"No, not at all. I've never been with a guy before. Not like—" Farah blushed, cutting herself off. Brian suddenly realised the point she was trying to get across, noticing how much he could relate to her words.

"I get it. It's new. It's new for me too." Brian looked over at Farah with a smile creeping up his lips. "I-It's okay to talk about it. If you want to..."

Farah wasn't sure how much she believed Brian when it came to his pursuits. Everything she knew about him and how skilled he had been all pointed to something incredibly different. Farah suspected this wasn't new territory for Brian...except it was.

"Don't you think we're moving a little *fast*?" Farah continued to play with the water bottle as she looked over at Brian, concern in her eyes.

"This is the longest relationship I've ever had."

"Right." Farah felt goose pimples on her arm at the word *relationship*. It was a strange thing to call it, but she knew what he meant.

They hadn't even been on a date. As far as Farah knew, this wasn't the order things happened. This wasn't the order she was used to. It felt as if they had already skipped so many stages in what she imagined would make a healthy relationship.

Was there a rulebook for this sort of thing?

Brian didn't think they were moving too fast.

"I'm not good with this stuff. I'm sorry. I'm *really* trying!" Brian felt nervous, he didn't want Farah to feel as if he was pushing her. That was never his intention.

"Oh no, it's not you. I have no idea what I'm doing..." Farah chuckled lightly, placing her hand on his arm without hesitation. It wasn't just Brian that had been taking things a little quicker than expected. Farah was a part of this too.

"Me neither. Isn't that supposed to be part of the fun though?" Brian smirked, getting back the happy expression he always seemed to get when Farah was around.

"I guess? I'm not sure."

"Hey, maybe we could figure it out together?" Brian suggested, keeping an eye on Farah's hand she had placed on his arm.

"I feel like such a loser." Farah blushed as she covered her face so Brian couldn't see her sudden change in expression. She felt embarrassed by everything, but that didn't mean she wasn't happy it happened.

Brian was quick to turn on the bench, lifting his leg onto the seat so he could face her. He disliked it when she spoke down on herself. It looked as if she was going to cry, and Brian wanted to do everything he could to prevent it. He couldn't help but feel as if it somehow spiralled down to being his fault.

"I don't think you're a loser! Why would you say that?" Brian panicked, unintentionally returning the favour of placing both his hands on her. One hand covering the top of her own and the other resting gently on her arm.

"It's silly."

"It's not silly! You can talk to me about anything. Really." Brian assured, his warm and comforting presence being one Farah could have never matched with anyone else in her life. She could get used to his emotional honesty.

Farah looked up at him, feeling ridiculous for getting upset about something she no longer had any control over.

"I just feel so embarrassed about it all." Farah sighed, trying her hardest to phrase it in a way that didn't belittle Brian's feelings.

Brian looked around the room, making sure nobody else was in their vicinity to hear what he had to say.

"About the...sex?" Brian whispered, only causing Farah to blush further.

"A little."

"We don't have to do that ever again if it made you feel uncomfor—"

"It didn't."

"I just don't want you to think that I'm hanging around just so we can have sex."

"I don't think that."

"I mean, I *do* want to have sex with you again—*someday.* If you wanted to then maybe we could? I don't think you need to mark it in a calendar or anything, but—" Brian sweated out his words as Farah's eyes widened. That was verbal confirmation he wanted to have sex *again.*

Farah stared at him as he threaded his fingers through his hair nervously with a small chuckle to accompany.

"Shit, I'm terrible at this. I'm so sorry. J-just, that's not why I want to hang out." Brian felt his words were falling short as he had a sudden case of verbal diarrhoea. "I'm sorry that happened a little...*quick.* I want to spend more time with you, like we did in Austin! I want us to watch a movie or something. Anything! I just want to spend some time getting to know you better."

Farah could feel his thumb brushing softly against the top of her hand. She smiled at the memory of their time together before things started to get a little complicated. Holding hands, kissing and eating ice cream was all part of their time in Austin and she had savoured the memory unlike anything else before it.

"I'd like that." Farah smirked, glancing back down at his hand on hers. She flipped her hand over so they could be palm to palm. Brian smiled at her as he held her hand at an awkward angle.

The way Brian smiled and the way his eyes lit up whenever he saw her made Farah feel special. It was nice to have someone look at her the way Brian did. Even when they had sex he had made sure she was comfortable and reassured her with how beautiful she was. She had never been a fan of her body and yet Brian had given her newfound confidence she had never considered before.

She was excited to spend more time with Brian before the tour was over. It wasn't long before all the shows would have been over, and Farah would travel back home to spend the remainder of her summer with her parents before going back to college for her last year.

She was interested to know what her parents would have thought of the quilt museum they were currently in. It was something different, but history regardless.

As much as Brian wanted to kiss Farah as she sat on the bench and looked back at him with a smirk he knew he couldn't make his move when the band and Max were nearby, ready to catch them at any moment.

"Are you guys coming?" A voice sounded on their way out from the other room.

Brian immediately sprung into a sitting position, taking his hands away from Farah as he balanced them back on his knees and swallowed his nerves. Farah sat in silence, placing her hands on the water bottle as Zoe stepped in from the other room and exchanged glances between them both.

"If you say anything about sleeping birds again, I will never forgive you." Farah whispered out the side of her mouth as Zoe approached.

"Got it." Brian whispered back in confirmation.

"Y'all are missing out on the quilts, come on! If I have to suffer, you do too." Zoe groaned as she gestured for them to join the rest of the band in their pursuit of looking at more quilts.

Brian and Farah smiled at one another before standing up and following Zoe.

Farah was pleased Brian wanted them to hang out more. That meant getting to spend more time with him before the tour was over and as the days passed by quickly, every second counted. Farah was having a good time. There was one other thing he had said that stuck to her mind like glue.

He had mentioned he wanted to have sex with her again. Sure, that was something he wanted to do, but it wasn't something that defined their relationship. It was simply a bonus.

He was *attracted* to her. Mentally and physically. It filled Farah with a confidence she didn't know had been within her this whole time. Where was it when she needed it in the past? The times she had been with guys in college. There were so many opportunities that if she was a little more confident she could have experienced her first time sooner and not inside of a recording studio.

Yikes.

The sort of sex she had participated in was the kind of thing she thought about late at night, not something she ever would have believed to have happened in reality.

The second time? The most intimate experience of her entire life. Exploration and adoration. Farah had valued their time together.

Brian had valued it too. Sure, he had sex plenty of times in the past, but none of them had been *romantic*. He had never shared that level of intimacy with someone before.

301

It felt as if he had allowed Farah to see inside of his soul. He was once an empty shell of a man and yet at that moment, he felt complete. He was *complete* with her.

At least, that's how he felt. That's how he had felt the night he had to stand up on stage and look down on the crowd. It was a small venue Stan had booked for them.

Brian stood in front of the crowd for the thirteenth time throughout the tour, everything came so naturally to him. Everything from the lyrics he shouted to the fluid movements he performed on stage. The band were professionals, and they didn't have a shadow of a doubt about their ability to perform.

Brian looked back at the crowd, getting ready to start the next song as he pressed his foot against the pedal to change the tone. He noticed Max in the crowd holding her hand above her head to get his attention, Brian nodded back at her in confirmation he had seen her support. Max threw him some finger guns in response.

He scanned the crowd for Farah, assuming she would have been at the back of the venue. He couldn't see her, but he knew she was there. As someone who hadn't enjoyed his music at first, it still surprised him she had no problem in showing up to his performances every night.

As the show ended, people began to leave the venue, allowing Farah to make her way to the front. Usually, the band would be there to greet them, but this time there was nobody there.

Admittedly, anxiety ran through Farah as she thought about all the things that could have caused the band to not ever want to speak with her or Max again. It would have been Farah's fault for sleeping with Brian.

As she got closer, Farah noticed Max in an altercation with a member of security.

"Hey! What the hell do you think you're doing?" A bellowing voice sounded over the speakers playing a pop song completely unrelated to the music that had just played.

"Oh, nothing! I *know* these guys." Max shouted back, a security guard gripping on the back of the flannel that was wrapped around her waist, attempting to pull her off the stage. Her leg was in the air as she was already in the process of lifting herself onto the raised platform.

"That's what they all say." The security guard groaned as he pulled her off the stage. Max found her footing, stood in front of him and folded her arms. She shook her head.

"You are making a grave mistake, Pal."

"Was that a threat?"

"N-no. More of a...friendly reminder? Like when your calendar app reminds you you're well over the age of forty and are yet to have that vital prostate exam. We all know it's embarrassing, but it's for your own good." Max chuckled nervously as she scratched the back of her neck, internally praying the band would turn around and see her struggling with security.

"Go on, the show's over. Get out of here before I drag you out."

"You *did* get that prostate exam, huh? Traditionally they use a finger, but it seems like you still have the gigantic *stick* they used stuck up your *ass*." Max snorted, pushing her luck as the security guard's expression dropped.

"Right, that's it."

"Max! What's going on?" Farah walked over to defuse the situation.

"Oh, this *dickcheese* won't let me see our friends." Max pointed behind her to the security guard who was holding onto the back of her t-shirt, more than prepared to kick her out of the venue.

"This *your* friend?" The security guard cocked an eyebrow towards Farah, holding Max in front of him. He was a tall man with a broad build, his authority shown through a fluorescent vest and earpiece.

"Um...yes?" Farah gritted her teeth together. "I am so sorry, Sir. We just want to get to our friends on stage. We're with the band." Farah apologised. She wasn't going to let Max out of her sight, it seemed as if she had a little bit too much to drink.

"Come on, it's time to leave." The security guard ignored Farah's request; one he had heard a million times from people wanting to get close to the bands. It was a security risk for sure.

"We're V.I.G's. Very Important Groupies!"

"Max, no!" Farah scowled, sweating nervously. "W-we're not groupies. We're just fans. F-friends! We're their friends!" She assured the security who was more than confused with the two women. Farah thought about her comment...would *she* have been considered a groupie now?

She shook the thought from her head.

Farah wasn't ready to leave the venue, they had already planned to meet up with the band afterwards. It was strange Brian hadn't come down off the stage and either spoken to fans or greeted her or Max as he had done in the past. They hadn't seen any of the other members either.

Just as bad thoughts began to run through her mind she noticed the back of Brian's red flannel just past the side of the stage. She dragged Max to the left to get a better look to confirm her suspicions. The security guard watched them carefully.

"Brian!" Farah shouted to the best of her abilities, but to no avail.

"Brian Blossom you beautiful bastard!" Max screeched to get his attention. This time, they were successful.

Brian stepped back to get a better look at whoever it was shouting his name. By the side of the stage stood Farah, Max and a grumpy looking security guard. His face lit up as soon as he saw them, practically jogging to the edge.

"What are you guys doing? Come on! There's someone I want you to meet." Brian kneeled and spoke to them both, Farah glancing up with a look of concern.

Someone he wanted them to meet? That didn't sound good. Although, from the look on his face she was sure it wouldn't have been anyone...bad. Could it? They were important enough for Brian and the band to skip out on packing their gear away straight after the show.

"Cool. New friends." Max slurred.

"Do we just...come up?" Farah questioned, looking at the stage she would have made an ass out of herself if she were to climb.

"Yeah, sure. Come on!" Brian held out his hand, ready to hoist them up onto the stage. Sure, they could have taken the steps around the side but that would have been too easy. It also meant Brian wouldn't have been able to offer to hold Farah's hand, even if just for a split second.

Max was the first one to reach out her hand for Brian to grab, allowing him to pull her up to the stage. Max immediately turned around and laughed at the security guard who was in the process of shaking his head with disapproval.

"Suck on those eggs, *son*! Friends with the band!" Max tittered, pointing down at the man in the fluorescent jacket.

"I can bring you right back down."

"Max, don't push it." Farah scowled, the last thing she wanted was a further altercation with the venue's security.

Brian reached down and held out his hand for Farah. She didn't hesitate to grab on, feeling his warm hand in her grip once again. Brian pulled her up onto the stage and held her a little closer than he had done with Max. It wasn't a mistake.

"Thank you, Mister Security." Brian nodded down at the man, still holding onto Farah's hand.

"Thank you!" Farah smiled politely.

"Thanks, professor dickwad of the security squad!" Max winked as she stuck both middle fingers up at the man who glowered back at them all.

Farah shook her head rapidly as she pushed Max's hands down so she was no longer making the crude statement. She used one hand, keeping the other hooked around Brian's fingers. Brian snorted at Farah's efforts to control her best friend's drunken behaviour as Max laughed at her panic before heading backstage. The security guard dismissed himself. There wasn't much he could have done.

"Here, come on! There really is someone I want you to meet. You're going to love her!" Brian grinned, keeping hold of Farah's hand as he practically dragged her across the stage with excitement. Max was quick to disappear backstage.

Her?

She would have been lying if she said uncomfortable thoughts hadn't crossed her mind.

Farah didn't question being led by Brian, happy enough to have followed as she held onto his hand. She had been craving his touch. She couldn't stop thinking about it. About him.

"Okay, sure!" Farah chose to believe his excitement as she followed.

As she entered the room at the back of the venue, her jaw dropped. It was someone she only recognised from the music streaming apps she used.

A beautiful figure stood before her, long wavy blond hair flowed past a brown leather jacket. She looked taller than her pictures, but that was likely due to the heels she was wearing that added a couple of inches. Her lips were doused in red lipstick and she sported a grin showing off her straight teeth. She was gorgeous and so was her voice...

A voice she had heard plenty of times on the radio.

Farah's jaw dropped when she saw who had been waiting backstage.

"This is Farah and that's Max. They're both following us on tour and it's super cool!" Brian grinned, excited to show the woman standing in front of them their new friends.

"*Bailey Craig*!?" Farah gasped at the sight, instantly recognising the person in front of her.

Pop-folk sensation Bailey Craig was standing little under six foot away. Never in Farah's life would she have ever imagined meeting one of the very few artists she listened to whilst studying. She had caught her music on the radio once and listened ever since.

"Wow, it's really nice to meet you both! Following a band? That takes a lot of dedication." Bailey grinned, excited to meet them both.

Farah balled her fists and brought them to her chest. She didn't want to be starstruck, but she could feel her hands shaking from anxiety. Was this how Max had felt when she had met Brian? Brian would have been considered famous, but not *Bailey Craig* famous.

"Um, I don't think you understand. I-I have every single one of your albums saved on my phone. I always play through them when I'm studying. I can't tell you how many times those albums have seen me through the night. I love everything that you've created—" Farah began, shocked she was stuttering in front of the current music sensation that appeared in nearly every music recommendation. The new big thing.

Farah loved Bailey's music, it was a lot calmer than whatever it was Brian and the rest of his band played. Farah couldn't have studied to Social Dropouts' music, or at least she had never tried to do so.

Max stood off to the side and squinted, trying her hardest to figure out who the person Farah was swooning over was.

"*Whomst the fuck—That's* Bailey Craig!?" Max whispered out the side of her mouth to Brian who glanced over at her in slight shock. Farah had spoken about her and Max had heard a few songs, but she wasn't a *fan* like her best friend was.

"Yep! That's Bailey!" Brian gestured towards Bailey; Farah stood beside her still in the process of drooling over the musician.

"What's Farah *doing*?"

"Freaking out the same way you did when you first met us." Zoe smirked as she butted in on the conversation.

"I did not!" Max defended herself.

"*Social Dropouts is my favourite band!*" Zoe mocked as she did a poor whiny impression of Max.

"Okay, that's accurate."

Farah was a little lost for words over the fact she was speaking to Bailey. Was Brian friends with many famous people? He seemed to know her.

Of course he was friends with famous people, his mother was one of the biggest pop stars of a generation. He must have had an abundance of famous contacts. She was somewhat intrigued to know who else was in his phonebook.

"Aw, that's super sweet. I'm so glad that I could help with studying. I know that feeling." Bailey placed her hands on her hips and grinned.

Farah turned back around and noticed the band had been watching her freak out about the musician. A part of her felt bad about knowing Bailey's music and not any Social Dropouts songs. She knew a few songs now after hearing them every single night for the past few weeks.

"Someone's a fan!" Zoe folded her arms and cocked an eyebrow as she stared over at Farah with a smirk. Farah held onto her arm, turning a little red with embarrassment.

"Bailey's music *is* really good!" Farah tried her hardest to prevent a small grin from creeping up her lips. It was to no avail as she smiled, excited to be in the presence of the musician.

It was hard for her to think of Brian as someone who was friends with people who were as famous as Bailey Craig. It didn't cross her mind much. Brian was the son of Cherry Blossom, an insanely famous pop singer. It blew Farah's mind whenever she thought about it and yet it never seemed to have any impact on their relationship. She hadn't thought too deeply about the fame and burdens he held. She didn't want to.

At least, not until that moment.

Admittedly, Farah had thought people who had any kind of fame within their lives were nothing but assholes. How wrong was she? Brian was far from the word and she had never even seen him in that light before despite adoring fans shouting his name every night. He wasn't like the famous assholes from television. He tried his hardest to stay out of the spotlight. As much as he loved the fans of his emo band, it was a niche genre and he knew he would never be as famous as his mother or as popular as Bailey. That was the plan.

"We should probably stop touring around the same time, it makes it hard for us to go to each other's shows!" Bailey chuckled, looking up at each of her old friends. It had been a long time since they had reconnected.

"You managed to come and see us." Russ smiled.

"Free night. Couldn't miss you guys!"

"You're too sweet, Bails! We're all going to have to come and catch one of your shows soon." Zoe stepped over to Bailey and threw her arm around her, excited to have been with an old friend.

"We'll start a mosh pit!" Catfish put his hands in the air.

"Um, we don't play the same kind of crowd anymore." Bailey laughed uncomfortably; her music didn't cater to the emo scene anymore. She didn't see many mosh pits at her shows.

"You want to hang out? I saw a super cool bar next door with an arcade...looked like it has those cocktails you liked too." Zoe nudged Bailey with a smile.

"Okay, maybe a few. I have a show to play tomorrow." Bailey rubbed her arm as she grinned.

"Yeah, so do we." Catfish huffed, holding a singular drumstick and spinning it between his fingers. Farah was always impressed by how he did that.

"How many people?" Bailey pushed, ready to show them all up.

"It's eight hundred cap." Russ inputted.

"Sold out?"

"Not yet."

"Okay famous pop star, what's your cap?" Zoe was intrigued to know the number of people Bailey was performing in front of.

"Four thousand. Sold out. We're flying to Chicago tomorrow." Bailey found satisfaction in letting the band know her pursuits. There was a certain type of luxury that came from flying to shows and yet a lack of authenticity. Being in a van was a whole different experience.

"That's insane." Catfish gasped.

Farah noticed Brian smiling, he hadn't had much input on the conversation. At least, not in the same way the rest of them did.

Nobody denied the idea of going to the bar with Bailey. They were all accepting of it. Even Farah was happy to have been in the vicinity of them all. She was hanging out with *Bailey Craig*!

"You didn't tell me you knew Bailey Craig." Farah whispered to Brian as they walked across the street to the bar after they had packed up their equipment.

"Oh, she's a good friend of ours. My dad's her manager now and probably one of his biggest clients, she really brings in a crowd."

"Wait, really?"

"Yeah, the guys used to be in a band with her in high school. They always used to play music together and then Bailey's solo stuff got big with the help of my dad and the guys took a different direction creatively. After that, they picked me up as their new frontman and the rest is history." Brian snorted as he kept his hands in his pockets, watching everyone walk in front of them.

"That's...really cool." Farah bit her lip. She always forgot how famous *Brian Blossom* was. He tried his hardest to stay out of the spotlight. That didn't mean that people didn't recognise him, bother him in supermarkets or even just talk about him in general conversation as they scanned up and down pages written about him on the internet. Max and Farah were both guilty of the latter.

"My dad could probably get you and Max tickets once the tour is over. You seem to be a pretty big fan." Brian was quick to make the offer.

"N-no, I couldn't. That's too much." Farah didn't want to take advantage of having a friend in a high place. She hadn't gotten close to Brian for the benefits of his fame.

"Okay, well, if you change your mind let me know. I'm sure Bailey would be happy to help out too. She's super nice." Brian grinned; Bailey would have happily given Brian as many tickets as he wanted if she could. She had always supported him.

"That does sound nice." Farah couldn't deny the kindness that came from the offer.

"Or maybe we could go together?" Brian suggested, pushing his shoulder against her as they walked. Farah blushed as she pushed him back, unable to control her smile.

"Maybe..." Farah diverted her attention from him as they approached the entrance to the bar. The last thing she wanted was to raise suspicion around their fling.

It felt weird knowing that only a couple of days ago she had woken up in a bed next to Brian Blossom. They didn't want things to be different between them, but the thoughts kept popping into her head that reminded her of the time they had shared.

That wasn't a bad thing, they had a great time. They had even come to an agreement that things had been moving a little too fast, at least for Farah.

That was all either of them could ask for. An understanding of one another.

It was nice to hang out in a bar with everyone, despite it not usually being a location Farah enjoyed. They had passed the halfway mark in LA and going on the tour had been something none of them would have taken for granted. Especially Max and Farah.

They all sat with one another inside of a booth, smiling faces all around. Farah had never been part of a friendship group before. This was the closest she had gotten. It felt nice to have been included in the conversation. They didn't leave Max or Farah out of the loop. Every trip of nostalgia came with a story to fill them both in, there were even stories from high school Brian wasn't aware of.

Brian occasionally nudged Farah to make sure she was okay, mostly with a tap of his knee against her leg under the table or a little shoulder bump. He was doing his best to make sure they stayed connected, he craved spending more time with her.

The band, Bailey, Max and Farah had started an air hockey tournament within moments of being inside the arcade. Russ and Zoe came out victorious against Catfish and Brian. Max and Zoe had kicked Bailey and Farah's ass. Farah had played air hockey with Bailey Craig and she couldn't wait to tell everyone she knew.

Farah watched from afar as Max snapped a few photos of the band by a skeeball machine for their social media pages.

Farah sat at a table on a tall stool as she watched everyone else order more drinks after their small photoshoot. If everyone else was drunk she needed to make sure she was level-headed enough to keep an eye out for them.

"Is the Sober Squad accepting new members?" Brian leaned his elbow on the table, Farah leaning on the opposite side. She looked adorable wearing his band's merchandise she had purchased the previous night. The hoodie suited her well.

"It depends if they're sober or not." Farah smirked as she removed her chin from her hands, no longer propping herself up.

"I'm hoping smoking doesn't count then." Brian shrugged.

"I'll let it slide...this time." Farah smiled.

Brian slid onto the seat opposite before tapping his finger against the table, looking over at the band and Max ordering drinks at the bar. Brian didn't mind drinking socially and prob-ably would have drank a lot more if Farah hadn't been there. He wanted to keep her company.

Farah looked over at Brian, he looked just as good as he had done every night. There had been something in Los Ange-les that had made him overly attractive. It could have been the alcohol in her system or even the stupid red shirt he had opted to wear. Farah wasn't sure what had gotten Brian under her skin, but she wasn't complaining.

"Do you play any video games?" Brian attempted to strike up a casual conversation relating to the arcade.

"Sometimes. Me and Max have a Switch in our dorm room we play together a lot." Farah shrugged.

"Really? That's cool!" Brian tilted his head, interested to know more. He hadn't expected her to be a fan of video games.

"Yeah, there's these two guys who live upstairs who always come round to play Mario Kart. I don't know why they bother; Max and I always win. They're *terrible*!" Farah snorted, thinking back fondly on her memories.

"Huh. Maybe you two are just really good?"

"Obviously." Farah laughed, noticing Brian's disconnect at the mention of the people who shared her building at college. There was nothing to it, but she understood the threat. "Hey, I bet I could prove my skills and beat you at *these* games." Farah added as he turned to look at her, shocked by her comment. She pointed over at the arcade.

"I don't think so." Brian sat up and shook his head.

"Really?"

"This is my field of expertise."

"I thought that was music."

"My *second* field of expertise."

"What makes you say that?"

"One of my mom's bandmates had an arcade in her house. Do you know how long I spent there as a kid?" Brian turned in his seat to speak to Farah, a seriousness in his tone.

"*Too* long?" Farah laughed.

"Yeah, it was a long time. A really long time. See, the moral of the story is...I'm going to beat you at any game you choose." Brian gave Farah a smug expression as if he had already won every game they were considering playing.

"You just told me you have a clear advantage." Farah resisted her smirk, leaning on her hand again so she could hide her expression.

"So? I'll go easy."

"Nope. If you want to play, we play *fair*. I want to be able to beat you at your best."

"Okay..." Brian chewed the inside of his mouth.

"What's the bet?"

"The *bet*?"

"Let's play for something. We can make it interesting."

"You don't strike me as a gambler." Brian tapped his chin.

312

"It's not a gamble if you *know* you're going to win." Farah scoffed, finding enjoyment in his smile turning to a frown. He hadn't expected that from her.

"Oh, okay. Sure. What do you have in mind?"

Brian had spent a lot of his time being the one to flirt, hoping she would flirt back. Despite that, it felt as if Farah was in control of their budding relationship. It was down to her what happened next and going off what he had said previously, she wanted a chance to know him better. Alone.

"Would you...uh...still be up for that date?" Farah asked nervously as she tapped her finger against the table. Brian blinked at the words, staring at her from the other side of the small table. *Nobody* had ever asked him on a date before. She noticed his mind wander, terrified she had said something wrong she attempted to get his attention. "Brian?"

"Yes." Brian answered without thinking, still in complete shock.

"Did you hear me?" Farah questioned, terrified he may have ignored her on purpose.

Brian stared down at the table, noticing her finger circling a grain on the wood. She was nervous, but he wouldn't tell her secrets. He swallowed hard before nodding his head multiple times, looking up at her with a smile.

"Yes. I heard you. I-I think that's a great idea." Brian held his hands together as he sat on the stool with a smile on his face.

She wanted to go on a date.

"Winner gets to choose where we go?" Farah tucked her hair behind her ear as she tilted her head, Brian entranced by how beautiful she was under the bar lights.

A million possibilities ran through Brian's mind on where he could have taken her. The possibilities were endless. He wanted to make Farah feel as special as she made him feel.

He *had* to win.

"Okay...deal." Brian nodded. He reached across the table and held out his hand for Farah to shake. Farah smiled as she shook his hand, feeling the warm connection of his skin on hers.

"Deal." Farah smirked.

She *wanted* to win...

He *had* to win...

"Guitar Hero? That seems a little unfair..." Farah shook her head as she folded her arms and looked down at the plastic guitar. With the rest of the band distracted by drunken Giant Jenga, they had an opportunity to sneak away.

"Oh, come on! This is different from a real guitar." Brian groaned as he held the guitar by its strap.

"But you're really *good* with your fingers. I'm not!" Farah spoke casually, moving her fingers to play the air guitar. She hadn't realised what she had said until it was too late. Her expression dropped as a huge smile crept up Brian's face.

"Oh, *really?*" Brian grinned.

"That's not what—"

"I know, but it's funny. Considering, y'know—" Brian snorted at the thought. He knew she was still embarrassed to admit how much she enjoyed having sex with him, but he didn't mind. It was fun to tease her phrasing.

"I know!" Farah snapped, her cheeks turning red. He chuckled as he put the guitar back in the spot created for it to sit perfectly, except it didn't. Years of erosion had caused it more harm than expected.

They played a few of the games, from racing games Farah managed to win by miles to more traditional games Brian excelled in.

"How are your skeeball skills? The final game to break the tie!" Brian pointed over at the machine in the corner.

"I could be a professional skeeball player if I wanted." Farah teased, pushing her hands into the front pocket of her Social Dropouts hoodie.

"I'm going to start thinking of ideas on where to take you now." Brian scoffed, not believing Farah in the slightest.

"Don't get too cocky." Farah shook her head and smirked. It turned out Brian was a competitive person and was going to do everything he could to have won against her.

He wasn't going to let her win.

They made their way over to the skeeball machine and Brian placed money in both the slots before smugly cracking his knuckles. He bounced on his heels and pretended to crack his neck as Farah shook her head and laughed at his enthusiasm.

"You should probably walk away now. It might be embarrassing to lose." Brian continued with his witty banter, Farah completely over the pretentious competitive side of him. She had to shut him down.

"Not a chance, Blossom." Farah winked, picking up one of the balls and preparing herself to throw.

Little did Farah know Brian didn't just spend a lot of time in the arcade when he was a kid, but he was pretty good at it too. Brian wasn't going to share the full extent of his history of playing the traditional games. He wanted that advantage. He wanted to be the one to pick where they went together.

Farah and Brian began to throw balls into the machine, laughing as they played. Farah was rolling what she believed were successful balls until she glanced over at the numbers in front of Brian, making her gasp in shock.

He wasn't even going *easy* on her! He was thrashing her score with little remorse.

Farah furrowed her eyebrows as she tried to aim the balls for the highest numbers, only hitting them on the off chance.

Brian had his victory handed to him on a silver platter. He placed his hands on his hips and beamed up at the high score on the small screen before looking back at Farah who had been defeated by her score.

"Um...I'm sorry—"

"You're *really* good." Farah's eyes were wide with shock.

"I guess. I mean, we can—" It was hard for him not to feel bad about his win when her score was...so...*low*.

"You won. It was *close*, but you get to pick." Farah stepped forward and poked him in the chest with a smile. She was interested to know what he would have decided on.

Brian had never been on a date before. If he had asked people before, they had never showed up. He had seen plenty of movies that involved dates in various locations, that was the extent of his knowledge. Did he have to dress up? How much was it going to cost? How long was it going to last? When would they have time to go on a date?

"Where do you want to go?" Brian asked, Farah began to laugh at his words.

"You get to decide, that was the whole point of winning. It's down to *you*."

"Can you give me a hint?" Brian bit his lip, nervous that he wouldn't have been able to think of anything. What happened to all of the ideas that had previously flooded his mind in a moment of excitement? What happened to his knowledge of romance?

"No, that's against the rules." Farah snorted, finding entertainment in his inability to decide. It looked as if she had caused his mind to go blank.

"Nothing?"

"Nope." Farah found satisfaction in walking away over to the pinball machines, Brian nervously following her. For a self-proclaimed romantic, he was struggling.

He had finally been given the opportunity and as much as he had thought about that moment for a lot of his life, suddenly he had nothing.

Farah posted a coin into the slot of the pinball machine. She wasn't much of a player herself but was interested in playing as Brian mentally panicked. Why was it so difficult?

He hadn't thought this through. He should have let her win. The sex part was *so* easy, but it was the only part he knew.

He had never been beyond that with anyone before and yet there he was pacing up and down the side of the pinball machine trying to figure it out.

Farah pressed the sides of the game and watched as the ball shot back up the machine. Out the corner of her eye, she could see Brian stewing on questions he wanted her to answer.

She could see it was torturing him.

"Does it have to be *fancy*?" Brian leaned on the side of the pinball machine, attempting to make eye contact with her.

He hoped she would have given in if puppy eyes were an option.

"It's *your* decision." Farah continued to stare down at the pinball, not bothering to look up at Brian as he pouted.

"What if I get it wrong?"

"You can't get it wrong. It's just...somewhere we can hang out. Talk. Y'know...a *date*." Farah shrugged. She had been on plenty of dates in the past. Despite that, *most* of them hadn't been through choice.

Brian looked around the arcade to see if he could see any of the band, Bailey or Max. They didn't seem to be around.

Brian crept behind Farah, standing as close to her as possible.

Farah noticed his presence, practically pushed up against her the same way he had done when he was attempting to teach her guitar. She had completely forgotten his first lesson, too distracted by the kiss he had given her not long after.

She felt his hands slide down either side of her arms and fall into the same place as her hands that were currently pressing the buttons on the machine. As the ball went to the top of the machine, Farah took a small break to also have a look around the arcade. She was nervous about the band seeing them.

They were alone.

"I probably should have let you win." Brian tittered softly beside her ear, watching the pinball over her shoulder.

"Yeah?"

"I've never been on a date before."

"Wait, *really*?" Farah was shocked to hear it, turning around slightly before focusing her attention back on the game.

He had mentioned his love for love in Austin, but the conversation was quick to trail off. He didn't date anyone he had sex with...mostly because *they* didn't want to.

"When I said I was new to this stuff, I meant it." Brian rested his chin on Farah's shoulder as he watched the ball bounce around the machine, continuing to hold onto the tops of her hands as her fingers repeatedly pressed into the buttons.

"You seem pretty confident."

"I'm pretty nervous." Brian admitted with a chuckle. He didn't want to mess anything up, but honesty was on his side. Farah respected his ability to admit his lack of knowledge on the subject. She hadn't been so confident in telling him her prior experience when it came to sex.

"I'm nervous too." Farah responded, with him resting on her shoulder she internally wished they could have cuddled up with one another as they did in LA.

"I really like spending time with you. I want to make sure it's perfect." Brian's words were a croaky whisper in her ear over the music and sounds of the arcade machines around them. He had repeated his previous fears.

Farah knew it was cheesy, but she wanted to tell him everything would have been perfect if he had arranged it. In her mind, it didn't matter what they did together. It wasn't a competition and he didn't need to impress her, he had already done that.

"I just think it'll be nice to spend time together. No pressure." Farah smiled, feeling the weight of his warm hands on hers.

"I don't know. I'm just..." Brian sighed, unsure of what he was supposed to say. His confidence in himself was near to none when it came to this kind of thing. There was nothing he could do to shake the thoughts. "...I'm scared." Brian finally confessed.

Farah allowed the balls to fall through the middle of the arms inside the pinball machine as she heard the words. She was desperate to understand his fears, she wanted to be there to comfort him. She had grown to care a lot about him the past couple of weeks.

Farah turned around as Brian stepped back, taking his chin away from her shoulder. Farah pushed the bottom of her back against the pinball machine as she gripped onto either side of Brian's shirt.

Brian felt nervous, he had never admitted his fears to anyone before when it came to relationships. There had been so much swimming through his mind since the first day of the tour when he had met her. How was he supposed to navigate romance when he was used to sexual partners that didn't even wait until the morning to leave him?

"I told Max." Farah announced, a little to Brian's surprise. "About...us."

"You—"

"I'm sorry, I needed to talk to someone about it. She won't tell anyone. I promise." Farah looked up at Brian's shocked expression, scared he may have been upset by her actions.

Farah was hoping by telling him it would have forced the confirmation she wanted to be around him. Something to help assure Farah was serious. She wouldn't have told Max otherwise.

"Y-you told Max?" Brian blinked, his entire evening had been spent feeling speechless after everything she had said.

"I'm sorry—" Farah felt the guilt build within herself.

"No, no, no! It's fine! You trust Max, she's your best friend. I get it." Brian held onto Farah's arms and nodded. "It would be *weird* if you didn't tell her."

"Right." Farah looked away before continuing. "Have you told the band? I wouldn't be mad..."

"No. Not yet. I think they *probably* know, but it's complicated. I don't want them to know. Not now. Not yet." Brian sighed, embarrassed by his past. There were reasons he couldn't get into with Farah why telling the band would have been awkward.

"Oh."

Brian didn't want them to judge him for his past mistakes, reflecting them onto Farah would have been the worst thing they could do. In his mind, he was convinced they would have repeatedly told him how bad he was for wanting to be with Farah. It wasn't as if this was the first time he was convinced he had fallen in love with a girl whilst on tour. Except, they didn't understand. This *was* different.

"Y'know what?" Farah moved so she could hold Brian just as much as he held her.

"What?"

"If there's one thing I've learned whilst being on this tour, it's that it doesn't matter what other people think of you. Sure, I'm still super anxious about everything, but I've done things on this trip that months ago I wouldn't have even thought of. Sometimes it's hard to meet these expectations people set for you. I study tirelessly in college and what does it get me? Sure, it gets me the education I want, but I've never *lived* like this before. It's such a different lifestyle and it's fantastic." Farah straightened the front of his jacket and smiled; she had become a lot more confident around the man that her actions shocked her.

"Wow. Yeah, you're right." Brian was struck by her words.

She caught eyes with Brian as he stared back at her, they looked great together under the ambient lighting of the arcade. The lights took his mind back to the hazy purple lighting in the recording studio. Farah bit her lip before brushing the front of his chest.

"There's only a few days left of the tour...so this needs to be a pretty good date." Farah smirked. She knew it wasn't the location of the date he feared. He was afraid of there being nothing after. She wanted to do what she could to assure that.

"I-I can do that." Brian stuttered his words.

"I can't wait." Farah leaned forward and planted a small kiss on his cheek, causing him to blush. "We should probably see what everyone else is up to."

"Yeah...sure."

Farah stepped past Brian and began to walk in the direction of the bar. Brian turned on his heel with his mouth slightly ajar from her actions. He lifted his hand to his cheek and smiled as he watched her throw her hands into the front pocket of the hoodie and spin around.

"Are you coming?" She shouted before tucking her hair behind her ear.

"Y-yeah!" Brian stuttered, noticing her little smile as she walked in the other direction.

He was completely smitten.

CHICAGO, IL

Farah stared down at her open shoes; they weren't the sort she should have been wearing somewhere so...*dangerous*. She held her hands together in the front pocket of her hoodie and looked around for the rest of her party.

It wasn't her outfit that made her feel out of place, with the hoodie and skinny jeans she fitted in perfectly. It was mostly her presence and lack of skateboard that made standing to the side of Grant Park skatepark a little scarier than she had expected. Brian had attempted to convince her that skaters mostly cared about themselves, their tricks and weed. There wasn't anything else on their agenda. They wouldn't have bothered Farah.

"Are you sure you don't want a go? I don't want you to feel left out." Max held the skateboard out for Farah as she shook her head to deny the offer.

"I'm fine! It's a lot of fun watching you guys, I'm just worried one of you might end up in the hospital." Farah pulled a face at the thought. The park was busy.

"Unlikely. These guys know what they're doing. They can fucking shred." Max stuck her tongue out and threw up a shaka sign with her hand.

Max was right, the band had been skating for as long as they could remember.

Max got back onto the board and pushed off past Farah, making her way back to the skatepark. Farah had to admit, it *did* look pretty fun. It had been a while since Farah had given skateboarding a go by practically stumbling off the board and falling into Brian. That had been embarrassing.

A great weight had been lifted from Farah's shoulders knowing she was able to speak to Max about Brian. It was awkward when she thought about it in detail, but for the most part, she was happy to have gotten it out of her system. There wasn't anything to worry about.

Farah watched as Brian kickflipped onto a rail before grinding down and landing on all four wheels. Of course, Farah had no idea what the skateboarding terms were, but the quick succession of his movements showed he was slick when it came to showing off another one of his talents.

Considering there were kids all over the park that could barely take four wheels off the ground when popping an ollie, it was hard not to compare Brian's fluidity in the sport to the new starters. He certainly knew what he was doing. Brian knew what he was doing when it came to a lot of things...

The previous night after the show they had been to the arcade and Farah had lost a bet. Brian still hadn't suggested anything else for a date. She could tell Brian was struggling for ideas.

After yesterday, it was weird for her to not see Brian in a different light. Knowing he knew Bailey Craig felt strange. She had never really considered him *famous* until that point. It was enough to reiterate he was very different from the rest of the people in the band. His mother was Cherry Blossom, the lead singer of the exceedingly popular nineties band, The Flower Children. That was hard to digest.

Farah watched as Brian climbed up the side of the bowl through a gap in the fences to join her. He tucked his skateboard under his arm and walked over, the bottom of the skateboard still showing off the cartoon image featuring alien abduction.

"Are you sure you don't want another lesson?" Brian breathed heavily as he spoke.

"And what happens if I hit another rock?"

"I'll catch you." Brian smiled proudly, Farah snorted in response as she shook her head. "Besides, the ground here is super smooth. There probably won't be any rocks."

"You really want me on that skateboard, don't you?" Farah laughed as she pointed towards the board.

"What's so bad about being on wheels?"

"I've been roller skating before, that's fun!"

Brian pondered on her words for a moment. That was a date idea! People go roller skating on dates all the time! It was *perfect*. It was the perfect date.

"I've never been." Brian admitted. Although, if Farah enjoyed the activity then it would have been the best place for them to go on their first date. Right?

"It's a lot of fun and there are more wheels and less...*board*. I used to go with my friends back in high school. I'd love to go again."

"Huh. You should do the things you love more often."

"I haven't been in years."

Brian smiled before walking over to the bench Farah was standing in front of. He had a brilliant idea.

Farah noticed where he was going and sat down. You could see the whole skatepark from the bench. Farah could just about make out Max and the others in the distance.

"Are you free?" Brian began to execute his excellent plan, placing the board on the floor beside him and leaning back on the bench before catching his breath. He decided to put his arm on the back of the bench behind Farah. She noticed instantly, feeling more connected to him without being subjected to his touch. At least he hadn't yawned before doing it.

"*Now?*"

"Right now."

"I think Max wanted to visit the Bean."

"The *Bean?*"

"Yeah, it's—never mind. I'm free." Farah snorted, seeing Brian's face full of confusion over her words.

"Do you want to go on that date now?" Brian found himself feeling giddy at the ask, allowing his cheeks to flush a shade of red. He watched as Farah blinked rapidly at his suggestion. Did he even have a plan?

"What about the band?" Farah was confused how his plan would have worked. There was very little planning involved.

"Oh. Uh. I'll tell them I don't feel great and that I need to head back to the motel so I can rest before the show. Yeah!" Brian snapped his fingers as he continued to come up with the idea on the spot. He should have been more efficient with his planning, but it was clear his excitement had gotten in the way.

"What about Max?"

"She probably wants to hang with the band anyway! We'll figure something out. We're always together." Brian chewed the inside of his mouth in a subtle plead of desperation. All he wanted was for her to agree to the date now he had a plan formulating in his mind. A very loose plan.

He hadn't even checked to see if there was anywhere in the area they could roller skate. Regardless, he was going with the plan. Anything to be with Farah.

"I don't know..." Farah was unsure what he was planning, but she was willing to follow whatever he had in store for her that afternoon.

She noticed the puppy dog eyes he gave her. She was practically powerless against them.

"*Please*? It'll be really fun!" Brian tried his hardest to convince her it was the right time for them to go on the date. Farah was the one who had asked him out to begin with, she wouldn't have wanted to deny it.

Farah turned to look at him, his face showing an expression of innocence as if he hadn't done anything to make her look at him that way. He wasn't as innocent as he made out.

"I'll have to check my calendar." Farah giggled as Brian smiled back, understanding her flirtatious humour straight away.

"Oh, okay. Sure. I can pencil you in though, right? Or can I use pen?" Brian asked, his arm remaining on the back of the bench. It took every fibre in her very being not to snuggle up beside him. The weather wasn't that great in Chicago and they had managed to catch one of the few overcast days in the city that July.

"Where are we going?" She chose to ignore his ask, curiously wanting to know his plan.

"Um...it's a surprise." Brian bit his lip. He had spent all day trying to think of something, even consulting old online forums.

Where do you take someone on a first date?

Was it even their *first* date? Officially, he guessed it was. He was glad she had mentioned something about roller skating otherwise he would have continued to be stuck for ideas.

Farah was convinced there was a chance Brian still had no idea where he was taking them.

"A surprise?"

"Yeah! We can go soon."

"I look forward to it." Farah smirked. She didn't have much planned in Chicago and as much as she would have liked to look around the Art Institute...Brian's offer was much more tempting.

Brian quickly shuffled away from Farah as he noticed a recognisable face approaching. Farah didn't know what was going on as he slid away from her on the bench and held his skateboard between his legs. Farah looked up and noticed Max walking over to them both.

"Jeez guys, you look guilty." Max sighed as she caught Brian's flustered expression. He didn't want to be seen with Farah, especially not by the band. They would have made assumptions he didn't want to deal with.

"Nothing. We're talking about music." Brian defended himself, anxiously coming up with some kind of excuse. Farah looked over to him again, he was terrible at lying.

"Dude, I know you're fucking." Max snorted as she shook her head and kicked up the board she had been skating on before catching it.

"Max..." Farah groaned, pushing her palm against her forehead in frustration.

"Oh right." In a moment of panic, Brian had forgotten Farah had told him about Max knowing the previous night.

"Cheek clapping aside, what are you losers doing?" Max questioned as she held onto the skateboard, exchanging glances between them.

Farah looked at Brian, he needed to ask Max to cover them if they went out on a date. It would be down to her to keep their trail clean.

"We were going to...hang out together." Farah wanted to be honest. Especially with Max.

"You're going to do the *do*?" Max felt no shame in allowing the smirk to creep up her face.

"N-no!" Brian defended with furrowed eyebrows. That wasn't his intention.

"Could you cover for us?" Farah suddenly piped up the question seeing as Brian seemed too caught up in his own anxieties to confront Max.

"Cover? Whilst you play hooky? That'll be expensive." Max checked her fingernails with a grin.

"Come on, Max! Just once. Please!" Farah fluttered her eyelashes at her best friend, causing Max to tut. She wasn't going to be able to say no to Farah.

"Just *once*! Never again." Max shook her head, there was no way she was going to cover for the couple every time they wanted to go off together. She wasn't going to keep up with the lies.

"That's good enough for me." Farah nodded.

"You want to go now?" Brian cocked an eyebrow as he realised the date was about to happen. He was still sweaty from skateboarding and didn't look his best. Either way, this was his plan. He needed to follow it through.

"I thought you wanted to go now?"

"Y-yeah! I do." Brian nodded. This was his one chance to prove to Farah he was much more than a man in a band. The one chance to prove he wanted to maintain what they had started to build over the course of the tour.

Little did he know Farah was thinking the same thing. If she had any hope in continuing the relationship she had built with the man then it would have to be complying to whatever plan he had in store for them that afternoon.

"What are you both waiting for? Go and have fun!" Max attempted to shoo them away. If they were going to go on a date, they may have well done it sooner rather than later.

Farah and Brian looked at one another for a moment. This was it.

"Go on! Have fun. Be safe. Text me!" Max pointed at Farah specifically.

"Yes, Mom. Always." Farah rolled her eyes. She had no idea where Brian was taking her, but she would have texted Max her location as soon as she knew where it was going to be.

Within moments, Max was winking and clicking her fingers before spinning on her heel and heading back to the skatepark. That left Farah and Brian standing beside one another ready to partake in their date.

Brian pulled out his phone and checked something as quickly as he could. Specifically to see if there were any skating rinks in the area. Luckily for him, there wasn't one too far away.

"So, what do you think?"

"Roller skating?" Farah questioned as she stood beside Brian inside of the dimly lit room. The carpet below her was reminiscent of an old bus seat. There were sounds of arcade games buzzing in the background. The musty smell of someone burning popcorn. The humdrum of chatter and wheels rolling against the rink.

This wasn't what she had been expecting, but she liked what he was trying to go for. She had been the one to mention it.

"Yeah! You said you'd done it before, and I thought you should go again! It looks easier than skateboarding." Brian stepped to the side as he explained his plan for their first date.

It wasn't to say it was a bad thing, but it wasn't what she had pictured Brian to pick.

"Is this what *you* want to do?" Farah snorted. His logic was sweet but confusing.

"I thought it would be fun. We could always—"

"No, it's okay. We can do this." Farah assured with a smile, noticing his face drop at her expression. He had to make sure he impressed her. This was his chance to prove himself.

How hard could roller skating be?

Farah was standing on the outside of a roller rink waiting for Brian to put his skates on. She glanced over to him, noticing he was sticking his tongue out slightly whilst tying up the laces on the front of the skates. It was the little things that made Farah find herself wanting to be with him. She smiled down at the man who was just as cute as he was when he asked her what her favourite Social Dropouts song was the first time they had met.

Brian undid his laces and tied them up again three times. His hands weren't working well enough to communicate with his brain. He had to make sure his date with Farah was perfect.

"Are you okay?" Farah questioned, looking down as he finally pulled the bow tightly. The fourth time's the charm.

"Y-yeah, I'm fine!" Brian looked up and smiled.

He gripped onto the edge of the bench and chewed the inside of his lip. He had to be confident in his movements. Roller skating must have been easy in comparison to skateboarding.

"Need a hand?" Farah smiled, trying to keep her snigger to herself. She didn't want him to think she was belittling him. She held both her hands out for him to hold if he so desired. He looked nervous, but she wasn't sure if it was the concept of the date or the fact he had wheels strapped to his feet.

"I'm okay." Brian nodded with a grin, pushing himself up off the bench and standing on two feet. He wobbled slightly. Easy.

"Are you *sure* you're okay?" Farah smirked, holding out her hands in case he was to fall. She could only imagine this was what she had looked like when he had gotten her to step onto his skateboard.

"I'm fine." Brian sighed before staring at Farah with a deadpan expression. "But you won't let me fall, right?"

"You've caught me a few times now, I think I should return the favour." Farah nodded. Desperate to make him feel comfortable. It didn't seem like Brian was confident in the sport, despite trying to cover his nerves with a heavy façade.

Roller skating was easy. Brian had managed to stand up. Now he just had to move.

Farah held out one of her hands and allowed him to grip on. His hand was clammy, and she was sure he was nervous about their time together. She didn't expect to be the one leading the date, but she was happy to do so as she attempted to pull him towards the rink.

"They're going pretty fast. Think we could go faster?" Brian cocked an eyebrow as he looked over at the rink where people were practically flying around.

"We have to get to the rink first." Farah snorted at his enthusiasm. She had already clocked onto his fears. By the way he held himself it was obvious he had never been on skates before.

Brian knew he could do it. Everyone made it look so easy. It *had* to be easy.

Except it didn't look easy. It looked terrifying.

Is this what Farah saw when they were at the skatepark? Why did roller skating look so terrifying in comparison to skateboarding? He had fallen off his skateboard countless times in the past that if he were to fall from the skates it shouldn't have bothered him.

Farah took a step back on the carpet, they weren't far away from the roller rink. She held him tightly as he slowly took each large step as if he were on the moon.

"You can hold onto the side if you like." Farah offered as they were about to approach the rink.

"It's okay! I've got this." Brian scoffed, Farah pulling him onto the slippery surface.

Brian was used to his skateboard. Farah had been on roller skates...a few times.

He hadn't been on them before.

"Careful!" Farah chuckled as Brian took one step onto the rink and nearly fell, immediately letting go of Farah's hand and throwing himself into the side of the rink. This wasn't anything like skateboarding! He held on tightly, not wanting to move his legs anymore.

"I'm okay! Beginner's jitters!" Brian felt his cheeks heating up with anxiety as he gripped on for dear life. He couldn't move. He had to move. He couldn't ruin this for them. This was supposed to be something Farah enjoyed that they could enjoy together.

"We can take it slow." Farah suggested, rolling over to the side of the rink to be beside him.

"N-no, fast is fine! I just need to find my footing."

"If you say so..." Farah smirked. She knew he was trying to cover his fear.

He moved his feet beneath him, half of his body practically thrown over the side as he held on. As he tried to adjust position, he felt himself slip again, causing his eyes to widen as he tightened his grip. He couldn't move.

"T-this is...oh *wow.*" Brian snorted nervously as he looked back at Farah in embarrassment. This wasn't how he had planned a first 'date' in his head. He hadn't planned it at all.

"Come on, I'll help you. It takes years of falling on your ass, remember?" Farah laughed as she held out her hand once more.

"Did you spend years falling on your ass?"

"Nope. I've only been roller skating a few times."

"Wait. *What?*" Brian's face dropped, still too afraid to let go of the side of the roller rink to place his hand in Farah's.

"I'm not a professional skater or anything. It was just a fun activity my friends and I did a few times in high school." Farah shrugged, suddenly understanding why Brian would want to take her there after the quick mention of it at the skatepark.

"Oh. Hm." Brian chewed his bottom lip. He had made a horrible mistake.

"Wait. Did you think I had done this as much as you've skateboarded?" Farah pushed her lips together in an attempt not to let out a small snigger. She didn't want to make Brian feel bad about it, but it was funny.

"Well...I...*yes!*"

"Oh. I mean, I've done it enough to know what I'm doing. Sort of. It's fun once you get used to it!" Farah held out her hand again, feeling guilty Brian had gotten the wrong idea.

Brian was embarrassed as he reached out and held onto Farah's hand, terrified to let go of the side of the rink. There was no way he was going to get anywhere without her help. He had to accept his failure.

He took a deep breath as he stood up straight, one hand on the railing and the other threaded between Farah's fingers.

"We don't have to—"

"I want to."

"As long as you're sure."

"I can do it." Brian assured.

He held a little tighter onto Farah's hand as he loosened his grip on the railing. Farah wanted to do whatever she could to make sure he was comfortable. He was trying too hard to pretend he was okay.

"It'll be scary at first, but you'll get used to it." Farah decided to push him with some reassurance. She wanted to be honest with how he felt about it. It was okay to be scared by new things. Brian had even helped her come to terms with the idea over the course of the tour.

"Was it this scary the first time you did it?" Brian's eyes widened as he stared down at the floor.

"How scary do you think this is?"

"Eleven."

"Out of?"

"Ten."

"Oh. Isn't skateboarding harder than this?" Farah questioned as she attempted to coax him from the railing by holding out her other hand. He hesitated before reaching over and holding her.

"I don't know." Brian looked at her with panic in his expression as he forced a slight smile. He was so embarrassed by his actions.

Brian wanted nothing more than to have made his day with Farah the best day she could have possibly had. She probably thought he was an idiot for the suggestion.

"One step at a time. Just pretend you're skateboarding." Farah shrugged as she let go of his other hand and began to skate, pulling him along behind her.

Brian took a deep breath as the skates began to move. *Just pretend he was skateboarding*, sure, he could do that. As much as he wanted to concentrate on the skates below him, he couldn't stop staring at the girl in front of him who was helping drag him around the rink.

Brian glanced down at Farah's skates, noticing how she moved. He mimicked the action, figuring out the best way to move his feet. Farah felt pride in her ability to show off her agility in the activity. His flustering over his skills were adorable.

"Look, it's easy." Farah smirked as she pulled him along. Brian grinned at his achievement as he watched her turn around to smile.

She was gorgeous and he was so lucky for the opportunity to spend the day with her. He couldn't put into words how much he enjoyed being with her. How much he wanted to *be* with her.

Farah found him cute as he fumbled around on the skates like a new-born animal. However, with each lap, she could see the improvement in his movements. He had started to concentrate on her more than the skating.

"Yeah..." Brian slurred. He focused his attention on Farah, her sweet smiles and soft hands. She was wonderful.

It didn't take long for Brian to start getting used to the sensation of being on the roller skates. It didn't feel like skateboarding.

He hated it.

He was grateful for Farah guiding him around the rink. He knew he wouldn't have done it without her. He was embarrassed about picking the activity, but it was the best he could do with what little time he had.

That didn't seem to matter after they had been around the rink a couple of times. Brian's nerves began to slip away, the whole experience making him laugh. He watched Farah laugh at him for the silly remarks he made or the nervous faces he pulled when he was about to slip. No matter what, she would have been there to make sure he didn't fall.

That made the anxiety worth it.

"See? You didn't have to be scared." Farah nudged Brian with her whole body whilst sitting beside him, taking off the skates as she spoke.

"I wasn't *scared.*"

"Oh, yeah?" Farah chuckled, not believing a word he was saying.

He pondered on what to say next for a moment.

"Okay, it was a *little* scary." Brian laughed as he nudged her back gently, undoing the tight knot he had pulled hard enough to never come undone.

"You did it though."

"I did." Brian nodded with half a smile, happy to have heard her encouragement.

Brian tied his shoes as Farah slipped hers on. Farah found it hard not to swoon over his date idea. He had listened to her and made an educated guess based on what he had heard thinking it was something they would enjoy. It was spontaneous, but sweet.

Brian checked his phone to confirm he didn't have any texts from the band questioning why he wasn't in the motel room resting after he had texted Zoe saying he didn't feel well. He felt a lot of guilt lying to the band, but he was desperate to hang out with Farah. There was still time before he would have to go to the venue to set up.

"Do you...want to grab something to eat?" Brian asked as they stood outside of the roller rink. He couldn't help but feel he had ruined their time together. He should have picked an activity that wouldn't have made him look like an idiot.

"Do you have something planned?" Farah cocked an eye-brow as Brian sat down on a small brick wall with deflation.

"Not really. No." Brian sighed, running his fingers through his hair as Farah sat beside him. He looked sad. Did he not *want* to be there?

"Are you okay?"

"I'm really sorry, Farah." Brian made his apology with a deep breath, feeling disheartened by his first-ever date. It wasn't what the movies made it out to be.

"What for?" Farah tilted her head, a few things running through her mind on what he could have been apologising for.

"I screwed this whole date thing up, didn't I?" Brian chewed the inside of his lip, feeling completely out of his depth. He liked Farah enough to be frightened of doing the wrong thing.

"What? No! I'm having loads of fun!" Farah insisted, quick to place her hand on Brian's arm to hold a connection between them. The innocence of their touches felt different from what they had experienced in LA.

"Really? I went with the first thing that came to mind. I was really struggling with ideas. I just wanted it to be perfect. I wanted you to have fun."

"I *am* having fun, Brian." Farah smiled sympathetically as she held him, seeing the sadness behind his eyes. She could tell how much he had struggled with a date idea, but she had appre-ciated his effort.

"I should have let you win skeeball." Brian held his head in his hands and grumbled.

"Yeah, you should have let me win skeeball." Farah confirmed before smiling. "—But, I've enjoyed hanging out with you. I don't think it matters what we do, I just like spending time with you."

The words hit Brian. Nobody had ever said anything like it to him before.

"I like spending time with you too. A lot." Brian looked up and smiled at Farah, placing his hand on top of hers as it balanced on his opposite arm.

"Also, you were very adorable on skates."

"You were really good." Brian complimented; he couldn't take his eyes off her as they sat together.

"You were really bad." Farah teased.

"Hey! That's uncalled for."

"True though."

"Hm, I guess you're right." Brian sniggered, enjoying the taunt.

He tilted his head slightly as he looked at Farah, not quite believing that out of everyone on the planet she had chosen him to go out on a date with. She had chosen him to spend time with. She had chosen him to kiss. She had chosen him to have sex with...

"Still up for some food?" Farah smirked back, noticing he had forgotten the premise of their original conversation. She was happy to remind him, excited for some food before the show.

"Always."

Brian felt proud to walk around the city with Farah's hand in his. Although there was no definition to their relationship it had been nice to be close to her in a public setting. She wasn't embarrassed about being with him and that felt *fantastic*.

Farah was once nervous about being with Brian in any capacity. She now felt as if she could be herself around him without any judgement. It was nice to have someone else she could rely on other than Max. She didn't know him as well as she wished she did, but in some respects, she hoped that would grow over time.

They had decided to head to a small café on a street corner, what they assumed would have been a quiet location. They didn't let go of one another's hand the entire time until they sat opposite at a table after ordering coffee and cake. Despite not holding hands, for anyone passing it would have been hard not to notice their legs tangled underneath the table.

Brian leaned his chin on his hand as he stared at her from the opposite side of the table, showing off his infatuation with the girl as she sipped on the coffee he had bought with his near-to maxed-out credit card.

"Do you always stare?"

"Only at you." Brian smirked as she placed the coffee down in front of her.

Farah mimicked his actions and rested her chin on the palm of her hand as she leaned forward and stared back at him. He grinned at the gesture, looking just as handsome as ever.

Going to the roller rink had been a fun experience for Farah and she hoped that in the end it was also a good experience for Brian. He was more anxious about making Farah upset or accidentally disappointing her with his lack of skills, both romantically and on roller skates.

He didn't want to mess it up.

"*Brian Blossom?*" A voice broke him from his trance of both romantic and sexual fantasies as he stared at Farah from across the table.

Brian blinked up in shock as he saw the figure of a girl standing beside him. Farah sat up straight, cocking an eyebrow at the rude woman who had decided to interrupt their time together.

He had no idea who she was.

"*Hi?*" Brian half-smiled with a wave, unsure of how to interact with the stranger.

"You're in a rock band, aren't you? *Deadbeats? Several Deadbeats?*" The stranger attempted to confirm her suspicion of who he was, not quite hitting the mark. It made Brian a little sad they hadn't even gotten the name of his band correct, let alone the genre.

"Social Dropouts?" He squinted.

"Yeah! Social Dropouts! Cool name!"

"Yeah, that's me." Brian grinned awkwardly. He never minded meeting fans, but they always seemed to appear at the wrong times. Farah exchanged glances between Brian and the fan.

She was pretty. *Really* pretty. Farah felt a little insecure with the girl's instant fawning over Brian. Were these the sorts of girls Brian was usually with? The people he *slept* with?

Farah was nothing like them.

"Can I get a picture?" The stranger asked. Brian was never a jerk when it came to his fans, and he was always eager to please. He didn't want to deny them the picture.

"Sure!" The sooner they took the picture the sooner he could have gotten back to being with Farah.

"Oh hey, could you take it for us?" The woman pushed her phone towards Farah, her expression dropping as she awkwardly took the phone from the stranger. She didn't have much choice in the matter.

"I guess..." Farah's eyebrows dipped as she held the phone up and watched Brian's awkward people-pleasing smile turn into a photogenic grin.

"Make sure you take lots of pictures. I want to be able to pick the best one for my Instagram!" The girl instructed as she kneeled slightly and got incredibly close to Brian. Close enough for Farah to have gritted her teeth.

Farah rapidly pressed her thumb against the capture button before holding the phone out for her to take back. She didn't want to have to abide by anything else the woman said, and she certainly wasn't going to sit around and watch as she got close to him. Farah was the one who was on a date with him, not the *stranger*.

She hoped the photographs came out poorly.

Brian sat uncomfortably as he watched the stranger scroll through the pictures whilst awaiting her approval. He looked over at Farah and gave her a sympathetic smile. Almost as if he were apologising.

"Wow, thanks, *Brian*! My mom is a huge fan of The Flower Children, she'll never believe I met Cherry's son! My mom was at one of the shows right before she died, how crazy is that? Sorry, by the way. About your loss. I read all about it, didn't your dad find her in the bathroom? That's fucked up. Damn." The fan explained casually in conversation, suddenly engrossed in her phone as she continued to flick through to find the best photo. "Well, anyway, thanks for the picture!" She waved before spinning on her heel and exiting.

Brian watched as the fan disappeared, biting on his lip before tapping his finger anxiously against the table. It hadn't been the first time that had happened to him, and he knew it wouldn't have been the last. There had been no respect or humanity for his situation as if his mother were simply just someone everyone knew through watching the music channel when they were younger.

She was his *mother* first before *anything* else.

Nobody else saw that. Nobody else respected that. Nobody cared about Brian for who he was...just what he *could* have been. He was Cherry's son and couldn't amount to anything else.

Brian didn't want the comments to get to him. It was harmless. It was insensitive, but they didn't know any better. He probably would have never seen them again in his life. He couldn't let little things like that get to him. They were just bad memories now. Bad memories he wished to forget.

"Brian..." Farah whispered, reaching over to place her hand on top of his for comfort. He stared out the window for a moment before pulling his hand away. He couldn't allow her to touch him after the interaction. He didn't deserve that.

Farah was in complete shock, unable to comprehend what had just happened before her eyes. Were people truly that insensitive towards Brian and his past? Had he dealt with similar situations before?

Although he would never be used to fans of The Flower Children seeing him as a piece of a heart-breaking story, he didn't want Farah to experience it. Why did it have to happen to him when she was with him?

His world around him was crumbling. It had been a terrible day. One he once wanted to be perfect.

"Yeah?"

"Does that happen—...I'm so sorry." Farah couldn't get to a point where she was ready to finish her sentence. She was struggling to fathom what she had witnessed.

"It's okay. It's...one of those things." Brian shrugged, somewhat numb to the experience. His mind was littered with bad memories of his mother in the weeks leading to her death. It was something he had to deal with for the rest of his life. That didn't make it any better.

"It shouldn't be...I can't believe she just—" Farah was seething with rage. Who could have possibly thought that what she had said was acceptable? She wished she was brave enough to stand up for him.

"Farah, it's okay...*really.*" Brian half-smiled as he held himself. He didn't want her to have been involved in whatever bullshit life had to throw at him.

"Brian...that wasn't okay."

"It happens. People can grieve, they're just not speaking to the right person."

"That wasn't grief. That was just...*rude!*"

"There's not much privacy when it comes to my mom's...death. Everyone knows and everyone speaks to me as if it hurt *them* just as much as he hurt me. It's hard when you can just look on the internet and find my life story. She was my mom...I—...nothing about her death changes that for me. I just...I don't get the same luxury they do about the situation." Brian spoke with a slight croak, obvious pain in the way he said his words.

"I'm so sorry, Brian." Farah allowed her heart to ache for the young man. Nobody should have gone through what Brian had been through. Especially not to have been reminded of it daily by strangers who believed they knew her the way he did.

"It doesn't matter. As if I couldn't make this 'date' any worse." Brian sighed with a small chuckle. He had failed. This wasn't anything like he thought it was going to be. It wasn't his fault, but he blamed himself for being...*himself.* Farah shouldn't have had to listen to the fan. Brian wasn't after sympathy votes.

"No, no! It's fine, none of that was your fault. Don't blame yourself." Farah attempted to reach out across the table again, but was swiftly rejected. She wanted to hug him. He didn't deserve any of that.

Brian sighed deeply, he wished he weren't such a sad sack around Farah when he was so happy to have her there with him. He didn't want to burden Farah with his emotional baggage.

"Thank you for understanding." Brian wasn't sure what else to say. He had never been with anyone before where they had to witness someone saying something like that to him.

Other than the band. He had been with people who had said things like that to him...after getting what they wanted.

Why would he have ever wanted to be with people who treated him like that when Farah was right in front of him? Maybe that was all he deserved. He deserved to be used and treated like shit. He didn't deserve someone like Farah to have even paid him attention. She was too nice to him.

"Anytime." Farah smiled back, wanting to understand what it was like inside the mind of Brian Blossom.

There were some things she couldn't ever understand. Although, everything she had seen him go through matched up with what she had seen online...he had lived a difficult life. Sure, being raised around money was one thing, but living a life under difficult circumstances was another.

"C-Can we go?" Brian swallowed hard at the suggestion, pushing the coffee cup into the middle of the table and looking out the window. He didn't want to be there any longer.

"Y-yeah, of course!" Farah was quick to respond, getting up out of her chair almost instantly. She saw the vacancy in Brian's eyes and knew she had to act on his words.

Brian shyly kept to himself as they got a ride back to the motel they were staying in. He had felt embarrassed that their time had been plagued with bad thoughts and feelings interrupting the good. Firstly, it came from not being able to roller skate, messing up his idea of a date and the anxiety that came with it. Just as he thought everything was getting better, a fan had made his life a living hell just with their words.

He hadn't planned to subject Farah to any of that. Perhaps how people interacted with him was one of the many reasons why people never stuck around? He didn't want to emotionally burden them and yet that was the only thing he was good at when it came to relationships.

Farah hadn't judged him. She had barely questioned his fame or brought up his past. She wasn't interested in any of that. She was interested in him as a person and that was more than Brian could have ever asked for.

Whilst in the back of the car, Farah had decided to sit closely beside Brian, she had noticed how quiet he had become after the interaction with the fan. A quick disconnect from everything as his mind flooded with thoughts.

339

No matter what he thought there was still a beautiful girl beside him that was more than happy to have held his hand. She leaned her head against his shoulder in the back of the car, showing him comfort that he hadn't felt in a while. He wanted to cry at the connection, but he held in his tears.

She was going to leave him.

It was all just a ploy to make him feel better about himself because she was a *nice* person. As soon as the show was over that night in Chicago she would leave and never speak to him again. Why would she ever want to speak to someone like him?

A loser.

They didn't speak much after the café. Brian was saving his words for the show in the evening. They made their way back to the motel without exchanging words.

Brian had told the band he hadn't felt well, which at this point was the truth. He wanted to crawl into one of the beds inside of the motel room and sleep through his emotions, but instead he knew he had a show to play.

When they both stepped out of the car, Farah felt the disconnect immediately. He didn't want to touch her, nor did he want to even face her. He couldn't. He had messed it up and it was going to hurt too much knowing this was it.

"I should go." Brian swallowed hard on his words before shoving his hands in his jacket pockets. He dug around a little deeper hoping he had weed on him. He didn't.

"Yeah...we don't want the band to suspect anything." Farah half-smiled, trying not to feel disheartened by his lack of engagement. She hoped she hadn't said anything that could have offended him.

"Sure." Brian whispered before staring down at the floor in silence. He didn't know what else to say.

Farah held her hands together, curious to know what to do next. They had a show to go to, but Brian didn't look well after his interaction with the fan. After their time together.

His past had ruined everything again.

"Thank you for the date." Farah spoke softly as she tucked her hair behind her ear and chewed on her bottom lip.

"Sure." Brian nodded as he clamped his teeth together and held back any emotion he needed to release.

Farah took a step forward, so she was directly in front of him before putting her arms around his warm body, giving him a hug. One he needed more than anything. She could hear his shaky breath as she held her head against his chest.

"If I don't see you after the show tonight, I'll see you tomorrow." Farah closed her eyes as she hugged him. She knew he wanted the connection despite him not asking for it.

Brian didn't verbally respond, holding back his tears for what he in his head believed would have been the last time he would feel her physical touch. She was providing him with false hope to make him feel better.

Farah reluctantly let go, facing him and watching his eyes fall on hers. He blinked at her, waiting for her to turn around and never come back with the same space in her mind for him like before. He was a failure in his pursuits. Nothing like his mother and nothing like people expected of him.

Farah could only assume he needed space to process the interaction. It had caused him a lot of upset and she didn't know how to solve it other than to let him deal with it in a way he understood. He admitted to having encounters like it before.

"Okay." Brian uttered, his thoughts and feelings overtaking his ability to speak.

Farah nodded; she wasn't sure what would have been best for Brian. She wasn't sure what would have been best for *them*. All she knew was that she had to give it time.

In her mind, the date had been fine. She had enjoyed her time with Brian until the fan had disturbed them. Even then, it wasn't his fault. He was only going to blame himself for all the things he had messed up. He was so prepared for it to be perfect, but his expectations only turned out to be lies.

Farah held herself as she walked back to the motel room she was staying in with Max. She would have been lying if she hadn't felt the sense of rejection from Brian. It couldn't have been over, not like that. She didn't know what she was going to tell Max about their time together and she had no idea when she would next speak to him. Even if she did, would it have been the right time?

Farah slumped herself down on the end of the bed when she entered, opening her phone and staring down at her messages. It had been seconds, but she was sure he would have texted her something. Anything. Confirmation of them having a good time together.

Nothing.

Her heart ached at the thought of him in emotional pain. An emotional spiral he was unable to escape from. If she had to battle with anxiety, she had no idea what Brian dealt with inside of his mind. He had been there to help her when she had been down and yet now he was struggling she was unsure how to help him.

Farah had all sorts of thoughts running through her mind when it came to Brian and his situation, finding herself scrolling through pages about him online as she waited for Max to return to the room so they could go to the show. It felt as if she was invading his privacy by doing so, immediately closing the page after reading a sentence. She didn't want to base her assumptions on the man from pages online. She wasn't like...*them*.

When it was time for the show, Brian still didn't look any better. After Farah had left him, he had spent the rest of his time alone smoking whatever pot he could find inside of his bag back in the motel room. It served to relax his thoughts, but this time only made him more paranoid.

His erratic behaviour helped their cause; the band were genuinely convinced he wasn't feeling well. They would have been able to pull through the show, but it would have been an early night for Brian.

He wanted to get the show over and done with and head back to the motel. Nothing more and nothing less. He wasn't even willing to stick around to meet any of his fans as he usually did. He didn't want to be in the spotlight for any longer than what was required of him.

This time, when Farah watched him play on the stage the emotion in which he exhibited were different from the previous nights. Although a lot of his songs expressed what seemed to have been pent up anger and frustration, he always ended them with a smile.

Until that night.

As Brian shouted into the microphone, Farah began to listen to the emotion in his voice. The sheer anger he held within him about his memories. He was singing about them. It was the only release he had from the pain he held deep within, covered up by twinkly tones and silly titles.

That night, Brian left the venue the moment they had packed everything away. Farah had texted him to ask if he needed to talk about it, but he had never responded.

Perhaps Brian was a fool for not texting back, but he knew it would only lead to heartbreak. He couldn't handle any more of that in his life. Instead, he chose to stare at the message with responses in his head, typing them out before deleting them.

There was no coming back from the ruined date.

It was all his fault.

GRAND RAPIDS, MI

"Why can't you just speak to him?" Max questioned, eating a chip from the bag she was holding as they sat in the parking lot of a museum they had just visited together in Grand Rapids.

"He's not responding to my texts, and he wouldn't talk to me when we were in Urbana either."

"Speak to him after the show tonight. We were all tired after visiting the house."

They had woken up early in Chicago to make a four-hour detour to Urbana to visit a house Russ insisted was a key part of emo history. Max was excited to visit the house with the number '704' on the outside. They all took photos on the street by the house, Farah stood in the background, confused why the white house that was falling apart was of any significance. Max had explained the significance multiple times in the car, but she had been distracted.

Brian hadn't spoken to her the entire time they were there. He couldn't face the final rejection she had in store for him in his mind. He was terrified that would be their last conversation before they parted ways.

"I just feel bad. You should have seen the look on his face. I've never seen him so *sad* before." Farah pushed her elbow against the door as she balanced her cheeks against her knuckles.

Farah sighed heavily as Max crunched another chip. She looked over and furrowed her eyebrows at her best friend's expression. She was torn up about the man's sadness and the separation it had caused them.

"I'm sure he's okay. Maybe he needs someone to be there for him?" Max didn't know a lot about relationships, but she did know her friend was one to blame herself for situations. "He's probably just having a hard time in his mind. You know how it is."

"You're right." Farah exhaled deeply. She knew Max made sense, but it was hard to come to that conclusion in her head. She went over everything she had said throughout their day together, trying to examine if it was something she had done that had caused him to close up. He had responded positively to nearly everything she had said, until he didn't respond at all.

It was hard going the entire day knowing Brian didn't want to speak to her. It was only a couple of hours before they had to go to the show, and she knew Brian would have inescapable thoughts. What she didn't know was how most of those thoughts involved her.

Nobody was perfect, but he had tried so hard.

Couldn't the world give him that?

"You seem real distant, dude. Everything good?" Catfish questioned as he stood beside Brian at the fire exit of the venue. They had only just managed to set everything up.

Brian balanced the unlit joint between his lips as he flicked the wheel of his lighter repeatedly. Just his luck, it wasn't working. He tried once more before noticing Catfish had pulled another lighter from his pocket and was holding it out for him to take. Brian looked up at his friend and gently took the lighter from his open palm.

"Thanks." Brian mumbled with the joint still between his lips, shoving his lighter in his pocket before using Catfish's to light up. He made sure to pocket Catfish's lighter for future use. They had loads of lighters in the van.

Brian took a long hit of the joint the moment he had lit it, desperate for the relief. It was enough to make him cough slightly before passing it over to Catfish who immediately took it from him.

"Yo dude, you good?" Catfish patted his back as he choked, repeating the words he had since ignored. Brian coughed into his arm and regained his breath.

"I-I'm fine." Brian winced, pushing his back against the wall as he readjusted his jacket.

He didn't want to admit any of his feelings to Catfish. He had a show to play and letting any of his emotions pour out beforehand would have been a mistake. For someone he cared about, he had done a good job at avoiding Farah all day. He dreaded that final conversation.

"Are you sure?" Catfish asked, taking a hit of the joint.

"Are you going to do that cool drum solo again tonight? I thought it was sick." Brian complimented, doing anything to speak to Catfish about something other than his mental health. That was the last thing he wanted.

"Hell yeah! It's going to be awesome. Some chick recorded it and put half of last night's show online already. It even has artsy filters and shit. We're amazing! You fuckin' shred, my man." Catfish bunched his fist and knocked Brian in the arm causing him to force a smile.

"Yeah, we're pretty good." Brian smiled, reaching out and taking the joint back from Catfish. There was no way he was going to let him keep it.

Admittedly, that night, he would have preferred not to have played. His dad wouldn't have been happy if he ever cancelled a show last minute. He would never forgive him.

That night, Brian Blossom went onto the stage and continued to stew on the thoughts he had formed in his head. Thoughts that had been plaguing him all day. He was scared. Scared of the reality that came with messing everything up. Why couldn't he have gotten the date perfect?

She would never want to be with him outside of the tour now. That was his final chance to prove his worth and he had ruined it completely.

He played the show as he did every night, with no intention of staying. He had searched for Farah in the crowd but couldn't see her. He was worried she hadn't bothered to show up. He didn't blame her; he didn't want to be there either. Especially not to see him play.

Once again, the band had opted to stay in a motel that was by the venue. Unluckily for Brian, it was the same one Farah and Max were staying in. It would have been impossible to avoid her, but in his mind he knew he wanted to be with her...even if he was afraid of the rejection.

Farah had decided to head back to the motel early, without Max. She had hidden herself at the back of the venue throughout the show, but she was determined to take Max's advice. Rather than continue to text him, she had to confront him in person to make sure he was okay.

She had gotten back to the motel a little sooner than Brian, allowing her to wait in her room and look out of the window, anxiously awaiting an arrival of a car. She had found his fiasco silly but wanted to understand why he couldn't just *speak* to her about what had happened. It wasn't as if the fan speaking to them had anything to do with Farah.

She wasn't to blame, and neither was he. They still had a nice date together. At least, that's what Farah thought.

Farah had put her Social Dropouts hoodie on and tied up her hair as she watched a car pull into the parking lot and drop off a tired looking man.

Brian sat down on a small wall that surrounded the parking lot of the motel. He needed somewhere to sit so he could roll the joint he deserved after the show. Another one. His mind was hazy, but he didn't care. Farah exited the room and made her way over to him.

He looked up and noticed her walking towards him. As beautiful as ever. He was such a fuck up for believing this time would be different. Nothing would ever change who he was, and he would always be reminded of it.

Brian took a deep breath, knowing the moment he had been dreading was finally dawning upon him.

This was it.

Farah sat beside him in silence, not knowing what else to do. She held her hands in the front pocket of the hoodie and watched him roll the joint. He had done it so many times before he did it without thinking.

Brian didn't say a word as he placed the joint between his lips and dug around in his pocket to find the lighter he had taken from Catfish. For someone who was once embarrassed about smoking in front of Farah, that fear had dissipated in his time of release. She didn't mind and even if she had, at that moment Brian wouldn't have cared.

"Did you get my texts?" Farah asked suddenly, wanting to know if he had read everything she had said. Most of which were just questions of confirmation to make sure he was okay. Texts that told him it wasn't his fault and that she had enjoyed herself. Things she thought he needed to hear.

"Yeah, I did." Brian flicked the lighter and Farah watched a flame spark.

"You didn't respond."

"I didn't know what to say."

"That's okay—"

"I know you're not here to smoke." Brian grumbled as he took an extended puff of the joint between his fingers before leaning his elbows on his knees for support.

"I thought maybe you'd want the company." Farah shrugged.

"When I'm smoking?" Brian cocked an eyebrow, knowing Farah was internally against his bad habits. She wasn't vocal about them...but he could tell.

"Yep."

"You hate smoking."

"I don't mind. I like being with you." Farah tried to smile. She had never seen him like this before, vacant and devoid of emotion.

This was the opposite of what Brian had thought in his mind. She wasn't supposed to *want* to be with him. Nobody *liked* being with him.

Brian couldn't understand why she was still there. After all the shit he had put her through. From a failed date where he looked like an idiot, being pounced on by a fan only to be triggered enough by her words to cause him to spiral. Brian was a worthless piece of shit who couldn't get anything right and he hated himself for it.

"Why the *hell* are you still here?" His words came out cold and a little harsher than he had expected. Most of all, Farah was taken back by his sudden change in tone.

"*Excuse me?*" Farah's eyes widened at his comment, her heart racing as he caught her off guard.

Brian took a hit of the joint before running his fingers through his hair. Farah didn't know what to do as she sat beside him, watching the young man dig his fingernails into his scalp.

He had fucked everything up.

Farah welcomed the silence until it was filled with Brian's loud sobs. He made sure to keep his eyes covered with his hand as he rested his elbows on his legs. Brian turned away the best he could, the burning joint in his other hand. He didn't want her to see him like this.

She didn't deserve that.

Farah had never heard anyone sob the way Brian was. It was heart breaking and put Farah in a position she didn't want to be in. She had no idea what she could do to help. The most she could do was be there for him.

"I-I'm so s-sorry." Brian choked through his cries, trying to compose himself in front of her. It was proving harder than he first thought. "I-I didn't mean that. I didn't—. Fuck! Shit!" Brian wiped his eyes to rid himself of whatever tears he had wept.

"Do you need me to go?" Farah held her own hands a little tighter for comfort. She pressed her lips together as he contemplated an answer.

Brian was a lot more complicated than just being the frontman of an emo band. His situation was far more complex. He had issues even years of therapy couldn't resolve.

"I don't w-want you to go." Brian shook his head, pinching the bridge of his nose as he attempted to collect his thoughts. It wasn't working. "I want you to stay. I mean, if y-you want to stay. I just don't understand why you would want to—"

"What?" Farah saw his isolation from the burden he carried that fell heavy on his shoulders.

"My mom left. My mom's bandmates left. My dad's barely around. The band's sticking around for now, but they'll leave one day too. Bailey left! It's not impossible! Max is going to leave! *You're* going to leave! *Everyone* leaves!" Brian raised his voice through his frustration, violently animating his hands in front of him.

She watched as he turned to face her, his eyes were red from his tears. He still held the joint between his fingers, but he allowed it to burn away as he focused his attention on his emotions.

"You're—"

"I ruin everything. I ruined *this*. People don't want to be around me, Farah. You're the first person to ever look at me like a human fuckin' being and I *ruined* it. I don't understand why you're still here. Right here...next to me! *Me*! Y'know...the guy whose dead junkie mom has all those shitty songs you hear on the radio!" Brian gritted his teeth together as he pointed at his chest, tears streaming down either side of his face. He blinked a few times to clear the water from his eyes. "T-that's all I am. To anyone..."

Farah sat there in silence, feeling nothing but sympathy for the man. She really had been the first person to stick around. His mother had left him when he was young. From what she knew, his dad didn't stick around for long either. Always on tours or managing bands in different states. The only constant in his life was the band.

"Brian..." Farah reached out and placed her hand on his shoulder as he breathed deeply. He had comforted her the first time they had met and she only wanted to return the favour.

She watched his body language shift at her touch, his leg beginning to shake as he turned away and took a long drag of the joint. He wanted to escape. He hated it when it didn't work, understanding why his mother chose harder drugs. He hated that realisation even more. His bad habits came in other forms.

They shared a moment of silence as Farah took in the herbal smell of the joint he was smoking. She wanted to worry about the amount of second-hand smoke she was breathing in, but it wasn't her priority.

In the silence, Farah decided to shuffle closer. Unlike when they were in the café, he didn't move away. Brian noticed her movements but didn't pay much mind until her arms wrapped around him. Another hug. He stared forward at the parking lot as he felt the comforting embrace. He let out a shaky breath with his mouth slightly ajar as Farah placed her cheek against his arm, holding him tightly.

"I know we haven't known each other for long, but you're not that to me. You're Brian Blossom, one of the kindest and sweetest people I've ever met. If people paid attention past what they wanted to see, they'd realise that too." Farah practically mumbled into his jacket. "I'm here if you need to...talk about things."

Brian attempted to digest the words. She was so nice to him and it broke his heart to know it could all be over in just a few days. Then it would have been like every other time.

"I'm not very good at talking about it." Brian practically whispered as he balanced his wrists on his knees, the joint slowly burning.

"That's okay too, but I'll be here if you ever want to try." Farah confirmed, offering her companionship beyond the tour. At least, that was how it sounded.

"I'm sorry I was an asshole." Brian chewed his lip as he stared down at the joint. "I-I typed out loads of messages. I was so worried you'd never speak to me again; I didn't think there was any point. I'm sorry."

"You don't need to apologise. I understand." Farah nuzzled her cheek against his jacket, feeling her glasses push against her face as she held him.

"I'm so glad I met you." Brian sniffed loudly before wiping his eyes, Farah gently let go of him.

Brian took another puff of the joint, the contents slowly going to his head.

He couldn't help going into a different headspace over the bad day he had experienced. Surprisingly, it had taken more days on tour than it usually did to have an emotional crisis. Brian was convinced that with Farah being there he had managed to suppress whatever feelings he would usually hold on tour, replacing them with a beautiful distraction.

"Me too." Farah whispered as she placed her head on his shoulder.

They sat there for a moment together as Brian smoked, consuming a little more in a short period than he should have. It felt nice to have Farah so close. He was lucky. The first good thing that had happened to him since the band.

She looked over to him, he was still scruffy from the show and where he had repeatedly run his fingers through his hair. His eyes were red from his tears and his shirt underneath his denim jacket was creased and curling at the collar. Farah sat up and he turned to face her, she adjusted his collar to make it neater. It wasn't so much about making sure the shirt looked good, it was about forming a connection between them.

Farah had admitted to Max that she liked Brian. It had been the first time she had confessed how far her little crush for the frontman of an emo band went. This felt like more than an innocent crush.

Brian bit down on his bottom lip as he caught her eyes in his line of sight, exchanging a deep stare.

His eyes were heavy as he took another hit of the joint out the corner of his mouth, torn between Farah and his bad habit. He finally turned back and stubbed the remainder of the joint out on the brick wall, part of him grimacing at the wastage. He stubbed it out just enough so he could relight it later.

He looked back towards Farah with hesitation, he was embarrassed by his actions. In a way, Farah understood.

"I'm so sorry." Brian spoke softly, his apology sweet and genuine. Farah heard it louder than ever as he reached out and gripped onto her hands. As per usual, his hands were soft aside from his calloused fingertips.

"I already said you don't need to apologise."

"I do. It's not right. I don't want you to think I'm taking advantage of you. I'm really sorry, Farah." Brian apologised again.

"You're not—"

"My problems are *my* problems. I shouldn't be sharing that burden with anyone." Brian shook his head as Farah felt his thumbs rub against her hands.

"You're allowed to have feelings, Brian." Farah attempted a smile. Brian stared down at her hands, they fitted so perfectly in his.

Farah was trying her hardest to look out for the man as much as he had looked out for her. It was clear he hid behind a façade, and it hurt her to know it had slipped. She didn't want him to be alone.

"Thank you for being...amazing." Brian smiled sweetly, finding it hard not to as he thought about everything she had done for him over the past couple of weeks.

Farah blushed at his comment. She wanted to make sure he was okay. She wanted to be there for him.

"Would you like to stay with me tonight?" Farah offered, her kindness coming through. All her pragmatic thinking fell through as she ignored the logistics of them staying together.

"With you and Max?" Brian cocked an eyebrow, he hadn't expected the ask.

"Don't you sleep in the van sometimes?"

"You want to sleep in the *van*!?" Brian blinked a few times at her request. Farah was just as shocked at her suggestion as he was.

Sleeping in the van? She wasn't sure how much she approved of the idea.

"I want to be with you tonight." Farah chewed the inside of her lip as she looked away. She wanted to be with Brian.

"I want to be with you too." Brian croaked. A realisation within himself that this was a moment he had always craved.

Someone was asking him to stay.

"Max will be happy to get the room to herself." Farah smirked.

"And the band won't even notice." Brian sighed; he had done it more times than he was willing to admit.

Farah wanted to say something inspiring, something that would make him smile. She was out of ideas. Out of anything that would have made things better.

There were just some things in life she couldn't make better for him. That was just fact. She didn't know him well enough to continue to comment. She didn't know nor would she ever be able to relate to what he had been through.

It was only an hour later that everyone had returned and Brian and Farah agreed to meet. Farah told Max what she was doing which resulted in an overly tired groan, she was barely paying attention. Brian went back to the room, briefly spoke to the band and then went out to the van.

Farah had kept the Social Dropouts hoodie on over some shorts, if she was sleeping in the van then she wanted to be as comfortable as possible. Brian was sitting at the side of the van with the door opened as she approached.

"Welcome to my humble abode." Brian chuckled nervously as he stepped inside of the van and out of the way, urging Farah to join him. She laughed as she climbed inside and pulled the sliding door closed.

They had spent the hour collecting their thoughts. It had been a strange couple of days between them and they still managed to smile.

The van was old and wasn't very aesthetically pleasing. The seats were ripped and stained from years of use. Farah was thankful the only real lighting inside of the van was the dim yellow light on the ceiling and the streetlamp outside. She clambered past the seats and into the back where Brian had laid down a blue sleeping bag. There wasn't enough room, but Brian was determined to make it work. He had already messed everything else up, what else could go wrong?

"It's not exactly a five-star hotel, but hey, it's better than the floor." Brian smiled as Farah recalled the memory from one of the first nights they had spent together. She didn't want to have to sleep on the floor again.

"Anything is better than the floor." Farah snorted as she sat down on the sleeping bag, Brian held himself between the two seats in the middle of the van.

Brian had taken off his jacket and had thrown it over one of the seats in the front, leaving him in his burgundy flannel shirt.

"I'm sorry about everything that happened yesterday. I didn't want you to see that. I wanted you to have a good time." Brian sighed as he brushed his hands through his hair anxiously.

Another apology.

"It's okay." Farah shook her head as she held out both her hands, he reached out and held on, slumping himself down in the seat beside her.

"Sometimes I get so caught up in my head. I hate it." Brian had spent the past hour attempting to rationalise his thoughts. He had come to a somewhat healthy conclusion.

"It's okay to have bad days." Farah shuffled closer to him, she wanted him to know he wasn't alone.

"I just don't want to bring other people down."

"You make emo music, Brian." Farah laughed at his comment, finding the irony in it.

"That's different, it's not about making people sad. It's about making sad people feel a little less alone." Brian spoke softly, his reasoning and wording were mesmerizing.

"That's...beautiful." Farah was taken back by his words.

"It's...yeah..." Brian held his hands together and twiddled his thumbs.

Farah smiled at him whilst shuffling closer. She let her hair down and took off her glasses. There was confidence in her movements as she touched his chest and cuddled close to him. Brian tried not to smile at her action but failed miserably.

Brian turned slightly, making himself as comfortable as possible as he lifted his arm and allowed Farah to lie down on his chest, hugging him around his torso. Other than the morning after their night together in LA, Brian had never cuddled with a girl before. He had never felt a connection this close with anyone before as Farah closed her eyes and listened to his heartbeat.

"Thank you for staying with me." Brian whispered.

"Anytime." Farah replied, nuzzling herself into Brian's shirt as she got complacent enough to sleep.

When Brian opened his eyes in the morning the first thing he noticed was his fingers being touched softly. Farah's fingers lightly brushed against his as he held her in his sleep. Brian's neck didn't enjoy the position he had been in throughout the night, but after looking down at Farah still cuddling him every instance of pain was destined to disappear.

He wasn't sure what time it was, but he knew it was morning from the light breaking through the front of the van. The rest of the windows were tinted. As by 'tinted', he meant they had been painted black.

Brian stretched slightly, Farah noticed his gradual movements, continuing to keep herself resting on his chest. She had gotten used to listening to his heartbeat. Farah continued to play with his fingers as they laid together in the back of the van. She had slept considerably well despite being in such a small space.

"Good morning." Farah spoke quietly as she noticed his breathing pattern change.

"Good morning." Brian grinned as he repeated her words, taking a deep breath in and stretching the best he could whilst seated.

"That was nice." Farah turned to look up at Brian.

"Think you could get used to sleeping in a van?" Brian chuckled.

"No, but I could get used to sleeping with you." Farah commented without thinking about the words coming out of her mouth. She immediately realised her words were forward and suggestive, gasping at her comment.

"That has two *very* different meanings." Brian snorted at the utterance, internally wishing both meanings were the truth.

"Yeah..." Farah laughed nervously. She would never verbally admit to agreeing with both meanings.

Farah sat up straight, pushing her hair out of her face and putting her glasses back on.

Brian leaned his elbow on the back of the seat and held his head up with his hand as he looked over at her with infatuation in his eyes. He couldn't believe how lucky he was to have been sitting in the back of the van with a girl he was attracted to. He had cuddled with her all night and she was still there when he had woken up.

It was a dream come true.

Even after the bad day Brian had experienced, Farah had been there the whole time to see him through it. She didn't mind, she wanted to be with him.

Farah adjusted her hair with her fingers, wanting to look somewhat presentable without a hairbrush. It wasn't working out the way she wanted to as she felt a certain person's eyes burning into her sweetly. She turned and saw Brian with his head against his hand staring at her as he always did. His affectionate eyes she had found herself falling for time and time again.

"You're the prettiest girl I've ever seen." Brian swooned, unable to comprehend his attraction for the girl. No matter what he did, he couldn't help but look at her.

Farah smirked shyly as she placed her hands on her knees. She shouldn't have been nervous around Brian, but she was. She watched as his hand balanced itself on top of hers. It didn't matter how many times he touched her, every time she felt that same sense of desire.

"You're not so bad yourself." Farah chuckled; Brian found humour in her words. Her words were coming from a place of genuine attraction and Brian knew that.

Brian coaxed her hand away from her leg, allowing him to trace circles with his finger around the top of her thigh as he looked at her. Farah wasn't sure what he was doing, but what she did know was he was a complete and utter tease. He had woken up with Farah in his arms, causing his mind to travel as he held her.

"I hope this makes up for a bad first date." Brian sighed; Farah felt as if he got a little closer with every word.

"It wasn't *bad*." Farah countered; she could tell he was embarrassed about everything that happened. The only thing that truly bothered her was how awful the 'fan' had been and the distress it had caused.

"I never got to kiss you." Brian pouted as he swirled his finger on her knee. Farah turned in the seat to match his position.

"You never asked."

Brian watched Farah's lips curl slowly, finding satisfaction in teasing him in return.

"Do you want to make out?" Brian bit down on his lip as he asked.

"That's a little more than a kiss." Farah chuckled, respecting his honesty. He was forward about it, but it didn't make her uncomfortable.

"Are we allowed to make out on our first date?"

"Brian, we've had...sex." Farah spoke in a slight whisper, confused by his flirtatious logic.

"Is that a *yes*?" Brian gave a cocky smile, pushing his luck.

Farah sighed heavily with a smile, rolling her eyes slightly and making Brian laugh. She leaned forward and planted her lips against his.

Farah took the opportunity to lead the kiss, confident enough to take control. It felt nice to know things were on her terms and Brian was happy to comply.

There were plenty of thoughts running through her mind, but one was dominating everything. She had never thought about sex as much as she had done that week with Brian. Now it felt like something she was struggling not to think about.

He was always on her mind.

Farah clambered onto his lap as she held onto the front of his shirt, her lips still on his. He hadn't expected her to sit on him, hormones flooding through his body at the touch.

Farah placed her hands on either side of his face, their kisses becoming deep and passionate as her palms pushed against his stubble. She was in a state of intoxication as his hands fell to her hips, this time he wasn't shy about touching her. Farah didn't mind, too focused on the feeling of her lips against him and the way her body slotted so perfectly into his.

Farah felt Brian's warm hands travel underneath the hoodie and touch her bare skin. His calloused fingertips made their way up her back, heading straight to where her bra would have sat. He was surprised to find she wasn't wearing one, continuing to kiss her with intent.

Farah gripped onto his shirt, taking note of the way she subconsciously moved her hips against him to the beat of their kisses. When she had woken up that morning, she hadn't expected to have been kissing him so soon after. She hadn't had the chance to wake up before horny thoughts dominated her mind.

The way he kissed her was soft and passionate, unlike when he had pushed her against the cabinet in the recording studio. The soft intimacy of their second time in the pool house had been much more rewarding. Brian had learned his lesson, making sure to go slower in the back of the van.

Farah held onto him as she felt his body pressed tightly against her, this wasn't the kind of thing she imagined when Max had suggested going on the tour.

He unlatched his lips from her neck and placed his hands back on her waist as he looked up to face her.

"I have to ask..." Brian pouted as he looked directly at her, he noticed her face had turned red.

Farah smiled as she threaded her fingers through the back of his hair, keeping her arms resting on his shoulders as they looped around him. She kissed him softly on the lips, wanting to be in control of the situation. Brian allowed her to kiss him a few times, still awaiting verbal confirmation.

"Yeah...I do." Farah breathed heavily as she pushed their foreheads together.

Brian fell back into the habit of kissing her aggressively at the agreement of what would have happened next.

He could have kissed and teased her all day, except at that moment he wanted nothing more than to pleasure her in a way he couldn't do solely with his kisses. Selfishly, he wanted satisfaction for himself too.

It wasn't long before they had switched positions on the back seat of the van, Farah lying down on her back as Brian held himself above her. As much as Brian wanted Farah to take control of the situation, he wasn't sure how confident she was. He was happy to take the lead.

She allowed him to put his hands wherever he pleased, granting him full access to her body for the third time since they had first met. Once again, it was a whole new experience for them both. Not only a little uncomfortable in the back of the tattered van, but different in the way their bodies found themselves intertwined. They were beginning to understand one another in ways they didn't before. The connection between them was growing in a way unmatched by anyone else.

Neither Brian nor Farah had ever experienced anything like it.

It wasn't long until they were both spent, both breathing heavily at what could have been rated as the best sex they had both had.

Brian laid lazily on her stomach between her legs and held her tightly as she brushed his messy hair with her fingers. As much as she was conscious of herself being nude, they had already shared a few times without any articles of clothing. She doubted it would have mattered much as they caught their breath.

Brian was a little shocked that sex with someone a third time could be so rewarding. He was more than ready to have stayed in the van all day holding her closely. They were both currently swept away in their post-sex high as Farah stared at the ceiling, threading her fingers through his hair and massaging his scalp as she felt his stubble against her stomach. His eyes were closed as he held onto her, she could feel the smile on his lips against her skin. She too could have stayed in that moment forever.

"I can't believe this will be over in a few days." Farah sighed as she got into a headspace where she could gather her thoughts.

Brian's eyes shot open as he looked towards her, balancing his chin on her stomach.

"What do you mean?"

"The tour. You've only got three more shows."

"Oh..." Brian felt a sense of deflation as he rested his head back on her stomach, not wanting to think too deeply about what that meant for them.

"Don't you have your own apartment in Nashville?" Farah suddenly questioned, taking Brian by surprise.

"Yeah, that's right." Brian balanced his chin back on her stomach, wanting to be an active participant in the conversation. "You'll have to come and visit sometime. I could show you some cool spots." Brian suggested with a smile as he reached over for her hand, threading his fingers between hers.

They knew they would have to get up soon despite neither of them wanting to. They had to travel to Indianapolis before late afternoon, although the journey wasn't that long in the car.

"That would be nice. You can come to my college too." Farah felt his fingers between hers, making the suggestion was the best way to get him to see her after the tour. She would have liked that.

"Yeah?" Brian's eyes lit up at the idea. She was suggesting plans with him, something he didn't think a girl he had met on tour would have ever done.

"Sure! You might have to put up with Max showing you through her vinyl record collection though."

"I'm okay with that." Brian grinned, happy to have been invited in the first place.

"Speaking of, we should probably get ready." Farah sighed. If she could have laid in that position forever, she probably would have accepted the offer.

Brian let out a long groan. The last thing he wanted was social interaction with anyone but Farah.

With much hesitation, Brian and Farah attempted to get dressed after picking up the clothes they had haphazardly thrown on the floor of the van. After spending the night on the top of the sleeping bag, Farah regretfully glanced down at the floor realising how disgusting it was. She preferred the van when it was dark outside and she couldn't see every discrepancy.

It was hard for them to get dressed without latching onto one another's lips. Each kiss was matched with a small giggle between sloppily putting articles of clothing on. Neither of them was paying attention to anything other than themselves.

Farah was wonderful and every moment Brian got to spend with her, he was going to savour. There was nothing better than being attached to her lips. Farah felt a sense of elation as he ran his hands over her body as they sloppily got dressed.

After the previous night, Farah had witnessed Brian in the worst mental prison he had been in for a while. A part of her was curious to know if the sex had helped distract him from his thoughts, something she had guessed he used as a coping mechanism in the past. Farah was smart enough to figure out if she was being manipulated and interestingly enough, this didn't feel like one of those times. His thoughts and feelings were genuine.

Neither of them wanted to leave, but they knew they would have to tumble out of the van at some point. Even if that meant they continued the kiss they never wanted it to end.

Brian slowly slid the door of the van open, keeping his lips on Farah's as they deepened the kiss, stepping out of the van whilst giggling. They were drunker on each other than they would have liked to admit.

They continued to kiss, completely unaware of what was around them.

Suddenly, a cough. Followed by...

"We just wanted to know if you wanted pancakes, man." The disappointed voice of Catfish sounded.

"I think I've lost my appetite." Russ sighed.

"Brian..." Zoe spoke in a low tone of disappointment.

"Woah! Brian and Farah? *Together?* What a shocking turn of events! The plot thickens!" Max was the last to speak as she pointed towards the couple and spoke sarcastically.

Brian disconnected his lips from Farah and turned around to see the band standing in front of him. His jaw dropped in shock as Farah buried her head in her hands at Max's response.

Oh no...

Busted.

"What a lovely morning we're having!" Brian commented as sweat began to trickle down the side of his face, suddenly not feeling so great about the wonderful morning he had experienced.

"What were you two *doing?*" Zoe placed her hand on her hip.

"Bird watching!" Farah blurted out as Brian's eyes widened at her response.

Shit.

"There aren't any birds in our van. It's the incorrect habitat!" Russ folded over his arms.

"Uh Brian, your shirt is inside out." Max pointed out bluntly as Brian stared down at his shirt, noticing the label sticking out of the side and in turn the upside-down collar.

"Whoops!"

"This is just like Portland..." Catfish gasped.

"This is nothing like *Portland!*" Brian countered in his defence, pointing aggressively at Catfish.

"Are you sure? It sort of looks like Portland."

"Yeah, it totally looks like Portland." Russ interjected.

"This isn't Portland!" Brian shouted, gripping onto his hair.

"What happened in Portland?" Max lifted a finger as she questioned, out of sorts with the conversation.

"Nothing!" All four band members turned around and shouted at Max, catching her off guard.

"Ooo touchy subject...remind me to never bring that up ever again." Max giggled nervously as she stepped back.

"You're *sleeping* together now?" Zoe questioned as she pointed at both Brian and Farah.

"Nope." Farah pressed her lips into a thin line.

"A little bit."

"Brian!?" Farah shot an intense glare at him as he held onto the label that was sticking out of the shirt. She should have noticed the misaligned buttons but hadn't been paying attention.

"What? I'm not good at lying!" Brian panicked as Farah took a deep breath and buried her head in her hands in sheer embarrassment.

"I am so shocked by this. Farah, I'm disappointed in your actions. Brian...you pervert. Fiend! How dare you dick down my best friend! Oh, the humility!" Max spoke in a sarcastic tone as she pointed at Brian and shook her finger.

"*Dick down*?" Brian blinked rapidly as he held his chest.

"What the—" Farah looked back up in horror.

"Woah. Tone down the melodrama. We don't have any grounds for judgement. Brian's free to be whoever Brian wants to be. If Brian wants to be Brian with Farah, then let Brian be free." Russ inputted into the situation as everyone exchanged glances, unclear of what he was trying to say.

Brian and Farah felt embarrassed by the situation. It felt as if it was a situation Brian had found himself caught up in throughout his past...but this was different.

"Band meeting!" Zoe instructed, as much as she loved Max and Farah's presence this was something that needed to be discussed without them.

The band spun on their heels and headed back towards the hotel room. Brian continued to hold the label on the side of his shirt in embarrassment.

"I'll see you later?" Brian half-smiled as he turned back, realising he was probably about to receive a lecture about sleeping around on tour. The same one he had received countless times in the past.

"Yeah." Farah smiled in response as she waved, watching him follow the rest of the band.

Max stood beside Farah with her hands on her hips and joined her in watching the band disappear behind a closed door in the motel.

"Well, that was an interesting turn of events." Max sighed.

"*Dick down*? Really?" Farah scowled.

"I was trying to hype the drama, y'know? This is some prime-time television emo Shakespearean shit. Oh! Maybe like one of those reality TV shows. *'College girl fucks emo boy— shocking story! Sad songs are written about a sad fuck.'*"

"It wasn't a 'sad fuck'."

"Oh, I see...you *are* going to tell me the details?" Max adjusted the beanie on the top of her head before pondering as she stroked her chin. "Wait. Save it. It'll make good television. All I need is a camera, and we can sell it for hella cash. At the very least, this is going to be the topic of a song."

"This is one of the most embarrassing moments of my life." Farah sighed, taking off her glasses and cleaning them against the Social Dropouts hoodie. A part of her was glad Max already knew, otherwise her anxiety levels would have been through the roof.

"How much do you think a Brian Blossom porno is worth?"

"Max..."

"I'm curious, y'know? How famous is he *really*? Could we be the ones to make him *famous-er*? Get the camera close enough and he could have a famous pe—"

"*Max*! Don't finish that!" Farah gasped in horror.

"That's the sort of thing you say to someone who's halfway through eating an under-cooked chicken, not someone who's going to make you big bucks off your boyfriend's peen." Max shook her head before smirking, too caught in teasing her best friend.

"I wish you wouldn't say that."

"Peen? Would you rather I said *ding dong big schlong*?"

"No! Boyfriend! Don't call him my *boyfriend*!" Farah shook her head, unable to cut off Max's inappropriate words before she spoke. Max's humour was hilarious at the best of times, but it grew frustrating to be around. Farah loved her no matter what but wished she wouldn't have to hear words like *ding dong big schlong* coming out her mouth in such quick succession.

"Sorry, it's a little early to be throwing the b-word around when you're only f-wording." Max sighed before throwing her hands in her pockets and rocking on her heels, both still standing by the van looking at the motel room door in the distance.

Farah dreaded to think about the conversation Brian was having.

"It's a little more than that."

"Ugh. You're not in *love* are you?" Max looked over at Farah with a huge grin.

Farah stared down at the floor before pushing her hands into the front pocket of the hoodie. Farah had never been 'in love' before. Was it possible to be 'in love' after just a couple of weeks?

"N-no. You can't fall in love that fast. It's stupid."

"Hm, you don't sound so sure."

"I really like being with him." Farah smiled at the thought as she gently scuffed the bottom of her shoe against the asphalt.

"That sounds like you love him."

"I didn't say that."

"You said it with your eyes."

"I wasn't even looking at you!"

"I know, but I can tell. Ha! My Rah Rah is in love!" Max cheered with a slight whisper, worried the band may have heard through the door. Max began to poke Farah in her sides to irritate her further.

"I'm not!" Farah chuckled, gently swatting her best friend away.

"You're going red!" Max teased.

"That's because I'm ticklish!" Farah pushed Max away harder, causing her to get the message.

Max stood still for a moment as Farah regained her breath before brushing the front of her hoodie. Max glanced back at the van and furrowed her eyebrows, connecting the dots in her mind.

"Hold the fucking phone..." Max took a deep breath.

"What?"

"Did you two get *frisky* in that van?" Max pointed behind her to the van as she pushed her lips together.

"I..."

"Farah! I'm the biggest Social Dropouts fan there is, do you know how excited I was to get to ride in that thing the other day? Too excited! But you...*you* got to have sex with one of them *in* there? What the fu—"

"Max! I didn't mean for that to happen, it just *did*!" Farah attempted to get Max to lower her voice, she didn't want unsuspecting members of the public to hear.

"You are blowing my mind."

Farah wasn't sure what else to say as she rested her back against the side of the van and groaned. Things didn't need to be this complicated. Things didn't need to be as they were. Brian and Farah were both adults and there was no reason why they couldn't have been together.

Was there?

Brian had been dragged into the room and sat down on the end of one of the beds as the band took their places. Catfish slumped himself down on the edge of a bed as Russ pulled up a chair, sitting on it backwards. Zoe remained standing as she began to pace back and forth in front of Brian.

"Why didn't you tell us?" Zoe questioned; a little hurt Brian didn't have the confidence to speak to them. They were all best friends, why couldn't Brian have told them? He had told them about women he had been with in the past, why was this so different?

Brian felt detached, taken away from something he was enjoying and being placed into a room of people who were there to belittle him. It wasn't fair. He chewed on his lip, reluctant to answer.

"Because of this..." Brian sighed, disappointed in his past actions.

"You told us you weren't having sex." Russ spoke with a disapproving tone; upset they had been lied to. Mostly upset Brian felt as if he couldn't speak to them about it. Were they that hard to speak to?

"I wasn't when you *asked*!" Brian threw his hands in the air. He couldn't have felt more embarrassed.

"Dude, we're just looking out for you." Catfish shrugged, on the same page as everyone else.

It wasn't as if the band were worried about what Brian did in his own time, but it was questionable with the number of women he had slept with on tour before. Brian had gotten himself in bouts of trouble a few times due to it.

Brian didn't want them to know about his newfound relationship he had built with Farah. They would have only related

366

her to all the girls in the past who had left him the morning after. The ones that had left him broken and alone.

"You can do whatever you want, Brian. It's not like we're mad about it." Russ nodded at Brian as he lifted his head.

"You're not?"

"Brian...I ain't one to judge your tour lifestyle, but if you screwed anyone in that van, I want it cleaned. That's disgusting." Zoe shook her head in disapproval.

"I'm calling shotgun." Russ lifted his hand.

"I didn't want to tell you because I'd only assume you'd think this is...like every other time. It's not! She's different! Really different! B-but in a good way! I promise!" Brian spoke with a slight croak in his voice. He had a track record for getting his heart broken, the band spending days consoling him until he moved onto the next girl who was ready to screw away his problems.

The band exchanged glances with one another, sympathy immediately being felt for their frontman. They knew how desperate he was for love. For any kind of companionship. He had always been on the pursuit of finding it.

"You like her. You really like her." Russ huffed with a smile as he leaned on the back of the wooden chair.

"Huh?"

"Farah. She's not like the other girls." Zoe smirked, feeling rather smug that her suspicions about the two of them had been correct. Brian wasn't particularly good at keeping things from people and he certainly hadn't been as cautious about sneaking around as he perhaps should have been.

"No. She's smart and creative and pretty and talks about really interesting things that I didn't know a lot about, but now I do! Ask me a question about *fracking*, I dare you!" Brian's face lit up as soon as he mentioned her, becoming expressive with his hands.

"Uh, I don't want to hear about you fracking Farah." Catfish gritted his teeth together.

"*Fracking*! It's—" Brian spoke slowly so he wouldn't get the wrong idea.

"Fracking? Since when have you ever cared about *fracking*?" Zoe snorted loudly.

"It's a serious issue, Zoe." Brian scowled at her.

"How long?" Russ asked, curious to know how long Brian had been holding onto this romance.

"I don't know how long the process takes. We didn't get to talk about that part—"

"He's talking about your relationship with Farah, nerd. Not fracking." Zoe flicked him on the cheek causing him to flinch.

"Hey! Watch the face!" Brian rubbed the side of his face and sighed.

"Your voice is the money maker, not your face." Zoe snorted as she flicked him on the nose, causing him frustration as Catfish and Russ laughed.

"Will you *quit* it?" Brian swatted her away, Zoe was the closest he would ever have to an older sister and that was a ticket for irritability.

"Tell us!" Zoe demanded, flicking Brian's right ear. He flinched in annoyance, shuffling over on the bed to escape her reign of terror.

"Alright! We kissed in Birmingham." Brian admitted as he rubbed the side of his face.

"Holy shit. That's why you were both up late at night!" Catfish pointed over at Brian from the opposite side of the room.

"You *saw* them?" Zoe gasped.

"Sorry, Catfish. I...um...I made up the thing about sleeping birds because I didn't want you to know about us." Brian blushed as he rubbed the back of his neck.

"Man, that blows. I've lost all respect for them." Catfish sighed with deflation in his tone.

"Wait. You kissed in Birmingham? J-just kissed?" Zoe cocked an eyebrow, completely blown away by his words.

"Yeah..."

"You've been with Farah since Birmingham?"

"That's what I said."

"So, you didn't just sleep with each other? You've established an emotional connection? An unbreakable bond based upon the structure of human intimacy and the boundless quest to discover your kindred spirit?" Russ sucked in a breath of air after he spoke.

"I guess..." Brian rubbed the back of his neck once more.

"Brian!" Zoe jumped forward and gripped onto either side of his face, taking him by complete surprise.

" *Yush—*" Brian could barely speak as he looked up at Zoe as she squeezed both of his cheeks together.

"You were with Farah in Birmingham and you didn't sleep together that night?"

"Nuh-huh."

"You've been with her since *Birmingham*? Nobody else? Just Farah?" Zoe was beyond elated for her friend; this was nothing like what they had witnessed with Brian before.

"Yuh-uh. Just Farah." Brian nodded his head as Zoe continued to squeeze his cheeks.

"Has that even...happened before?" Catfish furrowed his eyebrows, wanting nothing but the best for his friend.

"I don't think it has." Russ inputted.

"Brian...Farah *likes* you!" Zoe practically cheered at her conclusion, releasing Brian from her grip.

Brian scratched the side of his face as he stared up at her before looking around at both Russ and Catfish who were smiling at him. He had come to this conclusion a few times in his mind, but it wasn't until he saw the faces of his friends that he realised it may have been the truth.

It was never about trying to get to him for his status.

It was never about using him to get drugs.

It was never about checking a box.

It was never about sex.

It was always about...*him.*

It was at that moment Brian knew this time was undoubtedly different. It was something that had been playing on his mind every single day on the tour.

He wanted to be with someone. He wanted to try.

"Yeah..." Brian allowed a small smile to creep up his face. Farah wasn't leaving him the morning after. Farah didn't run away at the first instance. Farah was there with him through his highs and lows.

It was just an hour ago he was having the most passionate sex of his entire life. He couldn't believe he would have thought anything else of Farah other than the fact she would have been more than happy to be with him. She liked him just as much as he liked her and that had been proven time and time again.

"You can't let her go, man." Catfish nodded.

After everything Brian had experienced throughout his life, he *deserved* someone at the very least. It had been a painful couple of years on tour as all the members of the band witnessed Brian's intense pursuit of companionship.

"Don't be afraid to show your true self, Brian. You're a beautiful person on the inside and out. I'm sure that no matter what you do, the power of emotional bonds and cellular devices will keep you together beyond the tour." Russ held onto his shirt as he spoke, becoming a little over-dramatic.

"Wow Russ, thanks." Brian smiled at Russ. He couldn't imagine what life would have been like once they had gone back to their everyday lives.

"Look, Brian...we figured something was going on, but we wanted you to tell us in your own time. It seemed like you two are getting on well with one another and we didn't want to ruin that. We didn't want you to be afraid of telling us! We want what's best for you and as long as you're happy we're happy with whatever you choose." Zoe placed her hand on Brian's shoulder. Brian appreciated Zoe's words beyond belief.

"We didn't want you to get hurt. We know now this isn't a situation like Port—" Catfish shrugged, his words immediately being cut off.

"No!" Russ snapped.

"We want you to be happy and y'know what? We've never seen you happier than we have on this tour. This tour is kickass!" Zoe chuckled, nudging Brian in the shoulder slightly.

"I think Max and Farah helped with that one." Russ grinned, more than happy to have adopted the two college students into their line-up. The tour wouldn't have been as fun without them.

"I lied in Chicago. I spent the rest of the day on a date with Farah. It didn't exactly go to plan though..." Brian sighed as he ran his fingers through his hair. It wasn't what he wanted it to have been.

"We figured you weren't sick."

"Not physically. We went to get coffee and some woman came and spoke about my mom. She asked for a picture and everything! It was so embarrassing. I made it worse because I freaked out about it and got super upset in front of Farah. I thought she hated me." Brian chewed the inside of his mouth, still upset from the events.

Zoe looked back at Russ and Catfish with concern.

"Uh...it didn't look like she hated you when she stumbled out of the van with your tongue in her mouth." Zoe gave Brian an uneasy look as she gritted her teeth together. Russ and Catfish felt satisfaction in laughing.

"Y-yeah, we, uh—it must be fine now. It's fine. She stayed with me when I was upset and that was...nice. Really nice." Brian gripped onto the front of his shirt, noticing it was still inside out. He looked up at Zoe and gave her a small smile, attempting to hide his blushes.

"I'm happy for you, Brian. Farah's super sweet and I've seen the way she looks at you. You're *in* there. You've got to keep in contact after tour!" Zoe spoke excitedly, happy to see Brian with excitement in his eyes.

"I will!" Brian nodded.

"And none of this sleeping around shit—"

"No! I wouldn't. *Never.*" He shook his head, if Farah were in his life, he wouldn't need to be with anyone else. He hadn't even thought about any other girl on tour. She was the only person on his mind.

"Look at our little Brian! He's all grown up!" Zoe aggressively ruffled the top of his hair, causing him to try and bat her away as he laughed.

"Zoe! Come on!" Brian laughed, pushing her away. Catfish and Russ sat in the background and didn't say a word, too busy laughing at Zoe tormenting him.

"I'm really happy for you, Bri." Zoe grinned as she adjusted her jacket. Just as Brian thought the torment was over, she leaned down and whispered in his ear. "But stop fucking in the van, otherwise I'll refuse to drive it."

Brian laughed at her threat, but he knew she wasn't bluffing. He had to put a stop to that bad habit. He hadn't done it often, but this hadn't been the first time.

It had been the *best* time.

When Brian finally came out of the hotel room he checked his phone and noticed Farah had sent him a text message.

'We thought we should get on the road to Indianapolis. I'll see you there? Max said the band would be chill with it. I hope you're okay. X'

Brian smiled at the text, taking note of the kiss at the end of the message, she hadn't sent one of those before without him sending it first.

Now, it had a little more meaning than just an 'X' at the end of a message.

INDIANAPOLIS, IN

The band piled into the van to head to the next state for the show in the evening. Zoe had forced Brian to sit in the back of the van, refusing to go anywhere near where he had spent the morning having sex. Russ subtly opened the window.

Max and Farah made their way across the states as per usual. Everything was starting to wind down now they only had a couple of days left of the tour.

There was one thing that kept bugging Farah in the back of her mind and as much as she wanted to speak to her best friend about the matter, she didn't want to continue to burden her with her newfound love life. Although Max would have been grateful to hear the gossip.

Farah couldn't stop thinking about everything that had happened between her and Brian on the tour, from the flirtation to sex. There was nothing strange about having sex with him the *third* time. It had been incredibly pleasurable and an unmatched physical experience.

They had gotten so caught up in one another that even just the thought of having sex with him again felt *normal*. It didn't have the same dirty feeling that it once held. Farah wanted to be with him, both emotionally and physically.

It was hard for Farah to picture them in a relationship but couldn't think of a life outside of the tour without him. Things were different now. She had mentioned him coming to see her when she was back at college and the thought lived rent-free within her mind.

Farah had slept with the frontman of Social Dropouts. There had been several points within the tour she had thought about how famous he truly was...meeting the one and only Bailey Craig cemented that. Brian was a star in his own right.

She had worried about it at first. Was she just a phase? Another girl he had been with on tour for the sake of it? Another tally to add to a chart? She knew he had slept with people in the past, but she didn't know how *many*. She was worried to know.

Now that the band knew, it meant that for the last couple of days of the tour they wouldn't have to hide their attraction to one another. It was an interesting concept they were willing to explore.

What would that have felt like?

To have been...*okay* being together?

To have been *open* about it?

It would have been strange.

It would have been—

"Race cars!"

"Huh?"

"We have nothing planned and we're in Indianapolis. We have to go to the Motorsport Museum!" Max insisted, realising that without her incredible input there wouldn't have been anything in Indianapolis other than conversations about Brian Blossom.

"When I said I wanted to go on a historical road trip—" Farah began, only to be cut off.

"It *is* historical! Race cars are super cool too, so I'm sure the band will want to come. We can all hang out." Max suggested before pondering on her words. "Unless that's awkward since y'know...you and Brian..."

"It's not awkward. Why would it be awkward?"

"Uh, I don't know. There's still the question in the air on whether the band snapped and finally decided to castrate him."

374

"They're fine with it. I think. It's not weird, is it? You're okay with it?" Anxiety coursed through Farah's mind, causing her to question everything. The last thing she wanted was to upset Max.

"You're having a good time and that's all I wanted from this trip. Sleep with Brian Blossom all you like, just not where I can hear it...*please.*" Max held onto the steering wheel and chuckled to herself.

Farah stopped for a moment, curious to know what Max thought about their *relationship.*

"Would it be weird if I kept in contact after the tour? Do fans do that or is that *weird?* I sort of maybe invited him to college and—" Farah rinsed her hands together as Max shot her a glare before rudely interrupting.

"You did?"

"Yeah."

"Wow, okay. You actually like this guy, huh?" Max gave her a look, concerned Farah had fallen too deep. As much as Max loved hanging out with the band and wanted to continue after the tour, she was trying her hardest not to get her hopes up only to be let down. She didn't want the band to ditch them as soon as the tour was over, but it was likely. They had lives outside of music.

"I think I do." Farah stared out the window before backtracking on her words. "It's stupid, my parents would take one look at him and...they'd hate him before he even opened his mouth."

"Dude, shut up about your parents. You do whatever and *whoever* you want to do. Fuck that noise." Max scoffed, knowing if she didn't push Farah there would have been no way she would have come out of her comfort zone and admitted to liking Brian the way she did.

"It's not that easy, Max."

"To hell it is!"

Farah kept quiet. There was no point in starting an argument with Max on the matter. She knew without a doubt her parents would not be welcoming of Brian Blossom, no matter how sweet or kind he was. It wouldn't matter if he turned out to be the love of Farah's life, there was no way they would ever accept him into the Vishwakarma family. They already had a plan for her. Nothing was going to change that, especially not a weed smoking emo boy with tattoos from Nashville.

Some things were worth fighting for and Farah knew if she ever wanted to be with Brian, it would take a lot of fighting. It wasn't as easy as Max thought it was.

The band had spent a lot of the journey pressing onto Brian about Farah. It wasn't so much about what they had been up to but more about how Brian felt. This was the first time they had ever noticed Brian acting that way around a girl. A lot of the people they were used to seeing him with were people they only saw once.

Farah had stuck around.

After Farah had mentioned she and Max were going to the Motor Museum, the band agreed with the idea and they would have loved to have hung out. As much as the band were interested in the fast cars, Brian had other things on his mind. He hadn't spoken to Farah since he had been abruptly pulled away by the band to be interrogated about his newfound connection and he was desperate to speak to her about it.

When the band arrived, Max and Farah decided to meet up with them. Brian was more interested in seeing Farah again in private. They had thought of a plan over text. A sure way to get together again after their time in each other's arms. Desperate to see her again after the beautiful morning they had shared.

"I'm going to the bathroom." Farah stated as she looked up from her phone, not managing to wait until everyone was together.

"You don't have to sneak off. I know you're screwing Brian. If you want to go and fool around just say that's what you're going to do." Max rolled her eyes as she took a pointless picture of a fast car that was part of the exhibit behind them.

"I—" Farah placed her phone into her pocket and sighed. Max wouldn't have cared; she would have been with the band soon enough and that was a dynamic she enjoyed.

"I'll see you later!" Max pushed Farah's shoulder with a smile, trying to get her to leave and enjoy herself.

"I'll see you soon." Farah nodded with confirmation as she began to walk to the bathroom.

It had been a couple of quick texts that suggested meeting up outside of the bathrooms. They were recognisable and easy to spot. The one thing neither of them considered was that the museum was large enough to have a toilet in a couple of locations throughout. Admittedly, Farah did need the bathroom which led her to go sooner than she was expecting Brian to meet her.

Upon exiting the bathroom her hands were still a little wet as she came out quickly so she wouldn't miss Brian. She scanned the area around her for him. Except, the only people she recognised were Zoe, Russ and Catfish all standing around a bench they had claimed.

"Farah!" Zoe shouted, taking her by surprise. She resisted the urge to turn around and go back into the bathroom to hide, but she knew that wasn't an option. Things were awkward between her and the band, even before she started hooking up with Brian.

Farah reluctantly stepped towards them, knowing she didn't have a choice in the matter. They had already seen her.

"Oh! Hi guys." Farah waved as she gritted her teeth together and pushed her glasses up the bridge of her nose. They hadn't gotten off on the right foot, but things had gotten better throughout the tour. The band was a huge part of Brian's life and if she *was* serious about him then she would also have to be serious about the people he treasured most.

"Have you seen Brian? We lost him amongst the crowd." Russ queried, a hint of concern in his voice.

"I haven't." Farah confirmed. Where was he?

"Did you lose Max too?" Catfish asked.

"Looks like it." Farah folded her arms and smiled, feeling a little uncomfortable in their presence. She had never really been around the band when Brian wasn't there. They were too cool for her.

"Want to help us find them?" Zoe put the question on her, forcing Farah to decide on whether she was going to spend time alone with the band.

This was bad. It would have been rude for her to leave them considering they were looking for the same people.

Following them was her best hope of finding Max and Brian. She had to buckle in for the ride.

"That sounds like a good idea." Farah confirmed, holding herself a little tighter. She shouldn't have been anxious around them; they were Brian's best friends. As cool as they looked, they were just as much a bunch of dorks as Max and Farah were.

As the band set off for their search for Brian, Farah made sure to trail behind slightly. The last thing she wanted was to force herself between them. She was there to find Brian and Max. Nothing else.

"Sooooo..." Zoe prolonged her word as she threw her arm around Farah. The sudden touch made Farah jump followed by a shiver. It wasn't what she had been expecting. "You and Brian, huh?"

There it was. The question she was afraid of. Their common interest. She didn't have anything fun or quirky to speak to the band about as Max did. Farah was uncool and boring in comparison. Of course they wanted to talk about Brian.

At least, Zoe did. Russ and Catfish walked ahead and managed to pay attention to their surroundings on their search for Brian and Max.

"Heh, yeah. That's...*happening.*" Farah rinsed her fingers together with anxiety before tucking her hands under her arms. Zoe still insisted on keeping her close.

"Can I just say that you two make an adorable couple!" Zoe pulled her in a little closer, Farah immediately being able to smell the strong perfume she had drowned herself in.

Farah wasn't sure if 'couple' was the right way to describe them, taking note of the connotations that came with it.

"Yeah? I guess..." Farah smiled with her teeth, not knowing how to formulate a coherent response.

"I've seen this boy with all kinds of people before, but not the way he's with *you.* I think he really likes you. I like you too, Farah. Perhaps not in the same way as Brian, but certainly in a way that makes me want to hang out with you more." Zoe pushed her fist against Farah's shoulder. It was strange for someone as pretty, kind, popular *and* intelligent as Zoe to have even been within reaching distance of Farah.

"Oh. That's so nice, thank you."

"I don't think I've mentioned it and if I have, not enough, but I want you to know how gorgeous you are. Brian's struck gold with you, girl." Zoe laughed as she nudged Farah once more, continuing to keep her arm around her new friend.

"You're really pretty too. I love your hair." Farah blushed, continuing to be jealous of the confidence Zoe held. Enough confidence to have half of her long black hair dyed teal.

"Stop it!" Zoe giggled, before continuing as they walked through the Motorsport Museum. "You go to Duke, right?"

"Yeah, same as Max."

"You girls are hella smart. You remind me of my sister, she went to one of those fancy colleges like you. I wish I was super into education and then maybe I'd be somewhere that wasn't with these losers. They're lucky I love them." Zoe chuckled as she pointed towards both Russ and Catfish walking in front of them, practically scrapping at one another for entertainment as they searched for the frontman of their band.

"You can be smart in lots of different ways. Education is important, but it shouldn't define who you are as a person. You're incredibly articulate and seem to manage everyone correctly, even from just knowing you for a couple of weeks I can see you're the glue." Farah began to explain, somewhat hypocritical in the way she spoke.

"The *glue*?" Zoe cocked an eyebrow as she snorted, removing her arm from Farah.

"Well, yeah. Max says the bass player holds the whole band together."

"Sure."

"I just think that translates well off stage too." Farah spoke softly, hoping her words didn't offend Zoe. That wasn't her intention.

Zoe smiled, pleased to have the opportunity to speak to Farah. Brian was right about her. She was smart, but not in a way Zoe found pretentious. Zoe had appreciated everything her friend's new love interest had said.

"Wow, thanks. I...*try* to keep all the guys from hurting themselves. I'm like a well-dressed babysitter." Zoe straightened her leather jacket before letting out a small laugh, Farah followed as she walked alongside her, happy to have created a relationship with Zoe. There had been plenty of times throughout the tour where Farah could have spent some time with members of the band but spent her time with Brian instead.

"You're good at playing. Have you played for long?" Farah attempted to strike a conversation, one that wasn't about boys.

"I started playing when I was about thirteen. My sister had a guitar and I wanted to be different, so I asked for a bass one Christmas. She didn't continue with it, but I did." Zoe grinned proudly. "How about you, Farah? When are you joining the band?"

Farah blushed at the request, it was something Brian had joked about too. She was not musically inclined.

"You wouldn't want that. I'm terrible with music." Farah snorted, tucking her hair behind her ear in the process.

"I find it hard to believe you've never picked up an instrument."

"Violin. Once. It was something my parents wanted me to do, but I wasn't interested. They pushed it, but I wasn't *good* and I think they accepted that. One of the only things they did allow me to stop pursuing. I think they *knew* I was bad and didn't bother." Farah chuckled, awkwardly looking away at the thought. Her parents gave up on her musical talents, pushing her that way wasn't getting them anywhere. Academics was where she shined her brightest.

"I'm sure you'd make a kickass violinist." Zoe assured, even if it wasn't something she wanted to pursue. It was nice for Farah to have that confirmation.

It made her smile, it felt as if Zoe only wanted what was best for her and that was freeing in itself. Farah held her hands together as she walked beside Zoe, following Catfish and Russ. She hadn't had a full conversation with Zoe up until that point, but she wasn't disappointed in the result.

"Thanks." Farah grinned, pleased to have gotten the opportunity to talk to Zoe.

On the other side of the building, Brian Blossom had made his way to one of the bathrooms, expecting Farah to be outside. After texting a few times out of sheer curiosity and anxiety, he was worried he had lost her. He noticed Max staring at one of the exhibits, an old red and white race car.

If anyone knew where Farah was, it was Max.

Brian walked over to Max and stood beside her as he looked at the car in front of them. Going to the Motorsport

Museum was a good idea and if Brian didn't have other things on his mind, it would have been super interesting.

"Hey Max, have you seen Farah?" Brian asked politely. This was already a lot calmer than when she had queried Farah's disappearance to him.

"Oh, Brian. I thought she was somewhere boning you...*again.*" Max snorted at the thought, Farah had gone elsewhere.

"N-no, I haven't seen her yet." Brian scratched the back of his neck, having to stick around with Max would have been awkward. It wasn't so much the fact she was a huge fan, but she was also an incredibly big fan of Farah and that meant she would break laws if she ever had to defend her best friend.

"That's weird." Max grew an inch taller as she stood on her tiptoes and scanned around the museum. She couldn't seem to see Farah.

That was it. They were stuck together. The only thing they could do was to leave to look for the rest of their friends. Wouldn't that have been considered rude? Brian wasn't sure, but he didn't want to get on the bad side of Max.

"Want to help me look?" Brian asked.

"Be a sidekick in your conquest for sex? Bro—"

"No! I-it's just so we can find Farah and the band." Brian shook his hands out in front of him.

"Yeah, I can do that. Let's do that." Max pointed towards the frontman of her favourite band. A part of her still finding the whole experience surreal.

Brian had spoken to Max a few times over the weeks they had been together. Although, with his attention focused on Farah it had been hard for him to give time to Max.

If it weren't for Max dragging Farah across the states to see his band then he never would have met her. It was rude of him to ignore his biggest fan.

"Do you like cars?" Brian was unsure how to start a conversation as they walked through the museum. Making their way through the exhibits to see if they could find the rest of their party.

"Not really. If you want to talk about cars, you'll have to see my brother. They are super cool though. I'm mostly a music person." Max nodded, knowing Brian would have agreed.

"That's funny. Me too." The frontman of Social Dropouts proudly pointed to himself with a smile.

"Dude, your music is—Is this *weird* for you?"

"Weird? What's weird?"

Max held her hands together for a moment as they walked. She had spoken to the rest of the band about the music they created but speaking to Brian was next level. Brian was everything Max loved about music and the creations that came out of Brian's mind had gotten her through the last couple of years of high school and the start of college.

It felt strange for her to have been hanging out with him for the past couple of weeks. It was even weirder to know that her best friend was *sleeping* with him. It was even weirder than weird to know they were holding a conversation as they walked through a museum together.

"I've been pretty casual about it. Especially around you, but...I'm a *really* big fan." Max suddenly blurted out, feeling guilty for doing so. "Your music is really good and...this is *super* weird for me." She began to trail off with her speech, adjusting the red beanie on the top of her head. A part of her was desperate to pull it over her face with embarrassment. How else was she going to befriend Brian Blossom the way she had befriended the rest of the group if she didn't *talk* to him?

Brian had heard it all before but coming from Max felt a lot more genuine than anyone else who had claimed to enjoy his song writing.

"Wow, thanks. Farah talks about how much of a fan you are, but I didn't want to bring it up. I didn't want to embarrass you or anything."

"What? No! Never. You could *never.*"

"It kind of feels like we're friends, or at least you're someone who I want to be friends with. The guys love you. You're cool." Brian smiled, knowing that with every word he was making Max's day undoubtedly better.

"No, *you're* cool!"

"No man, you're cooler."

"I'd say you're as cool as the north pole, but greenhouse gases ruined that one." Max laughed at her joke, Brian catching onto the humour and joining in.

There was a silence as they looked around once more, trying to see if they could find either Farah or the band. Nothing. They both let out a sigh.

"Do you play any instruments?" Brian pushed, attempting to start a conversation with Max. The only things he really knew about her were things the band and Farah had mentioned.

"My dad got me a guitar when I was younger. Unlike my brothers, he probably thought I'd actually use an instrument. I did. I can't play like you, but I *can* perform a pretty mean version of *Greensleeves*." Max scoffed.

"That's awesome. I bet it rocks."

"I can play Russ' parts on two of your songs. Your parts are *way* too hard!"

"Oh yeah, which two?" Brian smirked, interested to know more.

"Uhm...'*What Was That About a Dog?*' and '*Foundations of a Brittle Body*'." Max looked up as she thought about the song names.

"Sweet, they're not *easy* ones! We'll have to get you to feature on a song when we're back in Nashville."

"Wait? Really?" Max's eyes lit up as Brian placed his hands inside of his jacket pockets.

"Yeah. We could hang out. Together. Us...and the band...and Farah." Brian chewed on his bottom lip as he casually mentioned his plan.

Max stopped in her tracks and started to laugh. Brian gritted his teeth together, wishing for the band to turn the corner any moment and free him from whatever conversation he was about to be thrown in.

"Nice try, Casanova. If you want Farah to go and see you in Nashville, just ask her." Max rolled her eyes, noticing what Brian was trying to do. He thought he was smooth, but not *that* smooth. Max was able to see through his bullshit.

"W-well, that's not entirely w-why." Brian began to choke on his words, followed by a small blush and a cough to clear his throat.

"Save it, dude. I get it, your dick is doing all the talking."

"N-no, it's not—"

"I'm not saying anything bad! You're good." Max laughed, noticing how flustered Brian had become.

Brian was lost for words. A part of him feeling awkward around Max and not wanting to admit anything. Especially not when it came to Farah.

"Right."

It was only then that Max's expression dropped as she got a little closer to speak in an aggressive whisper.

"But you do anything to hurt my best friend and you're a dead man, got it?"

Brian nodded. Understanding loud and clear the threat was potentially one that held substance.

Just as Brian was about to defend his corner, he looked up and noticed on the opposite side of the hall Farah was walking with the rest of the band—laughing. The sight immediately put a smile on Brian's face. Max stopped and looked past the exhibits surrounding them to see the people they were searching for as well.

"There they are." Brian grinned; happy he was finally reunited with everyone.

"We make pretty good detectives."

"We just walked around in a circle for the past ten minutes."

"Exactly, and we solved the case. Great detectives!" Max smirked as she began to walk towards their party.

Now was his chance, before they managed to get back to the band.

"Hey, Max?"

"What's up?"

"We should jam sometime. Guitars and all. Nashville, maybe? You have a great taste in music, and I'd like some opinions on some new stuff. For *real* this time." Brian tried his hardest to make a new friend. Indirectly apologising about his time in LA.

Max's eyes lit up at the comment. This time it sounded like he did want to hang out.

"Can I bring Farah?" Max smirked.

"She doesn't really like my music." Brian snorted, realising how silly he sounded. Farah probably wouldn't have wanted to sit there and listen to them make music.

"No, but she likes *you*."

Brian's heart skipped a beat at the sound of Max's words.

"Yo! We found them!" Catfish suddenly threw his hands up and pointed towards Max and Brian.

Max took Farah by surprise as she pulled her in for a hug, a little concerned she may have lost her best friend in the museum. Luckily, they hadn't been apart for too long.

"You left me with Brian!" Max pretended to sob on Farah's shoulder. Farah gently pushed her away whilst laughing.

"Oh yeah? How did that go?" Farah chuckled, a little worried about what they could have possibly spoken about. They had a couple of common interests, but she knew one of them was her.

"I found out he's the frontman of the band we're following on tour. Insane, right?" Max winked as she held onto Farah's shoulders.

"That is pretty crazy." Farah smiled as she looked over at Brian who was currently caught up in a secret handshake with Russ which looked overly complicated and long for no good reason.

"Right?" Max patted her friend's shoulders as she took a step back and greeted Zoe and Catfish.

Admittedly, it was nice for Farah and Brian to have spent some time with the people that were important to each other. Brian was grateful for his awkward yet important conversation he had with Max. Farah was happy she had gotten the chance to speak to Zoe more so than before.

Just hours ago, Brian and Farah were in the backseat of the van getting to know one another better. Now they were stood side by side.

"Hey."

"Hi." Farah responded as she glanced over at Brian.

"I hope Russ didn't bore you with a conspiracy theory or something." Brian smiled, wanting confirmation that his friends hadn't scared her away from him.

"No, I mostly spoke with Zoe."

"Oh, yeah?"

"Yeah. It was nice. She's nice." Farah folded her arms as she looked at Zoe who was now laughing with Max about something. "What did you and Max talk about?"

"Mostly our concern about losing everyone, music and *you.*" Brian began to mark off the topics on his fingers.

"Me?" Farah acted surprised as if there wasn't a chance she would have come up in a conversation between her best friend and the guy she was seeing.

"Mostly about you and Max coming to Nashville after the summer. I-If you're free. Maybe." Brian spoke quietly, not wanting the rest of the band to hear how nervous he sounded.

"I'm sure we'll love that." Farah grinned, the idea of being able to see Brian after the tour was exciting.

Brian smiled back. It felt nice to have confirmation from Farah herself, despite Max already mentioning it was something they both would have done regardless.

They spent the rest of the afternoon looking around the museum at the exhibits. They were willing to stick around until Max could find the one she could sit in and take photographs with. She had seen it on their website.

Brian and Farah stuck close throughout their time inside the museum. It felt strange to be close and not hide it. After having the conversations with their friends, it felt a little less awkward than it had done before.

Things felt different now. Although, it was a good difference that neither of them minded. Something they had gotten comfortable in accepting. It should have been weird, knowing that their friends had stumbled upon them after having sex.

It felt as if they were happy for them more than anything. A confirmation that their relationship was okay. There wasn't a need to hide.

Brian felt confident, enough to stand close to Farah as they stared at an old car. Brian gently flicked his fingers against the top of Farah's hand, wondering if she would have taken to holding him in return.

Brian continued as Farah stared ahead with slight hesitation, before allowing for their fingers to slip together in front of everyone. Nobody was paying much attention and even if they were, they didn't care.

The whole day up to the point where Brian had to go on stage...the two of them were holding hands whenever they could. It was nice to know the people around them weren't judging them for their choice.

When the show came to an end in the evening, Brian and Farah sat together with their fingers interlocked again. They exchanged smirks as the band began to tell stories and jokes about previous tours. Farah found it hard to concentrate when his warm hand was wrapped tightly around hers, never wanting to let go.

Nobody said a thing.

COLUMBUS, OH

"I'm glad today is the hottest day of the tour. This is going to be awesome!" Max squealed excitedly as they all walked along the path shaded by trees. It wouldn't have been long until they reached the lake they had been told about.

"Hottest day? Don't you remember practically *frying* in Texas? I'd never seen the van's AC work so hard!" Zoe sighed, wiping her brow at the thought of their time in the huge state. It hadn't been fun cooped up in the van with everyone for days.

"This is a good kind of warm." Russ commented, he had already reduced himself to nothing more than khaki shorts, a white tank top, his usual baseball cap, sunglasses, and flip flops. It was going to have been a good day.

The band appreciated having Max with them, one of the many reasons being her ability to have thought of fun activities for them to do together.

This time, Max had suggested the band go swimming. It was a little different from what they were used to, but it was something they hadn't done yet. Max had seen far too many coming of age teen movies and needed the satisfaction that came with jumping off a dangerous cliff into a lake.

Brian and Farah had spent the day being more open about their newfound relationship. It was nice to know they didn't have to hide anymore if they didn't want to.

Brian had taken that and ran. Meaning that every opportunity he got he was holding her hand and occasionally pecking her with kisses when nobody was looking. He didn't want to be one of those people who showed a ton of public affection, but he couldn't help himself. He wanted Farah to know how much he cared about her. How much he wanted her in his life. He only had a day to prove it.

Farah was in two minds about the affection. Brian's confidence certainly spurred her on to accept his kisses, but it still felt awkward. Her anxiety got the best of her.

"This must be Lake Sprinkle Sprankle!" Max threw her hands in the air as they reached the edge of the forest and revealed the lake in front of them. Max's reference had been wasted on Farah. Everyone else appreciated the alternative humour.

The lake was huge and glistened under the sun. Farah was nervous about swimming. She had mostly been nervous about having to wear a swimsuit she had purchased on the way there. She hadn't expected to go swimming on a music tour.

Farah didn't have much body confidence, which had pushed her to wear the swimsuit over the bikini Max had tried to convince her to buy. Brian excelled her confidence, but it wasn't just Brian there.

"Are you much of a swimmer?" Brian questioned as he leaned in closer to Farah.

"I can swim, I just don't do it much." It was fun when she didn't feel so self-conscious about her body. Something that prevented her from going swimming over the past couple of years.

It would have been fun for the crew to have spent their day at the lake. Not only was it incredibly warm, but they only had two more shows to play before the end of the tour. Things were starting to come to a close and they were all pretty sad about it...especially Brian.

Catfish placed a small speaker on the grass by the side of the lake and began to blast beats through it. Farah was surprised to hear that what came out of the speaker wasn't emo, but more everyday pop hits with pep. It was interesting to hear how different the band's taste in music could be in comparison to what they played.

They had set up a picnic for them all. From a cool box full of beer to every variety of chip you could purchase from a gas station. Farah knew the band mostly lived on sour candy, pizza and weed, but she hoped they'd have brought something in addition to that for their penultimate day together as a unit. They didn't.

As soon as they had gotten to the side of the lake everyone had stripped down to their swimwear. Everyone apart from Farah who was sitting by the speaker with her legs tucked to her chest, watching as everyone else prepared themselves to swim.

Farah couldn't help but stare at Brian in his red swimming trunks and black and white checked sliders. She had seen his chest a couple of times now, but his bulky yet somewhat muscular build was always nice to look at. His tattoos were on full view, from the ones scaling up and down his arms to the chameleon on his back. He was an unconventional kind of handsome and was a treat for the eyes. Farah was incredibly attracted to him.

"Not coming in, Rah?" Max cocked an eyebrow down at Farah, not intending for the rest of the band to turn around and be a part of the conversation.

"You guys have fun. Someone has to play the role of the lifeguard." Farah chuckled nervously.

"Lifeguards can go swimming too!" Max insisted, wanting her best friend to join them on what could have been their last day all together.

"Usually only when someone is drowning..." Russ gave everyone an uneasy look as he adjusted his sunglasses.

"Oh. I mean..." Farah's eyebrows dipped at his comment, feeling a little unnerved.

"We can tell you what the water's like." Brian shrugged with a smile. He was torn between going swimming with everyone and sitting beside Farah.

"I bet it's cold." Zoe groaned.

"I hope there aren't any leeches." Catfish scratched the back of his neck at the thought.

"I doubt there are any leeches." Max laughed nervously; worried Catfish's words would bring on a wave of leeches that consumed them all.

"I mean, there probably *are* leeches in there somewhere." Russ shrugged.

"Hm, yeah."

"Why is everyone talking about leeches and not jumping in the lake?" Brian groaned as he exchanged glances between them, confused with their behaviour.

"Okay. Cool. Farah, you've got to be the judge of this." Max pointed down to Farah with a grin.

"What? Of the leeches?" Farah looked up with an expression full of confusion.

"What? No! No leeches!"

"Okay, what is it then?"

"Alright, everyone hold fire. I need silence in the room." Max held out both her arms and took a deep breath, everyone in the circle intrigued to know what she was doing.

"We're outside and if you think I'm jumping in, you've got another thing coming." Zoe sighed. The last thing she wanted was to be contending with her hair curling when she had spent so long straightening it to how she liked.

"Shut up and get ready!" Max took a deep breath and pulled her bunched up hair tightly before yelling. "The last one in the lake listens to *Nickelback* unironically!" Max shouted before immediately sprinting to the edge of the water. Everyone stared at one another at the sound of her words, realising the game they had all been opted into without a chance for denial.

Farah laughed as she watched everyone run at full speed towards the lake, Max being the first person to dive off the edge. Each of them followed, splashing into the water one after the other until Zoe who ran down to the edge of the lake and climbed in without jumping. Max was first to resurface, raising her hand in the air and squealing happily. Everyone else found themselves above the water laughing at the jump they had just completed.

Zoe was right about it being cold, although it was cooling in the heat.

"Hey Farah, are you sure you don't want to come in? The water's great!" Max splashed on the surface.

"No leeches!" Catfish laughed as Russ splashed a large amount of water towards Brian.

Farah stood up and walked over to the edge of the lake, smiling at them below her. She thought back to her first encounter with the band and how they had been pushy.

They weren't trying to convince her because they wanted her to feel peer pressure, they wanted her to have a good time. They wanted her to be a part of their group. A part of the band.

She looked down at them smiling back at her. She had no reason to be shy around any of them. None of them had judged her as harshly as she judged herself.

Brian smiled at her the widest, his internal voice screaming how much he wanted her to join them in the water. He nodded up at her, a subtle telepathic 'you've got this'.

Farah took a deep breath and stood back away from the water, quickly trying to get both her shirt and shorts off as rapidly as she could so they didn't spend too long watching her undressing. She kicked her shoes to the side and took off her glasses. She wasn't going to be able to see much without them, but it was better that than to risk breaking them.

Brian didn't get to see her outfit as she leapt off the side of the lake and into the water. They all covered their eyes and laughed as she splashed water in all directions, everyone letting out a little cheer as she came up to the surface and brushed her hair back with a smile.

It wasn't long before everyone was swimming, chatting, and splashing one another aggressively whilst in the water. Mostly the boys. Zoe was trying her hardest not to get her hair wet. Max should have taken the same consideration, but was having too much fun to care.

"Do you guys go swimming in lakes often?" Farah questioned as she floated in the water beside Brian. They had been next to each other the entire time. Farah was already mesmerised by the hilarity in the flatness that came with Brian's hair once it was wet.

"Nope." Brian admitted as he made his move to swim a tiny bit closer to Farah. "I like swimming with pretty girls though."

He swam nearer to her in the hopes he would have gotten what he wanted if he asked nicely.

He didn't have to ask nicely; Farah was already more than happy to allow him to place his hands on her back underneath the water. By this point, she was used to his touch. A weight she welcomed. His hands felt strange under the water, but she didn't mind.

"Do you want to get any closer?" Farah sarcastically snorted with a smile, Brian taking her words as a question.

"Yeah." Brian smirked as he pulled her towards him. They were practically chest to chest as they stared at one another for a moment. Finally, he was close enough for her to see the features on his face. Only yesterday they had been cuddling up in the van. Brian was still feeding off the high of the moment.

Farah placed her hands on his chest, both wet and warm from the lake and the heat that surrounded them.

Farah looked over towards the band and Max who were distracted by one another. She looked back at Brian and smiled sweetly.

Brian smirked before attempting to make his move, tilting his head as he went in for a kiss. Farah was surprised his kiss wasn't just a peck and immediately shut her eyes as he led one of his usual romantic kisses. Farah clenched her hands against his chest as she felt his hands sit comfortably in the middle of her back.

Farah could have kissed him all day, thoughts running through her mind about how little time they had left together. It wasn't fair.

"Oh my god! Get a room!" Max cupped her hands over her mouth as she shouted at Brian and Farah. The rest of the band laughed, finding hilarity in the situation.

Farah pulled away from Brian with a smile, holding her hands against his chest as she chuckled. He noticed the red in her cheeks, realising he had embarrassed her in front of their friends. She didn't mind, despite the anxiety, it gave a good adrenaline rush that made her want to kiss him again.

"I...really like kissing you." Brian chuckled sweetly as he kept her close, regardless of what others would say.

"I like kissing you too." Farah blushed.

"I don't care what they say." Brian smirked, pushing his forehead against hers as she laughed. It was hard to deny his attraction when he was set on showing it to everyone.

"Me neither." Farah beamed before pressing her lips against his, allowing him to pull her in so their bodies were against each other under the water. Brian had given her enough confidence not to care about what other people thought of her.

It didn't matter what anyone else thought of them being together.

It was between them.

The band were on a tight schedule and going swimming wasn't the most sensible way to have spent their afternoon. They wanted nothing more than to have sat around the lake drinking cheap beers all afternoon as it bled into the evening.

They would, but they had a show to play.

They clambered out of the water to get themselves dry and somewhat clothed for the journey back to the motel. Brian didn't see Farah in the swimsuit for long, but he made sure to savour every moment he did.

There wasn't much time before they had to head over to the venue and begin their sound check. They hadn't even been to the venue to begin to set up and it was already late in the day, it was likely the venue was going to be pissed with their behaviour. It didn't matter though; they had been having too much fun together at the lake.

They got into the van and headed back to the motel they were staying in not too far away from the venue.

With the limited time they had, Zoe had directed everyone to the two separate rooms. Naturally, she paired Max and Farah off with Brian who would have to shower in their room. Brian didn't mind the direction and much to Max's discretion, he went into their room to shower.

Once they had all gotten back to the rooms, Max was the first one to hop into the shower as Brian and Farah sat on the edge of the bed speaking about just about anything they could.

Brian's mind was racing when it came to the thought of the tour nearly ending. Columbus was their penultimate show, and he wasn't sure how to feel about it.

It wasn't so much the music that was painful to think about, but he could have possibly been leaving Farah forever.

She wouldn't have done that to him, *right?* She would have wanted to have seen him after the tour, *right?* She had already expressed that was something she wanted to happen, but plenty of people had lied to him in the past. Why not someone else?

This was different.

"Feels weird being...y'know..." Brian sat at the end of the bed beside Farah, they both felt a little disgusting in their damp clothes. They had to wait for Max to finish.

"Open about it?" Farah half-smiled as Brian took her hand and held it tightly.

"Yeah...it's...nice."

"It is pretty nice." Farah chuckled, seeing the nerves spread throughout his face. His hair had mostly matted to the top of his head, the lake water didn't do him any favours. Farah didn't mind...it was cute.

Brian gently rubbed his thumb against the top of her hand as he smiled. He loved being close to her after everything they had experienced.

"I really like hanging with the band, but I love hanging out with you too. It's so...different." Brian was unable to stop himself from smiling, just thinking about it gave him chills.

Before the pair could continue to swoon over one another Max came out of the shower. She was incredibly grateful she hadn't walked in on anything. That was her new worst nightmare.

"I'm glad things were kept PG whilst I was gone. Although, I don't trust them to remain that way." Max sighed as she attempted to cover her hair with a towel, walking across the room to grab her bag containing various hair products. There was no way she was going to have stayed in the room with the two of them.

"Where are you going?" Farah questioned as Max picked up a few of her things.

"I'll come back when you're done showering, whether that's together or individually. I don't want to hear or see anything. It might corrupt my innocent mind." Max held various bottles of hair products in her arms and nodded towards the pair on the end of the bed, still holding hands.

"*Innocent?*" Farah cocked an eyebrow.

"More innocent than you." Max winked before opening the door with her elbow and pulling it closed with her foot.

There was a silence in the room, one that Brian and Farah didn't know how to combat. It had been strange for Max to suggest they would shower together. They had slept together multiple times now, but the idea of a shower felt too intimate.

Farah decided to take hold of the situation and stand up. If she didn't get the ball rolling on showering, then it never would have happened. Besides, to conserve water and time, she was usually fast at it.

"Are you okay if I go first?" Farah spun on her heel and questioned, not mentioning anything about the idea of them showering together.

"Yeah, sure, that's cool." Brian nodded as he watched her gather her things and disappear into the bathroom.

Brian sat in the room alone, hearing the showerhead begin to spray the water onto the shower floor. He made sure to take his shoes off before sitting in Farah's bed with his back against the headboard. She probably wouldn't have been too happy with him sitting in her bed in his gross clothes, but at least they weren't *completely* wet.

He pulled out his phone and began to flick through social media, seeing all the nice things people were saying about his band online. Not only that but seeing all the things he had been tagged in throughout the day was interesting. Some days, he enjoyed interacting with his fans.

As Brian began to scroll, the phone on the bedside table began to ring. Brian looked over and noticed Farah's phone vibrating against the wood, a name flashing up on the screen. It didn't bother Brian at first, so he ignored it. What he couldn't ignore was when it rang again.

Worried it may have been her parents or Max, he glanced over at the phone and took note of the name 'Hasan'.

Farah hadn't mentioned Hasan before.

Brian diverted his attention back to his phone and tried his hardest to ignore the ringing. Whoever it was, they wanted Farah's attention. Desperately.

Brian's heart sank at the name. Who was Hasan? Why was he calling her? Was it a family member? Her brother? She hadn't mentioned any siblings.

Her *boyfriend?*

If that were the case, it wouldn't have been the first time Brian had been caught in the middle of a relationship he wasn't aware of. Including one that ended in a bloody nose.

He tried not to think about it as he kept his attention on his phone, noticing the ringing stopped. A few moments passed before the ringtone started again, giving Brian copious amounts of anxiety. He would never want to think the worst of Farah, but with his past experiences, it was hard for his mind not to go to that place.

He waited patiently, desperately wanting Farah to be done with her shower so she could shut off the taunting ringing. It rang through Brian's mind over and over. He started to find it hard to concentrate on his phone screen, desperately wanting to call for Farah. Desperately wanting the ringing to *stop.*

After only a couple of minutes, it sounded like Farah was already done with her shower. It was such a relief for Brian to have heard the lock on the door click open and for Farah to step out, instantly noticing her phone was ringing.

"Someone keeps calling you." Brian chewed his bottom lip as he held onto his phone with both his hands.

Farah stepped over to her phone and immediately snatched it off the nightstand, declining the call that was currently on screen. She grumbled at the notification that claimed they had called her seven times since she had been in the shower. Considering he was probably used to her picking up the phone on the second ring, he must have been concerned.

"Are you sure you don't want to answer it? It seemed pretty important." Brian sat up, noticing Farah's distaste for the caller.

"Trust me, it's not." Farah sighed, frustrated he felt the need to call her. She had given him so many signs she wasn't interested. Most of them included the one-word answers over text and the tendency to try and ignore his calls.

Farah had already dressed inside of the bathroom but had taken to drying her hair on the end of the bed. She half-expected Brian to go straight into the bathroom, but he was still focused on the phone calls. Just as she was about to turn around and explain her phone began to ring again.

"Are you kidding me?" Farah groaned, staring down at her phone and instantly declining the call. She held her finger against the button and turned it off before throwing it to the bed on the other side of the room. "I wish he would just leave me alone..."

"Is everything okay?" Brian shuffled to the end of the bed to be beside her, concerned someone was bothering her. Farah didn't want to have to explain it. It was embarrassing to her and something she didn't want Brian to know about. Despite that, she wasn't prepared to lie to him.

"I'm sorry, he's just some guy I know."

"*S-Some guy?*" Brian cocked an eyebrow at her phrasing, his words coming out in a higher pitch than usual.

"It's not like that. W-We're friends. Not really. We're not friends, we're just *expected* to be friends. Technically, we're expected to be together. As if I have nothing better to do than to eventually marry some man with credentials. It's ridiculous." Farah pushed her glasses out of the way as she covered her eyes, embarrassed she was telling Brian this after everything that had happened between them.

"Oh. That's—"

"It's stupid. His parents know my parents, it's a whole thing. I don't even like him; he hugs me like he's trying to suffocate me and he's constantly bombarding me with calls and texts. It's like he doesn't get a hint! At least, my parents don't get the hint. I've given him nothing but one-word answers for months and he's *still* trying! I'm dreading graduation. It'll just be another excuse to get us together, but this time there won't be any distractions from school. Easy. Just another archaic tradition!" Farah ranted, allowing Brian to sit and listen to her speak intensely about the subject.

"I-I'm sorry." Brian didn't know what to say. It was a complex situation he was afraid of getting involved in. With the sounds of her family dynamic, was it even realistic for the two of them to be together?

It made him think that maybe he *was* just a phase. A phase to get away from the reality that faced her back home.

Farah felt terrible speaking about Hasan in front of Brian. Even so, she felt as if he were someone she could trust. It was nice to have someone to speak to about the situation that wasn't

Max. Max had already heard enough about Hasan that she was ready to kick his ass if she ever met him.

"N-no, I'm sorry. I'm sorry I'm bringing you into it, I should have told you. I know it's weird and I hate it. It's not my choice, I promise." Farah showed Brian a sad expression, one he hadn't seen before. She felt so embarrassed.

"It's okay..." Brian tried his hardest to comfort her as he turned and placed his hands on top of hers.

Farah knew it wasn't okay. She had no plans to ever be with Hasan in any respect. She hated that the idea was even something she had to consider. She was worried she would have never been able to find someone and end up with a man she was pressured to be with.

That wasn't...*love.*

Brian was so sweet in everything he did. It was hard to deny her attraction for him and even harder to deny that Brian was the sort of person she would have wanted to be with if she ever had the choice. With Brian, it felt as if she had that choice.

A choice to be herself.

"Please don't get the wrong idea. It's nothing like—"

"You just *have* to be with this guy?" Brian furrowed his eyebrows, trying to get his head around the tradition he wished he weren't so ignorant in.

"It's not my choice." Farah shook her head. Brian couldn't seem to understand the concept. Why hadn't she brought this up before?

"Why does he keep calling?"

"Because he wants to know what I'm doing and act as a messenger for my parents to get on their good side."

"Can't you just block his number?"

"Then my parents will *know* I don't want to be with him."

"But...you don't want to be with him?" Brian swallowed hard, his quick-fire questions becoming persistent.

"It's more complicated than that." Farah didn't know what to say on the topic as he held onto her hands. She could feel his grip loosening after every word.

She hadn't taken him to be a jealous type, but she could see the desperation for connection in his eyes. He was afraid she was slipping before he even got a chance to be with her.

"You *do* want to be with him?" Brian questioned as his lips parted with anticipation. Farah noticed his voice crack as he asked, clearly torn up over the idea she could be with someone else. That wasn't the case.

"No! No, I would never!"

"I'm really confused." Brian pulled in a shaky breath. Farah didn't owe him an explanation, but she knew he deserved one.

Farah turned to face him completely, gripping onto both of his hands and holding them tightly. She watched him divert his eyes as she tried to make eye contact. It was clear her mention of Hasan had caused them discomfort.

"There are certain formalities I have to...*do* for my family. I didn't mention him because he's not important. Not to me. When I'm home I usually have to go on 'dates' with him, but it's not like when we went roller skating. It's...an awkward conversation on opposite ends of a couch with our parents in the room next to us. It's not the same. This...*this* is different." Farah nodded, pressing her palms a little tighter against his hands. She felt guilty at his inability to look back at her until her last word.

"Okay. I think I understand." Brian chewed his inner lip. This blew up his chances of being with her after the tour. He knew it.

"This doesn't change anything." Farah assured.

"N-no, I...it's fine. It's something you have to do, not what you want to do."

"Exactly."

"Alright." Brian half-smiled as he held onto her hands. She immediately moved her hand to the side of his face. She placed her palm against his cheek and gently touched the scratchy beard on his jawline.

She would never forget the last few weeks spent together. Thinking about Brian was the one thing that she wanted to do, on tour or not.

"Besides, he's not really my type." Farah smiled, taking note of Brian's lips curling at her comment.

"Yeah? What is your type?" Brian smirked.

"Uhh, well, they have to be kind, honest and charming. I like it when they have a good sense of humour because you can't be serious *all* the time. I'm a big fan of facial hair and scruffy yet adorable hairstyles. I like the kind of guy who's confident, but a total dork around me because he's not afraid to be himself." Farah spoke in a soft tone as she ran her fingers against the side of his face, unable to resist his eye contact.

"Uh-huh." Brian was content with listening.

"I like guys who are passionate about things."

"*I'm* passionate about things." Brian immediately pointed out, making Farah laugh at his enthusiasm.

"Want to know what I'm super into?" Farah tried her hardest not to laugh.

"What?"

"Guys in bands who I follow on tour because my best friend likes their angsty music." Farah chuckled, unable to hold it in any longer.

Brian pondered for a moment before grinning.

"I like to think I'm humble enough not to say it, but I think I match your description."

"Oh, yeah?"

"Yeah."

"Did I mention I like guys who are good kissers?" Farah spoke with confidence as if she had been with plenty of guys before who had kissed her. That wasn't the case, but she knew that out of everyone she had kissed, Brian had been the *best* at it.

"No, you didn't mention that."

"Oh. I probably should have."

"How will I know if I meet that criteria?" Brian cocked an eyebrow, knowing exactly what the conversation would have led to.

This was much better than speaking about a guy Farah would have to go home to...

Farah didn't bother to reply with words, instead, she confidently pressed her lips against his. Their kiss was slow yet sensual, like what they had experienced in the past. It was a nice confirmation for Brian to have, knowing he was the one she was interested in and not the person who consistently called her as if there was an emergency.

It was the best confirmation Brian could have asked for. If anything, it was perfect. There was nothing he wanted more than to prove how much he adored her company. The taste of her lips was one he had gotten used to and one he knew he could no longer live without.

Although, their kiss didn't last anywhere near as long as they wanted it to.

"Please don't be fucking. Please don't be fucking. Please don't be fucking." Max whispered as she slowly opened the door to the motel room, her fingers crossed, and her eyes closed. It took her a moment of anticipation before she opened her eyes and looked across the room at both Brian and Farah who were sat tangled in one another. She witnessed them detach their lips and look towards her with a shocked expression.

"Max..." Farah groaned, slowly removing her hands from Brian's face and focusing her attention on her best friend who had casually interrupted them.

"Uh, okay, not what I was expecting, but still no better." Max was a little lost for words, finding a lot of entertainment in catching the couple. It would only make for great material to use against Farah for comedic purposes in the future.

"I should probably shower." Brian laughed. He wanted to seem productive. After all, they were on a schedule.

"You didn't shower together? Thank god." Max touched her palm to her chest with a sigh of relief. "Anyway, I'm here for my phone. I left it behind by mistake." Max reached over to her bag and picked her phone out from her pants lying on the side.

"Right." Farah nodded, awkwardly pushing her glasses up the bridge of her nose.

Brian pressed his hands together as he stood between the two friends.

"Later, losers. Don't do anything on my bed! You've got ten minutes before we have to bounce." Max threw up the peace symbol with her hands before leaving, pulling the door shut behind her.

Brian looked down at Farah who was still sitting at the end of the bed, her hair was wet and she was as wonderful as ever. She looked up at him with a sweet smile.

She wished Brian didn't have to find out about Hasan. It only served to make things awkward. It wasn't as if she wanted to be with him. Never. Even before she had met Brian, she wasn't interested. Now, she was only interested in one person.

"You met the criteria." Farah grinned as the words fell from her lips. Brian blushed, feeling giddy from her comment.

He smiled widely, holding both of his hands together before leaning down and pressing a quick kiss against her lips. He stepped back and kept his eyes locked on hers as he moved towards the bathroom. Farah snorted at him, being the dork that he was and not looking where he was going he was pretty shocked to find the bathroom door was open, causing him to stumble backwards.

"I'm fine!" He laughed as he held onto either side of the door to regain balance.

Farah laughed at his silliness, unable to control herself. Brian wanted to be embarrassed about falling, but the way it had made her laugh only served to make his heart pound.

There was one more day on tour before they would have to go home. One more day to spend time with the person they had grown close to over what was nearly a month of them being together.

Whilst Brian was showering, Farah turned her phone back on and texted Hasan to let him know she was alive but busy. Once again, the same excuse she had used plenty of times in the past. An excuse that allowed her to get away from him, if only for a little while.

The evening swung around quickly, and everyone attended the show as per usual. It was clear just by the view from the side of the stage that Brian was having the time of his life. There was so much energy in his performance and after every song, he turned to Farah with a smile.

There were some things neither of them could change. Particularly things about their pasts that weren't their choice, but that didn't seem to matter. Sometimes, things couldn't be forced.

Sometimes it was just better to wait for things to happen.

SAYREVILLE, NJ

"We started this trip super against the idea of being labelled as groupies and yet here we are. Max and her sidekick, *Groupie Farah*." Max cocked an eyebrow, a small smirk creeping up her lips. Her hands were gripped tightly onto the steering wheel as she attempted to get her point across.

"What are you talking about?"

"You're a groupie! A Social Dropouts groupie!" Max pointed at Farah.

"I'm not a groupie!" Farah gritted her teeth together.

"You slept with the lead singer of the band—multiple times! You're a groupie!" Max teased, getting more enjoyment out of it than she should have.

"I'm a fan!" Farah sighed, bringing up the same phrase that Max had continued to make early on during their trip. The same phrase that Brian had picked up on.

"You don't even like the music that much! How can you *possibly* be a fan?" Max snorted loudly.

"I've grown to like it..."

"I know what it is...you're a fan of Brian's dick!"

"*Max!*" Farah shouted, despite it being just them inside the car she still felt a twinge of embarrassment from the situation.

"Okay, sorry sorry! You make it far too easy for me." Max chuckled; Farah was an easy target. Max happily accepted retaliation.

"Trust me, it's not intentional." Farah sighed.

"Are you keeping in contact with Bri-fy once this is all over? Or is this like...only a sex thing?"

"It's more than that!"

"Are you going to confess your love before leaving tomorrow morning?"

"Uh...no. I've told you, we're not in love."

"Pfft. Reject all that fairytale bullshit you want, but it'll catch up to you one day. When it does, I want to be the first person to say *I told you so*." Max pointed over at Farah aggressively.

"I swear you don't even believe in love!"

"Nuh-uh, I do *believe* in love. What I don't believe in is the reality of myself being in a long-term relationship that doesn't end up with my name on the title sequence of a true-crime documentary. Therefore, my current technique is the 'fuck and flee'. You could do that with Brian too...if you're not into the whole romantic side of things." Max explained, giving Farah what she believed to have been sound advice.

Farah had never been in love before, she didn't know what it felt like. Most of her so-called relationships were built around who her parents wanted her to be with. She had never thought about what it would have been like to...love someone.

"How do you know if you're in love? Isn't it rather tropey? Y'know? Love." Farah questioned, confused on the matter.

"Floating babies with kickass crossbows, puppies, yada yada roses? Yeah, I haven't got a clue. Something about being warm and gooey. Man, love is weird." Max furrowed her eyebrows as she stared out at the road ahead. She didn't know how to describe a feeling she hadn't experienced either.

"Nothing insightful?"

"Hey! You can't keep getting insightful Max Kayori advice for free. Ping me some cash, I also accept tips." Max paused for a second, realising she should probably give her best friend some more free advice. "Look, I'm sure love is that same feeling you get when you drink too much coffee. The desire, the

warm feeling at the pit of your stomach, the caffeine high you get from it, followed by the eventual diarrhoea and regret..."
Max sighed heavily.

Farah was lost. Max usually had all the answers.

"Oh...wow. You're not getting any tips for that one."

Farah pondered on it longer, realising she knew little about love. She turned around only to see Bryan Dande-Lion strapped in the backseat. Max hadn't forgotten their new travel companion. She had claimed he had become the band's mascot.

As excited as Farah was for the last show, she was also sad. She had been reluctant to go on the trip in the first place, it had opened her eyes to things she had never seen or done before. Max was right about one thing, if she told her future kids about her adventures across the states, they wouldn't have found her boring.

Max had been so convincing when it came to inviting her on the trip that as uncertain as she was to go, she was happy she did.

She had collected enough pictures of every museum and historical landmark they passed for her parents to view upon her return. They would have enjoyed the ones from the quilt museum. She had already sorted through the folders on her phone to make sure her parents didn't see any of the photographs of her and the band. Of her and Brian.

There was one they had taken together in Austin. Brian had held the phone up high above them both as they stood under a streetlight by the hotel. It was simple. Just the two of them smiling as they looked up at the camera. Just from looking at the picture you wouldn't have been able to tell if they were romantically involved or just friends. It didn't give any hints. All you knew was the two people in the photograph were close.

They were happy.

Something neither of them could honestly say before they had met. Something they had learned over the course of their time together. Happiness was hard, but it was harder to achieve alone.

Brian had opted to drive from Columbus to Sayreville. It was a long drive to get done in a single day, but he was convinced he could do it. It was a shame the drive was so long that they didn't have time to hang out before the show with Max and Farah. It would have been nice to have wished them well and said goodbye. Farah had already told her parents when she was going to be back home, so it was hard for them to stick around.

Brian pondered on a lot as he drove across the states.

Brian found it hard to think back to being on stage where he wasn't putting all his attention on his guitar and Farah. Even his memories when he wasn't on the stage were flooded by Farah. He simply couldn't get her out of his head.

"Next time, we're saving up and getting more motels. I'm getting pretty sick of the whole floor shit." Zoe groaned as she rested her head on the back of the seat.

"We stayed in motels in the end. Mostly." Catfish countered. It had been true; nearer the end of the tour, they had spent most of their money on somewhere to stay for the night. A lot of the time it was wherever Max and Farah ended up staying.

"My bank account is aching." Zoe complained. Touring was expensive. Most of the money they had gotten from the venues they had burned through already.

"Maybe we could do more camping? That was fun." Brian inputted, despite barely getting any sleep the one night they did camp.

"Is that because you spent the night with your *girlfriend*?" Zoe teased, gently prodding Brian in his stomach as he kept his eyes on the road ahead. She watched him flood a shade of red.

"She's not my *girlfriend* and no, that's not why. It was very pretty underneath the stars!" Brian huffed. It felt weird with Zoe referring to Farah as his girlfriend.

He had been worrying about the end of the tour from the moment they had become a little more than acquaintances. What would happen when it ended?

"I'm sure it was." Russ continued to speak in jest as the rest of the band chuckled lightly. Brian scratched the top of his head as his cheeks remained heated.

"It was, *stars* are pretty!" Brian insisted, now with his eyebrows dipped into an angry position.

"*Sure.*" Zoe snorted.

"We love you, Bri." Catfish grinned as Brian checked the rear view mirror. They loved him and he loved them back, even if they were annoying.

"I love you guys." Brian couldn't hide his smile as he gripped a little tighter on the steering wheel.

Social Dropouts were stronger than ever, and it was all thanks to the tour.

Surprisingly, Max and Farah didn't manage to get to the venue as quickly as the band. They knew they should have woken up earlier in Columbus, but they had spent the night before getting pizza and chatting until the early hours of the morning. There was no chance they would have woken up sooner.

"One drink. It's the last show, it's going to be fun!" Max attempted to sway Farah's opinion on alcohol as they stood at the back of the venue together awaiting the band. Farah had texted Brian to let him know they were there and that she would see him at the end of the show.

Brian had a lot to do before their last show of the tour.

"You're really trying, aren't you?" Farah folded her arms and chuckled, knowing how badly Max was trying to get her to drink.

"You drank with Brian. I felt a little hurt by that, y'know? I've seen you tear shit up in our dorm and yet you won't even have a teeny tiny bit of alcohol with me here? Let us have fun before we grow up and become boring gin moms. Fucking end me if I ever have a 'it's gin o'clock' doormat." Max groaned. "Please, my lovable best friend and roommate, let's make this a *Ra Ra Riot*!" She placed her hands over her heart and batted her eyelashes. Farah couldn't resist the pouting expression that Max pulled.

"One drink." Farah sighed. "I mean it!"

"Okay, but I get to choose what it is."

"Depends on what you choose."

"That's a surprise."

"Max, I won't drink it."

"Come on..."

"Hmm..."

"Please? Do you want me to get Brian to ask you instead?" Max pouted.

"Oh, come on!"

"I'm offering to pay for something! Isn't that so...*unlike* me? Take that opportunity and run!"

Farah grumbled slightly.

"Alright, fine. Nothing too bad. Please."

"It won't be *bad*." Max rolled her eyes before giving Farah a thumbs up as she backed away in the direction of the bar.

Farah stood on her own and looked around the room. Nobody looked as intimidating as they had done the first show she attended. Despite everyone standing around and laughing, they were all docile and didn't look threatening in any sense of the word. Perhaps once the music started they would have bashed into one another as they formed a mosh pit, but that was all part of the fun. They weren't there to harm one another.

There was one thing she noticed at every show she had been to. If someone fell inside the mosh pit—everyone *stopped*. It wasn't a selfish act of trampling on people who had fallen, it was a communal effort to make sure that person was safe and enjoying themselves. Farah enjoyed watching from afar, it was reassuring to know that the scene would protect you.

Like one big...family.

It didn't take long for Max to come back with a concoction of a sort. Farah didn't question it too much. They both took the shots as if they were back in their dorm room on a Friday night celebrating their test results.

They stood at the back of the venue and waited for the lights on the stage to flash, signalling Social Dropouts onto the stage. Max let out a scream as Farah followed with one just as loud. It filled Farah with a feeling of elation. Max had a huge smile across her face, she was so proud of Farah for the anxiety she had overcome during her time on the tour.

Each band member entered the stage one by one. It was hard to see them with inadequate lighting. The crowd continued to shout as the band took their places.

This was the eighteenth time they had played on the tour.

Brian closed his eyes and took in a deep breath. The air around him was stuffy with the number of people in the room, but it was the atmosphere he craved.

He was ready.

A red pair of skating shoes pressed gently against a pedal that had been drilled onto an old skateboard deck, an abundance of leads trailing from each colourful device, the final lead feeding into a red Fender Telecaster. There was a slight monotone drone over the speakers as everyone in the room waited patiently with anticipation.

A drumstick bounced on a cymbal, enough to make it hum with impatience. Fingers twisted the pegs of a guitar as one of the digital pedals lit up a bright green colour. A simple pluck of a bass string.

The build-up to what would have been a fantastic gig.

The stage was dim, just enough lighting to see the band's silhouettes outlined in blue. They could see the lights pointing at the crowd. Every face was a person who wanted to see them play. Excited. Thrilled.

Ready to rock.

The frontman took a step forward, brushing his fingers through his messy blonde hair. It wouldn't have stayed in position long once he had sweated his way through the evening, but it was a nice start. He looked at each member of his band before looking towards the back of the venue.

He could see her. Farah Vishwakarma. The college student who had reluctantly decided to tour with Social Dropouts. She stood beside her best friend Max, patiently awaiting the show just as she had done for eighteen nights.

He approached the microphone that had been adjusted to match his height. As he looked at the crowd, he noticed the girl in the back wave at him. He held up his hand and waved back causing the whole room to erupt into a loud cheer. They may have thought he was waving to the whole crowd and perhaps he was, but his smile was directed to someone in particular.

"Everyone's here to have fun tonight, huh?" Brian spoke into his microphone. It was a simple question and one that elicited quite the response.

The crowd responded with a roar louder than the last.

"I don't think that was loud enough." The second guitarist stepped up to his microphone and commented on the crowd's performance before adjusting his glasses.

"I didn't think it was too bad. Seems like Russ is pretty hard to please though. You're going to have to do better, so, I'll ask again—is everyone here ready to have some *fun*?"

The crowd shouted much louder than before. The sound was deafening. Max and Farah laughed as they joined in with the screaming.

"Hey, that's better!" The bassist laughed as she stepped to her microphone and spoke with confidence.

The lights on the stage sparked on, allowing everyone to see the band. Brian Blossom held onto the microphone and coughed into it slightly, scanning his eyes across the crowd and smirking. Catfish kept his drumsticks rapidly tapping against the snare as he awaited his cue.

"Yeah...*much* better." Brian winked before stepping back on one foot and grabbing the guitar that was hanging on him by the strap.

Catfish hit every drum on his kit as each guitar began to play their parts. As per usual, Brian tapped his fingers against the frets. Russ played complex chords that he couldn't name in a practically unknown tuning. Zoe kept them all together with a solid and catchy bassline.

"*I've made a mistake! All my errors have come crashing down, my confidence has gone away!*" Brian began to shout into the microphone as everyone in the room started to jump around at the start of the song. There was nothing they enjoyed more than how their music made people want to dance.

Max gripped Farah's hand. Farah glanced down at the gesture with wide eyes.

"Come and mosh with me—*please*!" Max tried her luck as she yelled over the loud music, pulling Farah towards the crowd.

Farah shook her head at Max. Moshing was not an activity she would have ever seen herself participating. But, after hearing Brian's music night after night she was starting to realise that perhaps it *did* have the danceability that she hadn't appreciated before.

"*I'm afraid that I'm not good for you, but even if I'm not I'd fight for you!*"

"You won't lose me, right?" Farah considered the idea of going into the mosh pit.

After all, wasn't the trip about seizing the day? What was the point of coming all that way without proving how much she had cracked out of her shell?

"Oh my god! No!" Max laughed as she pulled Farah a little further forward much to her hesitation.

"Promise?"

"I love you, man. Trust me, if this was dangerous, I wouldn't let you do it!" Max winked as she began to jump along to the music, continuing to hold onto Farah's hand to convince her to do the same.

Farah began to nod her head to the beat. The song was catchy. The same one they had opened with for most of the tour. She recognised it. Max nodded back, encouraging her to bounce on her feet until she was laughing with Max as they jumped up and down on the spot to the beat of the song and Brian's manic shouting.

"*I'm gonna lose to the bad guy. Put your fists up in a fight as I just sit and cry—I'm the good guy! In a fight against myself, so please just save yourself because I'm not good for you.*" Brian's lyrics were hard to hear over everyone's screams inside the crowd.

Max dragged Farah into the masses, she focused all her energy on her best friend. She didn't want to lose her.

The pit was already warm and jumping around with Max was a lot of fun, she bumped shoulders a few times with the people around her, but other than that everyone was sensibly bouncing to the song. It was a lot calmer than Farah had expected after viewing it from afar. It may have been down to the song having reached a calmer part as Brian slowed his shouting to sing.

"*I can't be alone with you. I can't be alone with you. I can't be alone with you.*" He whispered into the microphone.

"Are you ready?" Max nodded towards Farah.

"Okay!" Farah wasn't sure how to respond as the beat in the song suddenly dropped.

Brian stepped back from the microphone before shouting the next few lyrics as loudly as possibly. Catfish smashed the drumsticks against the drums as hard as he could as both Russ and Zoe plucked at the strings of their guitars in quick succession whilst pacing the stage.

"*I'm an addict for my own self-deprecation...taking it out on you for my own validation...I cannot be alone in this room...I don't know what I will do...to myself...*" The room erupted into a sea of jumping Social Dropouts fans, screaming the lyrics as they all bumped into one another.

Max and Farah laughed together as they got swept away in the commotion. Farah was having the time of her life, something she hadn't expected to have done at one of the shows.

Brian repeated his words, this time a lot slower as the whole crowd gently stopped jumping and caught their breath.

"*I'm an addict for my own self-deprecation...taking it out on you for my own validation...*" Brian sang softly into the microphone as he allowed the crowd to take the second half of the verse.

"*I cannot be alone in this room. I don't know what I will do to myself.*" The crowd sang back at the band. Even Farah had picked up on the lyrics and sang them back with her finger pointed in the air, copying Max.

"*To myself...*" Brian repeated the last lyrics as he pushed his pick against one of the strings of the guitar to signify the end of the song.

The crowd exploded into the overbearing sound of applause as they listened to the band perform. Despite being the first song of the night, they were already pumped to have heard the rest of what Social Dropouts had to offer. It was off to a great start.

Farah took a moment to regain her breath after the song had finished, realising she had been missing out on a lot of fun being at the back of the venue.

Brian looked towards the back of the venue and couldn't see Farah. He scanned the crowd and noticed Max waving her arm in the air before lifting Farah's hand for her.

Farah was in the pit.

Max could see the excitement in her eyes as the show continued. Farah didn't stop jumping around the whole time. She was having the time of her life. She wasn't sure if it was the small amount of alcohol she had consumed that was making her feel this way or the adrenaline that ran through her. Either way, she was having fun.

"*I ran out crying without ever saying a word. All your friends laughed because you couldn't get with a girl. Regrettable decisions that make you the villain.*" Brian neared the end of the set with one of the last songs of the show.

"Want to go up?" Max pointed upwards as she shouted over the music.

"What?" Farah shouted back, not bothering to stop her rampant jumping on the spot as she danced to the rhythmic tones. Letting her hair down for the last show was an unbelievably memorable experience.

"Up! Do you want to surf?" Max explained as she pointed up again.

"Me?"

"Yeah, you!"

"Oh...I don't—"

"Come on, it's super easy! No kicking and no scratching! Let yourself be carried." Max instructed before bending down and interlocking her fingers together so Farah could be boosted up onto the crowd.

Farah stared down at the gesture. There were so many things in her life she was terrified of. Crowd surfing looked scary, but over the nights on tour she had seen many people do it. It couldn't have been *that* scary.

It did...look fun.

"It's cool, hold on." A stranger gestured to Max, noticing what was going on. Farah couldn't deny the offer now that strangers were involved. She had to accept.

Farah smiled down at Max as she placed her shoe on her best friend's hands and stepped up as she held onto the stranger's shoulder. Max helped boost her onto the crowd as the tall stranger allowed Farah to hold his shoulder. Farah practically fell on top of everyone, noticing that without hesitation the crowd held her up. No matter how big or small they were, everyone made the effort to lift their hands in the air to help carry her forward.

"*Sitting in the corner, but you're pulling me forward, I tripped on my intentions. Oh fuck, this is awkward!.*" Brian continued to shout, glancing into the crowd and noticing Farah balancing on an abundance of people.

He couldn't help but grin as wide as possible, realising he was about to reach the peak of the song. A guitar solo that couldn't be matched. Farah had gone out of her comfort zone, laughing and screaming as she pointed her finger towards Brian. She was having the time of her life.

"From the wisp of your breath to the tip of your tongue. You were on my mind, but you weren't just anyone..." Brian yelled into the microphone with sweat dripping down either side of his face. He had written the song a long time ago, but some of the lyrics resonated with his current situation.

Brian assured his guitar lead wasn't caught on anything as he took a running jump onto the crowd. He had been in plenty of crowds before and was sure everyone would hold him up, he closed his eyes as he jumped, hoping he didn't land on the venue floor.

The band stopped playing for a moment in anticipation of the guitar solo. Brian opened his eyes, realising he was being held up by a sea of hands, security holding the lead of the guitar that was trailing back to the stage.

Brian looked over at Farah who was also on top of the crowd and smiled. She smiled back at him and began to laugh; the experience was like no other. This was the moment they wanted to be trapped in forever.

Farah could feel the people below her with their hands on her back, holding her above them as she was pushed to the front of the crowd. She held her hands out to balance herself, noticing how fluent her movements were across the sea of strangers.

Brian nodded towards the band as he began to shred on the guitar, continuing to tap on the frets to create the twinkly tones the genre loved. The crowd held him in position as he played, teetering back and forth.

Farah had been thrown off the crowd and was now in the arms of a member of security. She chuckled awkwardly as he held her before he instructed her to go to the back of the venue after taking a sip of water. Farah practically sprinted back around, pushing her way through the crowd to find Max. Brian was still playing his solo when she got back to Max.

"Holy fucking shit!" Max screamed as she threw her arms around Farah and screamed in her ear. Farah couldn't stop laughing as she held Max back, both practically swinging one another around in the middle of the crowd.

Max was so proud of her best friend.

Brian held his head back and held his arms out as he was pushed back to the front at the end of his solo. His guitar balanced on his stomach as he was swept back. He was quick to hop past the security guard and struggle back onto the stage with the guitar still hung around him, he scrambled over to the microphone to continue the song.

"*I want you to wake up, covered in makeup. I want you to go home, wearing my old clothes. Lying next to you just hours ago, I begged you to stay the day. You said I was wrong for wanting something different, but it's okay for someone like you...*" Brian breathed the last words of his song heavily into the microphone, the crowd singing every word. Brian raised his hand in the air before listening to the screams of the crowd in front of him.

He loved playing shows. Music was everything to him.

He panted heavily as he turned to each member of his band who had done a fantastic job throughout the tour. Brian couldn't have been more grateful for them all.

Behind the screen of the hazy smoke machine and blue lights, Farah could see the sweat beading from his forehead as he breathed deeply. His stance was one of confidence as he held the microphone with both hands.

"We're Social Dropouts and it's been a pleasure playing for you tonight and every night on this tour. I hope you all get home safely."

There was a slight pause.

"...and I'll see *you* tonight!" Brian nodded towards the section of the crowd where Farah was standing.

Farah smiled up at the man on stage as her best friend gripped onto her arm and shook her violently. She watched him wave as he exited the stage. Farah's heart fluttered knowing he was talking to *her*. This wasn't just a crush on a boy in a band, it was so much more.

Nobody in the crowd felt the same as she did.

Once the show was over Max and Farah continued to freak out about it all. Farah battled her fear of mosh pits and Max had gotten her wish.

Max and Farah were invited backstage on the last night of the tour, making their way to the room with a singular couch, a table and a broken chair. It wasn't anything special and was pretty much the same as every other gross looking venue they had played at throughout the states.

"Home tomorrow." Max sighed as she leaned back on the couch and glanced around the room at everyone. Zoe was sitting beside her on the couch, Russ was on the broken chair, Catfish was sitting in the middle of the table with his legs crossed and Brian and Farah were sitting on the floor with their backs against the wall.

"It was a great tour though." Russ put his thumb up as he spoke.

"It was killer, man. We smashed it." Catfish grinned as he nodded at everyone in the room.

"We were amazing. Did you guys see Farah surfing?" Brian laughed before pressing the back of his head against the wall and looking over at the girl who had won his heart. She chuckled lightly as everyone's eyes fell on her. She noticed Brian's open palm resting on the top of her thigh, offering to hold her hand.

Farah slipped her fingers between Brian's. She didn't want it to end when the morning came around.

"My best friend, Farah Vishwakarma is the coolest crowd surfer you have ever seen!" Max practically shouted across the room as she pointed towards Farah. Farah blushed at the comment, feeling Brian's thumb gently brush against her hand.

"Yeah! I saw you. You're good at that! You have to come and rock out with us in the future." Zoe chuckled.

"It was a lot of fun." Farah continued to blush.

"Can I make a toast?" Russ stood up from the broken chair, everyone in the room looking concerned as the chair creaked, a piece of plastic dropping off the back as he got up. The venue was falling apart.

"We don't have any bread." Brian snorted.

"Ayeeee." Catfish pointed finger guns towards the frontman. Russ sighed heavily before continuing.

"Anyway, carbohydrates aside, I wanted to say thank you to our new friends that we made along the tour. Max and Farah have helped make this tour everything it needed to be. I'm incredibly grateful that you both joined us on our adventure, and I hope you can do so again in the future." Russ nodded, clapping his hands together as he finished talking.

"Aw Russ, that's so sweet! Thank you for inviting us." Farah commented, her heart full of love for the whole band.

"Man, that's awesome." Max grinned, exchanging glances with Farah. She was glad they had gotten close to the band. "You guys are the best."

Farah smiled, nodding her head in agreement with Max whilst keeping her fingers intertwined with Brian as she looked around the room at everyone.

They were all unique in their own way and she respected them all for the kindness they had shown her and the talents they held. They had a bumpy start, but she had learned to love them.

She truly hoped it wouldn't have been the last time she got to speak to them all.

They eventually got kicked out of the venue and made their way back to the motel they were spending the night in. It would have been the last time they all stayed together. It was a momentous occasion and everyone was sad to leave in the morning—especially Brian and Farah.

As everyone got ready for bed Brian texted Farah and asked her to meet him outside by the van. Brian was nervous, knowing it was possibly the last time he would have been able to see Farah. He didn't want that to be the case, which is why he had called her outside.

He wanted to...talk.

"It looked like you enjoyed the show." Brian smirked as he leaned against the side of the van with his hands in his denim jacket. Farah stood beside him, folding her arms and looking up towards the sky.

It was a clear night. Perfect for stargazing.

"I did..." Farah snickered as she shuffled closer to Brian as they looked up at the sky.

"Do you think you'll come to another Social Dropouts show?" Brian turned his head as he cocked an eyebrow at the question.

Farah shrugged, struggling to stop herself from smiling.

"Of course. You guys are really good."

"Thanks..."

"The stars are pretty tonight." Farah sighed as she looked up again.

"So are you."

"Thanks." His compliments never failed to make her smile.

"Do you...want to sit on top of the van? We'll get a better view." Brian suggested, continuing to keep his hands inside his jacket.

"Is that safe?"

"I don't know, but it'll be fun!" Brian pulled open the side of the van and climbed inside before stepping on the seat and hoisting himself up onto the roof. It probably should have dented from the weight, but even if it did—he didn't care. The van was already far past its expiry date.

"Please don't fall."

"The only falling I'm doing is for you." Brian leaned over the edge and held out his hand for Farah to grab onto, making the offhand comment that only served to make Farah laugh. "I-I'm sorry. That was bad." He blushed as he practically laid on the top of the van waiting to pull her up. He was sure he had used that one on her before.

It had worked.

"You're a dork."

Farah reached up and gripped onto his hand, allowing him to pull her onto the roof. Brian shuffled to the back of the van and sat on the edge with his legs over the side, Farah followed and sat beside him.

"You're right about being able to see the stars better." Farah looked up at the sky and searched for any constellations she knew.

"You were right about it being dangerous." Brian looked down at his legs hanging over the side of the van and gulped slightly. It wasn't a huge drop, the stage he had dived off a couple of hours ago was taller. That didn't stop his trepidation.

"It's okay, silly." Farah snorted as she held out her hand for Brian to hold, just as he had done for her previously. Brian didn't hesitate to grip on.

He sighed heavily as he held Farah's hand on his lap, beginning to draw small circles on the top of her hand. She looked at him with a smile, taking note of his innocent action.

His sad expression told another story.

They gazed up at the stars above them. There was a silence shared as they held onto each other's hand. A cool breeze crept through the air. Brian took a deep breath as his eyes scanned the night sky.

"It's pretty lonely in space." Brian spoke in a whisper as he studied the stars above.

"Only if you choose to go alone." Farah held Brian's hand a little tighter. He glanced over at her comment, a sadness in his eyes. Her words spoke volumes.

Brian didn't want to be alone and Farah was giving him the option not to.

"This is it, huh?"

"The end of the tour?"

"The end of *us*?" Brian looked away, trying his hardest not to cry.

"Oh..." Farah let out a short breath, she wasn't sure what to say. It wasn't as if they had ever put a label on the relationship they had built over the tour.

"I've never had this before." Brian chewed his bottom lip nervously, trying to stop himself from breaking out in a flood of tears. He continued to circle the top of her hand, this time a lot softer and slower than he did when he was flirting with her.

"This?"

Brian lifted his head and looked towards Farah with sadness in his eyes, somewhat glistening under the streetlight as he fought back the urge to cry. His eyes watered simply at the sight of her. How could someone be so beautiful? Why would someone like Farah ever want to be with someone like *him*?

"I...I've never liked anyone the way that I like you." Brian sniffed with a slight smile, he had nothing to lose. If she rejected him like everyone else throughout his life then it wasn't as if they would ever have to see one another again.

Farah's heart pounded at his wording. The way the words fell so softly from his lips and the meaning that was behind them.

He *liked* her.

"Me neither." Farah smirked back at him, noting the cracks in his voice. It was something he had spent a long time pondering on and something he struggled to say. Something he had practised within his mind...and in mirrors in motel rooms.

"I really like you, Farah." Brian's words were practically a whisper as he looked into her eyes. Farah stared back, taking in the information. Brian's heart beat fast enough to jump out of his chest as he awaited an answer.

Nobody had ever said those words to her before. Not with the same meaning that was behind Brian's breath. They had the same feelings about one another. It was a beautiful feeling.

"I-I really like you too, Brian." Farah let out a small sigh of relief, something that had been hanging over her head was finally out in the open.

"Really?" Brian's eyes widened, shocked by her answer.

"Y-yeah!" Farah laughed at his reaction.

"Oh...wow." Brian looked off to the side, his mind stewing on her answer. As much as he wanted her to have said the same in return, a lifetime of rejection had taught him otherwise. He held tightly onto her as he used his spare hand to wipe his eyes as they began to water.

"Are you crying?" Farah reached out and placed her finger underneath his chin to force him to look up at her.

"N-no." Brian laughed as he wiped his tears away from his eyes.

"It's okay to cry! I promise." Farah gently brushed her thumb underneath his eye to remove a stray tear.

He placed his palm over her hand that was on his face, slowly bringing it down between them so they were now holding both of their hands. They stared at each other deeply for a moment, there was so much for them to take in.

"I'm crying because I'm happy." Brian finally responded with the same dorky smile he had given her time and time again.

"The best kind of tears."

"Yeah..."

"You're going to come and visit, right?" Farah tilted her head to the side slightly. She couldn't bear the thought of this being their last night together.

"Yeah!"

"If I'm super busy with college, you'll still call?"

"Only if when I'm busy you call too."

"I will!"

"Okay." Brian nodded with a smile, happy to hear they had come up with a plan together.

Farah thought back on all the times they had shared throughout the tour, from meeting him at the back of a venue, skateboarding, kissing him for the first time in Birmingham, eating ice cream in Austin, spending a night with him in the City of Angels, visiting museums, roller skating, sleeping in the van, being lakeside lovers to surfing on the top of a crowd. They had a wealth of memories together, none of which could ever be replaced.

It went without saying that Brian had a special place in his heart for Farah.

"Wait until Max hears that Brian Blossom of Social Dropouts told me he *likes* me." Farah snorted, unable to stop teasing.

"Lawrence."

"Huh?"

"Brian Stanley Lawrence. It's my...*real* name." Brian half-smiled, looking at Farah with glistening eyes. "I haven't told anyone that before."

The only people he had told before were his band. The people he sought permanence from. He wanted permanence from Farah too.

"*Lawrence.* I like that." Farah chuckled softly. Brian had enough confidence to tell her something personal about himself. He trusted her. It was a sure way of guaranteeing he was serious.

"Yeah, *Blossom* is...a placeholder. A stage name." Brian shrugged.

"That's smart."

"My dad encouraged me to use 'Blossom'. It was what my mom used. I could drop it if I wanted to, but I didn't want to disappoint him. He's still torn up about Mom and I know he wants to hold onto whatever parts of her he can. If this helps him somehow, then whatever, it's just a name." He shrugged slightly as he spoke in a soft tone, leaving himself open for Farah to listen to.

"That's sweet you would do that for him."

"Yeah, sometimes I think it's all about appearances, but I can never be sure. He expects a lot from me, so I should give him this at the very least."

"I understand. The expectations of our parents are ones we have to fill, yet ones we don't want to. They always have something big set up for us when the reality is...we want something else." Farah sighed, knowing that she could relate.

"I probably should have changed 'Brian' whilst I was at it. It's the name of my grandfather I've never met. My dad's a man of tradition or some shit."

"I like the name Brian."

"Don't lie. Nobody likes the name *Brian*." Brian rolled his eyes.

"That's pretty offensive to everyone named Brian." Farah teased as she nudged his shoulder.

"As part of the Brian committee, I can assure you none of us would take offence." Brian shook his head and laughed.

They shared a moment of silence as they looked up, scanning the night sky for something, anything that could have given them more time together. Perhaps something to extend the tour? Anything would have been better than knowing in the morning they would have parted ways.

After their time on the tour, sitting on top of the van encapsulated a lot of how they felt. Farah could feel the warmth of his hand on hers, but it felt so special. She had fallen hard for the frontman of the emo band and she liked him more than anyone she had ever had feelings for in the past. Nothing was ever like this.

Farah shuffled closer, Brian lifted his arm and placed it around her—holding her close. Farah could feel his hand on her waist before she pulled it upwards so she could lightly run her fingertips against his. She felt his lips press against her head as she leaned against him.

She could have stayed in his arms forever.

"I have a show in Atlanta next month, it's my solo stuff, you should come! It's uh...I *sing*. Y'know, instead of yelling."

Brian suggested as he explained his solo act.

"I hope I'm back at college by then, I'd love to see you *sing*." Farah commented, only then realising her words could have come across as offensive.

"Still not a fan of the shouting?" Brian grinned as he felt her cuddle up to him. It was the nicest feeling.

"It's very loud."

"That's the point."

"I know, but I like hearing you talk. I like hearing you sing. You have a nice voice." Farah closed her eyes as she held onto him. She listened to his breathing as she smelled the sweet cologne on his jacket. He was warm and she loved the way he held her in return.

She never saw him as the man on stage with the adoring fans. Or the man who had a famous mother. Or even the man who was recognisable enough that people were willing to disrupt their time together to get to him. She always just saw Brian for Brian.

Brian Lawrence.

Brian turned and planted a small kiss on Farah's head for a second time that evening. It was sweet. Sweet enough to have said goodbye without the desire for more, but intimate enough to have meaning.

"I'm going to miss you." Brian admitted, still torn about not being able to see her, potentially not for a while.

"We'll still see each other."

"I know, but it's not the same when it's not every day." He sighed.

"I heard video calls are good for this kind of thing." Farah inputted, attempting to think of a solution.

"Not as good as the real thing, but I'm happy to do that. As long as I still get to see you." Brian shrugged with a smile spread across his face.

"You'll see me." Farah laughed, resting her head on his shoulder as she spoke.

There was no telling how long they spent outside sitting on top of the van, but most of it was in silence. Gently brushing their fingertips against their hands, listening to their heartbeats and playing with their hair. They didn't need words to show their affection for one another.

Brian's heart was no longer heavy with sadness, but a new-found feeling of bubbling happiness that he never wanted to shake. Farah made him feel so special.

Farah hadn't expected to spend the journey across the states becoming infatuated with the frontman of an emo band and yet there she was, cuddled up tightly beside him as they stared up at the night sky.

On that night they only cared about one thing and that was one another. Brian had admitted his attraction to Farah verbally, something he had never done before.

There were lots of things that Farah could have done throughout her summer but choosing to go with Max had been one of the best decisions of her life.

Life didn't have to completely consist of stress and textbooks, there was so much outside of college that Farah was yet to experience. So much of the world she wanted to see.

Farah Vishwakarma had always been an introvert, so when her best friend, Max, suggested following a band on tour, it wasn't something she thought she would ever agree to.

Except, she *did* and she didn't regret it for a second...

THE ENCORE

The repetitive sound of the needle scratching on the runout groove of the vinyl record echoed through the small apartment, gracefully accompanied by the sound of the broken ceiling fan clicking as it spun. Bags yet to be unpacked laid in a line from the door over to the bed in the middle of the room.

There was a slight grumble to be heard as Brian Lawrence laid flat on his face in the centre of the bed, barely making it to his pillows. He was still wearing the clothes he had been in when he had been driving back home after the tour. The only thing he remembered was piling into the door of the tiny studio apartment with an armful of bags, making himself a coffee and putting on one of his favourite records to relax.

Nearly twelve hours later the record continued to spin and the mug of cold coffee sat under the coffee machine, untouched. Brian had barely made it out of his shoes before he had slept the day away. He had never been so exhausted from a tour before.

It was without saying that it had been the best tour of his life. A tour where he found himself playing some of the biggest shows he had ever played. A tour where he had hung out with some of his favourite people. A tour where he found what some people may have described as...

Brian's eyes shot open as he rolled over, spending the next few minutes staring up at the broken ceiling fan, paralysed with thoughts of the past couple of weeks spinning through his mind. Everything from buying a girl a drink at a bar to having the most passionate sex he had ever experienced. He internally scowled at himself for allowing his mind to drift.

He reached into his pocket for his phone, happy to find it was still there. He had received texts from nearly everyone he knew asking if he had gotten back home safely. It didn't help that he had been dead to the world for the better part of the past twelve hours. Texts weren't going to be able to wake him from his deep slumber. He had been exhausted and it was a privilege to have slept in his own bed as opposed to the floor, a shady motel or someone's couch, even if he hadn't gotten to the point of being able to tuck himself in.

Everyone had texted him. Zoe. Russ. Catfish. His dad. Was that....*Max*? Oh, and there was one text hidden at the bottom.

Farah.

Brian held the phone above his head and flicked through the messages, ignoring them all to go to the contact with the emoji of a pile of books beside it. His new favourite contact. His new romantic interest who liked him back! He grinned widely at the thought, adjusting the phone slightly as he scrolled.

Just as he balanced it above him, the phone was quick to slip from his fingers, falling straight into the middle of his face and causing him to groan in pain. He was too tired for that kind of abuse from his clumsiness. Brian rolled over onto his elbows to avoid any further embarrassing phone-to-face scenarios.

He finally got a chance to read Farah's text.

'I hope you got home safely. I can't wait to see you again soon xxx.'

His heart was full as he read multiple times. He beamed at his phone, what a wonderful start to his day. He hoped future 'mornings' would have been welcomed with texts from Farah.

Brian thought about responding, instead, debating whether she would have preferred a phone call.

Was it too soon to call? Was that needy? *Desperate*?

She had mentioned that people liked video calling, but his hair was dishevelled, and he hadn't shaved in a while. He wasn't feeling as well-rested as he should have after the amount of time he had slept. Perhaps he would keep a call to voice? Just for today.

He debated on calling Farah for a moment longer before scrolling through his other text messages. Mostly from the band group chat.

There was a text from his father.

'Hey Bri, I know you're probably sleeping off your post-tour blues, but I have news! Your old man just scored you some points with the big leagues. Call me ASAP.'

If his call were band-related Brian would have rather been with everyone else when he called. He wasn't sure what the news was and he wasn't sure he wanted to know. He needed to speak to his dad about the tour and query when it was he would get his guitar back from the people who helped transport it around the country.

Brian sat up on the side of the bed, making his head spin. He shouldn't have sat up so fast. His phone was flashing with a low battery warning, but he was sure he would have enough to call his father and then maybe even call Farah. If he had enough courage...

Today was all about relaxing from the tour and unpacking his bags. He already knew he was going to be ordering food for dinner, suddenly thinking about the milk he had left in the fridge before he went. He had to remind himself not to open the top.

He pressed the green telephone icon on the screen and placed his phone by his ear, listening to it ring as he stood up and twisted open the blinds behind his bed. He squinted at the sunlight bursting through his singular window as the tone within the speaker changed.

"Hello, Stan Static speaking." Stan spoke in a serious tone down the phone.

"Hi, Dad!"

"Brian! How was the tour, kid? Did you have a good time?" Stan was quick to jump on the question. He wanted to hear all about it. Brian didn't communicate with Stan as much as he should have throughout the tour. Especially this time.

Brian had been...distracted.

"It was great! We had crowd surfers every night!" Brian grinned. It was mostly Max.

"*Every* night?"

"Yeah! It was pretty fun."

"It sounds like it. I'm glad you had a good time. Speaking of, have you looked online?" Stan spoke with excitement in his voice. Brian could tell that he was working, a distant hum of chatter in the background. He didn't like to disturb him when he was working with everyone else, Stan had a lot more bands to manage than just...his son.

He hated bothering him, but Stan always made time for Brian.

"I haven't had the chance." Brian admitted. It was usually Zoe and Catfish that managed the Social Dropouts social media pages. Stan had taught them how to best promote their pages, but Zoe and Catfish usually did their own thing with as many pictures and memes as possible.

"Good news. There's a lot of people that are reviewing your shows, including some of the big dogs in the scene. So, your old man managed to rustle you guys a deal." Stan spoke proudly, happy with what he had gotten for his favourite band.

"What is it?"

"The front cover of AlternativeChaos magazine. They also want to do a ten-page feature on you all, including reviews of some of your shows for your first cross-country tour. Someone must have been scouting for content and was blown away by what you could do!" Stan was incredibly enthusiastic in his speech.

Brian smiled at the thought, it was nice to know there was someone who appreciated the effort he and his band put into making and performing their music. It always seemed to shock him that there were a lot of people who enjoyed their music.

However, to hear that a large magazine wanted to do an interview? That was certainly something.

The band was going to be ecstatic.

"Ten pages?" Brian stared at the floor at the thought.

"You won't have to do much talking, it's mostly just pictures. Big shots of your face and whatnot, like a Rockstar!"

Brian wasn't sure what kind of fame he wanted to achieve from the band. All he wanted to do was to have fun with something he knew well. He didn't want the band to reach the same amount of fame as his mother's band, but he didn't mind them gaining *some* popularity. He mostly did it for the rest of his band, not himself.

"Woah. Okay. Cool."

"I saw a review online and then shuffled around a few dates. Looks like you're going to LA again in a few weeks for a photoshoot with the whole band. They'll snap a bunch of pictures, even the one for the front cover. How does that sound?" Stan questioned, he was so excited. This was one of the first big opportunities the band had gotten without much of Stan's encouragement. They had been in magazines before, but not in the same capacity.

"That's...it's cool." Brian stared out the window of his apartment, the only view he got was of a pizza place across the street. He one day wished for somewhere with a nicer view.

"It's not *Rolling Stone*, but it is a *stepping* stone. Right?" Stan laughed a little more enthusiastically than he should have.

It would have been strange to see his face on the front cover of a magazine. He suddenly remembered his mother's face on the front of all the newspapers the day after she died...

Brian took a deep breath as he looked around his apartment. It felt so lonely there after spending so long with his closest friends.

It was strange to be alone. Again.

He stepped over to his record player, worried he had ruined the needle after having it spin on the runout for so long. He gently released the arm and put it back into position.

"I think I have an idea for an album." Brian sighed, his words slowly leaving his lips. Brian had been pondering on what he could have written about for a while, exhausting all of his ideas of depressing lyrics months ago. He wanted to make sure he was in the right frame of mind to continue writing. He wanted his heart in the right place.

He knew he probably shouldn't have mentioned it to his father, his excitement getting the best of him. Stan would have blown it out of proportion and that was the last thing Brian wanted.

"Yeah?"

"Yeah...being on tour gave me a new perspective on a few things. I want to start writing the new Social Dropouts album." Brian grinned, knowing exactly what kind of experience he wanted to focus his energy on. Using one hand, he took the record off the player and put it back into its sleeve as he listened to his dad speak.

"Well, shit, Kiddo...that's great! Give me a shout if you have some demos and I can get you all in for some studio time. I have no idea what it's going to sound like, but I already know that this new album is going to be killer! You've got to talk about it during the interview along with your solo album in the works! Early promotion can get some interest in this, make a single, perhaps even release it when the interview is published!" Stan instructed, being more of a manager than a father. "Think you can throw together the best fucking song I've ever heard?"

"I can try."

"Amazing. You're going to smash this! If things go well with this album, then I'm making sure you go overseas. How does that UK tour sound now?" Stan questioned.

Brian had never thought about touring outside America. He had played in nearly every state throughout his career, one-off shows or supporting other bands through half of a tour. It would have been exciting to leave the country to play shows.

"That sounds...fun." Brian smiled. His mind immediately jumped to the thought of Farah joining them on tour again.

Would she go overseas with him?

"Yeah, it would be!" Stan noticed the conversation trailing off before finally adding. "I'm proud of you, Rockstar."

As much as Brian didn't want to accept the praise, it was nice to hear the words from his father. A confirmation that he was doing a good job in his field. He just wanted to make sure that everything he was doing was where he needed to be in life.

His dad always gave him good confirmation of that. It wasn't always a reliable source, but Brian needed to hear it anyway.

"Thanks, Dad." Brian smiled as he walked over to his small kitchen unit. The apartment he lived in was so small there was barely room for anything. He only had the basics.

Brian opened a cupboard and took note of its emptiness. He was starting to get hungry and knew that the only thing he would have been able to eat was the tin of beans at the very back. He opened the fridge and stared down at the expired milk, he wasn't going to open it to check. It was too far gone.

He picked up the mug of cold coffee before pouring it down the sink.

"Hey, do you think I could pick up some more hours at the studio?" Brian flipped onto a new month of his calendar and noticed his rent was due in less than a week. He wouldn't have been able to afford that.

"Brian, you have enough for this month's rent, right? Do you need money?" Stan spoke with concern, he often found himself transferring money to Brian without him asking. Brian would have done everything he could to avoid his father's material affection, but sometimes he had to let it happen. He had to swallow his pride.

"I'm fine, I just want to work." Brian insisted, not wanting any special treatment.

"You blew all your tour money on weed? *Already?*" Stan's tone came through as one of disappointment.

"What? No! I didn't!" Brian defended, not happy with his father's claims. His lack of funds was mostly due to his insistence on the band staying with Max and Farah in motels towards the end of the tour.

"Brian..."

"What?"

"If you're blowing your money on anything more expensive than—"

"I'm not doing drugs, Dad. Jesus." Brian accidentally slammed the kitchen cupboard a little harder than anticipated.

His dad must have heard.

"You know I—"

"No, you don't."

There was a moment of silence shared on the phone call. Brian leaned on the kitchen counter as he took a deep breath.

"How are things with that girl?" Stan questioned, changing the subject suddenly.

"Good. Things are good." Brian spoke bluntly, the conversation with his father leaving a sour taste in his mouth. He would have eventually spoken to Stan about his newfound interest in the girl, but now wasn't the time.

"What was her na—"

"Farah. It's *Farah.*"

"Farah. Right."

"Yeah..."

"Things are going well? You're not just...y'know..."

There were many moments Brian wanted to curl into a ball and die, this was one of them.

"Dad...I said things are good. Better than ever actually." Brian nodded, despite his father not being able to see him. "I really like her and she likes me back. I'm going to visit her at college and she's going to come to one of my shows...I hope."

"That's great, Bri. I'm happy for you."

"Thanks."

Brian could hear shuffling in the speaker of his phone, followed by the sound of whispers. Someone was trying to get his dad's attention.

"I've got to shoot now, Kid. Important business to attend to. You'll have to tell me about the girl later."

"Alright." Brian sighed, he hadn't even bothered to mention her name. He was sure he had forgotten it again.

"I'll see you soon, Buddy. Try and get some rest."

"I will. See you later, Dad." Brian sighed before hanging up the phone and listening to the silence surrounding him. It was so loud.

He slumped himself down on the end of his bed and fell backwards, staring up at the broken ceiling fan. He wished it did more than just click when he turned it on. He should have spoken to his landlord about it, but he was too tired for anything.

He was exhausted, but he had to combat his hunger first.

After being in New Jersey, it didn't take long for Max and Farah to get to Delaware. Max had decided to drop Farah home before heading back to Michigan to spend the rest of her summer with her family.

Due to the length of the drive, Farah's parents were willing to accommodate Max for a night. They understood the dangers of driving when tired and didn't want dear Maxine Kayori to impact the safety of herself and other drivers.

Max slept on Farah's sleeping mat on the floor of her room. She had rustled staying one night into two. Farah wanted to show her around the coastal town in Delaware. Max had come to visit before, but there were always new things to explore. Plus, she was always up for an adventure.

After Max had made her pleasantries with the Vishwakarma family the day before, Farah sat with her best friend in her bedroom. Max had slumped herself down on the bean bag in the corner of the room as Farah sat on the edge of her bed with her phone in her hands. Max sighed heavily at the sight.

"He's going to text you back, what are you worrying about?" Max groaned, her friend had been staring at her phone for the past few hours. Ever since she had sent a text to Brian Lawrence.

"Did I phrase it wrong? Should I have put something different?" Farah rubbed her forehead as she read over the text she had sent again. It was incredibly generic. There wasn't much to it and yet she couldn't stop thinking about whether or not it was wrong. Maybe it was the kisses? He usually put kisses!

He hadn't texted back, it *had* to be wrong!

"He's probably asleep." Max checked her phone, scrolling through the Social Dropouts tag on each social media page to search for herself crowd surfing or moshing in any of the photos.

"It's two in the afternoon!" Farah protested, feeling a little upset Brian still hadn't texted her back. Max sighed heavily, having heard her best friend go on about the same subject for hours.

"Dude had a long drive, cut him some slack."

"Am I being weird? Is this...*weird?*" Farah held her phone up and looked over to Max with concern. Farah had never told anyone she liked them before and that was the only thing that kept going through her mind. How the hell was she supposed to feel? The internet didn't have the answers either.

"I wouldn't say that. You're certainly...something—but *weird* is the wrong word." Max grumbled.

Farah took her glasses off and rubbed her face, feeling somewhat exhausted by the scenario. As if she wasn't already tired from the trip. It was nice to have slept in her own bed the previous night though, despite her room being empty since she had moved to college.

"I feel stupid."

"Stupid is the wrong word to use to describe you. Smarty-pants." Max teased, attempting to cheer up her best friend.

"What if he was just...well...he is pretty *famous*, right? He might..."

"Don't finish that. You're special. Stop it." Max instructed, realising where Farah was about to go with her words. She never wanted Farah to feel down about anything, especially not her new romantic interest. Especially not when it was the lead singer of her favourite band.

"It's the end of the tour. This is the easiest way for him to cut his connection from me. Easy. Done. He never has to speak to me again!" Farah attempted to raise her voice as much as possible without her parents getting any hints of what she was talking about from downstairs. The last thing she wanted was for them to find out.

"Far away Farah! You're spiralling!" Max shook her head. "He told you he *likes* you!"

He did. She had replayed the moment in her head the entire way home. He *liked* her and that made her feel giddy inside. It was a different feeling from when they kissed, this time the butterflies in her stomach fluttered tenfold. She was terrified of losing that connection.

"It just seems...unlikely." Farah felt unknown fear within the pit of her stomach. She had never felt this way about anything or anyone before.

"Wrong. It's very *likely*."

She worried she was just a phase in Brian's mind. He had said so much to her that could have been scripted. She couldn't think like that. That he was famous and potentially would have said these things to any girl. He didn't. He had told *her*. Unless that was a lie. He was so kind. What if it was an act? There wasn't any way it could have been an act. He was so genuine.

Unless he was a good actor along with a musician?

"Sure..." Farah sighed heavily. Her thoughts spiralling more than she could handle. She looked at the message on the screen again. She should have used different types of punctuation.

"Just call him."

"What?" Farah's expression dropped, anxiety flooding her mind.

"If he's not responding to your texts then just call him."

"I only texted him once. I don't want to seem needy."

"No way. If you like one another you're probably both nervous. You're both giant fucking dorks." Max shrugged.

"Yeah...I guess." Farah chewed nervously on her fingertips as she stared at her phone again. She wanted the confidence to call him.

Farah glanced over to Max with an anxious grimace. She wasn't sure what to do. Max had given her solid advice, but it wasn't the advice she wanted to take. She was too nervous.

"So, are you going to do it?" Max cocked an eyebrow.

"What?"

"Call him."

"Uh."

"*Farah...*" Max gave her a stern expression.

"Maybe he's busy..."

"Come on!" Max groaned, growing impatient with her best friend's inability to make a phone call. Max hated speaking to people on the phone too, but she was pretty good at forcing herself to do it. Well, Farah was pretty good at forcing Max to make phone calls.

Farah looked at the text message she had sent as a hand suddenly came out of nowhere and grabbed her phone from her grip.

"*Yoink!*"

"Hey!" Farah exclaimed in shock, Max showing no remorse for the situation. She was going to get them to talk to one another whether they liked it or not.

"If anyone is going to fuck with destiny—it's me!" Max growled as she touched the green phone icon at the top of Brian's name with the stupid guitar emoji beside it. Farah gasped as she attempted to reach over to Max to get her phone back. Max pushed out her arm, making sure to keep it as far away from Farah as possible.

"Give it back!"

"It's ringing!"

"No! Max, come on! You can't!" Farah reached over once more as Max fought her off, listening to the phone ring like a ticking time bomb waiting for him to answer.

"It's for your own good!"

"No, it's not!"

"Get off me, absolute fiend." Max kicked Farah gently in the scuffle, holding the phone away from her the best she could.

"Max, this is serious!"

"Nuh-uh, Rah, this is fate. Destiny, bitch!" Max snapped back, hoping that Farah's parents didn't hear them verbally fighting or whacking one another as they stretched across the beanbag. Farah had Max pinned, but still couldn't reach the phone as she held it away from them both.

"What the hell am I supposed to say?" Farah argued as she reached over, this time Max's hand pushed her face away as they battled over the distant rings of the phone. It was going to go to voicemail before she got it back.

"Well, a *'hi, Briaaaaaaan, it's been thirty hours since I last saw you and I want to hear your gorgeous voice again'* would be nice, wouldn't it?" Max mocked.

"Max! Give me the phone!"

"Not until you promise not to hang up and speak to him like a goddamn adult."

"Oh, screw you!" Farah growled at Max as she went to swat Max out of the way, aggressively lunging for the phone.

"Someone's feisty!"

"You're *pissing* me off!" Farah finally snatched the phone back from Max.

"Uh...hello?" A voice sounded through the phone. Farah fell backwards on her ass into the middle of her bedroom floor as she gave Max a look of concern. Max stared back with wide eyes as she adjusted the beanie on the top of her head. She slowly sat up in the bean bag and furrowed her eyebrows.

Farah looked down at the phone, her hand shaking slightly as she held it. It had taken so long to get the phone from Max that she hadn't even thought about what she was going to say.

"Farah? Is anyone there? *Hello?*" Brian spoke down the phone, perhaps wondering if the line had broken up.

Max nodded towards Farah, moving her arms in quick succession to get her to speak. Farah shook her head rapidly. What was she going to say? She froze.

"Hello? Oh." Brian sounded slightly disappointed he couldn't hear her speak.

Max immediately reached over and snatched the phone away from Farah before hanging up the call and throwing it across the room. Farah gasped at the sight, Max committing the act through sheer desperation.

"Max! What the hell?" Farah threaded her fingers through her hair as she stared at her phone on the other side of the room.

"That was too awkward! It was killing me! Oh boy, I had to get you out of that one." Max chuckled, pulling at the collar of her t-shirt.

Before either of them could gather their thoughts there was a sudden vibration on the carpet, followed by a melodic tone coming from the other side of the room. Max and Farah exchanged glances.

"Oh no." Farah's heart dropped, knowing exactly who the phone call would have been from.
Brian. He was calling her back.

"Answer it! You have to answer it!"

"I can't!"

"If you don't, I will!"

"No!"

"See? Just do it!"

Farah swallowed her nerves, giving Max a look of fear.

She reached over to grab the phone, regrettably spinning it around to see the screen. It was Brian.

She took a deep breath before sliding the green circle across the screen and lifting the phone to her ear.

"Hello?" Farah spoke nervously.

"Oh hi, Farah! D-Did you just call me?" Brian questioned, a little confused.

"Oh yeah, sorry, the signal here is pretty bad." Farah laughed, Max sat contently on the other side of the room listening carefully to the conversation.

"No problem, I understand. Is everything okay?" Brian asked, she noticed there was background noise to his phone call and was curious to know where he was.

"Everything's fine. I just...I thought I'd call you to see if you got home okay."

"I slept for far longer than the average person and I was sad to see my milk expire, but it's nice to be home. I'm sorry I didn't respond to your text; I was going to call you but then my phone died and I needed to go to the store first otherwise I'd keep putting it off. I'm currently shopping for anything that isn't pizza." Brian snickered down the phone, the tour making him sick of the meal.

"I don't think I'll be eating pizza for a while either." Farah laughed, matching his mood and realising she had called him whilst he was in a grocery store. He was doing errands and she had disturbed him.

"How about you? Did you get home okay?"

"Yeah, the drive was short in comparison."

"Driving never gets any easier. It's always super long and tiring."

"Yeah, I figured that out pretty quickly." Farah snorted, watching Max give her a simple thumbs up. She wasn't being a complete dork on their phone call and that was good. The last thing she wanted was to sound like an idiot in front of the guy she liked.

"Hey, Farah?"

"Yeah?"

"Could I call you back? I...really want to talk to you but it's kind of hard in here." Brian laughed nervously, he hated having to tell Farah he couldn't speak to her right then and there. He could, but he didn't want to be rude to the cashier. It was his turn next.

"Oh, yeah, of course!"

"I'm sorry, I don't want to be rude. I really want to talk to you! ' *You've never seen someone go through a checkout so fast'* want to talk to you. Just right this moment...I can't." Brian panicked, feeling as if he was coming off abruptly.

439

"No, it's fine! Honestly. I'm free later, you can call whenever." Farah smiled, flattered Brian wanted to give her his full attention. She could talk any time as long as Max was willing to cover for her whilst she was there.

"Amazing. Quick question...what's your opinion on ketchup?"

"Ketchup?" Farah sounded puzzled as she stared across the room at Max. Max shrugged her shoulders, curious to know what Brian was saying.

"Yeah, I'm buying some now and I realised that I have no idea if you like it or not." Brian snorted, realising how ridiculous he sounded. "Sorry, I just want to get to know you better. I thought—"

"I...like ketchup." Farah grinned as she held onto one side of her face, feeling herself getting warm in her cheeks. It was a sweet and simple gesture to show he cared.

She *was* different.

"Okay. Awesome. I like ketchup too. Cool." Brian created a quick awkward silence between them. She could tell through the phone he was flustered by his own words, feeling embarrassed as he faltered. "I-I've got to go, but I'll call you in a little while?"

"Sure. I'd like that."

"Great! Talk to you soon." Brian added a perky tone to his voice.

"Bye!"

"Bye!"

Farah smiled before hanging up the phone. It was nice to know that he was going to call her back. All she had to do was wait.

Farah sighed as she put the phone down, looking over at Max with a small grin.

"How was it?" Max cocked an eyebrow, only able to hear half of the conversation. From her friend's smile, it seemed to have gone pretty well. "Other than that weird thing about ketchup, which I'm hoping isn't some kind of rude analogy."

"He's shopping at the moment, but he's going to call me back." Farah double-checked her phone before pulling her knees to her chest as she sat in the middle of the room with a smirk on her face. "...He wanted to know if I liked ketchup."

"Right, okay then. There was nothing to worry about, you're both weird!"

"Sure..."

"I heard what you said about pizza. Does that mean we're not getting pizza today?" Max pouted, wanting to spend the last day of her time with Farah through the summer with a memorable meal.

"Hm, I might be able to bend the rule slightly."

"Okay, good, because I really want mozzarella sticks." Max sighed with relief.

Farah laughed, she had one of the best summers of her life. Things were looking up. She checked her phone again and noticed a text notification flash on her screen.

'It was nice to hear your voice again. I'll speak to you later. xxxx'

Farah smiled down at his text.

She couldn't wait for her phone to ring again.

DATES

7/11 - BROOKLYN, NY
12 - WILMINGTON, DE
13 - WASHINGTON, DC
14 - ASHEVILLE, NC
15 - CHARLESTON, SC
17 - BIRMINGHAM, AL
18 - NASHVILLE, TN
20 - AUSTIN, TX
23 - SCOTTSDALE, AZ

26 - LOS ANGELES, CA
27 - DENVER, CO
28 - OMAHA, NE
29 - DES MOINES, IA
30 - CHICAGO, IL
31 - GRAND RAPIDS, MI
8/1 - INDIANAPOLIS, IN
2 - COLUMBUS, OH
3 - SAYREVILLE, NJ

Art by Ronnie Cason

Dear Reader,

I want to start by saying thank you for reading that entire novel. It's a long one, right? Crazy. Something I put together when the world was crumbling around us and the only thing I could think about was how much I wanted to be in a mosh pit because for years now, being in a crowd is the only place I find comfort.

Without gigs, I got back to something else I love—writing and emo music. I blended the two and Social Dropouts was born.

2020 was one hell of a year for a lot of us and I wouldn't have been able to make it through without some of the fantastic people I met throughout that continued to encourage me to write for the first time in years. It was the first time I'd ever had such a mass amount of influence around me. I'd had internet friends in the past, but this was different. We had the spare time to talk to people digitally for a year without breaking that connection, I grew closer to people than ever before. It wasn't always about just liking the same things; it was about who we were as people and how our lives differed pre-pandemic and beyond. Both culturally and through our life experiences. Yes, I know you all love my British accent and how I say Tuesday, *innit*.

If anyone read my last novel, you'll know the previous author's note was a depressing tidal wave of my various mental health issues. Well, it turns out that all of those were wrong. In February 2020 I was officially diagnosed with autism at the age of twenty-one.

It made me realise ignorance really is bliss...or sometimes causes more distress than it should. Finding out was one of the best things to ever happen to me because now I knew the root cause of the things that made me question myself. Afterwards, I surrounded myself with neurodivergent people and my life was better for it. Groups of people who *understood* what it was like to be me. People who saw the world through the same-coloured glasses. It was important to me and in this case...it helped me write again.

I couldn't name them all because I'd be writing a list that would feel longer than this book and none of us would want that. However, the biggest shout-out goes to my internet friends, who are a blessing to us all.

From sharing your experiences and influencing the story, to

us all dressing up like the characters and having a laugh. It's been wonderful and one of the best experiences of my life.

I love you guys.

I want to thank everyone in my server. You know who you are, and I love you for it. But here's to the ones who heard the most:

For Liam, thank you for supporting my endeavours and putting up with us all ranting about it for a very long time. So much love to you.

For Ronnie, you legend, you. Let's turn water into Pepsi and talk about how great you are. Pouring a *cawfee pawt* out for you. Thank you for the tour *promotion.* Looks sick!

For Brittney, thank you for bringing my characters to life. Visually and through our quirky conversations. You're a very talented individual. Also, thanks for putting up with my musical influence, my excessive ranting and just me in general. Lots of love to you, nerd.

For Ramen, your influence has been fantastic. You encouraged me throughout this entire thing, even when I was scared to go ahead with it. You made me realise this story was one that needed to be told and for that, I'll forever thank you.

For Kahle, I dedicated this book to you. That's enough—right? I'm kidding. You know I love you. (That's a receipt!) This project wouldn't have been possible without your input. You've helped a phenomenal amount throughout the process and helped me become a better writer overall. I can't even begin to put into words how grateful I am. Thank you for being my friend and my number 1 fan. You're the best.

For everyone reading, thanks for putting up with my emo references for 440 pages. You're awesome.

All the best,

@KayCBarrow
PS. What happens in Portland, stays in Portland.

JOIN SOCIAL DROPOUTS ON
THEIR NEXT TOUR.

COMING SOON...

Printed in Great Britain
by Amazon